When the World Was New Again

Mitchell R. Dunker

PublishAmerica
Baltimore

First printing

All characters appearing in this work are fictitious. Any resemblance to real persons, living or dead, is purely coincidental.

At the specific preference of the author, PublishAmerica allowed this work to remain exactly as the author intended, verbatim, without editorial input.

ISBN: 1-4241-0469-6
PUBLISHED BY PUBLISHAMERICA, LLLP
www.publishamerica.com
Baltimore

Printed in the United States of America

Kellan Foster...

On the eastern shore of the island, the surf pounded the beach with great, frothing billows, one upon another endlessly. But in the sheltered southwestern cove where the lieutenant idled, the palm trees grew down to the shore and the waves washed the sand with a sound like the big tabby cat lapping milk from the tin pan by the back porch, at home.

The thought of home seemed to dissolve time and space, and he could almost feel his bare feet on the enormous, flat creek stone that served for a step to the back porch, a sagging appendage of tattered screen that housed rusted buckets and miscellany equally dilapidated. The Fosters never threw away anything.

He would never go home again, except for token visits. When the war was over, he would transfer his college credits to a university. He had had enough of the quiet, church affiliated college in the hills. At a university he could finish his undergraduate degree in a semester, and with the G.I. Bill, he could get a Masters. And then...

Abruptly the lieutenant was warily alert. Noises. They were coming from the base. The entire outfit was in an uproar. He jumped to his feet and hurried up the jungle path. No one had to tell him. He knew.

The war was over.

Joanie Welles...

The shadowy light of late afternoon came through the long windows and dappled the blue colors of the bedroom and the reflection of her nude body in the full length mirror. She appraised herself, turning this way and that, satisfied with the deep tan of her face, arms and legs but displeased with the white skin that was a pattern of her bathing suit. Then in the mirror she caught a glimpse of her father standing in the doorway.

Unaffected by his presence, she turned to face him and ask, as though he were aware of what she had been thinking, "Don't you think I look awful? I hate this patchy tan."

Her father's face and voice were mocking. "Just how, pray tell, do you propose to remedy this dire situation?"

"Sunbathe stark, stark, naked."

"Mind you don't get arrested for public indecency."

"My body is not indecent."

"I agree. Unequivocally." And then he said what he had come upstairs to tell her. "The war is over, Joanie. Listen. Don't you hear the church bells ringing?"

They were silent. Listening.

"Oh, yes, Charles, I do." As she spoke, a siren blast drowned her words, and no one heard her say, "Now we can have fun again. All the guys are coming home."

Bill Dietmeier...

Only minutes ago a downpour of rain had hit the island, but as quickly as it had come, it ceased. The jungle steamed, and the buildings glared hotly in the clearing where the Navy's spare parts base was located. Sweat ran down Lieutenant Dietmeier's youthful face as he headed toward the Officers' Club. He pulled open the screen door, entered, tossed his unopened mail on an empty table, and strode over to the bar where the bartender, an enlisted man, had already opened a beer and was holding the bottle out to him.

The bottle was cold, but it wouldn't stay that way long in the tropic heat. The lieutenant sat down at a table and took a thick piece of toweling out of his pocket and wrapped it around the bottle, ignoring as he did so the jeering voice that called out, "Diapering your beer, Dietmeier?"

He doubled a rubber band around the toweling, took a swig of beer and was satisfied. Let the dumb asses drink their hot beer and think they were smart. He shuffled through the letters from home, knowing they would all be good news.

Suddenly the recognition of Polly's handwriting on an envelope stunned him like a blow to the head. In the erratic way of service mail a letter from Polly had come to him long after her death. For a second or two he thought he was going to be sick, but he pulled his head up, tried to breathe deeply and bit his lower lip until he was in control of his emotions.

At that juncture, the announcement came. The war was over.

Kellan...

Kellan closed the book on Edward III and the Hundred Years War, leaned back in his chair, and relaxed. As was his habit when he finished studying, he looked out the second story window that was crisscrossed by the bare branches of a sycamore tree. On the campus below, a few students, chins tucked into coats against a cold March wind, hurried along the path that led to Julian Hall, one of the many dormitories. Further away a line of Quonset huts stretched out in military-like precision toward the horizon, housing for the GI's who had thronged back to begin or finish their education, and like the khaki shirts or Navy pea jackets sometimes seen on the men, were reminders of the war.

He seldom thought of home. When he did, his recollections seemed to be in shades of gray, solemn and grim. His family had waged a war against Hard Times which meant pinching pennies and doing without, but holding their heads high, genteel and refined, proud of family, sustained by faith. There had been good times and bad times,but Kellan found it difficult to remember any outrageously fun times.

More than any other way of life, Kellan liked university life. He liked the somewhat international flavor, the resources,the intellectual stimulation—all so different from the straitlaced college that had seemed like an extension of home with too many restrictions, too much preaching, too insular.

Contrary to what he had anticipated, he liked living in the big fraternity house even though aspects of the fraternal organization bordered on juvenile. But as Bill had promised when he urged Kellan to join the Chi house, the accommodations were comfortable and the food was excellent. Also there were enough vets like Bill and himself to offset the teenage mentality.

Kellan turned from the window as Bill Dietmeier came into the study room. "What's up?"

"Not much." Bill dropped down in a chair, lit a cigarette, and picked up a deck of cards from the beat-up end table.

He shuffled them once and began a game of solitaire.

"Does anyone ever win Idiot's Delight?" Kellan asked, having tried the game a couple of times and gotten nowhere.

"Hell, I won two games last week."

"And you also lie a lot."

"Very true," Bill agreed. "but never maliciously; only for the good of

8

humanity." He changed the subject. "I came in here to see if you want to go over to the hyper building and get up a game of basketball."

"Don't you ever study?" Kellan was sardonic.

Bill was smug. "I didn't know I was supposed to." And then, continuing to move the cards in his hand, he asked, " How's the thesis coming along?"

"Slowly."

"What the hell are you going to do with a degree in history?"

"I've been asking myself the same question."

"You're working your tail off and don't know what you're working for. Me? All I'm doing is getting a diploma so I can go home and mess around in the beer business with Dad. Go hunting and fishing. Go to the track." Finished with Idiot's Delight Bill put the cards back on the table. "Well, are we going to play round ball or not?"

"I've got a date," Kellan answered. "A girl from the Delt house asked me to their sock hop."

"Oh, hell," Bill groaned, "what a miserable way to kill time."

The Delt who had asked Kellan to the dance was neither more nor less good looking than a hundred other girls on campus. He had met Marjorie in a math class. She was a physics major. "There aren't very many girls who major in physics," he had said to her, and her quick, but good-natured rejoinder was, "And I've never met many history majors who were smart enough to understand matrix algebra."

Kellan liked Marjorie without being sexually attracted to her. He liked her for the person she was, and their encounters were always agreeable. Nevertheless, he was surprised when she asked him to the sorority dance. He accepted her invitation because he did not want to be unkind. So, leaving the frat house with a feeling of duty rather than exhilaration, he drove over to the Delt house.

From the outside, the sorority house was a house of blue lights; inside, the lights were dimmed, the rugs rolled up in the downstairs lounge where the crowd danced to records. *Jukebox Saturday Night, String of Pearls, Stardust...* more slow numbers than fast, probably because one of Marjorie's sorority sisters got penned that night, and the sisters were in a sentimental mood.

Because of the dance, the upstairs rooms, normally off-limits for males, were accessible, and when Marjorie and Kellan were tired of dancing, they took glasses of punch and went up to her room. Conversation that had been so free and easy in the classroom was now awkward. Kellan offered her a cigarette, a useless gesture for he was sure that she did not smoke.

"I do have an ashtray," Marjorie said, "an over-sized one that's perfect for catching odds and ends." She found a place to dump the odds and ends and handed Kellan the ashtray.

Kellan asked about the framed picture on her desk.

"My parents and my dog," she explained bringing what was an enlarged snapshot closer to Kellan's view. An attractive, older couple and an Airedale posed before a background of shrubs.

"Where do your parents live?"

"Arlington, Virginia. My father is in the patent office."

"What brought you to Indiana?" Kellan asked, trying to keep the conversation going.

"My parents are Hoosiers. Both graduates of IU. And both sets of grandparents live in Carmel."

When she asked about his background, Kellan was sorry he had brought up the subject of home-sweet-home. Bluntly he told her that he was from Kentucky, that both his parents were dead. People were reluctant, he had found, to ask questions after such a dolorous statement.

"Let's go for a ride," Kellan suggested, for that was the accepted ending to a sock hop. They night neck a bit, and with Marjorie, Kellan suspected that would be all. And all he wanted.

"I'll get my coat," she said.

Downstairs, as they passed by the dancers in the lounge, the most beautiful face he had ever seen seemed to peek at him from the embrace of her dancing partner. Had she been here all along? How could he have not seen her before? She had to be a late arrival. I'll find out who she is, he vowed, before the end of the semester.

His efforts were in vain.

Kellan did, however, see her again.

Feeling the heady relief of no more studying, no more exams, no more papers, Kellan said to the gaggle of men lolling on the porch in the spring sunshine, "I've got good news…"

"Free beer at O'Malley's Tavern?" a burly brother suggested as he flipped a cigarette butt across the porch railing on the yard.

10

Why should these dolts care that he had received a four point grade average? Most of them were satisfied with a C. He would keep his mouth shut about his grades.But before he could suggest they all go to O'Malleys—

"Hey, Foster," Bill yelled from inside the house, "you've got a call."

The phone call was more good news. Thinking that he might get an instructor's position while he continued to work on a doctorate, Kellan had applied to several universities, and while this telephone inquiry was not from a university but from a small college, at least he was being offered an interview. And that was good news. He could see himself on the faculty of Houghton College for a year or two.

"What's up?" asked Bill who had been unabashedly listening to Kellan's end of the conversation.

Damn it, Kellan thought, nothing is sacrosanct to Bill except his own personal affairs. Answering Bill, Kellan tried to sound blasé. "That was Houghton College. I have an interview Monday morning at ten."

"Whoo-ee." The way Bill said it, it was neither praise nor putdown. "And you're so excited you're about to piss your pants."

"No way. I might be excited if it were...say, Duke or Northwestern..."

"The hell you aren't excited. You're so excited your ears are red."

"Get out of here."

"Hey, not so fast. You know where Houghton is? It's only about eight or ten miles from the folks' house. Twelve maybe."

More like twenty, Kellan thought, knowing Bill's tendency to exaggerate.

"Tell you what," Bill went on, "since I don't have a car and since somebody at home will have to come get me, you can drive me home and stay over with us. Come Monday morning you can get yourself over to Houghton."

"Won't your family be coming over for commencement?"

"Hell, no. They don't know what the word means."

Kellan wanted to think that no one at home cared that he had earned a Masters, but he knew that wasn't true.

Grandmother, the whole family, would be filled with pride. He wished they didn't care. He felt guilty. Obligated.

"Well, what do you say?" Bill was impatient. "You going home with me or not?"

"I'd like to. If you are absolutely sure it is okay with your mother."

"I'll phone her."

A hot muggy wind whipped through the open windows of the black Forty-one Chevy and rattled the boxes, suitcases, and miscellaneous items stashed in the back seat. Kellan was driving, and Bill Dietmeier slept in the front seat with his long legs extended as far as possible and his arms folded across his stomach. His head lolled to and fro with the motion of the car and caused trickles of sweat to run down his tanned face. Off and on he snored.

The radio blared away in competition with the noise of the wind and traffic and was more irritating than entertaining. Kellan turned it off which caused Bill to rouse.

"Why'd you turn the radio off?" he mumbled.

"Shut up and go back to sleep." Before the words were hardly out of Kellan's mouth, Bill was snoring.

So Kellan drove on in dogged discomfort, not particularly looking forward to arriving at his destination.

"Wake up, Dietmeier," he called out when he realized they were approaching Bill's home town. He punched Bill in the ribs. "Wake up, Stupid. Give me the directions to the Dietmeier mansion."

The Dietmeier house was not far from the business section of town. Located on a wide street that was lined with maples, it was one of a line of square, two-story, white frame houses with front porches.

Kellan was uncomfortable about this visit, in spite of Bill's assurances that he had phoned his mother. Kellan knew Bill: maybe he had made that call and maybe he hadn't.

Uncertainly, Kellan said, "I hope I'm not a surprise to your family."

As they got out of the car, a baseball glove dropped out on the driver's side of the car, and a sack of dirty gym socks fell into the gutter on the other side.

"You worry too much. People dropping in don't surprise Mom. Happens all the time." Bill picked up the sack of socks and stuffed them behind the front seat. "It's too hot to unload now. We'll do it after supper. When it's cooler."

Kellan was so peeved he couldn't talk. Now he knew for sure that Bill had never said a damn word to his mother about bringing a visitor home with him. Kellan reached to take the keys out of the ignition, thinking as he did, that it would serve Bill right if he turned the engine on and left with all Bill's gear still in the car.

"You can leave the keys in your car around here," Bill advised. "No one will bother your car. I'd bet a hundred dollars that the key hasn't been taken out of the ignition of Dad's pickup since the day he bought it."

Nevertheless, Kellan pocketed his car keys and followed Bill to the back of the house. At the end of the well-worn backyard, there was a big, concrete block garage with a dog pen on the side that faced the house. A penned up dog barked and pawed at the fence until Bill walked down and let the dog loose whereupon the dog ran directly to Bill to have its head rubbed and its sides patted.

"This is Falls," Bill said, introducing the dog, a black and white setter with brown spots. "Falls City Beer. Dad always names his dogs after whatever beer is selling best when he gets the dog. The dog before this one was named Oertles '92. I think, maybe, this is the best dog he ever owned. She hunts close, right along the fence rows, doesn't streak to hell off like a field trial dog. She'll track a single or hunt down a cripple, and she's got a really soft mouth. When Falls brings a bird to you, you, can bet your life's savings it won't have a tooth mark on it."

"English setter?"

"Llewellyn. Well, let's go inside and see what's cooking."

The screen door was unlatched. "Anybody home?" Bill called out as they went inside. "Nobody's home, but they'll be wandering in before too long. It's close to supper time." Bill went back to the subject of keys. "Hell, we don't even own a set of keys to this house. If Dad sold the house tomorrow, he would have to get new locks before the new owner could take over.

Want a beer?"

"I never want another beer as long as I live," Kellan answered tiredly. "What happened last night before you threw me in the shower?"

Bill was nonchalant. "You were just being obnoxious."

Kellan did not want to know how obnoxious. He was in no mood for exaggerations.

Bill was still wound up on the subject of keys. "When Burt, my youngest brother,was in Lutheran school, he locked Teacher Krauss in the storage closet. He didn't do it on purpose, he was just fooling around, but he got licks anyway. Then when he got home, he got more licks from Dad." Having paid no attention to Kellan's refusal of a beer, Bill set two uncapped beers on the kitchen table. "Sit down, Kell, and relax. Nothing formal at the Dietmeier mansion." He fumbled at an empty shirt pocket. "Got a weed?"

Kellan took a pack from his own shirt pocket and slid it across the oil cloth toward Bill. "I don't have a light."

"I've got matches." Bill helped himself to a cigarette, lit it, and threw the pack and matches to Kellan. "Woops. No ash tray." He got a saucer from a white metal kitchen cabinet and dropped it on the kitchen table.

Bill was finished with talking. He got that way frequently, and Kellan was never put off by it. Silence seldom bothered Kellan. Perhaps it came from being an only child in a house of quiet people. But Kellan was bothered. Bothered by the fact that he was barging in on Bill's family. He didn't relish the thought of meeting new people and minding his manners. And worse, being obligated. He felt like an intruder in this place. This place of red geraniums. For the kitchen wallpaper was clusters of red geraniums and green leaves winding about white trellises. Holding him prisoner. Having come home with Bill was definitely a mistake. Come Monday morning he would be long gone.

Ten o'clock. Houghton College. Kellan Foster to see Dr. Watters. If Dr. Watters offered him a position—and Kellan believed he would—he would make the obligatory visit to Grandmother Foster, and then come back and look for a place to live. Chances were the college supplied housing for single profs.

A squeaking screen door broke the silence as a short, stout woman in a floral dress and a beribboned white hat atop her auburn hair stepped into the kitchen.

"Here's Mom," Bill announced as he got up to take the filled grocery sack from his mother and put it on the kitchen counter. "The hobo sitting at your kitchen table,Mom, is Kellan Foster. Can he sleep in the garage for a couple of nights?" Bill was unloading the sack and storing items in the cabinet.

"If anybody sleeps in the garage, it will be you, William Dietmeier." She snatched an apron off a hook by the sink, wrapped it around her middle and tied it. Her hat stayed in place. She went to work as if she had the room to herself, taking a round steak out of the refrigerator, laying it on a cutting board on the table, dredging it with flour, and pounding it mercilessly with the edge of a plate.

Wanting to get out of her way but not knowing exactly where to remove himself,Kellan got up from the table and leaned against the sink as Bill plucked the hat from his mother's head and stuck it on his own.

"You ruin my hat," Mrs. Dietmeier threatened, "and you'll be in big trouble." But her words were lost in the ringing of a telephone somewhere else in the house, and Bill went off to answer it.

Kellan was trying to think of something to say when a person—most likely Mr.Dietmeier—came into the kitchen from the back door. Mrs. Dietmeier who obviously did not remember Kellan's name said, "This is Bill's friend."

Kellan got a nod from Mr. Dietmeier who asked, "Who let Falls loose?"

14

"I did," said Bill, coming back into the kitchen. "You keep that dog penned up too much."

One remark led to another between father and son until they started discussing the fortunes of Bill's older brother Karl who was playing minor league baseball. All the while Mrs. Dietmeier was going around first one and then another as she prepared the meal, and Kellan was trying to get out of everyone's way. He had the urge to say, it's been nice meeting you and leave when Mr. Dietmeier bet Bill two hundred dollars that Karl would be called up to the majors before the season was over.

"Oh, mein Gott in Himmel," Mrs. Dietmeier groaned as she stirred a boiling pot on the stove; "if you two spendthrifts have found a money tree, I wish you would let me know where it is."

No one paid her any mind.

"Hey," Bill said as if he had just been reminded. "That was Burt on the phone. He and Max are at the swimming pool and want a ride home. Burt said someone stole their clothes." Which brought no response from the parents. "I'll go get them." Bill offered. "Is it okay if I take your new Buick, Dad? I haven't had a chance to drive it."

Kellan was never in his life so glad to get out of a kitchen. The dog followed them down the backyard walk toward the garage but turned back reluctantly and when Bill ordered, "You get back where you belong," slid on her belly to crawl under some convenient hydrangea bushes.

The Buick still had the new car smell, but no key in the ignition.

"I thought your family never took the key out of the ignition.," "Kellan taunted.

"Mom's the only one does that," Bill replied with complete aplomb and jauntily headed back to the house.

The town was crisscrossed by railroad tracks. The B&0, the L&N, the Pennsy, and the New York Central. At the B&O tracks, they had to wait for a long freight train to rumble and rattle by.

"Mom won't be in a good mood if we're late for supper," Bill remarked.

An ominous note, Kellan thought, considering the disgruntled state she had seemed to be in when they left.

At the swimming pool they waited in the car for the brothers.

"Wouldn"t it be reasonable to expect them to be ready to hop in the car?" Bill complained.

A perky little face appeared at the driver's side of the car. "Hey, Burt—oh, my gosh. You aren't Burt. You must be Bill.All you Dietmeiers look alike. Sorry."

"Nothing to be sorry about, honey, since we're all so good looking."

She giggled and strode off, enticing whoever would be enticed by her gyrating little rear end.

Kellan was enticed. "Cute kid," he commented.

"But who likes kids?"

Normally, Bill's cynicism amused Kellan or he ignored it, but not now. The combination of heat, hangover, and discomfiture made him so irritable he could hardly keep his mouth shut. But he did.

Kellan was made aware that Bill's attitude toward his younger brothers was almost paternal, for as soon as they, dripping water, were in the backseat lighting cigarettes, he growled at them for smoking. "If you've got any intentions of going out for football, you better lay off the cigarettes."

"Ah, shit," one brother was smug, "you smoke."

"I'm older than you. I've been through the war," a hint of teasing in his voice, "and I'm not going out for football come August."

"Bullshit," the other brother scoffed. "Don't tell me you didn't smoke when you were playing football in high school."

"These two smart alecks are my brothers," Bill said to Kellan. "Burt the younger; Max the older." And to his brothers, "This is Kellan Foster; he's going to be bunking out at our house for a few days."

"Hey, Bill," Burt's voice was as loud as if he were a block away. "We had this car out last Saturday night and really opened her up. We got the speedometer up to the max. Don't tell Mom."

Bill's voice changed to quiet intensity. "How often do you guys pull stunts like that?"

"Only when somebody's got a new car," Max answered. "You gotta try 'em out."

"Stupid." Bill was angry. "Utterly stupid. I ought to stop the car and beat the hell out of both of you. Beat some sense into your thick German heads. Polly died in a car accident. Or have you forgotten that?"

Silence.

Kellan had not heard Polly's name pass Bill's lips since that early morning in the South Pacific when Bill got the message that Polly was dead. Whatever agony Bill had suffered then—perhaps still suffered—he did not allow anyone to share. In the war Kellan had seen men react to grief in a variety of ways: some wanted to talk, some cussed and raged, some cried. Bill got sick. He vomited out his guts, and then, exhausted, he retched until he passed out. When it was over, he put away every reminder of Polly and never again mentioned her name. Until a moment ago. That moment's hush rode with them all the way to the Dietmeier house.

Supper was ready and waiting. Max and Burt pulled out chairs. "No, you don't," Mrs. Dietmeier ordered. "Go get shirts on if you want supper." No one mentioned the missing clothes. Which Kellan thought was odd.

Supper time at the Dietmeiers was noisy. A large oscillating fan whined and purred from atop the refrigerator, and a radio played in the background even as the family said in unison, "Come, Lord Jesus, be our guest and let these gifts to us be blest."

End of ceremony.

Load your plate.

Kellan let the bread basket pass without taking a slice, but Bill reached over and put one on Kellan's plate. "You can't turn down Mom's homemade bread," he explained, "best bread in the world."

As each person finished eating, he left the table without asking to be excused. Something Kellan was never allowed to do at home.

Mr. Dietmeier went to the front porch, and Mrs. Dietmeier followed after she had admonished Max and Burt not to put off washing and drying the dishes.

Bill was restless. "Let's unload the car, shower, and get the hell out of here. If we stick around home, Dad will want to play euchre. It's too hot for cards. We'll go some place air conditioned, like the country club, and drink beer."

Which is what they did.

The country club, though small and crowded, was cool. And evidently the place to be. See and be seen. Kellan wanted no permanent part of it. Raised on a farm and not a part of the snobbish, small town society, he had rejected both. What he wanted was to live where people were interested in ideas instead of gossip, where the environment was intellectually stimulating, a place that made things happen. Like New York.

As the two of them sat at the bar, Bill was hailed with raillery, back slaps, and handshakes like a person who had always been at the epicenter of small town life. Dullsville and welcome to it, Kellan thought.

While Bill jawed with his friends, Kellan dreamed about his future. He would take the position at Houghton, stay a couple of years—three at the most—get his doctorate, and take on the world.

Bill interrupted Kellan's musings to introduce him to the man who was hanging on his shoulder. "This is Robert Fulton. Steamboat."

This is a name I won't have trouble remembering, Kellan thought. And, as he listened to the one-sided conversation, the man struck Kellan as being as implausible as his name.

"Bass are hitting," Steamboat was saying, "a fellow came in the Sports Shack with a six-pounder to show me, but he wouldn't say where he caught it. What I know for a fact is that they're catching them on top-water baits." His face was boyish and his voice too loud. "I can't keep 'em in stock. Man, is business good right now. Get this, I got the contracts for the basketball uniforms for every school in the county. Hard to believe, ain't it? And I'll tell you a little secret. I'm selling more golfing equipment than the pro shop— how about that? Well, I gotta move on. You know how Helen is." And now he looked directly at Kellan for the first time. "My wife gets madder than hell if her Bobby is gone too long." He laughed. "The women just can't seem to do without me. Hey, nice to meet you…uh." and he was gone.

"Ho-lee shit." The tone in Kellan's voice said it all. Stupefied disbelief.

"Yeah, I know," Bill agreed nonchalantly. "But he's not a bad guy. Just takes some getting used to. He was a hell of a good athlete." As if being a good athlete made up for any shortcomings. "Growing up, Steamboat never had a pot to pee in.

"Now he's got something to brag about." Bill switched subjects abruptly. "Let's get the hell out of here and go fishing. I got a feeling the bass will hit tonight."

Kellan was indifferent to the suggestion.

Bill, in his habitual way of assuming a person was going to give him the answer he wanted to hear, was off to the men's room without waiting for Kellan's reply to the suggestion of fishing.

The high laughter of women, the deeper male voices, the hum of a crowd floated from the main dining room into the barroom and hung like the swirls of smoke in the air. Someone in the other room began playing the piano. Whether he stayed in this slack environment or spent the night fishing made no difference to Kellan. He was merely biding his time until Monday.

Houghton College needed him.

"You look like Laurence Harvey." The voice was feminine self-assurance.

Kellan turned to the voice and saw the face, the memory of which he had held in his mind since a certain sorority dance last winter. Somehow he managed to keep astonishment out of his voice as he came back with. "I am Laurence Harvey."

"No," she said matter-of-factly, and then to the bartender, "Chesterfields." And to Kellan, "You don't actually look like Laurence Harvey. I suppose it was the angle of your face when I walked up."

"Who is Laurence Harvey?"

There was no answer because the girl left before Kellan had finished asking the question.

"Who is Laurence Harvey?" Kellan asked Bill when he sat down on the bar stool.

"How the hell should I know who Laurence Harvey is?"

The bartender had not been deaf to the dialogue. "Laurence Harvey is a movie star." He spoke without looking at either Bill or Kellan, disinterestedly, his attention was directed to taking an order.

Clown or leading man? Kellan wondered.

Bill was pressing the issue of fishing. "What do you say?" He made a quick little motion as though he were casting.

Kellan ignored the suggestion. "I saw a girl here that I want to meet."

"Here? What girl?"

"That girl," Kellan said.

Bill turned toward the direction Kellan was indicating, a spot where glimpses of people entering or leaving the club could be viewed. The girl was leaving with her escort. "Oh, that's just Joanie Welles."

"*Just* Joanie Welles? She's ..." Kellan didn't finish. Anything he might have said would have sounded as corny as 'she's a vision of loveliness.' But she was that. The most beautiful girl he had ever seen. Bar none.

Because of the strange environment or the cool breeze that was blowing across the bed, or both, Kellan awoke early on Sunday morning. Around five, judging from the exuberance of the twittering birds. He thought about Joanie Welles and tried to remember her face, but the pink roses on the blue wallpaper kept interfering. He wondered what kind of Sunday routine the Dietmeiers followed. Late sleepers or early risers? He hoped the family did not sit down to a big breakfast. Maybe they would all go to church and leave him alone. And he would do what? He would telephone JoanieWelles and say, this is Laurence Harvey. And she would—slam, bam the receiver down. Best to sleep away the morning. Kellan closed his eyes, and the silence of the house and the hypnotic pace of Bill's light snoring caused him to drift back to sleep.

He slept until the aroma of boiling coffee and frying bacon drifted into the room. Kellan was hungry. And thinking of Joanie Welles. He would make Bill arrange an introduction. No matter how conceited she was, she wouldn't spit in his face.

Chances were that she would be a tad interested in him, for Kellan, no longer shy and unsure of himself, knew that he was attractive to women.

A rhythmic pattern of a ball slapping into leather came from the yard

19

below, lasted awhile, and stopped with a demanding yell from Mrs. Dietmeier. "Get in the house right this minute."

All was again quiet, but Kellan was wide awake and couldn't go back to sleep.

Thump, thump, thump, heavy footsteps pounded up the stairs.

Max stood in the open doorway; dressed in white shirt and tie, he looked older than he had the previous night. "Get up, Bill. Mom said for me to make sure you are awake. We're going to early service, and she said you better be sure you get to second service."

No response from the sleeping Bill.

Kellan reached across the space that separated the two double beds and yanked the pillow from under Bill's head and tugged loose the pillow he had between his knees.

"What's going on?" Bill sat up, rubbing his eyes.

Max repeated his message and vanished.

"You going with me?" Bill asked Kellan.

If I stay here, Kellan thought, I'll be in the house when the rest of the family returns from church, which will be awkward. If I go with Bill, Joanie Welles might be there. Accompanying Bill seemed the better alternative.

"Mom and Dad always go to early service," Bill explained as he and Kellan ate pieces of freshly baked coffee cake, "because it's in German. Well, it used to be in German. Until the war. People in town got nervous hearing all that German pouring out of church. The dumb asses. There was a rumor going around that Pastor Emhuff had a transmitter in his basement and was sending information to Berlin." Bill took a swallow of coffee. "People are so damn stupid."

They were late to the second service and had to sit in the overflow side pews where Kellan had a cross view of the whole congregation. He was able to sit very unobtrusively in the crowded church and scan the faces, not that he realistically expected to see Joanie Welles.

It had been years since Kellan had been in any church—he did not have a reason for not going to church—he had sort of drifted away and never felt any remorse for his indifference. This was the first time he had ever been in a Lutheran church. That the Christian religion was still a viable force in 1948, he thought, was something miraculous. Imperial Rome should have stamped it out in its infancy. It should have died in the ignorance of the Dark Ages. So many wars, so much persecution had been done in the name of Christianity that a jaded world might have rejected its teachings. Yet as he sat and watched, pews emptied and men and women filed up to the altar to receive the wine and bread of Holy Communion; to see cynical Bill—who never humbled himself to anyone, who was as pragmatic as arithmetic, who scorned sentimentality—on his knees with his head bowed was the epitome of incongruity.

When church service was over, and Bill and Kellan were heading for the car, Kellan, fumbling to loosen the knot in his tie, said, "Do me a favor, Bill."

Bill pulled his tie off and twisted his freed neck around. "What?"

"Get me an introduction to Joanie Welles."

"Sure. No problem."

Sure you will, Kellan mentally added, if I hit you in the head with a two-by-four to remind you.

Bill had driven no more than eight or ten blocks until he pulled in the long driveway of a Federalist style house with bricks so old they were faded to a soft, pinkish color.

"Why are you stopping here?" Kellan was suspicious.

"Because this is where Joanie Welles lives."

"You can't do this, Bill. Get the hell out of here."

Wasted words for Bill was already out of the car, walking toward the front door. *If she's at home and comes out of the house with Bill, I can handle it.* Kellan was angry enough to be stubborn. *I will not let Bill make a fool of me.* He watched Bill tap the brass knocker and then punch a doorbell. No response.

'They're not home," Bill said as he got back in the car. "Might have gone to the lake to spend the day."

"You knew all along that there was no one at home, didn't you?"

Bill shrugged his shoulders. "Now how would I know that?"

"You tell me."

Sunday dinner was ready when Bill and Kellan returned to the Dietmeier house. This time they ate in the dining room, and the meal was more subdued, chiefly because they were listening to Wait Hoyt call the Cincinnati Reds baseball game, brought into the home courtesy of Burger Beer.

After dinner, Bill and Kellan went fishing. They seined minnows from a brook—Kellan called it a branch and got laughed at—and then they went to Big Sandy Creek where they waded the stream, pausing to cast into areas where they thought a hungry smallmouth might be lurking under a ledge. The sound of riffling water, the murky, still pools of deep water, the willows that hung low over the bank, the old hollow sycamore with enormous roots that spread into the water, the very smell of the place reminded Kellan of home.

Summer Sunday afternoons Kellan and his cousins were allowed to go down to the creek to swim. That creek was much bigger than this one, with one hole so deep and wide that they could dive off a makeshift diving board without fear of hitting rocks. Swimming or fishing, he could never understand how time could slip by so quickly as it did at a lazy old creek.

When Bill and Kellan quit fishing, they had a full string: rock bass, a couple of bright sunfish, several smallmouth bass, and one big channel cat.

"Enough for a meal," Bill commented. "Mom's going to be happy with us. We'll eat fish tomorrow night. Mom doesn't cook on Sunday nights. It's every man for himself."

"And by the way," Bill said as they were riding home. "we have to clean what we catch."

So they drank beer and cleaned fish out in the hot, muggy backyard until almost dark.

"Tell you what," Bill began, "I'll fix us a sandwich while you shower. Then I'll shower, and we'll cut out of here and go to the coolest place in town. The Aurora Theater."

By the time they got to the theater, the first showing of the movie was over, and they had to stand in the lobby while the groggy crowd ambled out of the darkened auditorium into bright light.

"Half the town must have been jammed in there," Kellan commented.

"Yeah. Everybody takes in a movie on Sunday night. Nothing else to do."

And half the people coming out knew Bill and seemed to want to ingratiate themselves in his good favor. Like the woman who was now talking to Bill.

"Esther Scott," said Bill, making introductions. "And the guy behind her is her better half, Scott. Homer Scott."

Esther was a dishwater blond with down-turned brown eyes, who was not pudgy now, but the too-tight yellow dress gave every indication that she soon would be.

"Honey," she said to Kellan, "a lot of single girls in this old town are going to hope you stay awhile."

Bill was direct. "Es, is Joanie Welles around?"

Kellan could have throttled Bill.

"Why, Bill," Esther teased, "this is quite a surprise."

"Hell, Es, it's Kellan who wants to meet her."

"Take a number and get in line." Homer Scott's tired sounding voice was without humor. He had the lean, dispassionate look of one of Bill Mauldin's dogfaces. Joe or Willie.

"Jeeze, Scott," Esther corrected her husband. "Joanie's a sweet kid, but she's not any more popular than a lot of other women."

Scott shrugged his shoulders in a have-it-your-way indifference, and let his wife go on talking.

"Joanie and Dr. Welles are in Indianapolis," Esther explained, "attending a champagne supper for the patrons of the Indianapolis Symphony Orchestra." She went prattling on, but neither Bill nor her husband seemed to be listening.

Kellan was certain that, with Houghton College only fifteen miles away, he would meet Joanie Welles sooner or later.

The hard chills began as Kellan was driving back from Houghton College. He had felt the attack coming on even before that brief interview when he had been informed by the cordial, stereotypical professor with the Eastern accent, clipped mustache, aromatic pipe, that there had been a change of staff in the History Department that mandated their interviewing only those candidates with doctorates. He was sincerely sorry that he had been unable to contact Mr. Foster by phone to cancel the interview.

Kellan was too sick to care. He was too sick to think about anything but getting back to the Dietmeier house, gathering up his things and finding a hotel room to hole up in until he was over this bout of jungle fever.

He was freezing cold, his body shaking and jerking. Hot as it was, he turned on the car's heater.

The illness was not new to Kellan. The first attack had happened in the South Pacific near the end of the war. The Navy doctor was not able to definitely diagnose the disease, so he treated Kellan for malaria. Since the attacks occurred periodically, Kellan hoped the Navy doctor was correct when he said that the attacks would come less frequently and be less severe until the disease wore itself out. Kellan had reason to think this was true. Which was of little help to him in his present condition. He hung on the steering wheel wanting to drive fast but driving slower and slower because of the chills.

Kellan never remembered getting to the Dietmeier house and getting into bed.

He was vaguely conscious of covers being piled on. A warm hand on his forehead. His mother. No, mother was dead.

Grandmother Foster. No, no. It was Mrs.Dietmeier. Or somebody like her. Reality was the shivering and shaking that racked his body.

After a long time, he felt warmth and could release himself from the tight fetal position into which he had drawn himself in an effort to control the violent shakes. He was aware of voices.

Bill was telling Mrs. Dietmeier that there was no need to call a doctor. "Take it easy, Mom; I've seen Kellan like this before. In five days he will be back with the living."

"Well, what does he have? Diseases have names, don't they?"

"Jungle fever. And it's not catching."

They left and Kellan slept.

He slept until the smell of cooking food brought him to a nauseous wakefulness, and he stumbled to the bathroom and vomited.

Knees weak as water, he found beside his bed a bottle of aspirin, a glass, a pitcher of water, and a small saucer of orange slices. He took three aspirin, tried an orange section, and gave himself over to the bed and sleep.

The next time he awakened it was pitch dark, and the house rocked with snores.He was hot. He threw off the covers, but the fever was burning him inside and out. He took two more aspirin and got up and used the bathroom.

Back in bed, Kellan was restless and beset with uneasiness. Unrelated incidents flitted through his mind like short subjects on a newsreel, jumping from New Caledonia to the university to home. He remembered his mother. Gentle, calm, long-suffering. She was beautiful, but he had never thought of her as beautiful until now. Remorse at all that he had left unsaid to her filled him with sorrow.

He dozed.

Winter winds blew outside, and the chimney draft pulled the fire into flames that made the big log, just thrown into the fireplace, crackle and pop. Grandmother sat in her little rocker in the corner, sewing together diamond-shaped pieces for her Lone Star quilt top. Mother and Father sat on either side of the lamp table, and Mother tatted while Father read aloud by the circle of light from the coal-oil lamp. Kellan played on the floor with his lead soldiers until Father was finished. "What is a bastard?" Kellan asked. "A dirty word," Grandmother shot out. His mother explained, "A child who can't claim a father." Kellan recognized those as evasive answers because no one added any more information as they usually did when he asked questions. As a rule, they explained to the point of tedium all manner of things—except for whispered subjects that had to do with mysteries of birth. The wrong kind of silence hung in the room, but Kellan went ahead with his questioning because it was so important for him to know what a bastard was.

"Why did Johnny McGlocklin call me a bastard? Like he did at recess."
"Sometimes little boys use that word when they are very angry at their
playmates," his mother explained.
"Johnny wasn't mad at me."
Father began, "Son, in this worldly life you must learn to ignore the
uncouth and the vulgar. The Bible says you must learn to live in the world but
be not of the world. Fix..."
Kellan didn't listen to the rest of Father's long admonitions. He didn't
have to. Whatever a bastard was, he was one of them. Tomorrow, he
would look the word up in the dictionary. The heat from the fire seemed
to scorch his face...
Kellan put old reveries out of his head.

He was soaked with sweat. The bed, his clothes, everything was damp with
his perspiration. Now he knew that the worst was over. When the sweating
finally stopped, later that afternoon, he got up and showered and shaved but was
too exhausted to do anything about the damp bedding but lie down.

He was, however, able to eat the supper that Bill brought in on a tray.

By Wednesday he was downstairs apologizing to Mrs. Dietmeier. "I'm
sorry I made so much trouble for you and your family. Bill should have taken
me to a hotel."

"A hospital, maybe. Not a hotel. So don't apologize. You're not the first
boy ever got sick in this house. We went right on with what we had to do. Dad
and Bill have gone to work, I think Max has gone to cut the grass for Mrs.
Jorvitch—I think it was Mrs. Jorvitch—and Burt has gone to....I don't
remember what he said he was going to do...You sit right down at the table,
and I'll make you some breakfast." She was already cracking an egg. " Bill
says you didn't get the job over to Houghton College.What you oughta do is
get on at the high school. There's a shortage of teachers because of the war."

"I don't have an Indiana teacher's license," Kellan said, "so that really
isn't an option." No way, he thought, am I going to be a high school teacher.
Or a grade school teacher or a kindergarten teacher.

On Thursday Kellan accompanied Bill to work and hung around the
Dietmeier Distributing Company, not doing much but getting in everyone's way.

Friday he announced that he was leaving. He felt well enough to drive to
California if there was any reason to drive to California. As it was, he was
gong to drive home. He owed Grandmother Foster a visit.

"No, you're not leaving," Mrs. Dietmeier said irritably. "You can rest here
a couple of more days. Monday morning I'll kick you out. Bag and baggage."

Kellan let himself be persuaded, although he knew he was fully recovered and able to do anything he wanted to do.

Saturday night Bill and Kellan went out to the country club unaware that a dinner-dance was in progress until they opened the front door and heard the band.

"Let's get the hell out of here," Bill grumbled; "we don't want to get caught in this mess."

The words were hardly out of Bill's mouth until a coterie of locals had begun to gather around him which resulted in Bill and Kellan's joining a larger group partying at a long table.

And Kellan found himself seated next to Joanie Welles.

She was direct. "Did Bill say your name is Kelly?"

"No. Kellan. Kellan Foster."

"I like the name Kellan." Even though the tone of her voice indicated indifference.

In spite of the fact that he already knew her name, he said, in an effort to keep a conversation going, "And your name is?"

"I'm Joanie Welles." She spoke with the self-assurance of one who thought the entire world should know her name.

The band, which had been taking ten, struck up again. Loud and brassy but not bad. "Pretty good orchestra," Kellan commented raising his voice to be heard.

She shrugged her shoulders. "Better than nothing," and turned an ear to the man on her right. Obviously her date.

As the outsider, Kellan was observer rather than participant in the goings on. Banal men and women, smoking and drinking, laughing and flirting— small town people, lords and ladies of their fiefdom. And Bill was king of the hill. Among the assemblage, Kellan recognized the Scotts—Esther and...who? Scott. Scott sat morosely beside his wife staring at his drink and taking occasional sips as though he were rationing himself. With a sudden jolt, he leaned across the table toward Joanie Welles and asked her to dance.

In the dim light of the room, it was hard to tell if Joanie's hair was light brown or blond, if her eyes were gray or blue, but the duskiness could not distort the perfect symmetry of her features or the lines of her body. Not shaped like a Petty pin-up girl, she was much too slender for that, she was nevertheless as curvaceous as Kellan wanted her to be.

The music was slow and dreamy, and Scott led Joanie in the deliberate, measured steps of a poor dancer.

"Damn," Esther Scott wailed out so everyone at the table heard, "Scott let me sit here all evening without once dancing with me, and now he's dancing with Joanie."

26

"She's a better dancer than you are, Es." This from another person Kellan recognized by name. Steamboat. Bob Fulton. "Joanie can follow any guy; a drunk or a peg leg."

"Big deal." Esther looked at Bob Fulton. "Dance with me Steamboat. You don't mind, do you Helen?"

Helen, who sat straight and almost primly in her chair answered with merely a compliant gesture of her hand, as though the matter too trivial to consider. As she put her hand to her face and returned to an on-going conversation, coruscating diamonds on her third finger, left hand indicated that she was Mrs. Steamboat.

Leaning across the chair vacated by Joanie Welles, the guy who was her date began a conversation with Kellan. "Don't think I ever saw you around campus," he said. "What house did you belong to—or were you not organized?"

"Chi Lambda. And I'm sorry," Kellan apologized, "I didn't catch your name when Bill was making the wholesale introductions."

The man's mouth dropped, and his expression was one of incredulity. "Larry Somner." He ran a finger under the collar of his white shirt as if it was too tight for his bullish neck "Thought you might have recognized me. I played football for the Hoosiers. Defensive end."

At the Chi House, Larry was known as The Gap. Or The Gapper. Or Big-Chief-Run-Right-Through. For obvious reasons. Opposing ball carriers too often found a convenient hole on Larry's side of the line. Kellan had never seen Larry out of uniform— unless he was the man Joanie Welles was dancing with when he first saw her.

Kellan let Larry do all of the talking which was mutually agreeable since Larry seemed to like talking about himself, and Kellan did not want to talk about himself.

When the music stopped, but before Joanie could return to her place at the table, Larry met her on the dance floor, took her hand and pulled her possessively to himself as a tune began. A jitter-bug. They were unquestionably the best dancers on the floor. When the band stopped for a break, Joanie disappeared—the Ladies' Room most likely—and Larry sat down at the baby grand and rippled off a strain of music.

Larry was no slouch at the keyboard, and a small group gathered about the piano to sing along. Joanie, who did not join them, came directly back to the table as the musicians started taking their places, ready to begin another session. Before Larry returned to the table, Kellan had asked Joanie for the next dance.

The confident, nonchalant attitude toward women which had been Kellan's for a long time, was gone. He felt an unsure excitement that he had not experienced since he was a kid. If she was so affected, it was not discernible. Joanie fit snugly into his embrace, just tall enough so that if he bent his head, he could touch her cheek with his.She moved so lightly, followed every nuance of his dancing so perfectly that it seemed she was a mere extension of his body, moving from his brain impulses. Before the band had put the finishing flourishes on *It's Been a Long, Long Time,* she said, "It's so stuffy in here. Let's go outside."

The night was full of white moonlight that made the grounds around them like a charcoal sketch: all shades of gray and dark shadows. Honeysuckle grew somewhere nearby; Kellan could smell its penetrating sweetness in the damp air.

"Where have you been all my life?" He had not meant to say anything so sophomoric to her; the words just slipped out.

"Waiting for you," she answered quickly with no hint of flippancy or sarcasm in her voice.

So he kissed her. It was the gentle, experimental sweetness of lips first touching It made him hungry for the taste of her, so he kissed her again. Then he simply held her, basking in the feel of her warm responsive body against his. "You feel so good," he said. "I knew you would feel so good close to me." They kissed again, and it was the new-kiss freshness once more, and without taking his lips from hers he felt the deep, warm wetness of her mouth.

Time out.

He got out his cigarettes. "Last term I thought I saw you at a party at the Omega House. Were you enrolled at IU?"

"Oh, lord, no. The extent of my college education was one semester at Houghton College. But I was often on campus. For parties. I always stayed over at the Delt House with a friend." She paused to light her cigarette from the flame of the lighter that Kellan held out to her. "But you went to IU, didn't you?" The question was an invitation for him to tell her about himself.

"Before the war, I went to a small college until I knew that I would be drafted; so,I enlisted in the Navy and the Navy put me in the V-12 program which meant a lot of schooling. I came out a 2nd Lieutenant and was sent to the South Pacific where I met Bill who suggested that when the war was over, I ought to go IU. Which I did. I got my Masters, but the GI bill ran out and now I'm job hunting."

"For what kind of job?"

"I'm not sure. My degree is in history with an emphasis on European history."

28

"So," she led him on, "what do you do with a degree in history?"

"Write scholarly papers for other scholars to read," he joked. "Nothing I would ever read. I'm no scholar."

"What are you interested in? What do you do?"

"Do? Me? I don't do anything. Unless you consider playing cards and partying and dating bores like Larry Somner a career." There was a tinge of bitterness in her words.

"*Beauty is its own excuse for being,*" Kellan quoted.

"Oh, don't go intellectual," Joanie groaned. "You sound like my father. You really do."

"Is that good or bad?"

"I don't know. Neither, I suppose—where are you from, Kellan?"

"Green Forks, Kentucky."

"Podunk."

"About like this town."

"Podunk." Abruptly, she threw away her cigarette and came close to Kellan so that he could put an arm about her. "Did you have a bad time in the war?"

"Not too bad. I was in the supply corps—critical parts—and we were always barely behind the front."

"If it had not been for the war, you might not have met Bill, might not have met me. Are you staying the summer with the Dietmeiers?"

"No. I'm leaving in the morning." Very much aware that he wanted too much of her too soon, he said, "We should go back to the dance, don't you think?"

"Oh, let's stay out here and let everyone wonder what's happened to us. Maybe Larry will get mad and leave without me, and you can take me home."

"I'm riding with Bill."

"So? I used to have a crush on Bill when I was a freshman in high school and he was a senior."

Kellan did not want to hear about Bill. He gave Joanie a friendly kiss and said, "Let's go back to the club house."

Holding hands as though they had known each other forever, they walked slowly toward the lighted building ahead. Suddenly Joanie stopped. "I don't want to go back to Larry."

"I don't want to take you back to Larry."

"Then why are we walking in that direction?"

"Because, I guess, it's the proper thing to do."

"The word proper is not in my dictionary."

Nevertheless, they reluctantly returned, stopping to kiss long and lingeringly before they opened the door and joined the hubbub inside.

Bill, looking skeptically at Kellan said, "Let's get the hell out of this place."

It was just as well, Kellan thought, nothing more would happen between Joanie Welles and himself this night.

As Kellan and Bill passed by the barroom heading for the front door, a woman accosted Bill. "Hey, you big ugly Kraut, what's the latest development?" She was tall with a large frame but not fat. Her face was plain and her brown hair close- cropped. Her clothes were elegantly simple. Her voice was penetratingly raucous. "Look here, Dietmeier, introduce me to your handsome friend." When Bill hesitated, she went on, "Don't look so pissed off, sweetness, it isn't as though you have to share me with him."

"Jesus," Bill muttered, in a way that sounded more reverent than irreverent.

"Really?" she responded in mock surprise.

"Kellan Foster," Kellan put in quickly for he could see that Bill was absolutely seething.

"I'm delighted to meet you, Kellan," her voice as politely correct as a dignified matron, and then, "I'm Elizabeth Perry Portland the town, quote, character, unquote.Known familiarly as E.P." The harsh banter returned, "And darling, you can put your shoes under my bed, any old night. Want to come home with me to my…"

"We have to go," Bill spat out.

"Don't wet your pants," as she pointed, "the men's room is that way." She cackled boisterously as they unceremoniously left.

"I'd like to cram my fist down her dirty throat," Bill said between clinched teeth.He slammed one fist against the palm of his other hand.

Bill's anger had dissipated by the time he was home, and his seemingly careless approach to life had returned. "Well, hell. Now that you've met Joanie Welles, do you like her?"

"She's all right." Joanie Welles was not a subject that he wanted to discuss with Bill.

"Is that it? Just all right?"

Kellan did not want to talk. He wanted to be by himself. He needed to figure out how an unemployed vet with a Masters Degree could arrange his life to be near Joanie Welles.

"Want a beer or anything before you hit the sack?" Bill offered.

Kellan shook his had negatively. "I'm going up to bed. Tomorrow I leave for Green Forks when you leave for church."

"Hey, you can stick around longer if you've got something going with Welles..."

One long ring of the telephone cut into Bill's words. "Oh, hell. I hope Max or Burt isn't in trouble. In a wreck or in jail." Bill was into the dining room where the only phone in the house was located.

The call was for Kellan.

Joanie Welles. "I got rid of Larry. Why don't you come over?"

"Do you know what time it is?" It was eleven-fifty.

"I don't care what time it is. Charles—my father— is tied up at the hospital. Even if he were here, it wouldn't matter."

The prudent thing, Kellan thought, was to beg off. But he didn't. He let her tell him how to get to her house, repeating the directions as she gave them.

"You'll find the house by instinct," Bill was droll, "like a dog going after a bitch in heat."

"Shut your dirty mouth." If he sounded annoyed, Kellan didn't care. Bill almost made a career out of keeping his own life private. But as for other people's lives—different story.

Joanie was waiting for him, outside, sitting in a wrought iron chair, smoking a cigarette in the glow of light from the carriage lamp. Recognizing Kellan, she threw away her cigarette and went to him, coming into the embrace of his outstretched arms like lovers who had been separated for a long time, who shared a need for each other.

"Joanie, this is too much," Kellan said.

"I don't think it's enough," she countered.

"It isn't, but you know what I mean."

"Yes, yes, yes. Let's go in. We've a lot of catching up to do."

In the foyer a cherry stairway led upstairs. On the right he caught a glimpse of an immense living room and to his left a room that appeared to be a library.

"Let's go back to the kitchen," Joanie was leading the way; "I made cucumber sandwiches. I can't cook, but I can make a sandwich and open a bottle of beer. I can pour a glass of wine if someone gets the cork out of the bottle. I always foul up when I try to make mixed drinks."

The kitchen looked as though it had never been used. Kellan sat down at a round oak table like the kitchen table at home except this one looked stylish while the one at home was just old. "Your house looks like it had never been lived in," Kellan remarked.

"You wouldn't say that if you could see my room. It's ..." she paused in her thought to say, "I'm having white wine. Okay for you?" as she poured two glasses.

The last time Kellan had had wine—and then it was very dry red wine—was in New Caledonia when a French planter invited several of the young officers for dinner. Kellan would never forget that meal because he suspected that the meat was bat. A bat was the only creature on the island with bones that would correspond to the bones in the meat he had been served.

He had consumed enough red wine to allay the distaste of having to eat bat meat and to make him vow never to drink wine again. But this wine was different. Lighter. But he would drink only one glass because it was late, and he needed to get up early in the morning. "Do I hear snoring? Kellan asked, certain that the steady noise he heard was snores.

"Oh, that's Miss Eddie. Our housekeeper. Her rooms are downstairs. We can go into the living room if you like. We can't hear the snoring in there."

"No, the snoring doesn't annoy me." He wanted to know about her family. "Tell me about your family."

"My mother died shortly after I was born. My father never remarried; I have no brothers or sisters. It's always been just Charles and I. And Miss Eddie. What about you?"

"My parents are dead. My mother died while I was in the South Pacific. We always lived with my grandmother. It's she I'm going home to visit."

"Don't go away tomorrow, please. Kiss me. Kiss me and you'll never want to leave."

He might have passionately obliged, but the sounds of someone approaching the kitchen caused him to cover her hand with his and whisper, "Later."

"Breakfast? With wine?" He was tall and thin with a slight stoop. The dark skin of his face was taut and smooth except for the lines around his eyes and mouth. Black eyebrows that almost met across the bridge of his thin nose lifted and lowered as his black eyes alternated from snapping to quizzical. His crew-cut black hair had grayed in patches of white that looked as though someone had dabbed paint here and there. His tongue was tart. "So you are a family friend of the Detmeiers," he remarked after Joanie had introduced Kellan. "Good salt of the earth people." His voice was condescending.

And then he asked all those boring questions newcomers are subjected to.

"I'm rather at loose ends at the present," Kellan answered in response to a question from Dr. Welles. "I've completed a Masters Degree in history with an emphasis on European history. I plan to work toward a doctorate, but in the meantime..."

"In the meantime," Dr. Welles butted in, "what do you do with a degree in history? Teach?" His tone was belittling.

I will do whatever I damn well please, Kellan wanted to say, although he replied very respectfully, "Teaching is a possibility. I've also considered re-enlisting in the regular Navy. I would go in as a full lieutenant." Which was a lie. He merely wanted the snob to know that he had been an officer. Time to change the subject. "You have a very beautiful home, Dr. Welles."

Charles Welles drew Joanie close and kissed the top of her head. "Yes. I have two beautiful things in my life. My daughter and my home." The words were without mockery.

Kellan thought the show of affection was stagy. Too much.

Joanie removed herself from her father's hold. "Would you like a glass of wine,Charles? You look exhausted."

"No, thank you, my darling. But you are correct. I am exhausted. I delivered a first baby, and it was a difficult delivery.

Difficult because the young woman chose to be uncooperative. If screaming can get the attention of God, she had God and all his angels aroused."

"Kellan will think you a heartless physician," Joanie was quick to admonish.

The black eyebrows lifted. The mouth twitched. The expression on Dr. Welles' face was disdainful.

Kellan was not accustomed to being disliked. He had not experienced such rejection since high school. In those days the line of demarcation between county students and town students was a sharp one. Painfully vivid in his memory was the degrading way Baby Lou Morrison—cheerleader and popularity queen—had turned him down when he asked her for a date.

He should not even remember those days for they had nothing to do with the person he now was.

Dr. Welles lingered on awhile being haughty and opinionated before he said good night.

There was an interval of silent waiting, making sure that Dr. Welles would not suddenly reappear.

Then breathless with love, Joanie rushed to Kellan, and he thought he could not let her go. Not for one night. Not for one day.

Joanie pulled away. "Do you think I'm too forward? That I'm a hussy?" She didn't wait for his response. "I'm twenty- one years old. I don't play dating games. I know what I want, and whatever I want I always get."

Realistically, Kellan knew the evening had to end here, in the kitchen, because everything was moving too fast too soon, Kellan said, "As much as I hate leaving you, I have to get a little sleep before I leave for Green Forks."

Joanie clung to him. "Don't go. Not yet. Not ever. Not till we...."

"Not until we know each other better. That's the sen..."

"Damn. Don't say sensible. I hate sensible."

"Reasonable? Judicious? Prudent?"

"I don't even know the meaning of those words." She took his hand, and they walked through the house to the front door.

Kellan would have kissed her good bye, but she turned away. "No. No kisses until you come back to me.

Green Forks. Kellan saw the profile of the town, the part not hidden by the rolling terrain, like an artist's imaginary sketch of a faraway, charming place one might like to visit. Then it became, as he drove into it, the familiar reality of prosperity and poverty; beautiful and ugly, good and bad, the reminder of a part of his life that he felt no joy in recalling,

The courthouse with its shady lawn was the hub of the town, and Main Street circled it, and the whole was known as The Square.

Vehicles weaving in and out went round and round as did Kellan, seeking an advantageous parking space. After he had circled three times, he settled for a parking space on the north side of the courthouse. A half-hour remained on the parking meter. Plenty of time to go to the drugstore.

Heading for Yates Drugstore on the south side, Kellan took the short cut through the courthouse yard. The old brick building was open to summer. As he walked by the half-open doors of the public restrooms—segregated by race as well as sex a odor of urine and disinfectant as familiar as the building itself assailed his nostrils. Not much progress in the sanitation department. Prominent in the courthouse yard was the statue of a Confederate soldier.

A rash of cold air hit Kellan as he opened the heavy door of the drugstore. There was something new in town. Yates Drugstore was air conditioned. But the center of the store held the same ice cream tables and chairs. Yates was the popular place where the popular kids hung out after school. The ones who didn't have to work after school. This was the scene of his high school humiliation from the mouth of a girl who thought she was above dating a boy from the country.

The fountain was the same, all marble and mirrors along a side wall. Shelves with miscellaneous items from vases to valet brushes lined the other side. Drugs and the pharmacist were in the rear of the store.

"Goodness, gracious, sakes alive—it's Kellan Foster."

Kellan recognized the most popular girl of the Class of 1941, no longer a teenage idler but an employee. She looked older, but the bubbly voice had not changed a whit. Purposefully hesitant, Kellan asked, "Aren't you Baby Lou Morrison?"

And felt a nudge of satisfaction in paying her back for all her conceited, high school snobbishness. "Or is Tingle?"

"It's Morrison, sugar. Tuffy and I are divorced. Since we didn't have any kids, I took my maiden name back. I like being Baby Lou Morrison better than being Mrs. Tingle." She smiled at him. *The Girl With the Million Dollar Smile* was the caption under her picture in the year book. "Can I get you something or did you come in here just to see little old me?"

She got the items Kellan had come in to purchase—a carton of Old Gold filters, razor blades, a couple of magazines.

"I'm not real busy now," Baby Lou said. "Let's sit down and talk about old times over a Coke."

Why not?

Obviously, her high school career was the highlight of Baby Lou's life. She knew a good deal about where and what many of her classmates were doing. Kellan knew that Arthur McElroy died in the Battle of the Bulge, but he did not know that Richard Tompkins had gone through the war without a scratch only to drown when his fishing boat capsized in a choppy lake.

"So, so sad," she sniveled. Then brightened up and said, "Sugar, tell me what you've been doing with yourself since the war. Are you married?"

"I've been getting an education. No wife."

"W-e-l-l, what do you know about that? Engaged?"

"No. Perhaps we can get together while I'm home."

Baby Lou gave him her old personality-plus smile. "I'm going to count on that—you hear? It's so much fun to talk over old times."

"We once had so much fun together, didn't we?"

She wasn't stupid. She recognized the sarcasm. "We were in classes together. Remember, I sat right across the aisle from you in civics class."

"And tried to copy off my test papers," Kellan reminded her.

"I did not," she laughed, but her laughter was an admission of guilt. "Now don't forget," she emphasized as Kellan took his leave, "we're going to get-together while you are home."

He left her with the idea that he would be seeing her again, but he was so vague that there was nothing definite that she could count on.

Which was precisely the way he meant it to be.

Kellan drove south on the Nashville Pike for a couple of miles and turned off onto a gravel road. The meadows, the tobacco patches, the houses, the woods, the unpainted barns, even the twisted growth of blackberry bushes and sumac in the fences and ditch lines were unchanged. It was he who had changed. Changed by the two years at Central College before the war, changed by his years in the Navy, changed by his time at IU. Or was it not so much change as having developed into his own person from his experiences away from the tight environment of home? Or was it because he had no blood kinship with the Fosters? His mother was a Kellan, but he had never met any of those relatives.And who was the never- mentioned, mysterious man who fathered him? Progress of a sort had at last come to Green County, Kellan thought as he drove over a concrete culvert where not so long ago vehicles had to ford the swift water of the shallow stream.

Ahead on a little hill stood the one-roomed school, and across the road in a locust grove was the white-framed Baptist Church. He had attended the school, but the Fosters, who were staunch Methodists, cranked up the car every Sunday and drove into town to go to church.

Down a hill, up another hill, and the road leveled and went past Uncle Kirby's place. A bit of a turn in the road, and there is was. Home.

Ancient maple trees shaded the house which was a rectangular, two-story, white frame structure with field stone chimneys at either end. Spirea bushes almost hid the wide porch. A wisteria vine wound around one chimney and grew across the porch roof to the other chimney. Grandfather Foster had planned an elegant home to grace what was to be called Pleasant Hill, but he died before his plans were completed and no one ever called the place Pleasant Hill. Grandmother was left with a farm to manage and children to raise. Father was fifteen when Grandfather Foster died, Uncle Kirby was thirteen, Uncle Edward was eleven, Aunt Emmy six, and Aunt Amy three. Kellan had heard it all so many times it was etched into his brain.

How Father and Uncle Kirby worked like men. How Grandmother made homemade soap, pieced quilts, canned, and got them through the depression.

Kellan veered his car onto the overgrown driveway and stopped near the back door. He got out. How quiet it all was!

Not dead silent, but quiet with the rustle of leaves, and the cooing of mourning doves which was the most lonesome sound in the world. Kellan was overcome with sadness. He was sorry he had lost his mother, sorry her life and his childhood had been such a somber existence, sorry that he had been so unmindful of his grandmother. Yet echoes of Joanie Welles lingered with him, and he felt guilty because he begrudged the time he would spend here until he could get back his world.To Joanie Welles.

Having heard the engine of a car, Grandmother came out of the house to see if friend or stranger had arrived at her doorstep. She said, when she realized who it was, "Oh, child, it's so good to have you home where you belong."

Kellan bent low to kiss her cheek as was the custom when the kinfolk arrived at Grandmother's house; stodgy old men to the littlest child gave Grandmother the token kiss as she greeted them at the door.

A flat creek stone, an uneven five feet long and an uneven two feet wide served as the doorstep to the tattered screened-in porch full of a miscellany of junk. Nothing had changed, Kellan observed, as he followed his grandmother into the house.

"I was just fixing to get myself a bite of supper," she explained, "when I heard your automobile. Go wash your hands whilst I lay another plate. The minister and his family took dinner with me yesterday so there's plenty of leftovers."

Layer upon layer of old linoleum softened his footsteps as Kellan went to the monolithic kitchen sink— a relic of the projected indoor plumbing that was never completed because of Father's death—to wash his hands. On the walnut table by the sink stood a bucket of clean water and a gourd dipper. Kellan poured water into the shallow wash pan in the sink, washed his hands and dried them on the rough huck toweling. Then he carried the pan of water out to the back step where, reverting to a childhood habit, he took aim at a stray hen and doused her with the soapy water. He was never reprimanded for that because the chickens were a nuisance around the house. Once, he got himself in trouble when he lured an old rooster into swallowing a grain of corn that was tied to a string and then yanked the corn out of the rooster. Father caught him in the act and stood him up by the smokehouse and delivered a long dissertation on kindness to animals and the whole of mankind, but Father never laid a hand on him in punishment. And only once had his mother spanked him, but she cried so pitifully that Kellan, who had hardly felt the blows, put his arms around his mother and comforted her. Grandmother was not adverse to smacking him or thumping his head with her thimbled middle finger.

Kellan took his place at the table with Grandmother."Will you kindly return the blessing, son." It was a directive, not an invitation. Kellan's mind went blank. A gap of silence. He simply could not remember the table prayer that he had heard three times a day for the better part of his life. He mumbled, "Thank you, Lord, for the food." For this effort he received a questioning stare from his grandmother.

The conventional spoon glass was the centerpiece of the table, surrounded by a plate of cold ham and a few pieces of bony chicken, bowls of leftover vegetables, a few biscuits and corn muffins in the bread tray, and the remnants of a pie and a cake.

"I hope, Kellan, that you have not become too proud to eat a cold meal. But you know that in warm weather I don't build a fire in the cook stove but once a day. In the cool of the morning. So, I've got no hot coffee. But I've some leftover iced tea. Would you care for a glass of tea?"

"Yes, Ma'am. Please."

Grandmother Foster moved about with the same alacrity she had always possessed. She was really a remarkable woman, Kellan realized, quickly figuring her age.Grandmother was seventy-six. Her black hair had only glimmers of gray, and her face was virtually without wrinkles. She had always been dumpy. She could quote long lines of poetry—Longfellow was her favorite. *Life is real! Life is earnest!/And the grave is not its goal/ Dust thou art to dust returneth/ Was not spoken of the soul.* She could split kindling, supervise the butchering, serve on the county school board and teach a Sunday school class. She had known much sorrow. A baby girl had died of whooping cough. Her husband died in his forties, her oldest son, Father, was burned almost beyond recognition under an overturned tractor. She had lived through the Spanish American War, World War I, and World War II. Through all these vicissitudes she kept her gentility and her faith. Her common response to tragedy was "The Lord gives and the Lord takes; blessed be the name of the Lord."

Grandmother was talking to him. "What do you plan to do with your education,child?"

"I haven't decided."

"There is no nobler profession than the ministry." A hint of a smile came with her facetious addition, "Especially if it is the Methodist ministry. However, not every man feels the call to preach, like your uncle Edward. Some men have the gift of medical healing. Teaching is rewarding. Have you considered teaching?"

Damn. teaching again. "I may…" and he named the first thing that popped into his mind. "enter law school." Which, he reflected, might not be a bad idea.

"Why, law school would be fine. Whatever and wherever we can serve the Lord. My brother, your great uncle Edward Kirby, was one of the most evenhanded judges that ever sat on the bench over in Montgomery County where my people came from. Was said of him that he never took up a gavel without first pausing for a moment of silent prayer. You see, you can carry the Gospel with you into…"

All too familiar with the substance of her thoughts, Kellan tuned out his grandmother's words. She spoke of morality, he thought of money. His inheritance was put into a savings account and never touched. The government bonds which he bought when he was in service had never been cashed. It was possible that he really could finance law school.

"You are wool gathering, Kellan," Grandmother reprimanded.

"No. I'm listening."

"Well, are you aiming to stay the summer here?"

Here? All summer? "I don't know, Grandmother."

Grandmother eyed his plate. "You seem to be finished with your meal. Excuse me, and I'll clear the table." She stacked the supper dishes in the big dish pan to be washed in the morning. She opened the refrigerator to put away the butter, and a bright square of light shown in the dusky gloom.

Now that they have electricity at the farm, why, Kellan posed the question to himself, is Grandmother still using a wood burning cook stove? They had weathered the Depression and no longer had to pinch pennies. They could afford a few conveniences.

Wanting a cigarette, Kellan went out to the front porch, for no one had ever smoked inside Grandmother's house. Kellan sat down on the squeaky old porch swing and thought of Joanie Welles. Remembered the way she looked.

Mentally went over every word she had spoken to him. The confident boldness of her voice.

Intruding into his thoughts came the well remembered sound of the pant legs of new overalls swishing, swishing, as they rubbed together. Uncle Kirby. And soon Uncle Kirby appeared, coming out of the blind spot where the hydrangea bushes cut off the view of the path that led around the house. Kellan tossed away his cigarette and stood up to greet his uncle.

Uncle Kirby, unlike Grandmother and Father, had a round, cherubic face, pink-cheeked and dimpled, with sky-blue eyes always clouded with grave seriousness. He was slightly taller than average, stout but not fat, stolid but not athletic.

"Good to see you, Kellan." He offered his hand. "How are you getting along?"

"Fine, Sir. I've a couple of college degrees but no employment so far."

"Well, we're glad to have you home and hope you'll see fit to settle here. Your aunt Sammie will certainly be happy to see you. I think she's as foolish over you as she is her own children. As for that, I don't think there was ever a mother who doted on a child the way your blessed mother doted on you. And my sainted brother, he loved you like you like you were his own flesh and blood."

Uncle Kirby's words made him feel guilty. The family had nurtured him, but for that did he owe them the rest of his life? And did they have the right to keep secret whatever knowledge they might have about his biological father?

" Uncle Kirby, I think it's time…"

"Yes. It's time to go inside. Mother will be wondering what keeps us from joining her."

They went into the sitting room which was also Grandmother's bedroom. It became a sitting room because in cold weather there was always a fire in the fireplace.Grandmother was sitting in her little rocker in the corner by the fireplace, cold now but still exuding the piquant smell of burnt-out beech logs. She put down the paper she had been reading by the one light in the room, a floor lamp that was purchased when the house was wired for electricity.

"Kirby, so good to see you, son," Grandmother spoke as her son bent to kiss her cheek.

It's like they haven't seen each other for months, Kellan marveled.

They, grandmother and Uncle Kirby, questioned him about his studies at the university and other aspects of his life.

"I trust you attend church regularly," Kirby said, and then as though he suspected Kellan's slack, "we grow through hearing the Word and through fellowship with other Christians, as well as through our private devotions."

Grandmother picked up on the theme. "Never a day goes by that I fail to ask the Lord to bless and guide you."

And what have I ever done for you, Grandmother? Kellan asked himself. Nothing.He was struck with a sudden resolve. Before I leave, he promised, I'll do something for you. She deserved an easier life. She needed indoor plumbing. An electric stove." Grandmother, tomorrow I'm going into town and buy you an electric cook stove."

A little smile of surprised pleasure came to her face, but she cushioned it with counsel. "Why, Kellan, you are generous, bordering on foolish. I've lived seventy-odd years without such modern conveniences, and I suspect I can finish my life without them."

Kellan became even more assertive. "And this house ought to have indoor plumbing."

Kirby's cherubic face wrinkled up with disapproval. "Where on earth would you get the money for all this? From your inheritance?"

"I have some government bonds I bought while I was in service."

"You best be saving with your money, Kellan," Uncle Kirby advised. "Times might get hard again, and you may need something to fall back on." He went on to another theme. "What disturbs me is the immorality and licentiousness, the crass unbelief that began with war and is spreading throughout our country like a contagious disease."

Wanting to be argumentative, Kellan put in, " I read that we should expect a great surge of religious fervor after the war. That there are no atheists in foxholes."

Uncle Kirby's face deepened into troubled lines. "Men who are in foxholes act from panic, not from the conviction that comes from studying the Word. I tell you, Kellan, this country is on a path to destruction. Moral destruction." Uncle Kirby drew a deep breath and sighed.

Grandmother caught the baton and went on. "Much of what you say, Kirby, is true; but never forget that *all things work together for good to those who love the Lord and keep His commandments.*"

Uncle Kirby lost his tenseness. "You are correct, Mother. *As for me and my house, we will serve the Lord.* That's about all we can do, isn't it Kellan? Just serve the Lord and trust in His infinite wisdom."

"And in His eternal love."

Hold! Enough! Kellan wanted to shout as Kirby and Grandmother continued their mutually pleasing commentary.

Could staid old Kirby Foster ever have been a child? Or did he like a mythical character spring full grown, spouting Bible verses and platitudes? Adversely, there was a child-like quality about him in the way he innocently kissed his mother goodnight and shook hands with Kellan before he departed for his own home.

"Bedtime, Kellan," Grandmother announced. "There're clean sheets on all the beds upstairs, but I daresay you'll want to sleep in your old bedroom. Sleep well, child."

Kellan went upstairs to his old room. Mementoes of his growing-up years looked tawdry in the glare of the bare bulb that hung in the center of the room. Kellan took down a framed picture of his high school graduating class and all the odds and ends of his teens and put them in a dresser drawer, and like catching the glimpse of a stranger,he saw himself in the dresser mirror. Objectively. The man he saw had the appearance of a person who had everything going for him. Then why, Kellan asked himself, am I so damned dejected?

He found the pint bottle of bourbon that he had packed in his suitcase and took a swallow of the warm, friendly liquid.

He found an old pin tray to use for an ashtray, stretched out on the bed and picked up one of the magazines. *Life Goes on a Picnic.* As he studied the pictures of the women in the magazine, he compared each face to his memory of Joanie. No comparison. Joanie Welles was the pearl of great price, the…he stopped short. His words were words that might have come from Uncle Kirby. Deliberately, he put thoughts of Joanie out of his mind. In this place, she was not miles away but a world away from him. So he mulled over his agenda for the next day.

Tomorrow he would go into town and buy the electric stove first thing. No. First he would go to the bank. Then he would go to the hardware store. It occurred to him that Grandmother would have no way to heat the kitchen if she lost the wood burning stove. An electric heater, maybe? Then he would see if the Odum brothers had made it through the war and were in the plumbing business with their dad. And if it suited him, he would go by Yates Drugstore. He and Baby Lou, he thought sarcastically, could talk about the good old days when she wouldn't give him the time of day.

Before he went to sleep, Kellan made a decision. He would not leave Green Forks until he made someone give him some information about his father. Why should go through life knowing nothing of his own father?

"We were fixing to go ahead and eat without you, Kellan," Grandmother said at noon the next day. "I was beginning to think you were taking dinner in town. Go on in the dining room as soon as you've washed up. Kirby's at the table all ready. Your aunt Sammie and I will bring in the dishes. Hurry up. Don't dawdle."

Kellan was in a decent mood. He had run into no problems with arranging the installation of the stove. The plumbing was a different matter. No water lines and no sewage system in the country. Ed Odum made it sound like an impossibility, but with three Odums depending on the plumbing business for their livelihoods they were willing to tackle the project at a reasonable price. All of this would cost Kellan double of what he thought it would, but he didn't care. In a way, it lessened the onus of the obligation that he felt to the Fosters.

The big dining room was cool and somber. Grandmother had baked that morning—two pies and a handsome cake stood on the cherry sideboard. The table was set like it was Sunday with the good linen table cloth, the sterling silver, and the best dishes. Aunt Sammie and Grandmother scooted—well, Grandmother scooted and Aunt Sammie plodded—between kitchen and dining room, bringing in the hot dishes. Kellan was the honored guest. He felt like the Prodigal Son.

Uncle Kirby marked the occasion by dispensing with the usual grace and offering up a long prayer that included the entire Foster family, the churches at home, the missionaries abroad, and the President of the United States.

"I've got so fleshy, I 'low you wouldn't a knowed me if you'd met me on the street," Aunt Sammie said to Kellan.

She lifted her glasses and wiped the corners of her eyes with her handkerchief. Aunt Sammie had weeping eyes. Conversely, she also laughed a lot, often inappropriately. Although she had carried the Foster name for over twenty-five years, she had never become like them in any way. Aunt Sammie liked to read true confession magazines. At a very early age, Kellan had sneaked some of Aunt Sammie's old magazines up to his room because he thought they would be filled with sex. He remembered that he had been terribly disappointed because they were merely boring. He could not understand why the family was so ashamed of Aunt Sammie's reading material. She liked gaudy clothes, frilly doilies, Grand Ole Opry music, and going to town on Saturdays to stroll through the dime stores or sit in the car and watch the people pass by. As a child, Kellan thought Aunt Sammie was special because she could play the piano by ear and pick out any tune someone hummed. She played every tune in the same rinky-dink style so that *Battle Hymn of the Republic* and *A Tisket-a-Tasket* came out sounding remarkably the same. Aunt Sammie always wanted things like everybody else had. and Kellan, in his own way, also wanted to be like mainstream America, which gave him a bond of sympathy with Aunt Sammie.

As the meal progressed, Kellan felt Aunt Sammie's eyes following his every move, and all her conversation was directed to him.

"Are you going to be a teacher?" she asked.

There it was again. Teaching. "No, Aunt Sammie. I haven't decided what I want to do."

"William Kirby was taking some courses down at Western State Teachers'College, and I was hoping he might make a teacher. But he don't like school. Him and his wife is visiting her kinfolks over in Texas right now, but when they get back, they're moving into the tenant house and William Kirby's going to help his daddy farm."

It surprised Kellan that William Kirby had even attempted college. It wasn't that he was stupid—he was just so damn slow. In high school, even though William Kirby was three classes ahead of him, Kellan had to help his cousin with his homework. William Kirby read so slowly that he could not completely finish the required reading; so Kellan, who was a rapid reader, would outline long assignments for William Kirby. Not without price, however. Usually the price was Kellan's share of the milking. Kellan disliked cows, hated the smell of the cow barn, and detested milking.

Kellan heard the news of all of Aunt Sammie's children. Lena Russell and her husband, who was farming over in Warren County, were expecting their first child. Edward Bales, like his uncle Edward, was considering a call to the Methodist ministry. Elizabeth Allen taught school over in Timmonsville. Larry Wayne was in electronics school down in Nashville.

Kellan remembered Larry Wayne's birth and the family crisis over his name. Uncle Kirby wanted him named after the Jennings and Hardy sides of the family, but for once, Aunt Sammie had her way. *This baby is going to have a name just because it's a purty name. And I like Larry Wayne.*

Uncle Kirby raised his voice, a habit he had when he wished to give importance to his words. "After you've finished this fine dinner, Kellan, I'd like to show you the new pond. That is if it doesn't interfere with your plans."

Plans? All he knew for certain was that he was going into town that evening.

As Kellan and Uncle Kirby walked past the smokehouse whose very boards reeked with the pungent aroma of hickory smoked hams and shoulders, sacked sausage and bacon, Kellan drew a deep breath and said, "God, that smells good."

"Thou shalt not take the name of the Lord in vain, for the Lord will not hold him guiltless who taketh His name in vain, Uncle Kirby reproached in a sorrowful monotone, and then went on brightly, "It sure would please me to give you one of the hams if you were settled in somewhere."

A big if.

"Hey, what's this?" Kellan asked as they walked by a field where slender,chartreuse plants nearly as tall as corn had come up at random, here and there in the field and along the wagon pathway.

"That's volunteer hemp. Can't keep it chopped out. You may recall that the government asked us to grow it for the war effort. For rope. We all had to sign papers pledging that the hemp would not be used for anything else." Uncle Kirby chuckled at what he was about to say. "Nothing would do that sorry Andy Meechan—he was our tenant at that time—nothing would do him but he had to try to smoke the stuff. He sort of reeled around a bit, sat down cross-legged on the ground like an Indian. He puffed away and looked silly, and then he started singing. Not loud which was fortunate since he didn't have much of a singing voice. Then he just sat there with a stupid smile on his face. I'll have to say this to Andy's credit: he wasn't a sneak. What he did, he did with me as a witness." Uncle Kirby shook his head in remembrance. "Once was enough for Andy."

Maybe, Kellan could have added.

"Well," Uncle Kirby said, dismissing one thought for another, "it's going to be mighty good to have William Kirby back on the farm. He is a good farmer and a hard worker."

The farm was prosperous. There was no reason that the Fosters could not live as other middle-class Americans. No reason except that they were Fosters, and the Fosters were not moved by the tides of change.

The pond was much larger than Kellan had expected. Newly dug, its water was muddy and its dam and bank were raw red clay.

"Have you stocked the pond?" Kellan asked. "Your state government will do it for you, I've been told."

"I'm not a fellow who wants every Tom, Dick, and Harry walking onto his place, and what I understand is that if I let the government stock the pond then I'm obliged to let people fish it. No. This is for cattle and for irrigation if or when we need it." Uncle Kriby took the straw hat that he had been holding in his hand and settled it on his head. "Well, I've got the lower field to cultivate this afternoon; so unless you're anxious to take a turn, I'll say good afternoon and get back to work."

Returning to the house, Kellan got as far as the vegetable garden and decided he would go to Aunt Sammie's house.

Approaching the back door, Kellan heard the twanging guitars and nasal singing coming from Aunt Sammie's radio and drifting off into the quiet countryside.

"Aunt Sammie?"

"Why, Kellan, come in. Come in." She pushed open the screen door to let him in. "My land, take a chair and rest yourself. It's a might sultry day." As if to emphasize the matter, she fanned herself vigorously with a cardboard fan. *Compliments of Thatcher Funeral Home.*

Kellan relaxed in one of the rockers. He had always felt comfortable around Aunt Sammie.

"My, my," she said, "you do get better looking ever time I see you." She laughed and then pushed up her glasses and wiped the corners of her eyes.

"You ought to be a movie star, I swear."

Now, there was a career Kellan had never considered. "Do you think Hollywood is ready for me, Aunt Sammie?"

She laughed self-consciously at her own foolishness. "Oh, I don't know about all that. But I could tell them one thing. Kellan Foster is a heap handsomer than most of them movie stars."

"Am I too handsome to be a Foster?" It was a bantering question to lead him to the purpose of his visit with Aunt Sammie.

"Yes, honey, you are. Now don't get me wrong. The Fosters is nice-looking people, my children included. But you've got the kinda good looks that just don't come down the pike but once in a coon's age. But then, your ma was purty."

"I never thought I looked very much like Mother."

"There's some resemblance. Course you might have taken after …you know, you're real father."

"Can you tell me anything about him, Aunt Sammie?"

"Seems like Mary Katherine locked the door on her past and throwed away the key. About all I know is what everone who was around here back then knowed.Your mother came from a proud, aristocratic family. Well-to-do. When Mary Katherine got in trouble, her folks sent her down here to stay with the Radcliffs. Who long since moved away, don't you know. The Radcliff place was where the Honeycutts live now.Radcliffs was some distant kin of your mother. One thing I do know. Radcliffs was well paid for taking Mary Katherine in. All the neighbors knowed Mary Katherine was in the family way and there weren't no daddy. When her time come, all the neighbor men was over to the Radcliffs for wheat threshing. Well, noon time came and all the men came in and took their dinner under them old maples away from the house. But the men could still hear the screams coming from the house where the doctor was with Mary Katherine. Kirby said Garret got up and left. He just couldn't eat with the poor girl in such agony."

His mother might have suffered, but she would not have screamed. Never. Kellan knew his mother too well to believe that. Mother said that well-bred persons never made a public display of their emotions—pleasure or pain. Aunt Sammie was surely adding to the story.

"What's the matter, honey? Have I said too much?"

"No, no. Go on, Aunt Sammie."

"I guess there ain't a body in the world that can be anything but happy after a baby gets into the world safe and sound and the mother is all right. Afore they left Radcliff's that day, Garret and Kirby got to see the baby. You. Kirby said he seen a change in his bachelor brother right then and there.Well, after a decent time, Garret started courting your mother. Land, how people did talk. And when Garret took Mary Katherine to a ice cream social at the school, people weren't overly friendly.

Well, the war's changed things. People ain't so hidebound as they once was. Course, the family was right startled when Garret announced that he was marrying Mary Katherine Kellan. At first Mother Foster and Kirby and Brother Edward didn't take to the idea, but Garret's head was set. And you know the Fosters ain't nothing if they ain't stubborn. Amongst the four of them they thrashed it out, and Lordy-Mercy, your grandmother never cared for me like she come to care for Mary Katherine. I used to feel sorry for Mary Katherine cause she didn't know how to do nothing but read and do fancy needlework.She never did learn how to wring a chicken's neck, did she?" Aunt Sammie laughed at that thought and wiped her eyes and fluttered her fan at her perspiring face.

"But didn't mother ever say anything to you about who or what my…my biological father was?"

"No sir-ree. That was a closed subject. Your mother—and I ain't meaning to downgrade her—she had her pride, too.

And she was stubborn, I'd say. The closest she ever come to saying one thing about your real daddy was one time I remarked on your purty eyes, and she said, I remember her exact words, 'Kellan's beautiful eyes are exactly like his father's.'

There were no answers here. And there would be none from any of the Fosters. As far as they were concerned, Kellan was Garret's son. Amen.

Kellan decided that the only thing he could do for himself at this point would be to spend an evening with Baby Lou Morrison.

As they say in Green Forks, Baby Lou was dressed fit to kill. She wanted to go to The Steak House; steak houses were newly popular, and this one was the first in Green Forks. "Everybody but everybody goes to The Steak House, sugar.

"Let's have a drink first," Kellan suggested. Green Forks was in a dry county; therefore no alcoholic beverages were served in any public establishments, but Kellan suspected there was liquor available in Mutt Morrison's house.

"Sometimes Daddy keeps a little bottle of whiskey for coughs and colds…" Kellan's burlesque coughing interrupted her.

Baby Lou giggled. "I thought all the Fosters were teetotalers. Well, let me see if there's a bottle under the sink."

Kellan followed her into the kitchen where she opened the doors of the white metal cabinet under the sink. She pulled out a bottle of bourbon. "This do okay?"

Standing in neat rows was a full cache of bourbon. The gossip of Mutt Morrison's being a bootlegger was undoubtedly fact."You want your drink in Coke, Kellan?" she asked.

"Water and ice. I'll mix it."

In the small area of the kitchen they accidentally bumped into each other. Baby Lou winked at him. Kellan remembered the spacious kitchen where he and Joanie Welles had white wine and cucumber sandwiches. A world away. A world he wanted to go back to. To Joanie Welles. Comparing Baby Lou to Joanie made Kellan wonder what kind of blind teenage foolishness had made him believe that Baby Lou Morrison was the cutest, most desirable girl in the world. She was quite ordinary. A few pounds more ordinary since high school. Except for one thing, he was completely indifferent to her. What still rankled him was the humiliation he had suffered when she made fun of him for asking her for a date.

How things had changed. Here was the once snooty little cheerleader striving to please him, sending out messages no more subtle than Mr. Barkis's *Barkis is willing.*

"Now let's go to The Steak House, sugar," Baby Lou whined as she watched Kellan drain off the last swallow of bourbon and water.

"Sure," he said with an enthusiasm that was not entirely fake.

The Steak House was jammed. Every table taken, people waiting to be seated, people standing in line.

Baby Lou made sure that everyone noticed her. She smiled and showed her dimples, chatted happily, held Kellan's hand as she led him to meet this person and that person. She hung on his arm. "Didn't Kellan turn out to be a big old dreamboat?" she gushed.

Embarrassing as it was to Kellan, there was a certain amount of satisfaction in her fawning behavior.

They waited for their order to be taken. They waited and waited to be served, making do with sips of ice water.

On Baby Lou's glass, red imprints of her lips lined the rim. Rather nasty looking, Kellan thought. Though her lips still showed the carmine color, she took out a compact and a tube of lipstick and repainted her lips. Had Joanie Welles worn lipstick?

Kellan took perverse satisfaction in being abstruse with Baby Lou who failed or chose not to recognize his gibes and who radiated verve and good humor.

Later on, as they entered her parents' house, Baby Lou invited, "The night is ours, sugar. Like I said, my folks are down in the Great Smoky Mountains and won't be back for a week." She put records on the phonograph. "I still just love to dance." And as if to underscore the statement, she swayed with the music, coming to Kellan with arms outstretched in invitation.

They had never danced together before and their movements were awkward. He had danced with Joanie only once, but the fluidity of her body against his was an exemplar that made Baby Lou seem more inept than she was.

As soon as the record ended, Kellan sat down in an overstuffed chair. The room was hot and stuffy. "Don't you think we ought to have a drink?" he asked.

"Sure thing."

The record player had automatically changed records and the mellow sounds of *Serenade in Blue* filled the room. Kellan took out his handkerchief and wiped the perspiration from his forehead, closed his eyes and listened while Baby Lou rattled about in the kitchen.

She came in with two glasses, set them down on the doily-covered end table and popped herself in Kellan's lap. She pouted her lips at him in a petulant gesture intended to be provocative.

"Go take off your lipstick," Kellan ordered.

"My lipstick! Is that all you want me to take off?"

Curious about her drinking habits, Kellan took a sip of her highball while she was out of the room. The taste of bourbon over-powered the taste of Coke. Much of this and she wouldn't be sober very long.

When she came back to his arms, he kissed her, her mouth widening under his as though he had touched a spring. She lay limply across his lap, being uncomfortably heavy on his legs. As he attempted to shift her weight, his hands felt the bare hot skin of her thighs. He could do with her as he wished. "Get your clothes off."

"I'm not that kind of girl, Kellan," she mocked in an ever-so-earnest little girl voice.

"Should I then be a gentleman and leave?"

"Oh, just kiss me again, sugar."

He obliged.

She obliged by starting at the top of her button-down-the-front dress and unbuttoning it all the way down. She stood up and quickly her garments joined her dress in a heap on the floor. Her nakedness revealed a bit lumpy, droopy body.

At that point Kellan ended the evening. "Eight years ago a shy kid asked you for a date and you humiliated him—not privately—but so that the entire school knew." Kellan stopped. There was no need to add more.

Red-faced, Baby Lou dropped her head, for her passion had turned to shame. She was grabbing at clothes as Kellan left. He felt vindicated.

Vindication soon turned sour. As he drove home through the dark night, watching the silent flashes of heat lightening in the northern sky, he felt no satisfacation in what he had done, felt disgust with himself, felt pity for the woman whom he had robbed of her self-esteem.

I'll get even with you, Frank Jordan, Kellan had yelled when Frank snatched his sack of marbles and threw them all over the wooded area behind the outhouses. And when he was home, Kellan said to anyone who would listen, I'll get even with Frank Jordan for throwing my marbles away. Mother had said, Retribution precipitates retribution. He had not known those words, but he knew what his mother meant. Grandmother did not correct him but went to the big trunk in the bedroom and got out a sack of marbles, and sparing him the story of who had once owned and played with them, handed the sack to Kellan. Only after he had thanked her and had some of the beautiful marbles in his hand did she say, Vengeance is mine, sayeth the Lord, I will repay. Just you always remember that, child.

Having heard the sound of his car in the driveway, Grandmother was standing on the back porch, ready to unlatch the screen door for Kellan. She had news. "You got a long distance telephone call. I did not understand what the urgency was."

The Fosters did not make or receive long distance calls unless there was an emergency. "The connection was bad, and I didn't quite understand the first name, but the last name was Welles. I wondered at the time if she might be kinfolks to the Welles over around Waterville. They are the only Welles I'm acquainted with. You have any idea what might be wrong?"

"There's nothing wrong, Grandmother. It was a student from the university."

Grandmother looked at Kellan as though she were trying to read in his face the answers to her unasked questions.

"Now, if you need to make a long distance call, son, it will be all right..."

"No. That's not necessary;. I'll see her tomorrow when I get back to Indiana."

"Why mercy me," surprise was in Grandmother's voice; "you're surely not leaving so soon. You just got here."

"I'm sorry it has to be such a short visit, but I've decided to take the second summer session, and registration is this week."

"Goodness knows we don't want to hinder your studies." She was not being sarcastic. It was that ingrained respect, almost reverence, that the Fosters held for scholarly pursuits. "Well, it's late, way past my bedtime, and you have to travel tomorrow, so I'll bid you goodnight, dear child."

Full of the mixed emotions of guilt and sorrow, impatience and aversion, he went upstairs to his old bedroom. Kellan looked for something to read. He was finished with the magazines. The books on the shelf were some he had received as gifts, too familiar to engage interest, a few old textbooks. Perhaps there was something in one of the other bedrooms.

His parents' bedroom looked as it had when they were alive. Same dresser scarf on the dresser, brush, comb, and hand mirror neatly placed. *A King James Bible, Collected Poems of Sara Teasdale* on a rough table that served as a night stand. As a young boy, Kellan had sampled those poems and found them too mushy to stomach. He opened the book to the flyleaf and re-read the inscription he knew so well. *To my beloved wife, Mary Katherine, Christmas, 1934.* The bookmark was always between pages 26 and 27. Did that mark a favorite verse or had she never read past that page? He could not remember ever having seen her reading the book. Mother's sewing basket which used to be a fixture beside her chair downstairs, had been brought up and deposited on the seat of a T-backed straight chair. Nothing brought back his mother's presence and the sadness of his loss so much as her sewing basket. Still in the embroidery hoop was a linen handkerchief with the letter K partially embroidered. Knowing that he was stirring up latent sorrow and should turn away from these things, he nevertheless lingered, picking up her tatting shuttle, remembering how fast her dexterous fingers could turn out yards and yards of tiny lace. He dropped the shuttle and picked up a packet of letters neatly tied with blue embroidery thread. Old letters, mostly from himself, a newspaper account of his graduation from midshipman's school, a recipe for a hickory nut white cake, a business envelope bearing the return of Sears, Roebuck, and Co. Wondering if it was a bill or receipt or by slim chance a refund check, he pulled that envelope from the packet. Inside was a folded paper of good quality linen paper, slightly yellowed.

He opened it gently. The old-fashioned script was legible.

Tuesday

Dearest Kitten,

The day after you left, I found a white kid glove which could only fit the dearest hand in the world. I'm keeping the glove. There! Now you've an excuse for a shopping trip. Your rented house is boarded up for the season, and it looks so bleak on the empty beach. The sea winds howled fiercely all night last night and again today. I've never been melancholy here, even in the meanest winters, until you left. I sail in eight days.

I've considered chucking the whole thing and coming after you. But I keep telling myself that what we decided was the correct approach. After I've made something of myself, maybe your father will accept me as good enough for you.

Wait for me, my darling girl. I'll hold you in my heart until I again hold you in my arms. Remember always how much I love you. If you get forgetful of my love or ever doubt me, read this letter and be reminded that I love you as constantly as the surf beats on the shore, as faithfully as the moon pulls the tides.

Yours forever,
Chaz

Awed by all that the letter implied, Kellan put it carefully back in the envelope. Then he meticulously went through the packet a second time. Nothing more.

He had an irrational urge to tear the place apart to find something else that would shed more light on the mysterious person who was his father, but reason prevailed and he knew that somewhere, with someone, there were answers to his questions, but not this night, not in this room.

Kellan thought that his brain was so over-stimulated that sleep would not come easily, but he was wrong. He fell into a deep, dreamless sleep and did not awaken until Grandmother called him to breakfast.

"I do declare, it's a shame you have to run off practically as soon as you got here," Grandmother said as she sat down at the kitchen table. "Return thanks, son."

Kellan mumbled the table prayer.

"Now when you get halfway settled somewhere," Grandmother said, "I want you to take the things you've inherited from Garret while I'm still alive and got my senses so's I can tell you the history of each item so's you can pass the heritage along to your own children some day."

Kellan found it impossible to envision himself with children. Or married for that matter.

"If I know much about a young man," Grandmother went on, "the one thing you're most interested in is that Kentucky squirrel rifle that hangs over the fireplace."

Like the pioneers who prized a Kentucky rifle above all other possessions, Kellan could think of nothing in the house that he would value more. There was a mystique about the long, muzzle loaders. They fired so true they were accurate at distances as great as 300 yards. Daniel Boone was supposed to

52

have loaded his "Tick-Licker" with six fingers of black powder and obtained a muzzle velocity as great as 800 yards.

"Owning that rifle," Kellan said, "is like owning a piece of American history."

"Yes, indeed. And you know, Kellan, my side of the family through the Edwardses goes back to 1640 when the *Deliverance* landed on the shores of what is now Massachusetts. And through the Hardys we can trace the family back to Wales. What you inherit from us, Kellan, is worth more than all the wealth you might have got from the Kellan family." She split a hot biscuit and spread it with butter and sorghum molasses. "I declare to goodness, it's heartbreaking that you got nothing coming to you from your mother's family. But Mary Katherine's father was a stiff necked blue blood who turned his back on his own flesh and blood. Mary Katherine disgraced him. She was the same as dead to him from the day he turned her out and sent her down to the Radcliffs."

It was a rare moment to hear Grandmother speak openly of what had always been a hush-hush subject.

"What would you have done, Grandmother," Kellan asked, "if she had been your daughter? Would you have forgiven her?"

Grandmother's dark eyes turned bright with conviction. "Seventy-times seven!" Her voice softened. "Oh, I'd have been sorely grieved, naturally, but did Christ turn his back on sinners? Didn't He forgive the woman at the well? And could I dare do less?"

Kellan groaned inwardly. Why did the Fosters have to turn every statement into a sermon? "Grandmother, do you know who my real father was?"

"Your real father was Garret Foster."

I deserved that, Kellan thought. And for once he not only thought it but said it.

Then Grandmother returned to his question. "I never knew anything about the man who took advantage of Mary Katherine. Or cared to know. We forgave her and never dwelt on it. Garret loved your mother so much that he hurt because she had been hurt. I tell you, Kellan, preachers and poets dwell on the depth of mother love, but there is no love outside of the love of Christ to equal that rare love that once in a great, great while a man has for a woman. Oh, I lack the words to explain it. Kirby loves Sammie, you know, but it's not a patch to the ethereal feeling that Garret had for Mary Katherine.It was, I tremble to say, a kind of worship.

As he reflected on the lack of information about his biological father, it seemed totally in his mother's character that she would have kept private anything that had to do with her personal life. His thinking had been all screwed up when he went to Aunt Sammie for information about that shadowy figure who was his father. Mother would never have confided in Aunt Sammie. It might have been, Kellan concluded, that she was just waiting for the right time to tell me.

And so, as he had done time and time again, Kellan told himself that it really didn't matter.

He felt buoyed up, exhilarated—he was leaving. Did it show in his face? Did he move with more purpose? Define purpose, he said to himself. Joanie Welles. If I see her one more time, I can die happy. Wrong, wrong, wrong. I want to live to have her with me every day of my life.

"Say good bye to Uncle Kirby and Aunt Sammie for me," he said as he kissed his grandmother. "I'm sorry I have to leave in such a rush. But I do need to get back to make certain of getting into the classes I need." Liar. I'm not in the least sorry to be leaving and I don't know what in hell I'm going to do. Except see Joanie Welles.

"Let me know, Kellan, as soon as you can, your new address and telephone number in case of emergency."

"Thanks for everything, Grandmother. And I won't stay away so long this time."

"See that you don't, son. *And may the Lord watch between thee and me, while we are absent, one from another.*"

It was good, putting the miles behind him, putting distance between himself and home. Good to feel the fresh morning air on his face, good to block out the lingering cadences of Scripture with radio music. Good to be answerable to no one, good to be free to do and go as he wished—yet all the while being pulled like a magnet toward Joanie Welles.

He regretted not having brought along the Kentucky rifle that was his, but he hadn't had the guts to snatch it off the wall. It would have seemed too greedy. Like snatching the best piece of fried chicken off the platter. If Bill could see the gun, he would drool like a fool. He would appreciate the lore behind the rifle, but he would marvel at the distinction of the firearm and its craftsmanship. Until this visit Kellan had never expected that the gun would ever be his. He knew that Father had inherited it because he was the eldest son. But Kellan, adopted son, had never thought the gun would be his. Kellan suddenly felt guilty. Guilty that he had no use for the farm or the family's way of life, guilty that he was glad to be leaving it all behind.

How could he exorcise this demon guilt?

As soon as he drove across the county line into a "wet" county, Kellan stopped at the first Cold Beer sign and bought a beer. A surrogate exorcist. The tug of home loosened its grip as the miles behind him increased.

When he arrived at his destination, that flat, unlovely Indiana town, a place that surely no one could think of as scenic, his spirits lifted. He drove straight to Joanie's house.

An old woman answered the door. Not ancient, not elderly, merely old as opposed to attractive. She had rather colorless eyes and sallow skin unadorned with cosmetics. Her thin gray hair was pulled tightly back from her face, giving her a bleak countenance. This surely was the housekeeper. Kellan asked for Joanie.

"She's at the bridge luncheon at the country club. May I ask who you might be?"

"Kellan Foster. A friend of Joanie's. When do you expect her to be home?"

"Well, she might be home first one time and then another, but I have an idea she'll be here for dinner. Doctor likes her here for dinner."

"Please give her a message. Tell her that Kellan Foster will phone her after dinner." Would the woman remember to relay the message? He thought so because she was accustomed to being responsible for messages to the doctor.

Kellan drove aimlessly. What now? Hunt up the public library? Play the Viking, storm the country club, and drag Joanie out by the hair?

As he approached the Pennsy tracks, the long arms of the warning signals dropped in front of him. He idled the car. The diesel engine went by picking up speed as it clattered down the tracks. It was a long freight and it would be a long wait. Kellan turned off the ignition and let his thoughts be lulled to nothingness as he watched car after car whip by. When he could see the caboose, he started the engine of his car so he would be ready to scoot over the tracks to nowhere.

"Hey! Where the hell are you going?" The voice was Bill's. He was traveling in the opposite direction but had stopped the big Dietmeier Distributing Company delivery truck to yell at Kellan. He was also blocking traffic.

"I'll pull over so I don't hold up traffic," Kellan answered.

Bill, on the other hand, let the truck idle in the street and ignored the vehicles which had to pull around. He leaned out the window. "Give me a hand, why don't you. Dad's got a man on vacation and one down in his back—I'm way to hell behind on deliveries."

"Sure." The perfect antidote for his aimlessness. Kellan got out of the car and was locking it when Bill called out to him. "Hey! You can't leave your car parked on a yellow line."

"At least I'm not blocking the damn street."

"Well, hell. You'd get a ticket. Not me. Follow me and leave your car at the house." Which Kellan, feeling like a trained pup, did.

The work was not easy. Bill's "get moving," "stack 'em up," pull 'em down," "load 'em up," "set 'em off." squelched introspection.

"Is there a state law," Kellan asked, "that requires beer cases to be stored in the most inaccessible place possible?"

Bill laughed. "Seems that way." They had at that moment finished the downtown taverns where every man they encountered, regardless of social standing, had a friendly word for Bill. "One more delivery. Last one today. Eleven miles into the heart of the Deutsch settlement. The Sportsman's Bar."

As they bumped along the poorly paved road, Kellan told Bill about the Kentucky rifle that was his.

"How much do you want for it?" Bill asked.

"You think I'd sell it? I might give it away, but I will never sell it."

"I'll accept your generous gift anytime."

In a hamlet clustered around a Lutheran church and school, Bill stopped the truck in front of what seemed to be a grocery store with one gas pump beside the rickety porch.

"This is the Sportsman's Bar?" Kellan was incredulous.

"Yep. Soon as we get the empties and set the full cases off, I'll buy you the coldest beer in Indiana. And you can listen to the biggest lies in the state. If all the game they claim to have bagged was killed, there wouldn't be a squirrel, rabbit, quail, or grouse in the county."

Kirkendorff's Sportsman's Bar was both tavern and grocery. Shelves filled with can goods and miscellaneous items covered two walls in the fore part of the long room. In the back were an ancient bar and four ancient bar stools. In the center of the room were four tables covered with checkered oil cloth; the unmatched chairs once belonged to chrome dinette sets. Presiding over it all was old Kirkendorff, taciturn and deaf to any words except those that dealt with money. The talk was a mixture of German and English.

Before they had finished their beer, Bill had struck up a conversation about fishing with a man he called Bud. It ended with Bud offering Bill the use of his boat on Voston Lake, practically begging Bill to use the boat.

Bill, Kellan thought, is the most uncommon common man I have ever known.

On the return to town, Kellan asked Bill, "Where's a good place to take a girl?"

"Depends on what you have in mind."

"You know damn well what I have in mind."

Bill assumed a mock air of contemplation. "Well, now, there's Dad's old farm. She might like to see the place."

Kellan let it go at that. The uncommon man had made him as mad as hell. They rode back to the Dietmeier house with the truck radio blaring out the opening game of a twi-night double header at Cincinnati.

"You might just as well stay over with us," Bill directed more than invited.

Kellan hesitated. Not a good idea.

"It's the only pay you're going to get," Bill added.

"In that case, I'd better collect what I can." Kellan made it sound careless, off-hand. Actually he was relieved not to have to hunt up a hotel room.

"My God," Mr. Dietmeier said facetiously when Kellan walked into the kitchen with Bill, "I thought we'd got rid of you."

Mrs. Dietmeier turned from the stove that was a cauldron of steaming vapors. "Looks like I've got you to raise, Kellan…somebody hunt up Max and Burt. It's about time to eat."

Kellan felt comfortably at home. And before supper was over, he had accepted the offer to stay with the Dietmeiers and work at Dietmeier Distributing Company for the remainder of the summer.

"Oh, it's been a hundred years!" Joanie exclaimed as she rushed down the wide stairs and into Kellan's open arms.

He could feel her heart palpitating in the same excited fervor of his own, and she filled him with mingled satisfaction and desire. They kissed again and again.

As sometimes happens when one is the object of an unsuspected stare, Kellan involuntarily turned to see Dr. Welles watching from the open doorway of the library.The expression on his face was like that of a jealous lover.

Joanie was not in the least disconcerted to be under her father's observation though when he suggested they have a glass of wine, she glibly put him off by saying that they were driving to Columbia, twenty miles away, to catch the first showing of the movie, *The Treasure of Sierra Madre*, and that she would not be home until very late.

Later, she said to Kellan in neither defense nor regret, "That's the first time I ever lied to Charles about where I was going."

Kellan was driving to where he did not know and asked, "And where are we going?"

"Out to the lake. To our cabin."

The lake was about fifteen miles southwest of town. The cabin was no cabin at all. Even in the dim twilight Kellan could see that it was spacious enough for a family home.

"Damn." Joanie was exasperated. "I don't have my key to the cabin."

"Never mind," Kellan said. The rising moon promised luminescence. He took from the trunk of the car the blanket that he always kept there, and with Joanie leading the way, they walked down to the edge of the lake where he spread the blanket on the grass.

They stood for a minute or so, Joanie pointing out certain landmarks—so and so's cabin, so and so's dock, this and that. She curled her fingers tightly around his and asked, "Do you love me?" She spoke the words catechistically, knowing the answer before the reply was given.

"I have loved you all my life." His words were hardly an exaggeration. She embodied all that he had ever thought of as ideal...she was the girl he should have taken taken to the high school prom instead of Velma Mae Woodson. Had it not been for his mother, who always wanted much for him, he would not have attended the prom. To please his mother, Kellan had asked Velma Mae, a drab, uninteresting girl. The prom might have been bearable if Velma Mae had elected to stay plain, but she had gone to a beauty parlor and had her hair set in a pasty style of stiff waves and tight curls that made her ugly. Velma Mae's dress had been wrong, too. The other girls' dresses swept the floor, but Velma Mae's was short enough to show her Sunday shoes. He thought he would forever remember those white shoes clobbering over the dance floor.

He kissed Joanie again, feeling her hands under his shirt caressing his back, her fingers like supplicants, her eagerness a match for his own. She shed her clothes with no shyness and stepped into the light of the moon so that he might better see her.

This without coyness but not without vanity. She was the proud giver of a gift of great beauty, and the gift was herself. With equal candor, Kellan claimed his gift. She flinched and dug her fingers into his back, and the realization that she had come to him in pristine purity was overwhelming.

He touched her face, his fingers tracing a smile and she said, "This is the supreme moment of my life."

And when she put her hands on his face, he was not ashamed of his tears that spilled on her fingers.

A chilling wind blew off the lake. Reluctant to leave the place, they sat for a long time huddled under the blanket.

"I love you," Joanie said. "And I could never, not in a million years, tell Charles about this."

"It never occurred to me that you would," Kellan said, somewhat disconcerted by her words.

"I've always told Charles everything. When I first started dating, I would come home and tell him all the silly, stupid things boys would try. And Charles would make fun of the boys and say things that would make me laugh."

Kellan felt an aversion to the relationship she had with her father. "Yours is not the usual father-daughter relationship, is it?"

"I guess not. But for me, I don't know the difference. I know, growing up, that I was the only young girl who knew absolutely everything about sex. Charles never wanted me to be ignorant."

No, my darling, Kellan thought. You just think you know everything about sex. We will never again match the purity of this night, but there will be other nights that in another way will be more satisfying than this.

Abruptly, Joanie asked, "When are we going to get married?"

She was ahead of him. He loved her, but marriage was some distant, future thing. He made his answer light. "When I'm gainfully employed and can provide for you in the style to which you are accustomed."

She said as matter-of-factly as if she were commenting on the weather, "Then we had better get you a job."

"I have a job for a few weeks—with Dietmeier Distributing Company." He was avoiding the serious. Events were moving much too fast. He realized she was shivering. "Come. We can't stay here all night." He would not have been surprised if she had replied, why not, but she didn't. He stood up, gave her a hand, and pulled her to her feet.

When they had found their way back to Kellan's old Forty-one Chevy and were closed in from the cool night air, Joanie stated, again matter-of-factly, "You need a new car."

"That's not high on my list of priorities," he replied quickly, surprised rather than miffed.

She went on as though she had not heard his words. "We'll have a new car to drive very soon. Charles has one on order for me, and it should be in any day now. You'll love it. I know you will. But if you don't, we'll get something you do like."

Joanie, Kellan thought, needs an object lesson in frugality. Some weekend I'll take her home with me. She needs to know where I'm from and what I am before things get too complicated.

59

In and out of the truck, loading and unloading, riding from tavern to tavern, from one stop to another, Kellan appeared complacently at ease with the job, but his inner mind was in turmoil. Events had happened so fast. Not so long ago he had not heard the name, Joanie Welles. Now she spoke of nothing but marriage. Marriage! The word would have sobered him if he were dead drunk.

"Down that road," Bill pointed to an intersecting blacktop, "a mile, mile-and-a half, Dad and I got up the biggest covey of birds I've ever seen. I got three birds on the rise before..."

Kellan was sure of two things: he loved Joanie. He wanted no part of this or any other small town life. He had had enough of small town snobbishness to last a lifetime.

Bill seemed unable to shut up. "Did I ever tell you about the little beagle that Dad used to own that would point quail?"

"No. And I probably won't believe you after you describe this phenomenal aberration."

"Hell. I don't know anything about aberration. Or phenomenal. I know this beagle would hold a point a damn sight better than most bird dogs."

Joanie's relationship to her father was damned strange. The man bothered Kellan. He was polite to the point of coldness and wore an air of superiority like a coat of mail. And he doesn't like me. He merely tolerates me like I was Joanie's pet dog.

Bill pointed to the Lutheran school. "Every year, and you can bet every dollar you have on it, every year the high school valedictorian will be a kid from the Lutheran grade school. When my kids..." he didn't finish.

College, Joanie had told Kellan, was the only thing she and her father ever fought about. She wanted to go away to go to school, but her father stubbornly insisted she commute to Houghton College. She lasted one semester, but her grades were so poor that her father allowed her to drop out. Kellan thought it out of character. Dr. Welles seemed the type who would send his daughter to Smith or Wellesley. Sarah Lawrence, perhaps. Not let his daughter stagnate in a narrow, provincial environment. It seemed to Kellan that Joanie needed to get away from small town life as much as he did.

By the time the day's deliveries were completed, Bill had been morose for a long time, and Kellan had privately decided that the best thing for him to do was to re-enlist—he would go in as a full lieutenant—and let the Navy make his decisions.

Decisions, however, were already being made for him, for when they got back to the Dietmeier house, there was a message for Kellan to phone Joanie. They were having dinner, she told him, at the country club with the Fultons.

When Kellan told Mrs. D. that he would not be at her supper table, she wanted to know why; where, and what for.

Subtleness made no home with her.

Nor with the other Dietmeiers.

"You're lucky," Max commented as he yanked open the refrigerator door and peered in, checking it out. "Joanie Welles is the best looking chick in town." He pulled out the water jug and gulped down water, spilling as much on the floor as he drank.

"She's a looker all right," Mr. D. agreed, and then when Max turned from the refrigerator. "Clean your water mess on the floor so your mother won't have to."

Burt was leaning over the stove where two skillets of chicken were frying. He was trying to pick off a crust without getting burned. "Joanie's the sexiest broad I ever saw outside of the movies." He burned a finger. "Shit."

Mrs. D. in one quick motion yanked the towel off her shoulder and whipped it across Burt's arm. "Stop that dirty talk and quit picking the crusties off the chicken."

From boredom or disgust, Bill had walked out on the talk. Though, perhaps, Kellan thought, it was not that at all, but envy.

Miss Eddie ushered Kellan into the library to wait for Joanie. Having to wait did not surprise him. He would have been surprised if she had been ready. The only girls, in his experience, who were invariably prompt were those who weren't worth waiting for.

Though he would have preferred to wait alone, Miss Eddie sat down to entertain him until Joanie presented herself. She commented on the weather in general and the climate of the library in particular. "This is always a cool room."

Kellan's full attention was not given to Miss Eddie's converstion— "Doctor said…Doctor did…Doctor likes…."

But when the housekeeper said that she had come to work steady for the doctor years ago when his wife went sudden, he was immediately alert.

"How did she die?" Kellan had not meant to be so blunt.

"How?" Miss Eddie looked as though she had been caught sweeping dirt under a rug.

"I mean was it accidental or…"

"Cerebral hemorrhage." Her face went sour.

Kellan could sense that she was afraid she had said too much.

At the muffled sound of footsteps on the carpeted stairway, Miss Eddie jumped up awkwardly. "Joanie's coming downstairs. Well, it was nice talking to you." She lurched out of the room.

Kellan went to the foot of the stairs just in time to swoop Joanie into his arms before she reached the last step. He kissed her hungrily. Never from her a "don't ruin my hair" or "don't spoil my lipstick."

"Oh, darling," she was breathless, "I never want to leave your arms. Never, ever. Do you love me? If ever you should tell me that you don't love me, I'd kill myself."

"Then I must write out a declaration of love and give it to you so you can read it whenever you have doubts." Kellan had stunned himself. Without consciously being aware of it, he had said virtually the same thing that his father had written to his mother: read this letter and be reminded that I love you as constantly as the surf beats on the shore, as faithfully as the moon pulls the tides. With his love for Joanie, he now understood his mother and father's love, a love without reason. For the first time Kellan felt a sympathetic bond with that unknown parent who was no more than a shadow in his life.

"You know, don't you," Joanie said as if to put a resolution to Kellan's thoughts, "we need nothing in life but each other."

"Then let's skip the dinner with the Fultons."

"No," she said reasonably, "we can't do that. I arranged the whole thing. I was the one who asked Helen and Steamboat to join us for dinner."

"So be it." And I hope I have enough cash to foot the bill.

Just as he opened the door for her, Joanie turned to him and asked, "Do you like this dress? I mean do you like me in white?"

"I'd like you better in nothing, but you've got this damned dinner…"

"Oh, shush. I only asked because I was wondering whether to get a stark white wedding dress or an off-white."

"You've plenty of time to make that decision." Kellan's words were low-key. What kind of time frame did she have in mind? He was afraid to ask.

Bob Fulton put a hand on Joanie's shoulder. "God, you look sexy tonight, hon." Joanie and Kellan had just joined the Fultons at a little table in the barroom of the country club. "Don't she look sexy, Helen?"

"Bobby, dear," Helen said mildly, "she may look sexy to you, but she certainly does not evoke the same response in me. Joanie looks quite attractive."

"Oh, oh, get that," Steamboat mocked. "She doesn't evoke the same response…" then petulantly, "For Christ's sake, Helen, you don't have to impress us." And laughed to make it appear he was merely jovial and got up from the table and went into the small anteroom off the bar and dropped quarters into a slot machine. Empty handed, he came back to the table. "The state ought to outlaw those damned one-armed bandits."

"I think that might happen in the next legislative session," Kellan commented. "At least that seems to be the mood of the legislators. If it happens, how are small clubs like this one going to survive?"

"Higher dues," Helen responded. "Which members can easily pay from all they save by not playing the slots."

Joanie had not been listening. "I'm famished. Let's take our drinks into the dining room and order dinner."

"Helen's on the school board, Kellan," Joanie said after the waitress had taken their orders; then added as if to give importance to her statement. "You're president of the school board also, aren't you, Helen?"

"Yes," Helen answered with no hint of self-importance. "But it is not a position of power."

"But you certainly should know, shouldn't you, whether or not the school system needs teachers?"

"There is a shortage of teachers. The war, you know."

"See," Joanie said with an air of I-told-you-so, "I knew all along the school system needs teachers."

Had he not been amused by Joanie's conniving—she had obviously arranged the dinner with one purpose in mind, getting him a job—he would have been angry. He did not want to teach. He would not teach.

"Do you have a teacher's license, Kellan?" Helen asked.

"No. No teacher's license." That would end Joanie's little scheme.

"But he has all kinds of degrees." Joanie refused to surrender. "Don't you, Kellan?"

"I've got a degree," Steamboat boastfully put in, "from the school of hard knocks." He guffawed loudly.

Helen gave her husband a look of disapproval that turned into an indulgent smile.

Helen's beauty, like her speech and manners was, Kellan thought, patrician.Neat, side-parted black hair framed an ivory-skinned, oval face; charcoal colored eyes were well-spaced across a rather prominent nose that did not detract from the symmetry of her features. She was asking Kellan what subject his degree was in.

"I have undergraduate majors in history and math and a Masters in European history."

"But Kellan can teach anything," Joanie interjected. "You will get him a job, won't you, Helen?"

"I'm not the person to contact." Helen was being very patient with Joanie. "You need to see the superintendent first.

The board acts on his recommendations."

"Oh, well, the superintendent. That's easy."

"Not if I don't want to see him." Kellan had had enough.

Steamboat burst out in a laugh. "You tell 'em, kid."

Discomfited, Joanie started to say something but stopped.

Kellan blamed himself for not making it clear to Joanie what direction his life must take. But that was the rub—he knew well what he did not want, but was not at all sure of what he did want. Except for one thing. And that one thing was Joanie.

"Gol durn it. I don't believe it." Steamboat was sitting so that he had a full view of the entrance to the dining room.

"E.P. just walked in with that kid. Lonnie."

Heads turned.

E.P. threw a jaunty wave in their general direction and chose a table—she hadn't waited to be seated—across the room.

The three of them—Steamboat, Helen, and Joanie—felt compelled to spell out to Kellan the details of the relationship between E.P. and Lonnie Lykins. Lonnie was a nineteen year old, soon to be twenty, as opposed to E.P.'s thirty years. He was a talented athlete who had accepted a grant-in-aid to play basketball for Purdue. Lonnie's father had killed another man in a tavern fight and was serving a prison sentence for manslaughter. Lonnie's mother had abandoned her young daughters, left them with their grandmother and gone off to Georgia with a man she met in a bar. Lonnie lived with an uncle and worked part time in his filling station. Lonnie was a fair student, an exceptional basketball player and had lettered in football and baseball.

E.P. had her car serviced at Lyken's Service Station.

"E.P. found out she could get Lonnie to pump something besides gas," Steamboat said.

"Bobby, please," Helen reprimanded without acerbity, as though she were instructing an erring child. "E.P. has simply been acting as a mentor to Lonnie. She allows him the use of her car on occasion—and if you didn't know, she paid for his tux and everything he needed for the senior prom. I'm quite sure that E.P. is merely acting as a surrogate sister."

Bob Fulton threw up his hands in a gesture of unbelief. "Oh, geeze, Helen, come off that crap. You weren't born yesterday." He spoke directly to Kellan. "Foster, let me tell you about women."

Kellan missed that bit of wisdom, for the waitress interrupted to clear the table.

The evening turned into an impromptu party as older couples gradually cleared out, and a younger, less staid group began to gather around the Fultons and Joanie and Kellan.

First Larry Somner. Who pretended not to remember having once been introduced to Kellan.

"Somner, you're a damn fool," Steamboat pronounced.

Then the Scotts. Homer, the Bill Mauldin dog face, and Esther, his bosomy wife. They had two toddlers with them.

"We can't stay," Esther said. "We only stopped off to see who's here and what's going on."

"Damnit, Scott," Steamboat urged, "take the kids home and phone a sitter."

"Can't," Scott answered firmly. "Gotta work tomorrow. The whole plant is doing overtime."

The children, a boy and girl were squealing and trying to gain release from their father who held each one tightly by a hand. Esther was oblivious to the disruption they were causing, not at all disposed toward leaving.

Scott was insisting they leave when the little boy escaped from his father's hold, and Esther had to corral him, and the Scott family exited with one child crying and the other one screaming to be let down.

"Helen," Steamboat looked to his wife as though she had answers to his forthcoming question, "Do they have to drag those kids in here?"

Helen did not answer his question. "It doesn't seem fair," she mused "for Es to have two children while I want a child so desperately."

Larry took the opportunity to pay back Steamboat for his previous put-down. "What do you need a kid for, Helen, when you've got Steamboat to raise?"

Bill Dietmeier, beer in hand, sauntered in.

E.P. Portland, who had previously left with Lonnie, now followed Bill to the table. "I'm buying, good citizens, whether you're ready or not. As for this paragon of virtue," she tousled Larry's blond hair, "he gets a large glass of wholesome milk."

She pulled out a chair and sat down next to Larry.

Bill, without a word, left.

E.P. noticed his leaving. She shrugged her shoulders expressively. "*C'est la guerre.*" She continued to needle Larry.

"How goes the night, Horatio? Lousy, huh? One must say to oneself, it's a far, far better thing I do than I have ever..."

"What are you running off at the mouth about?" Larry asked crossly.

"Knowest thou not of what I speak? Methinks thou hast not fully comprehended nor yet understood that which those amongst thee most surely find as obvious as yon handsome nose that doth protrude from the face of that gentle man who hath so recently supplanted you in our lady's fancy. Love's labor..."

"What put a burr under your tail?" Larry sneered; "is your toy boy out with a young chick?"

"Go clean the shit off your saddle shoes, kid," E.P. said in an expressionless voice.

It seemed to Kellan that the crabby exchange between Larry and E.P. was the norm for the crowd paid little mind, and Larry and E.P. did not appear to be at the point of exchanging blows.

When the waitress arrived with drinks, she put a large glass of milk before Larry who stood up, drained the glass, smacked his lips and flexed his muscles. "Chug-a-lug."

"I know how to play that game," E.P. challenged. "Tell you what; I'll match you a glass of beer to a glass of milk, and I bet you a hundred dollars I drink you under the table. You'll be sick when I'm still thirsty."

"I'll buy," a new voice said, and another couple joined the party.

The new voice belonged to Davis Courtney who, almost scoffingly, introduced his date, Lynda Davis. "No relation, just a coincidence of names," Davis explained. We're not even engaged." He was smoothly sarcastic. "We do not even know each other very well, do we, dear?"

Lynda Davis looked about sixteen. She explained, "This is our second date. But I mean, well, you know, we kinda know each other pretty well. Living in the same town and all."

Davis was an ex-Marine, Kellan learned during the course of the evening, a product of an Eastern prep school who would graduate from Princeton next year. He had black, wavy hair and icy blue eyes and a little smirk that passed for a smile.

No matter what he said, even when he was being polite, the words sounded like ridicule.

Watching Joanie stride off toward the Ladies' Powder Room, Davis,disregarding Lynda, said to Kellan, "There goes the most fantastic female ever formed from human coupling. If there is a blemish on that body, only the sinister Dr. Welles knows where."

"Sinister?" Kellan kept his voice expressionless.

Davis's smirk was broader. "One could cast him in a horror movie, could he not? Strange young doctor arrives in town, young wife dies under, shall we say, suspect circumstances, exhibits rather unseemly affection for his only child…"

Lacking attention, Lynda said to Davis, "I should have worn my pink dress, the one you like…"

"The one that is so easily removed?" Davis sounded as though he were talking to a half-wit.

"Oh, Davis," Lynda was blushing. "you make jokes about absolutely everything and everybody."

To Kellan it was obvious that Davis did not make jokes. He made mockery.

Other couples joined the group, but in the alcoholic euphoria of near midnight, nobody bothered with introductions.

They closed the club.

"Where are we going?" Joanie asked when she realized that Kellan had not taken the route to her home.

"You'll see."

"The pump house!" she exclaimed when the road suggested the destination."Who told you about the pump house?"

"Burt. He said that's where he takes a girl when he wants to make-out." Kellan assumed Joanie would think that comical.

She didn't. "All right for him. But if you think we're going to make love in the back seat of a car, think again."

"When you said that you could be rather cruel to some high school Romeo, you really meant it, didn't you?"

"Absolutely. I was intimidating. And then there is Charles who can really be intimidating."

The pump house was no more than that: a pumping station for the local water works. Gas lights gave a soft glow to the structure, protected by a utilitarian iron fence, and to the adjacent grounds that had been landscaped into a small park with ornamental shrubs and plants, park benches, and a three-foot high stone wall that separated the area from the steep, shaggy bank that dropped off to the river, a smooth surface of pallid light that flowed quietly until it rushed over the dam in a noisy gush.

Holding hands, Kellan and Joanie walked down to the wall and sat down.

" The Wapahani," Kellan said.

"White River," Joanie corrected.

"Wapahani is the name the Miami Indians gave the river. Their favorite camping grounds were along its banks."

"How do you know that?"

"Well, it wasn't passed down to me because I'm a surviving member of the tribe. I read it in a history book."

"I don't like to read. In school I read what I had to read to make an A. Sometimes I get a best seller that everyone is talking about, but I skim around, and then turn to the back to see how it ends."

"At one time I read anything that came my way. I read more selectively now.Reading is one of the great pleasures of my life." Kellan offered Joanie a cigarette, flicked the lighter. As she bent to catch a drag, a strand of her hair fell dangerously close to the flame; in one quick motion Kellan caught the wayward strand of hair and pushed it away from her face.

The touch of his fingers on her face brought her into his arms, and she clung to him." Let's go away together now," she said. "Just leave everything and everybody and go away and make life one long, passionate love affair."

"Are you serious, Joanie?"

"Yes. I know what I want."

"How does New York sound?"

"New York, New Jersey, New Hampshire, New anywhere."

Kellan was struck with the idea of eloping. He had enough money for them to live on until he found employment. With his Navy credentials and his academic degrees and in the right environment, he knew he could easily find a job. "How soon," Kellan asked, "can you be ready to leave?"

Joanie was on her feet. "I can be ready in about twenty-five minutes."

Kellan laughed, pleased with her enthusiasm. "I wish we could leave on a moment's notice, but..."

"Tomorrow?"

"We will need money. And my money is in a savings bank in Green Forks.We have to make plans; we can't ride off in the sunset like..."

"Oh, don't be so practical."

"You were being practical when you arranged a dinner with a member of the school board to finagle a position for me in the local school system. Something that I can't thank you for because I have no intention of teaching."

"Take me home," she said, pushing herself away from him.

"Don't be angry; Joanie. We must always be honest with each other."

She was already walking toward the car. "Forget the whole thing. We couldn't go anywhere in this car anyway. It's too old."

That honesty, Kellan thought, hurt.

Summer sun filled the upstairs bedroom, and it was like waking up in an oven.Kellan got out of bed and walked to the open window. He had awakened thinking of Joanie. Not in specifies, it was more or less a consciousness of her. Echoes of her voice stayed in his head. Her very being seemed to touch him; he could look down at the yard below and at the same time see her in his mind's eye.

Bill was hanging up wash on the clothes line. Old Mrs. Lox, the widow who lived next door, stood at the fence watching. Kellan could hear the sound of their voices without being able to understand what was being said. However, when Bill jerked a sheet off the line and re-hung it, ends together, Kellan figured that Bill was receiving instructions from Mrs. Lox.

Amused, Kellan turned from the window and went to the bathroom to shower. He regulated the water to a pleasant spray and lathered up. Joanie, Joanie, fantastic Joanie. The water suddenly went cold. The shock took away his breath. Damn.

Too many loads of wash had used up all the hot water. Now he would have to shave with cold water.

Kellan looked at his face in the mirror. He had no reason to be displeased with the image he saw. But he was disgruntled with himself. Why didn't I get a degree in something marketable? Something I could auction off to the highest bidder?

When he went downstairs, Kellan found the kitchen in a chaotic condition. There were dirty dishes stacked in the sink, clean dishes drying in a wire rack, dishes scattered over the kitchen table which held the remnants of several previous breakfasts—a saucer of soft butter, toast crumbs, a butcher knife and a loaf of homemade bread, a pitcher with a small amount of warm looking orange juice, a pint of jelly dotted with crumbs. On the stove a pot of coffee was perking pleasantly along, and Bill stood over a skillet and turned food that was frying in sputtering grease.

"Did you get a lesson in how to hang sheets?" Kellan greeted.

"Oh, that. As soon as I hear Mrs. Lox open her back door, I do something to make her know she's alive. Like throwing wet clothes across the line. I bet she's told me how to hang shirts and sheets a hundred times. She never catches on."

"She probably thinks you're retarded."

"I am. Otherwise, I never would have brought you home with me." Bill turned from the stove. "I put a piece of blood puddin' in the skillet for you."

"Blood pudding?"

"Blood puddin'," Bill corrected.

"What's it made from?"

"Guess."

"Really?"

"Yep. When the old German farmers butcher, they drain off the hog's blood and cook it with rye meal and some of the head meat. Maybe add some side meat. It's gotta be cooked real, real slow. When it's thick, it's packed in cloth sausage sacks and laid by."

"Who butchers in the summer?"

"Nobody, you knucklehead. Ever hear of a frozen food locker? Or don't they have such modern conveniences in Green Forks?"

Kellan did not like the looks of blood puddin'. Not the raw variety he saw on the kitchen counter nor the black discs frying in the skillet.

"Some old Dutchmen eat blutwurst raw," Bill said when he saw Kellan studying the blood puddin'. "Take a taste."

Without any enthusiasm, Kellan replied, "I'll wait for the cooked product."

Bill took slices of homemade bread, spread them with blackberry jelly, and made sandwiches of the blood puddin'. Kellan got a couple of cups from the drying rack and poured coffee. He had a notion that he would need a lot of coffee to wash down breakfast.

Bill eyed Kellan as Kellan bit into the sandwich. "You don't like it, do you?"

"It's all right."

"It's all right, but you don't like it."

"It's different. Where's the morning paper?"

Bill handed the front section to Kellan and took the sports section for himself, propping it up beside his plate. "Well," he commented, "old Joe Louis kayoed Walcott in the eleventh round. Did you listen to the fight on the radio?"

"I forgot about it."

"How in hell could you forget a Joe Louis fight?"

"There were other activities that were engaging my interest at that time."

"Hell." The one word dismissed Kellan's activities as irrelevant. "Dad bet me twenty bucks it would go the full fifteen rounds. Hell, I was surprised it went eleven. Boy, did it hurt Dad to shell out a twenty dollar bill."

"I must need a hearing aid," Mrs. Dietmeier said as she came into the kitchen. "Last night I thought for sure I heard you and Dad agreed on a two dollar bet." She paused for a response but there was none. "If they gave a prize for the biggest liar, it would be a tie between you and Dad."

Bill was unruffled. "Mom, you exaggerate. Did you ever catch me in an out-and-out lie? I might stretch the truth a little…"

"I'd ask you to explain the difference," she interrupted, pushing away the wisps of auburn hair that were curling around her face, "but I don't have all day to listen. Will you two hurry up and finish so I can clean up the kitchen?"

Bill was unconcerned with her vexation. "Don't rush us through your good food, Mom."

Kellan was more than happy to quit the table. "I'll be out of your way all day, Mrs. D. I'm going to Moon Lake."

Bill looked puzzled. "Where the hell are you going?"

"Moon Lake. Joanie's father has a cabin up there."

"You mean Loon Lake. Though I don't know why the hell they named it Loon Lake. So far as I know, no one ever saw a loon around there. Mallard ducks. I've killed a lot of ducks on that lake."

"I suppose Mallard Lake doesn't sound as euphonious as Loon Lake."

As Kellan left the room, Bill called after him. "There are a lot of big bass in the lake. You're welcome to take some of my fishing gear if you want to fish."

Fishing was not what Kellan had on his mind.

Far off, the sky was hazy and soft against the purplish green hills, but directly overhead the sky was pure blue with an intense sun that dazzled the water and baked the shore. The smell of the lake hung in the heavy summer atmosphere. The only sounds that could be heard were the noises of children playing in the yard of a distant cottage and the squabbling of red-winged blackbirds in a nearby pine tree.

Lying beside Joanie, all his senses gratified, the beatification of her love flowing over him like an unction, Kellan thought that life could never be better than this.

A motorboat gunned across the center of the lake, and its wake slapped against the Welles's boat that was moored to their dock. The sound of fun. Small town life, Kellan was forced to admit, when experienced from the top was indeed enjoyable.

Earlier that day, as soon as Kellan and Joanie had arrived at the cottage, they sought each other—hungry to make up for the hours they had been apart—and made love in front of the fireplace whose burnt-out, pungent smell of last winter's fires reminded Kellan of home. Later, they swam and romped in the water with the free abandonment of careless children until they tired and went to the house for lunch—sandwiches, fruit, and wine—which they ate on the screened-in porch. And then they made love again.

Now they lay in the sun, lethargic and content.

Joanie, trying to expose as much of her body to the sun as was decent, had pushed the bottom of the two-piece swim suit into a white strip and unfastened the bra top and turned it into a white strip. Without moving another muscle of her body, Joanie reached a hand to Kellan's face and touched a streak of stubble. "You missed a spot when you shaved," she said idly.

And just as idly he answered, "There wasn't any hot water when I got up. I had to shave with cold water."

"Poor baby." Then she turned to him, one hand with a token hold on the upper strip of white, and ran her tongue over the beard. "Um-m-m."

" A touch of mercy, please."

With a gentle sound of triumph, she brushed her lips very, very lightly across his until he demanded, "Quit teasing and kiss me."

"Only if you'll promise me one thing."

"Anything."

"Promise that you will see Mr. Zeikoff, the superintendent, about a teaching job."

"That's a painless promise. I'll see him. But I won't promise I'll accept an offer to teach."

"Listen to me, Kellan. Don't interrupt. If you could get a teaching position, you would have a reason to stay here all summer. Plus, we would have a whole year to decide what you really want to do. Plus that will make it easy for Charles and me to plan the wedding."

There were definite advantages to what she proposed, he conceded to himself. "We'll see what happens," he said.

"Is that a yes?"

"It's a yes that I'll see this Mr. Zeikoff. Then we'll make decisions. Now kiss me,you little Circe."

"Who's Circe?"

"An enchantress that Odysseus…"

"Save it for some cold winter night when we're bored." Rolling from her back to her stomach, she said, "It's time for me to turn again."

"Are you timing yourself?"

"I have to be methodical. I want an even tan."

Kellan took up a book. *Petits Contes de France.*

"What are you reading?" she asked.

"I'm trying to improve my French."

"Charles speaks French."

"Really?" Kellan was thinking that her father had probably amused her with a few stock phrases.

"Yes. He lived in Paris for awhile. That's where he met my mother."

"Was your mother French?"

"No. She was an American. Charles said that there were a lot of young Americans in Paris after World War I."

It was fitting. If Joanie had told him that Charles Welles once lived on a ranch in Montana, that would have been beyond Kellan's comprehension. "Have you ever been to Paris, Joanie?"

"No. But Charles has promised me a trip to Europe. As soon as things are more normal over there. Think, maybe Charles will give us a trip to Europe for a wedding present. Wouldn't that be neat? I'll start working on that." She sighed sleepily. "If I go to sleep, don't let me sleep over fifteen minutes. It will be time for me to turn."

Kellan went back to the story of Sergeant Pidoux. Soon the steady, slow breathing told him Joanie was asleep. Unable to stay as passively in the sun as Joanie, Kellan went down to the dock, dived off and swam out to the deeper, cooler water.

When he figured fifteen or so minutes had elapsed, he swam back, toweled off, lit a cigarette and roused Joanie who took a drag off his cigarette and then positioned herself more advantageously to catch the sun's rays.

Just as Kellan took up his book and went back to Sergeant Pidoux, a raucous voice called out, "Hey, you people look like you could use a cold beer." It was E.P.Portland approaching them with Lonnie Lykens tagging along like a younger, albeit tall, brother who had been dragged to a place where he did not want to be.

Startled at the unexpected voice, Joanie deftly hooked the bra top of her bathing suit, tied the halter straps and pulled the bottom half of the suit up to its normal fit at her waist. Without the least frustration.

Lonnie stared openly at Joanie as he might have at a risque picture in a girlie magazine. Astonishment, lust, covetousness on his face. And the boy's face was a rare combination of masculinity and beauty. His black hair was shaggy: he needed a hair cut—but its shagginess softened his face as the black lashes shaded and softened the hard, aquamarine eyes. The cheek bones were high, the jaw-line firm and strong, the mouth full and feminine.

"I fail to understand," E.P. said, "why reasonably intelligent people want to broil themselves. "Do you think we could possibly find a bit of shade on yon porch where we can partake of a cold libation?"

And Kellan and Joanie like dutiful students gathered up their gear and went with E.P. and Lonnie to the screened-in porch.

Lonnie seemed incapable of taking his eyes off Joanie. And Joanie deliberately—at least Kellan thought it was deliberate—responded with the subtle body language that suggested her charms. He was offended by her lack of modesty. Jealous possessiveness, that's what he felt. For modesty like many conventions was relative. Not with Grandmother.

Not with the Foster clan. Their right was right, their wrong was wrong as they perceived it to be, without exception.

Try as he might, Kellan could not imagine Grandmother Foster with these people. And yet some day Joanie and his family would meet. It was an unsettling prospect.

Kellan wasn't superstitious. He did not believe in signs and omens. but when the tie—Joanie had said he must wear a suit and tie—refused to form a perfect knot and his neck suddenly felt a size larger than his collar, and his face broke out in a sweat, he knew it would be a bad evening. What kind of sadist would have an affair that required a suit and tie when the temperature had been ninety and above all week? The Fultons.

Ironically it was a house-warming party.

To Kellan's surprise and great relief, the Fulton house had central air-conditioning, and the interior was wonderfully cool and dry with a pleasant smell of newness that mingled with the scents of candles, perfumes, and tobacco smoke. Possibly the only private home in town with central air. Or at least one of the few.

Helen Fulton, who had met them at the door, showed Joanie and Kellan through the house, starting with the formal living room where a group of older people were listening to an E.P. monologue about her parents' experiences on their voyage on the *Queen Mary.* "When pater and mater return, I might go to Europe. I could do as much for Europe as the Marshall Plan."

They ended the trek through the new house in the dining room where a table laden with punch bowl and assorted dainties, gleamed under the bright light of the chandelier. It might be a very long time, Kellan knew, before he could provide Joanie with this sort of life. And could she be happy with less?

"Some lay-out, huh?" Steamboat came into the dining room. "Cost me one hell of a lot of dough. You know what? Helen wanted to do the house is French Providence..."

74

"French Provincial, Bobby," Helen corrected.

"Well, some damn French thing. I said not on your life. Everything's got to be strictly modern, or I don't….hey, don't drink that punch." Helen had started to ladle cups of punch. "That's for the old ladies. I got an open bar downstairs. Come on, let me show you my rumpus room. We'll let Helen entertain the old folks."

"Hey," Larry Somner called out to Steamboat, "we're all waiting for you to tune in the television you've been bragging about.Good enough to see the hair on a wrestler."

Davis Courtney, who was annoying his date, Lynda, by untying the bow on her halter dress as soon as she retied it, said in a soft, acerbic voice, "If you can't get a better picture than they get on the set at the Elks Club, you might as well use the damn thing to display your bowling trophies."

Steamboat fiddled with the aerial box and the dials until a picture emerged from the *snow*. Four entertainers in long wigs were doing a take-off of a popular singing group noted for their crew-cuts.

"Won't be long," Steamboat boasted, "until I'll be able to sit in my lounge chair and watch the State Basketball Tourney in Indianapolis."

The novelty of the television was short-lived. Davis suggested poker. "No, no, dear," he said to Lynda. "You don't get to play. You may watch me and keep your little mouth tightly shut."

Steamboat turned from the television set to a radio-phonograph console. "Pick out records, Joanie. It's got a beautiful tone."

As the beat of *String of Pearls* began, Steamboat claimed Joanie. "You and me, baby, let's show 'em how." And Kellan overheard him say as they started dancing, "Hon, you sex me to death."

And that, Kellan said to himself, calls for a drink. A stiff drink.

Homer Scott was behind the bar mixing a drink for himself. "Steamboat's got some damn good Scotch," he said to Kellan. "Damn good everything as a matter of fact." He held the glass out to Kellan. "Scotch and water. I'll make myself another one. It's a pleasure just to pour stuff this good."

The Scotch was superb.

"Look at that crazy Fulton dancing like he was seventeen." Scott nodded his head toward the dancers. "Does he look like he's got a bad knee?" Scott rubbed the jaw line of his hollow face as though feeling it to see if he needed a shave. "Yeah, he's got a bad knee from an old football injury. Hard to believe Steamboat was 4-F while a beat-up guy like me crawled all over Europe on his belly." Scott took a long drink. "That fool has been lucky all his life. Like marrying Helen McKintly and her money. Tell me," and Scott looked appraisingly about the room, "what the hell is a factory foreman like me doing around all this money."

"Or me," Kellan sympathized, "a farm kid."

"Joanie's old man has plenty of money. The Dietmeiers have money—they don't live like they have money, but they have money;. But that one—"

" Scott pointed with his glass to E.P.—she's got enough money coming to her from the Perrys and the Portlands to buy out the whole town."

Listening to Scott, Kellan missed the change of records, and so Joanie stayed on as Steamboat's dancing partner.

More people were coming downstairs, among them Bill who was immediately hailed by E.P. "Come on, Dietmeier." she challenged as she shuffled the cards, "I'm ready to take your money."

Bill pulled out a chair at the poker table, as Kellan knew he would. Bill might detest E.P., but he loved poker.

"I want to dance with you." Esther Scott laid a heavy hand on Kellan's arm. He was trapped.

Dancing with Esther was like dancing with a sack of potatoes. She leaned against him heavily, and he could feel the pillow softness of her bosom. She missed steps. She was prone to lead. After the music stopped, she held on to him.

Was he going to have to dance with her again? Abruptly, Esther put her arms around his neck and kissed him, pushing her tongue inside his mouth. All Kellan felt was anger as he realized that all eyes were on them. He saw Joanie turn her face away as if she were dismissing him from her life.

Kellan's mouth felt as if it had been smeared with rancid grease, so obnoxious was Esther's lipstick. I must look like a clown he thought, feeling like a consummate ass.

The lower level bathroom was occupied so Kellan went upstairs to the luxurious little powder room that Helen had displayed on her house tour. The lipstick came off after some hard rubbing, but it left a stubborn stain.

Approaching the living room, Kellan saw a recumbent form on the elegant couch, and a man, standing with punch cup in hand, sort of staring down at the sleeping form.

"He's not drunk, you know," he said of the sleeper who was Homer Scott; "tired to death." He put out a hand to Kellan. "I'm Kenneth Warwick. You haven't met me, but of course, I know who you are." Either assuming that Scott was sound asleep or not caring if Scott heard him, Kenneth said, "Scott's a good man. He works damn hard so Esther can live above her means. Too bad he's a Democrat."

"Oh?" Kellan was non-committal.

"The only thing worse is an Independent."

Kellan liked to talk politics, but this was not the right time or place. He didn't know Kenneth Warwick well enough. He seemed too dogmatic, too narrow-minded.

"The god-damned Republicans are going to lose the race."

"The pundits don't seem to think so."

"That's why the bastards are called pundits."

"What makes you think Dewey will lose the election?"

"It's that shitty mustache."

Kellan laughed.

"Don't laugh. Heroes don't wear mustaches. At least in 1948 heroes don't wear mustaches."

"Just villains like Hitler?"

"Of course." Ken touched Kellan's arm lightly. "Let's have some more of Helen's punch."

Raised in a traditionally Democratic county where Republicans were a maligned minority, Kellan now thought of himself as an Independent. Above partisan politics. Even so, politics interested him, and he liked talking to someone who knew the issues, even if he was rabid in his party loyalty.

"Now, if the Republicans had only nominated Taft." Ken was saying as he dipped into the punch bowl to fill two cups.

"Too many people associate Taft with isolationism," Kellan said. "And do you honestly think he has more charisma than Dewey?"

"Oh, dear God," Ken moaned, "has it come to the place that American voters vote for charisma rather than character?" He looked appreciatively at his cup. "Good stuff, isn't it?"

Not after Scotch, Kellan thought, not responding to Ken's remark but going on with politics. "Every poll gives the election overwhelmingly to Dewey." Kellan continued to sip on something he did not like.

"Polls don't vote," was Ken's cynical reply.

"There you are, husband mine." It was Juanita Warwick, Ken's wife. She was no great beauty, but her face was warm and friendly. Even though she was probably no older than twenty-five or so, Kellan thought she had a somewhat matronly air. "Oh, darling, you aren't drinking that sweet, sweet punch, are you?" Her words were a reprimand.

"I hadn't noticed."

She cautioned, "Don't over-do, darling. Why don't you join us downstairs?"

"I will, dear; very shortly."

And Ken and Kellan resumed their discussion of the current political situation.

Then Joanie came into the dining room looking for Kellan and suggested they leave.

Kellan put her off as Ken had Juanita. For at that moment it seemed very important to correct Ken's idea of why Eisenhower had disassociated himself from the Democrats.

Finally, when the green punch seemed to have soaked into his brain, and Kellan wanted to leave, he couldn't find Joanie.

"She left with Larry Somner," Steamboat told Kellan.

She should not have done that to me, he thought, and wanted to be angry but the punch got in the way.

Kellan had no trouble driving to Dietmeiers, at least he thought he didn't. But when he got upstairs to the hot bedroom, the room swam sickeningly around and everything was double. He tried to be quiet. He got in bed, and the nausea hit him. His head was whirling. He had to get to the bathroom. He threw up. Not once. Many times.

At last relieved of the venomous punch, he got back in bed.

Before he got out of bed again, the family had been to church and returned before he got downstairs.Mrs. Dietmeier eyed Kellan crossly. "Somebody was sick last night."

"Somebody never wants to see green punch again as long as he lives," Kellan replied.

"Well-I-hope-to-the-good-Lord-that-you-learned-a-lesson."

"The hard way. Never drink anything that's green."

"From now on you stick to goot beer." Mr. Dietmeier had heard the conversation as he came into the kitchen to take a cold beer out of the refrigerator.

"Oh, mein Gott," Mrs. Dietmeier groaned, smashing the potatoes hard enough to make the kettle ring. "Alcohol is alcohol, and a little goes a long way."

Burt, who had sauntered into the kitchen to check on what was for dinner, said mockingly, "Listen to Mom, the voice of experience."

Mr. Dietmeier was stern. "You speak with respect when you speak to your mother, Burt Dietmeier. And don't think for a second that you're too old to get the belt."

"What did I say that was so wrong? You kid around all the time. With Mom and everybody."

"Don't sass me. Now get outside and don't come to the dining room table until you ask permission of your mother."

From the submerged layers of his past that always seemed to lie just under the surface of the present, Kellan remembered one of the few times that Father had ever chastised him. It was an autumn day, the dusky barn was full of the musky smell of hay and feed, a good place to slip off so he wouldn't have to do chores. Somebody else was already there.

His cousin, Lena Russell. She called down from the loft, saying she had something to show him. Thinking it might be a nest of mice or something like that, Kellan climbed the ladder and there was Lena Russell all spread out on the hay. When he got close to her, she grabbed his hand and guided it up her thigh. He disliked everything about Lena Russell; she was ugly and hateful, yet in spite of that he felt a quickening response. A response that died a sudden death when he heard Father call for him in a voice that vented irritation. Lena Russell put her finger to her lips signaling him to stay quiet, but he ignored her and scurried down the ladder. Father began rebuking him for running off and leaving his poor mother to carry up water from the spring house, going on and on until he filled Kellan with so much pity for his mother, and so filled with remorse that he wished Father would switch him. But all he ever got from Father was a tongue lashing. Kellan loved his mother. And that was the day, although he didn't know it at the time, that he learned the difference between lust and love.

Kellan loved Joanie Welles as purely as he loved his mother, and she had left him and gone off with Larry Somner.

"Hey, man," it was Max who seemed to have taken the place of the exiled Burt, "you're going to have to eat fried chicken for breakfast, if you don't get up, aren't you?" He was talking to Kellan.

"When I was a little kid on the farm," Kellan told Max, "my grandmother used to fry chicken for breakfast every Sunday morning. We would have fried chicken, milk gravy and hot biscuits with honey or sorghum." He would not think of Joanie.

After Sunday dinner he played H-O-R-S-E with Burt. That kept his mind off Joanie, for as hard as he played, he could not out shoot a high school kid. But then, Kellan rationalized, he didn't grow up with a basketball goal in his backyard.

And later he said, "Sure" when Bill asked him if he wanted to go fishing.

The quiet of the creek let his thoughts range out like the line he cast toward the rock ledges. Why had Joanie walked out on him? And why with Larry Somner? All he was doing was talking politics with Ken Warwick while she danced with Steamboat. Did she think she had him wrapped around her finger and could pull the string any way she wished?

Kellan reeled in his thoughts as he reeled in his line, checked his bait and threw out another cast. He loved Joanie more than anything. Her oft repeated phrases—oh, I'd die if I ever lost you—oh, I'd kill myself if you left me—tugged at his heart like the bass that was running against his taut line.

"Got a big one?" Bill called out as he noticed the action of Kellan's line.

"Feels like it—-yeah, a great big one!"

"Hell, you're going to lose him if you don't watch out!"

The hook was set in the fish, no doubt about that, but Kellan knew that sometimes a bass would get off the hook just as it was being pulled out of the water. This one didn't get away. It was a smallmouth bass that would probably weigh no less than four pounds.

Bill thought closer to five pounds. "Hell, you've got the catch of the day. Catch of the summer most likely. Let's move upstream."

Joanie will have to prove herself to me, Kellan decided. He slipped on a slick rock and almost went down in the thigh- high water. Prove herself?

They fished until late in the afternoon, for Kellan's big bass was one of many fish—rock bass, bluegills, sunfish.

In the middle of the mess of cleaning the catch, Joanie telephoned.

"I've waited all day for you to call me," she accused.

"I didn't feel like talking to you."

"Kellan!"

Was she crying? "As soon as we finish cleaning the fish, I'll get showered and come over."

She didn't respond.

"Joanie?"

"Do you have to finish cleaning the damn fish?"

As it turned out, he didn't. "I'll finish dressing the fish," Bill offered as he cut the head off a bass and split it open. Get the hell out of here."

Showering and dressing, Kellan planned what he would say to Joanie, what he would do. Let her come to him with a contrite apology.

Instead, the second they saw each other they rushed into each other's arms as though they had been apart for years.

Her first words, "I was angry that you kept talking to Ken and ignored me. And you were drunk."

"Why did you leave with Larry?"

"Because he offered to take me home."

"Am I supposed to believe that nothing happened between the two of you?"

"Would I be so stupid as to tell you if it had?"

"Then I should assume the worst?"

"And if I should say yes—will you forgive me?"

Kellan could hear his grandmother's voice when she talked to him of forgiveness.Seventy times seven. "I would forgive you."

"Kellan, nothing happened. And you can believe me. Because I am not a liar. I have a lot of faults, but lying is not one of them. *I* don't have to lie about anything."

He took up her hand and kissed the palm, and her fingers limned his face. She said, "Let's go where we can be alone. There is no one at our cabin."

By the time they got to the lake, the day was almost done, and dark shadows were enveloping the houses and trees and only the lake reflected the last red rays of the sun. And by the time they were closed inside, locked away from the world, embraced in love, a shaft of moonlight from the undraped window made their bodies silvery forms in chiaroscuro. This, Kellan thought, is beautiful. But Joanie said it, "We are beautiful,aren't we? And the extravagance of their passion matched the extravagance of their promises to each other.

"You won't forget what you promised me, will you?" Joanie prodded as they rode back to town.

"To behave myself at parties and avoid green punch?" He was the happiest he had ever been in his life.

"Be serious. You promised that you would see Mr. Zeikoff." She took a deep breath. "And after you get the job, it will be time to tell Charles that we want the biggest, most beautiful wedding this town has ever seen."

The superintendent's office was located in a residential section of town in an old home that had been renovated for the purpose of housing the administrative offices of the school system.

Hiram B. Zeikoff. The B, Bill had told Kellan before he left for the interview, was for brainless. He had a mental image of a pudgy, round-faced, bald, loquacious man.

Zeikoff was thin, hook-nosed,with thinning gray hair and mustache to match. Zeikoff got the formalities over in a hurry.

"It's not often we have a first year teacher with a Masters. Too bad it's in social studies."

Look again, Kellan wanted to say; it's a history major. But he kept his mouth shut. To Zeikoff it was social studies.

"Social studies is sort of the prerogative of the coaches. Right now we need an assistant football coach and an assistant basketball coach. I've already got all the social studies teachers I need, but I wager the men I hire will both have a degree in social studies, and I'll have to do all kinds of shuffling around with the schedule. What's your minor?"

"I have an undergraduate major in math and a minor in English."

"You sure do have an odd transcript here. People with history and English usually don't have a major in math."

"I got so many math hours at Harvard that I thought I might as well get a major."

"Harvard?" Zeikoff gave him a sudden appraising look.

Don't I look like a Harvard man? Kellan felt like asking but answered, "The Navy V-12 program sent me to Midshipman's school at Harvard."

"Oh. Well, I could use a math teacher. We don't get many coaches who teach math. Any chance you could coach track? We're beginning to push track even though the town doesn't give much support to any sport except basketball. And football—but not to the extent of basketball. By the way, we're going to be mighty tough in basketball this year." Zeikoff relaxed. "We will win the sectional for sure, and we've got a good chance at the regional." Obviously he was a basketball fan. "Last year we should have gone to the State Finals but our best player, Lonnie Lykins—did you maybe read about him in the *Star?* Lonnie could work miracles with a basketball. He sprained his ankle in the last game of the regionals and we lost.

This year we've got the two Dietmeier boys. One's a senior but the other is a junior. They are really good players, but the coach is going to have to bring them down a peg. They'll pass up a player who is wide open under the basket to pass off to each other. I put some good teams on the floor when I was coaching but that's neither here nor there—think you could handle high school algebra?"

"Sure."

"Could you teach junior high English?"

"With no problem."

"Now wait a minute. Let me tell you something. One smart aleck kid can make you wish you'd never seen the inside of a classroom. Kids are brash these days. No respect. I guess it's the war."

Obviously, he had irritated Zeikoff with his smug attitude. Kellan, who at this juncture did not care what kind of impression he made on Zeikoff, said curtly, "I was not referring to discipline. I was referring to subject matter. I have never had any difficulties with any academic subject."

Now it was Zeikoff's turn to display smugness. "That may be. But the fact is that you do not have an Indiana State Teacher's License."

"No, I do not."

"And you are not currently working toward a license?"

"No."

"The only way we could possibly hire you is on a permit, contingent on your working toward a teacher's license. In this school system, we want fully licensed teachers."

"I understand," Kellan said. He understood very well. He had provoked Zeikoff, and Zeikoff would never hire him under any circumstances.

"Well, that's how it is in Indiana. Albert Einstein couldn't teach in Indiana public schools until he took his education courses and was granted an Indiana State Teacher's License." Zeikoff looked down at his desk and picked up his pen. He might as well have barked out, dismissed.

Kellan felt like saluting.

Zeikoff could take his job and stick it, as far as Kellan was concerned. He didn't give a damn. He had not wanted the job in the first place. It was Joanie's idea, not his.On the other hand, he could not help feeling the let down of another rejection.

Houghton College didn't want him. The public school system didn't want him. "Oh, that's the way Zeikoff is," Joanie said when Kellan recounted the meeting to her. "He likes to act important. It doesn't mean you won't be hired."

Bill's reaction was much the same as Joanie's. "You never know. Zeikoff's been known to change his mind more than once."

As it turned out, they were correct. Zeikoff phoned Kellan. He had reconsidered. The shortage of teachers was forcing him and a lot of other superintendents to issue temporary licenses. He wanted to set up a meeting with Kellan and Mr. Jacobs, the high school principal as soon as possible.

The second meeting with Zeikoff was a different ball game. They met, along with Jacobs, only briefly in Zeikoff's office and then toured the high school and junior high school facilities. Zeikoff, with Jacobs providing the chorus, pointed out the best features as though they were in real estate trying to make a big sale. They went back to the sperintendent's office where Zeikoff expounded on the various philosophies of education, the teacher's role in the community, blah, blah.blah. Just as Kellan thought he would choke on the bullshit, they got down to specifics. Kellan would teach three classes of freshman algebra and two classes of sophomore English. Subject to change, of course. Zeikoff still needed two coaches. As soon as the school board approved the hiring, a contract would be drawn up for him to sign.

"The school board goes by my recommendations one-hundred percent," Zeikoff bragged.

Someone had leaned hard on Superintendent Zeikoff.

Influence. Kellan was well acquainted with that. But from a different perspective. Warming the bench, watching Allan Crenshaw, son of the president of the Green Forks National Bank, play quarterback, Kellan knew that he could out pass, out scramble, out run, out smart Allan. And from the front row of graduating high school seniors, he had to listen to Judge Honeycutt's son, Robert Case, stumble through the salutatory and Dr. Adams's daughter, Alma Jean, squeak through the valedictory, all the while knowing that his grades were on a par with theirs.They were A students; he was an A student.

Perhaps it was not a coincidence that Kellan had been invited to Dr. Welles's house for dinner this very night.

Dinner began rather stuffily with cocktails in the living room before dinner, Dr.Welles's biting remarks directing the course of conversation. Kellan wondered how the doctor kept up a practice if he was as caustic with his patients as he was with his guest. With Joanie, however, he showed himself to be the indulgent father. With her there was a tactile closeness that made Kellan uncomfortable—as now, when Dr. Welles reached across the dinner table and covered Joanie's hand with his own and said what most fathers would say under the same circumstances. "Marriage? You hardly know each other."

I've known her all my life, Kellan wanted to say, because that's the way it was.

Joanie spoke out in the forthright way she did when circumstances interested her."We're not teenagers, you know. We love each other and there's nothing any person can say or do that will change that or change our minds."

"But marrying so soon?"

Joanie was quick in her response. "We'll just live together then, until you think we've known each other long enough to get married."

"While I could condone such an arrangement," Dr. Welles lightly scoffed, "I suspect a great number of the parents would be outraged to think that a teacher of their children was living in..." and here his voice became belittling... "sin, and Kellan would lose his hard won teaching position." A scoffing look on his face when he said *hard won.*

"All that aside," Kellan began, determined to make his position clear, to declare his intentions, "I promise you that I will always take care of Joanie, love her and protect her. I will never leave her. I come from a family which believes that marriage vows are a sacred commitment. That divorce is not an option." Kellan didn't like what he was saying. It sounded hokey.

Dr. Welles was curt. "Divorce is a necessary option. There are cases where it is utter stupidity—maybe even dangerous—to remain in a loveless or abusive marriage."

Kellan had been taken to task and knew he deserved it. But coming from the Fosters, the words he had spoken were not cant; they were creed: statements of belief as strong as the belief in the orderliness of the seasons, of day and night. But who could explain the Fosters? They had to be experienced.

Kellan wished to divorce himself from the Foster family. From their way of life. He wanted Joanie to know, thought that her father should know, that he was not a Foster by birth but by adoption.

So it was not with shame but with a sense of the loss of privacy that he told them the circumstances of his birth and his adoption by Garret Foster.

Miss Eddie came into the dining room to clear the table for dessert, and from the look on her bleak face, Kellan surmised that she had been listening to the conversation.

He hoped that the dessert would be better than the main course which he rated as one of the worst meals he had ever eaten.

Dr. Welles reached out to his daughter, turning her face with his hand so that she looked directly at him. "So you really and truly want this Kellan Foster?" he asked, stroking her cheek.

"More than anything I've ever wanted in my life."

"Then you may have him."

Kellan was indignant. "I am not," he said heatedly, "a marketable commodity."

Charles and Joanie burst out laughing as though he were joking. He wasn't but his words changed the atmosphere from somber to salubrious, and for the first time Kellan felt easy in the company of Dr. Welles.

The dessert which Miss Eddie brought in had the horrible look of tapioca pudding. Kellan more or less toyed with his dessert until Dr. Welles and Joanie finished theirs, and then he put his spoon down.

Kellan was mentally groping for an excuse to cut short the evening when, as a result of a telephone call, Dr. Welles announced that he was needed at the hospital.

"We may not be here when you get back," Joanie said. "Kellan hasn't driven my new car. Hasn't even seen it."

Her new car was a white Olds convertible.

Kellan slid under the wheel on white leather upholstery and inhaled deeply of the fresh, brand-new-car smell of the interior. "You will never want to ride in my car again, will you?"

"Why should we," she responded sensibly, "when we have this one?"

Kellan conceded that she had a point. What he really wanted her to say was that she liked riding in his Forty-one Chevy.

She sat close to him, her head on his shoulder, one hand touching his hand, and he wanted her. His negative feelings about her father, Miss Eddie, the way they lived evaporated in his desire. "The lake?" he suggested.

"It will be a long drive for nothing," she answered. "I can't tonight."

"Oh."

"Oh, what?"

"Oh, damn."

"Damn, damn, double damn." She straightened up and poked in Kellan's pocket for his cigarettes. "A little bother that interrupts our plans. I'll make it up to you."

Kellan thought the Reds might be playing baseball. "I haven't heard the radio on your car," he suggested.

Joanie switched on the radio. Music filled the car. "Good music," she said and turned up the volume. "Let's dance, Kellan."

"Where?"

"Here."

Leaving the headlights on and the door ajar, they danced on the empty street. Kellan felt that there was no trouble in the world that could touch them. He said, not to trivialize their actions but to compliment them, "If any one comes this way, he will think we're crazy."

"He will be jealous of us."

"Can you imagine what Bill would say?" And Kellan imitated Bill's voice, "Hell, someone ought to sell tickets to this show."

Joanie made those delicious low sounds that came when she was thoroughly happy. "I've always loved Bill Dietmeier."

Kellan stopped in his tracks. He held her tightly by both arms as he might a recalcitrant child. "If you meant that, say it again. If it was idle talk, don't ever say it again."

"Kellan don't be paranoid. I love chocolate. I love my father. I love the picture of my mother that hangs in his bedroom. I love to dance...don't you understand? Oh, Kellan, I love you so much there isn't a word for what I feel. Invent me a word and I'll use it."

Kellan drew her close and hugged her warm sensual body. Why had he been unreasonable? They were going to spend the rest of their lives together. "I'm sorry," he apologized and kissed her. And kissed her again. "The Greeks had three words for love. Or was it four? Agape was the word for...."

"I don't give a damn how many words the Greeks had for love." Her voice broke in tenderness. "I love you in a very special way. And that's all I need from you—for you to love me in the same special way. A love that is more than love."

"I love you," Kellan said in words that he had said before, "without reason."

Bill was getting himself a beer from the refrigerator when Kellan walked into the kitchen. He took out two instead of one when he saw Kellan.

Thinking of what Bill's reaction might be if he knew that Joanie had said she loved him, Kellan could hardly keep from laughing.

"What the hell is wrong with you," Bill mumbled, not expecting an answer. "I'm going out in the backyard where it's cooler than Mom's kitchen. You coming?"

They sat in metal lawn chairs near the peach tree in an area of the yard that was illuminated from house lights. The sky was clear with a high, white moon. Among the infinite stars, the Big Dipper stood out above the pointed roof of the garage.

Some day, Kellan said to himself, I'd like to take a course in astronomy. To Bill he said, "How did your softball game go?"

"We won." Bill flicked away his cigarette, and the red glow arced out into the grass. "I've got a hell of a problem."

"Hitting or fielding or both?"

"Portland."

"Oh, shit, Bill—tell her to go find Kilroy."

"Damnit, she dogs me everywhere I go. She came to the softball game, and hell, in that industrial league we don't have a handful of spectators. Just wives and dates. She stuck out like a sore thumb. Jumping up and clapping every time I came to the plate."

"Her toy boy, Lonnie what's his name, does he play in the industrial league?"

"Why hell no." Bill was getting irate. "He plays Legion baseball. All I want is for her to stay way the hell away from me. I never did like her. When I was in high school, she tried to put the make on me."

"Tell her to peddle her ass somewhere else."

"She's going to get her ass burned if she doesn't stay away from me."

Kellan's mind was on his own situation. Marriage. He wanted Joanie for the rest of his life, but marriage? He had always carried a vague idea that eventually marriage and family would be part of his life, but it was without substance like thinking about old age. Retirement. The realization that he was taking on a lifetime responsibility of another person was awesome. Was he making a mistake? As if to accustom himself to the idea, he said, "Joanie and I may get married."

Bill didn't respond for so long that Kellan thought he hadn't heard. Then he said in a totally serious tone that he so seldom spoke in, "You haven't known each other very long."

"That's what her father said."

"I bet that's not half of what he thought."

"He said," Kellan began, thinking that verbalizing the thoughts that kept running through his head like a hateful tune, might get them out of his brain, "that she could have me, if she wanted me."

"You're kidding me." Astonishment had dropped the level of Bill's voice to quiet unbelief.

"I wish I were."

"You better set that man straight, Kel. I'm glad he's going to be your father-in-law instead of mine. Best thing you can do is get a place of your own. Quick. He's likely to want you to move in with them."

"Never." So now he had a new problem. Finding a place to live.

Finding a place to live in a time of housing shortages was not as difficult as Kellan thought it would be. Pleasing Joanie was the difficult part. And Kellan could understand that. Compared to her father's house, anything they looked at seemed shabby.

In spite of all the delight he found in Joanie, he felt burdened with the obligation of trying to please her. She had no conception of being what Grandmother called "hard up." He wished he had never taken the teaching job. It would be so much better if they could move away from this town.

However, Joanie found, in her words, "the perfect solution." There was a fully furnished house, owned by Joe Fredericks, Dr. Joe, that he had purchased for his daughter, an army nurse who came home from the war with a GI husband. As civilians, they found themselves at war with each other. The erstwhile soldier departed for California, and Dr. Joe's daughter entered med school. Dr. Joe would rent the house to Kellan and Joanie. Dr. Joe was in no hurry to sell the house until his daughter moved her things out.

Kellan declined the offer.

"Why?" Joanie shook her head in disbelief.

"Because I don't think I can afford to rent a furnished house."

"But you don't understand. We would more-or-less be house sitting. The rent will be only a token. And," she hesitated as if not sure as to how her next words would be received, "Charles might buy the house for us."

"No."

His refusal put energy into her words, "Well, why not? Someday I will inherit everything. Why not have some of my inheritance now? My father doesn't need the money. He owns blue chip stocks—whatever they are—and bonds, and lots of investments." Her voice became soft and beguiling, "Will you just look at the house? For me?"

Kellan agreed to look at the house.

To him it seemed like a three-bedroom, two-bath palace.

"On the smallish side," Joanie commented, "but at least I can entertain in it. That last place that you said we might be able to make-do with was so cramped I wouldn't be able to set up two card tables in the living room."

In the end, she got her way.

The view of a small town was a lot nicer from the top of the heap. The rub was that Kellan wanted to make it to the top on his own. He was uncomfortable with getting the good things of life handed to him because he knew the right people. He did not want to be beholden to anyone.

One very pressing duty was to take Joanie to meet his family. Which would be nothing short of a total disaster. He knew her reaction would be one of distaste, and he could hardly blame her for that. Her family and his family lived in different worlds. The sooner the better.

The visit to Green Forks was delayed because Bill asked Kellan to work another week while his parents were in Memphis watching Karl play baseball.

"I must have taken leave of my senses to agree to leave four boys loose in my house," Mrs. D. complained. She was standing in the living room with her hat on and a suitcase by her feet. "No bouncing a basketball in the house, no...." and she went through a long litany of don'ts before she got to a do. "Keep up with the laundry. I don't want to come home to a basement piled up with dirty clothes."

As Kellan heard Bill tell his mother that she worried too much, he retreated to the kitchen to get a glass of water and allow Bill and his mother a measure of privacy. No sooner had he heard the front door screen slam shut behind the departing Mrs. D. than the telephone rang.

"I've got it," Bill called and Kellan heard him say, "Dietmeier's Slaughter House, what can I do for you?" And then, "It's for you, Kell. Dr. Welles."

As he picked up the phone and said hello, Kellan heard a click, and the line went dead. "We got cut off," he said.

"Guess my smart-ass answer made him mad." Bill shrugged his shoulder, not the least bit apologetic.

Dr. Welles did not call back, and Kellan forgot about it

Bill and Kellan put in long work days in Mr. Diemeier's absence, and Kellan thought that it was probably a good thing that Joanie and Dr. Welles had gone to Chicago. Otherwise, he would be working all day and staying out late with Joanie.

It was the Saturday before Mr. and Mrs. Dietmeier were to return on late Sunday or early Monday morning, and no laundry had been done.

"Look at that cloudless sky," Bill said on his way to the basement, "I ought to be out on the golf course."

Kellan was right behind Bill. "If it had rained today, we'd have a hell of a time getting the clothes dry."

Bill was the straw boss, telling Kellan what to do and making Max and Burt hang the wet wash out to dry. As soon as they found the opportunity, the boys disappeared, followed shortly by Bill who suddenly remembered he'd promised to make a foursome at two o'clock. The job of taking down the dry clothes fell to Kellan.

Mrs. Lox came out her back door and stood across the hedge and watched Kellan.

She adjusted the hair net that covered her thin, white hair and folded her arms over her sunken bosom.

"You enjoying yourself here?" she asked.

"Very much. It's a fine town." Snobbish, monotonous and insular like a thousand other small towns.

"Have you met a lot of young folks?"

"A few." Obviously she had heard gossip about Joanie and himself.

"I sure am glad Bill has kept a tight rein on Max and Burt while Herm and Gertie are on their trip. Last time Max and Burt stayed alone overnight a party went on till daybreak. I told Gertie I'd be the last person in the world to call the police on her boys, but I couldn't answer for the neighbors. Some of them were mightily upset."

"Well, you know how it is when you're a teenager." He doubted her memory went back that far.

"In my time youngsters had respect for their elders. For older person who might need a peaceful night's rest."

"Well, we were all young once. They'll grow up sooner than you think."
Thank God for platitudes.

"I sincerely hope so. If they don't get killed in an automobile accident.
Burt—and Max, too—they've got the reputation of being reckless in
automobiles. Oh, course I've never ridden with one of them under the wheel.
Don't want to. All's I've seen is them tearing up the alley spewing gravel into
my yard. Personally, I wouldn't ride from here to the courthouse with either
one of them."

Kellan took down the last T-shirt. "Kids of that age have good reflexes."
He picked up the wicker basket.

"Careful," Mrs. Lox warned. "You're about to lose the top clothes."

The kitchen was so hot that the red geraniums on the wallpaper seemed to
droop.Nobody had bothered to pull the blinds against the sun that poured
through the west windows. Kellan sat the basket on the kitchen table and
turned off the gas under some unattended hamburgers that sputtered in their
own grease. The doorbell was ringing. It was Joanie. She stepped inside the
uncharacteristically quiet house. "Are you the only one here?"

"As far as I can tell. Bill is playing golf." he gave her upturned face a kiss.
"Max or Burt came in while I was outside taking down clothes and started to
fry hamburgers and then vanished. They are the epitome of irresponsibility."

Joanie looked about the living room. "Everything's so Dutchy," she
commented."Crocheted doilies." and then she walked to the upright piano…
"photographs on an embroidered piano runner."

Kellan was disappointed in her attitude. What would she think of his
home, Grandmother's house? Let her think whatever she wants to think,
Kellan resolved. I'm not going to be embarrassed for what I am or the family
I came from.

"Oh, look at Karl's graduation picture… the haircut. Did you ever have a
haircut like that?"

Grandmother had cut his hair.

Not expecting an answer, she picked up a picture that was lying face down
and set it upright. "Polly Emhuff. Do you think she was as pretty as I am?"

Kellan ignored that question also. Remembering how Bill had put away
reminders of Polly, he said with authority, "Put the picture back the way it was."

"I wonder if Mr. and Mrs. Dietmeier knew about Polly."

"Knew what about Polly?"

"That she was dating an officer from the air base when she was killed."

"Is that gossip?"

"A few people in town know. E.P. knew the officer. And she saw them together on the air base. The night Polly was killed she was driving back from a dance at the base. It's all been hush-hush. It was bad enough that she was killed—nobody would want to add to that grief. It wouldn't bring her back…E.P. said that the officer…"

Joanie never finished for Max bounded into the living room breathlessly, saying, "I forgot to turn off the gas under some hamburgers I was gonna cook."

"Relax," Kellan said, "I turned the gas off. But the two hamburgers are still in the skillet."

And just as though a bell had been rung for mealtime, Burt came, and Bill soon followed.

"Well, look who's here to cook dinner for us," was Bill's greeting to Joanie.

"Sorry," she said. "I don't cook."

Bill cooked. Hamburgers. They had hamburgers and beer and a lot of fun. They might all have been the same age.

"How would you guys like to drive my new car?" Joanie asked the boys.

"You have to ask?" Burt was smiling.

"Don't smoke, eat, or drink in my car. And don't fool around with the top.Okay?"

She could have given them a ticket to paradise, and they wouldn't nave been any happier.

"What are we going to do?" Bill asked after the flurry of the boys' leaving had subsided.

We? Kellan's plans for Joanie and himself did not include Bill.

"Let's go skinny dipping," Joanie suggested drolly.

"Bass fishing," Bill countered.

"Dancing?"

"None of the above," Kellan interjected but his words were lost.

"I'll fill the cooler with ice and beer," Bill said.

Nobody asked where they were going.

They drove out to the lake. The night was warm and still with a sky full of stars.They spread a blanket out near the edge of the water, and Bill and Kellan swapped stories of their experiences in the Navy for the entertainment of their audience of one. Joanie sat in the circle of Kellan's arm, and when his face touched the top of her head he could smell summer in her hair.

"You need a girl, Bill," Joanie said languidly, her fingers gently caressing Kellan's arm.

"I'll get a girl, Joanie," he replied, "when I can find one like you."

Whether the remark was meant seriously or facetiously, only Bill knew for sure. In Kellan's opinion, they were careless words, but Joanie accepted them as genuine.

"That's the nicest compliment I've ever had."

By the time they got back to town, the night had turned dark and windy. The streets were deserted, and only an occasional house showed a lighted window. The street lights hardly penetrated the blackness. As Kellan caught a glimpse of a white car in front of the Dietmeier house, he at first thought it was Joanie's car. Then he saw that it was a State Police car.

As did Bill. "Dear Jesus."

Bill tore out of the car before it had come to a complete stop. Kellan and Joanie followed. There were the stilted greetings of law officer to citizens. They went into the house.

In the correct tone of official concern, the officer explained that there had been a one-car accident. The vehicle in which the Dietmeier boys were traveling had left the highway at an excessive rate of speed, turned over twice and was virtually demolished. Both boys were injured.

"How bad?" Bill asked.

The officer could not be precise as to the exact extent of the injuries, but they were serious.

"And no one else was in the car?"

"No."

There were other matters associated with the accident—car ownership, insurance; all handled smoothly with respect to the gravity of the situation. Routine. Solicitude without emotion.

The hospital operated with the same impersonal concern. Care without caring. White uniformed politeness in perfect calmness.

The preferential treatment began when Dr. Welles met them in the waiting room and escorted them to a private room where he explained the medical conditions of Max and Burt. Burt was thrown from the car and suffered a broken leg and shoulder as well as lacerations. Max had a skull fracture and concussion. In the initial impact the brain was still and the skull moved against it. After the blow, the brain continued to move against the stationary skull.

"There is bleeding and pressure inside the skull," Dr. Welles explained, "and an operation will be necessary to relieve the pressure. Brain damage is a calculated risk. In cases like Max's there is no other option. The swelling must be alleviated. If he were my patient, I would recommend moving him to Indianapolis where a neurosurgeon can do the surgery. However, he's Joe's patient. Not mine."

"Has anyone phoned Pastor Emhuff?" Bill wanted to know.

"He is in the hospital now. With one boy or the other."

"The State Policeman said that they are trying to locate my parents," Bill said. "I can't make any decisions until they get here."

"You may look in on Max," Dr. Welles offered. " But he is sedated and won't be conscious. Burt, however, is fully conscious except for the effects of pain killers."

They went down a corridor, up in the elevator to the fourth floor, and down the corridor. Dr. Welles opened the door of Room 12. Kellan caught sight of the rigid, still form of Max in the utterly quiet room. Pastor Emhuff in an attitude of prayer, was at the bedside. Bill went in while the others waited in the corridor.

Joanie slipped her hand into Kellan's perhaps for comfort, yet her warmth was reassuring to him.

Shortly, Bill and Pastor Emhuff came out, and they all went to Burt's room.

Burt was groggy but awake. His first words were abject apology. "Oh, gosh, Joanie, I'm so sorry we wrecked your new car." Realizing that the pastor's presence was an indication of the gravity of the situation, Burt's face turned fearful and tears rolled down his face as he struggled to ask the question, "Is my bother dead?"

"Your brother is alive, Burt." The pastor's voice was firm. "But he very much needs the prayers of you and all of us."

Bill and the others stepped out into the hall and left Pastor Emhuff with Burt.

"I'm staying here tonight," Bill said. "If there is any change, I'll let you know. There is no need for anyone to stay or do anything else until Mom and Dad get home."

Kellan, Joanie and her father went back to the private room. The phone was ringing as they entered.

"That was Joe Fredericks," Dr. Welles said when he had finished talking on the phone. "He's on his way to the hospital. He and his wife had gone out of town for dinner." Dr. Welles lit a cigarette. "Kids and cars." His words were an indictment.

"You can imagine what they were doing," Kellan added, "Trying out a new car to see what it would do."

Joanie's face went white. Her voice was hardly more than a whisper. "I never should have let them have my car."

Nothing—no words that Kellan or her father said could persuade Joanie that the wreck was not her fault.

She was wholly distraught.

Dr. Welles took her home.

Kellan went back to an eerily silent Dietmeier house. A house whose very emptiness suggested the futility of "being up and doing."

Before he went to sleep, Kellan thought that he too should pray for Max. And for Joanie.

Kellan phoned Joanie the next morning. Not that there was anything new to report on the conditions of Max and Burt.

"She's still sleeping," Miss Eddie informed him.

He called her at one-thirty. Now he could tell her that Mr. and Mrs. Dietmeier were home and at the hospital and Bill had come home and gone to bed.

Joanie was showering.

He phoned at two-thirty.

Joanie was napping.

Obviously he was being given the run-around. Why? To answer that question he would have to go to Joanie's house.

Miss Eddie answered the doorbell but remained standing behind the screen door as though she were a sentry on duty. She said, "Joanie's still asleep."

Taking Miss Eddie off-guard, Kellan said as he pulled open the door and stepped inside, "You don't mind if I come in, do you?"

The woman was so taken by surprised that she hardly reacted when Kellan said, "I'll just go up to her room and see her for a few minutes."

He had never been upstairs before, but he would find her room.

At the first closed door, he stopped and barely opened the door.

The room was dark and stuffy with pulled drapes and strewn clothes and bedding. Joanie lay across the bed on her stomach, her face toward the door.

"Kellan." His name was spoken as though it were habitual for him to be in her bedroom. "What time is it?"

"About three-thirty."

"Morning or afternoon?"

"It's afternoon, sweetheart."

She shook her head and moaned a little.

He raised her up. She was as limp as a rag doll. She let him kiss her and hold her without making a response. "Are you sick, Joanie?"

"I couldn't sleep last night. Charles gave me something."

Kellan couldn't stand seeing her in this zombie-like condition. "You need to get dressed and get out of this stale smelling room." He looked about and saw the shorts and shirt she had had on the night before. Her bra and underpants in a wad alongside. "I'll help you get dressed."

It was like helping a child. "Did you take any kind of medication this morning?"

"No. Yes. Maybe, I don't remember."

"Bill's parents are back," to spark her interest. "They are at the hospital now.Burt is coming along okay."

She was a tad more alert. "Max?"

"No change."

"It's all my fault. Oh, God, I wish I'd never let those kids have my car."

"It's not your fault."

"If I had not offered them the car…"

"If." Kellan was bluntly decisive. "If I had not fallen in love with you, you would not have been at the Dietmeiers' house. If Bill had never brought me home with him, I would never have met you. If there hadn't been a war, I would not have met Bill. It makes about as much sense to blame the war as to blame yourself. Grandmother would say…" he trailed off.

Grandmother would say all things work together for good to those who …

"What would your Grandmother say?"

"She would tell you to be optimistic. She would say things could be worse."

"It didn't have to happen."

"So we can't change what's happened, but we can accept the situation and do what needs to be done for the Dietmeiers. We're going to the hospital to see them and the boys."

"I don't think I can."

"Of course you can. Because I will be with you."

The first stop was Burt's room, filled with flowers, magazines, games, cards. A fan stirred the air and fluttered loose papers. A radio put forth tinny music.

Burt had the impression that his brother was improving. Whether it was his innate optimism or he had purposely been led to believe that his brother was in no danger, Kellan had no way of knowing.

Max's hospital room was also filled with expressions of well-wishes, but it was too quiet. There seemed to be no change. Mrs. Dietmeier was with him. She greeted Kellan and Joanie with the same composure she would have had if they had walked into the kitchen where she was cutting out noodles. Their stay was brief, leaving when Bill and his father came into the room.

"She doesn't blame me," Joanie said when they had quit the hospital. "None of them blame me. I could tell. I could feel it."

"They only want Max to live and be whole in body and mind."

From all indications, that would never be.

Mrs. Dietmeier was adamant. No surgery. No surgery though the alternative might cost him his life.

The response of the town to the accident was overwhelming. Enough prepared foods arrived at the house on a daily basis to feed a battalion. The telephone and doorbell were constantly ringing. Female relatives descended on the house to clean and scour, to vacuum and dust, to do laundry and to clean again where no cleaning was needed. The house was under a constant barrage of benevolence.

Kellan felt extraneous. In the way. Yet to leave town with the fate of his friend's brother hanging in crisis was unthinkable. The work force of the business was now normal, and it was better for Bill and his Dad to be occupied with work. Clearly, Kellan needed to leave the house but not the town.

The simple solution would be to move into the house he and Joanie would live in after they were married.

"How soon will I be able to move into our house?" Kellan asked Joanie. They were sitting on the screened-in porch of the lake cottage, having coffee and Danish rolls.

"The house is ours whenever we choose to move in. It does need a thorough cleaning. You did notice the musty smell, didn't you, when we first looked at the house?"

He had not.

"As soon as I can get our cleaning lady for an extra day, I'll take her and Miss Eddie over and they can get it ready."

"The sooner the better. Until then I'll get a hotel room."

"You could stay here, but Charles demands that this place be kept for his retreat. Sometimes he entertains here. Like next Sunday. He is having his bridge club out for supper and cards." Her eyes sparkled. "I'll share my room with you." And then seriously, "Why is that so horribly wrong? We love each other."

"Convention. Conventions of one kind and another." Thinking of finances as he now did quite often, "I'll move into the house the way it is. It won't be any worse than camping out. And I promise not to get in the way of those who are going to clean and sanitize the house." He waited for her answer, knowing her well enough now, to know that she was weighing her idea against his, coming around to his way of thinking.

"Do what you want. I don't care." Seeming now more interested in another Danish. Kellan took the roll from her hand and put it on the plate. He kissed her fingers and tasted sugar. "I love you and I want you."

"I want you and I love you, too." Her words were as fierce as her love-making.

As they lay in bed together, utterly satisfied, Kellan said, "We should get up and get dressed before we get caught."

"I don't care. I'm no hypocrite."

How paradoxical, Kellan thought, how glorious that this most uninhibited female had come to him a virgin. He teased her. "You don't want me to get fired before the first day of school, do you?"

"Why is a marriage ceremony necessary at all? All it amounts to is a humongous party."

"Marriage provides stability to the tribe."

"How do you know?"

He realized that it was not a question that begged an answer, and he would have sounded pompous if he had informed her that from the reading he had done, successful societies whether primitive or advanced had some sort of ritualistic commitment between men and women that insured children the protection of family. What would she think of Grandmother Foster's idea that marriages were made in heaven? He lit a cigarette."When I was little kid...."

Joanie reached up for his cigarette, took a drag and handed it back.

"When I was a little kid, I heard my grandmother tell my mother that matches were made in heaven, and I thought she was talking about the box of stick matches that they kept on the mantle above the fireplace. When I asked my mother about it, she explained that Grandmother was speaking about love matches. That two people truly in love were made for each other. At that stage of life love was not a subject that interested me."

"Was our match made in heaven, Kellan?" She was being overtly depreciatory but a subtle seriousness lay under the warp of her question.

"Does it matter?"

She got up. "No. The only thing that matters is that I have you. If I ever lost you, I'd kill myself."

"Don't ever say that again." Looking through the window of the cottage bedroom, Kellan could see thunderheads gathering and moving in from the southwest."The barometer is moving. That means fish will bite." Remembering the new fishing equipment he had seen on the back porch,

Kellan made a suggestion. "Let's take the boat out and catch some fish before the rain hits."

"I've never fished."

"Hasn't your father ever taken you fishing?"

"No. I've never known him to go fishing."

"Whose fishing equipment is that on the back porch?"

"I don't know. But I know it doesn't belong to Charles. It might be Dr. Joe's. Dr Joe does a lot of fishing. He goes to Florida every winter and goes deep sea fishing."

"Well, you and I are going fishing, and you will find out that fishing is a lot of fun."

Kellan took the boat across the lake and into a cove where willows grew out to the water and their long branches trailed out over a fallen timber that lay barely submerged. "This is a good spot," he said.

He gave Joanie a rigged-up casting rod, but she had trouble. He threw it out for her, but she got caught on a snag. He got her lure off the snag and cast out sending the lure to a perfect spot. She reeled in too soon, tried to make a cast and almost caught the barb in Kellan's ear. The confinement of a small boat was definitely not the place for her to learn to cast a fishing rod. Kellan took the lure off the rod and lay it in the tackle box.

"Why did you do that?" she asked. "I was having fun."

"Let's just say that you are a great deal better at making love than fishing. Anyway, I don't think the fish are going to bite today. We'll come back another day. Just look at those clouds; we might get caught in a cloudburst."

"I'm glad you didn't catch any fish," Joanie said when they were back on shore. Now we don't have all that mess that goes with cleaning the fish."

"We could stand here on the shore line and let you practice casting until you get the hang of it. Get the rhythm of throwing out and reeling in."

"Thanks a lot, but no thanks. It's time for a beer, don't you think? No, scratch that suggestion. Let's make it gin and tonic."

"Go ahead. Mix the drinks. I'll be in after I've put away this fishing gear in as good shape as I found it."

He could hear her in the kitchen, heard the ringing of the telephone but paid no attention to the conversation. When it ended Joanie came to the porch. "That was Charles on the phone. There has been a change in Max."

"For better?" Bad news would have been delivered in person.

"Yes. He said that Max spoke to his mother today. The swelling has gone down—there's no pressure. And Charles said he is coming up here as soon as he leaves his office."

It turned out to be the most relaxed occasion that he had ever had with Dr Welles who seemed to have sheathed some of his arrogance as they discussed the topic that was upmost in their minds, Max's recovery. Dr. Welles had no explanation for the boy's unexpected recovery except to attribute it to the power of a young body to heal itself. Kellan knew that the Dietmeiers would attribute the healing to the power of prayer.

And now, Kellan knew, it was time to take Joanie to Green Forks.

Slightly uneasy, Kellan wondered off and on as they sped along to Green Forks how Joanie would respond to Grandmother, to Uncle Kirby and Aunt Sammie. "You may not feel at ease," Kellan warned her, "when you meet all the kin. It's a different way of life from what you are used to. The Fosters are staid people with about as much frivolity as you would find in a monastery. The house…"

She broke in. "How can it be that different? It's still the United States, isn't it? Everyone speaks English don't they?"

Kellan didn't have to wonder about how the Fosters would react to Joanie. He knew it would be one of two ways: dumbfounded or preachy. Dumbfounded, he hoped.

"I wish we had my new car. We could have the top down with the wind blowing through our hair—I'm about to swelter."

"Want to stop for something cold to drink?"

"No. I'd just have to be hot that much longer."

"It's only a few more miles."

As they drove into the city limits, Joanie observed that Green Forks looked like any other small town.

"True. But we are not stopping in Green Forks. We're going on to the farm."

The route to the farm took them around the square and onto Highway 36 where after a couple of miles they turned off onto the winding, gravel road that led to the Foster place. As they passed the white frame one-room school, Kellan pointed out that it was the school he had attended for the first eight years of his education.

"Really? You went *there?*"

Reality was setting in.

Have I made a mistake, Kellan asked himself, bringing her here? Joanie could be so careless of others. He remembered her condescending remarks about the Dietmeier house. As much as he did not want to be like the Fosters, as much as he wished they were more mainstream, he did not want his grandmother shamed or hurt.

"Oh, look at the big chimneys," Joanie exclaimed when they reached the house."Do you still use the fireplaces?"

"Yes. We don't have central heat."

Just before Grandmother came out the back porch door to see who had pulled into the driveway, Kellan said something to Joanie that he had not intended to say. "Joanie, no one smokes in Grandmother's house. You'll have to smoke outside."

"Okay." She didn't seem to be listening.

Grandmother met them as they got out of the car. She received the token kiss from Kellan who introduced her to Joanie. Grandmother's gentle manners and her warm welcome, genuine but not effusive, brought the one response from Joanie that Kellan had never expected. She put her arms around dumpy little Grandmother, and the two embraced each other with instant affection.

Joanie displayed an artless curiosity about everything—what's this? of the cream separator, and admiration, oh, what a handsome sideboard, and the quilt on Grandmother's bed——you sewed this all by hand? and unrestrained amusement—that telephone really works? you have to crank the handle to get the operator?

She divulged more information about Kellan and herself than he would ever have revealed. And in the course of conversation there were casual references to all the social practices that were anathema to the Fosters: dancing, card playing, smoking, cocktails.

Not a word of reproach from Grandmother Foster, only a tolerant smile.

Perhaps, Kellan thought, Grandmother used up all her sermons on me.

"Grandmother's gold wedding band is so elegantly simple, isn't it, Kellan? We've decided, Kellan and I, since our engagement will be such a short period of time, we'll have only a plain gold wedding band when we marry."

"When I was young," Grandmother commented, "diamond engagement rings weren't in fashion. It's only been since the twenties that every girl has thought she must have a diamond engagement ring to seal the troth." Grandmother was setting out the cold supper. "We'll have a hot dinner tomorrow noon with Kirby and Sammie here, so we can be together as a family." She was apologizing for the meal, explaining that as a rule she did not cook a hot supper. "I will, though, make some hoecakes to make the leftovers a bit tastier."

"What is a hoecake?" Joanie wanted to know.

Kellan did not hang around for the explanation but went outside for a cigarette.

The cats—there were always cats, but these were new residents since he had left home—took Kellan's measure and decided his legs were acceptable for rubbing. With an involuntary foot action, he lofted the cats into the air. He was thinking of the ring discussion. All of Joanie's remarks were new to him. *We* hadn't decided not to have an engagement ring. Joanie had. And why? It sounded like a notion, but he was learning that very often her whims had reasons behind them. He would find out. The cats came back, focused on his legs, and this time there was a good deal of malice aforethought when he sailed them through the air.

"Want to go into town with me this morning?" he asked Joanie at breakfast. Kellan was in the best of moods. Their separate bedrooms were upstairs far removed from Grandmother's downstairs bedroom. Joanie came to his room, and they slept the night together for the first time, waking in the morning to see each other as if it were the first time they had ever seen each other. Kellan thought her more beautiful than he had ever before seen her.

"No. I'll stay with Grandmother. She can catch me up on all the years I didn't know you."

Oh, God, no. Kellan's thought was almost a prayer.

"Children," Grandmother began, and it sounded to Kellan that a sermon was on its way. "I am struck by how much you favor each other."

Relieved, Kellan said, "Joanie can't look like me. She's beautiful."

Joanie teased, "Didn't anyone ever tell you you are beautiful, Kellan?"

"Not lately," he said sarcastically.

Joanie licked at a dribble of sorghum molasses that had fallen on her finger. "I love hot biscuits and sorghum. I'll get fat if I stay here very long."

Grandmother eyed Joanie with a maternal look. "Seems to me, you could stand to put on a few pounds, Joanie." Then she turned to Kellan. "Kirby was down early this morning after milking. He's got business in town, and if he may ride in with you, it will be a savings for him. Said he'd be ready whenever you saw fit to leave."

Not exactly what Kellan had in mind.

As they bumped along the country road, Uncle Kirby gawked at the farms as they passed by, straining to see what neighboring farmers were doing and how their crops compared to his.

"The Lord has blessed us with a fine growing season this year," Uncle Kirby remarked. "We should prosper well this year if we aren't hit with hail or a long drought."

Kellan knew exactly what Kirby's next words would be. *Well, we'll take what the Lord sends. It rains on the just and the unjust.* But Uncle Kirby fooled him.

"What denomination is your intended?"

Damn. Good question. They had come into town and were passing the First Presbyterian Church. "Presbyterian." Kellan answered.

"I don't hold with all the Presbyterian doctrine. Like election. If I did, I'd be a Presbyterian." Uncle Kirby involuntarily leaned back as if to brake the car as Kellan veered the vehicle into a parking space. "However, I'm sure you can reconcile your individual beliefs and find a common faith." Kirby fumbled with the strange door handle and awkwardly got himself out of the car. "My business will take roughly an hour."

Kellan put a dime in the parking meter. "We'll meet at the car."

Kellan's purpose in coming to town was to withdraw his inheritance money from the savings and loan bank where it had been drawing three percent interest and transfer it to an Indiana bank. Before he got to the bank, he passed Drane's Jewelry Store. He heard Joanie's bright voice. *We've decided not to have an engagement ring.* Was she subtly telling him that he should give her a diamond ring? She didn't have to do that; he had already planned to get her a ring when they got back. But it would have been more in Joanie's character to say very business like, *It's time for you to buy me a ring, Kellan.* He stopped to look at the ring sets displayed in the window. He went in and priced several rings. Even the small ones seemed obscenely expensive.

Astonished at the price of diamond rings, he was shaken when at the bank he looked at the cashier's check and realized that the scrimping and saving of his parents could be substantially squandered with one purchase at Drane's. He felt guilty. Maybe prices would be more competitive in the city.

But the guilt feeling lingered, and the persistent preaching of Uncle Kirby who droned on and on as they road along about how his parents had sacrificed so that their son could attend a good college and have the things a young man needed, how he ought to use wisely and unto the Lord his small inheritance. Kellan gritted his teeth and tried to tune out Kirby's words until…

"And now, son, I want to talk to you about the estate of marriage."

Oh, no. What was he going to talk about? Sex? If he so much as says one word about sex, I'm going to shock the hell out of him. I'm going to tell him about the opulent place in San Francisco where a man could get sex in any language, where things were done that have never been written about.

But Uncle Kirby spoke of the responsibilities of a Christian marriage. How each should carry the other's burdens and forgive each other's shortcomings as Christ forgives sinners. "And," Uncle Kirby concluded, "remember to bring your children up in the nurture and admonition of the Lord. Bring a child up in the way he should go and when he is old, he will not depart from it."

I departed, Kellan thought.

Uncle Kirby expressed many of the same sentiments again at the table prayer as they stood before their places in the dining room. Grandmother, Aunt Sammie, and Uncle Kirby stood with heads bowed and eyes squeezed shut. Kellan and Joanie stared at each other.

At the amen, Joanie said, "If you get all you asked for, Uncle Kirby, there won't be any problems left in the whole world." Smiling happily, she added, "Now I know why Kellan is such a good person."

Accepting her remarks as a compliment, Uncle Kirby grinned in pleasure, his pink-cheeked, round cherubic face the antithesis of his dolorous disposition.

Aunt Sammie pulled up her glasses, wiped her eyes, and asked Joanie, "Was it love at first sight with you all?"

Uncle Kirby spared Joanie the trouble of answering by admonishing his wife. "Love at first sight only happens in those cheap magazine stories you read, Sammie."

Aunt Sammie didn't listen to her husband. She had spent more hours than Kellan under the sentence of a sermon, and she, like Kellan, automatically shut them out. Perhaps, it occurred to Kellan, that is why I used to feel more comfortable with Aunt Sammie than any adult in the family except my mother.

Kellan sensed that Joanie did not particularly like Aunt Sammie. And seeing Aunt Sammie through Joanie's eyes he could understand why. Aunt Sammie ate with her plate pushed forward and her left arm resting on the table and she ate noisely; in contrast to Grandmother and Uncle Kirby who ate with dignity. Being poor, Grandmother often remarked, should not keep a person from being genteel. And genteel folk never left the table without asking to be excused. And in the Foster family no one asked to be excused until the head of the table excused himself and only then could they turn and ask Grandmother to be excused. But Joanie did not know this.

"Kellan told me that no one is allowed to smoke in the house," Joanie said blithly, "so I'm going out on the front porch for a cigarette. But I will come back in and dry the dishes or something."

There it was, right out in the open, Kellan had brought home a girl who smoked. No thunder crashed. The earth didn't shake. Grandmother and Aunt Sammie insisted that they did not need Joanie's help in the kitchen.

Joanie wanted to see the spring house.

Holding her hand, Kellan walked her down the steep hill to the place where a fast little trickle of water flowed out from under the spring house door that was framed into the side of the hill and made its way into a stream of water that flowed off toward a distant creek. Kellan opened the creaky wooden door and showed Joanie the inside where there was a rough bench on which they once had stored perishable foods. "It stays cool enough in here that Jello will set," Kellan explained, but she didn't seem to be impressed by that information. She would never have made Jello.

"I'll bet you had lots of fun here—when you were a little kid," Joanie said.

"Somehow I never thought carrying buckets of water up that damn hill too much fun."

"But look at the muscles it gave you." She ran her hand up the length of his arm.She put her mouth to his to be kissed, and he felt the sensuous lips and tasted her goodness. "Oh, God," he groaned, pushing her away. "what you do to me."

Her half-laugh was both seductive and triumphal, but she did not tease him. "I want to see the rest of the farm," she ordered.

When they got to the tobacco patch, Joanie asked, "Why does your uncle raise tobacco if he is so opposed to its use?"

"Because it's the money crop."

"Aren't there any other money crops?"

"Raising tobacco is what he does best. That and curing hams."

"Is your uncle Kirby always so serious?"

"Always. He probably would have been more comfortable as a contemporary of Jonathan Edwards."

"Who was Jonathan Edwards?"

"A colonial fire-and-brimstone preacher who wrote a famous sermon entitled *Sinners in the Hands of an Angry God.*" When she made no reply, he added, "You don't like Aunt Sammie."

"I was polite to her."

"Too polite. That's how I knew you didn't like her." He added as if to give her a reason for liking his aunt, "Aunt Sammie plays the piano."

"So does Larry Somner and I don't like him either."

As they approached the edge of the woods, Kellan who had been thinking about Joanie's statement that she didn't want an engagement ring, sounded her out. "I almost bought you an engagement ring today, but I didn't know your ring size."

She stopped short. "I-do-not-want-an-engagement-ring."

"I thought every girl wants an engagement ring."

"I am not **every** girl."

"True. Yet there must be a reason."

She closed her eyelids deliberately as though to shut out the question, and her dark lashes lay against her cheeks like fringe. Then she opened her eyes and looked directly at Kellan and said pointedly, "I don't want a rinky-dink little diamond ring, and I don't think you can afford anything else."

"To hell with it."

They walked through the woods in silence. "This way," Kellan directed. He put his foot on the bottom two wires of a barbed-wire fence and held up the top two wires so that she could slide between. "We'll take the short cut back to the house." Kellan was curt as he easily straddled the fence to the other side.

"I'm sorry if I upset you," Joanie was apologetic, "but that's exactly how I feel."

"Forget I ever mentioned a god-damned ring."

"Let me remind you that you once told me that we must always be honest with each other."

"Congratulate yourself. Your honesty is overwhelming."

"Don't be so sensitive."

"You will get your plain gold band. That's the end of the matter. Subject closed."

They finished their walk in unhappy silence.

In the house, Kellan picked up the *Courier Journal* which had come in that day's mail and went out to the porch swing, leaving Joanie with Grandmother.

For a few minutes he read only to assuage his resentment and ire, but then he became interested in Truman's maneuvers in Congress. The feisty Truman was calling Congress back into session on the day Missourians called Turnip Day. Kellan thought he knew exactly what Truman would do. He would ask Congress to pass all the reforms that the Republicans had put into their platform. Congress would not do that, and then Truman could call them a do-nothing Congress. Would the plan work? Maybe…

"Joanie," Grandmother said as she came out on the porch, "is mightily distressed."

"She'll get over it."

"She's hurt. Now there's not an ounce of deceit in that girl—you are not listening to me, Kellan Foster."

"Yes, I am."

"Then put that paper down and give me your attention. Joanie is a fine girl. Granted she had a different upbringing...."

You can't possibly imagine how different, Grandmother. She's got a father who acts like her lover and gives her anything her heart desires.

...and she's been used to finer things like your mother was...

She's spoiled and self-centered. Mother wasn't.

...where's your Christian charity, Kellan?"

I never had any.

"You swore angrily in her presence."

Now we are coming to the crux of the episode.

"Never in this house have you heard God's name used in vain. Never have you heard one family member raise his voice in anger against another family member."

We choke on sermons.

"I understand. It's that rough element you were exposed to during the war. That can't be helped. You had to serve your country. And you did. Honorably. But Kellan, you've been taught that we must live above the sin of the world." She paused, expecting him to concur. When he said nothing, she went on. "Child, child, you are as dear to me as any of my own flesh and blood. And I know you love us dearly even if you find it hard to express your inmost thoughts. Well, so be it. Here's something that I should have given you some time ago. Your dear mother's jewelry box. What happened was I put it up one time when we were having a big family gathering because I feared some of the children might thoughtlessly get into the box and lose her valuable little trinkets." Grandmother handed Kellan an old cigar box.

The box was instantly familiar to Kellan, in spite of the fact that he had forgotten that it once set atop Mother and Father's bureau. He knew that his mother had kept some jewelry in the box, but he was never interested in its contents. They were women's things.

Kellan opened the box. The items were wrapped in soft cloth. There was a gold locket which he could not remember his mother ever having worn. Hoping to see a revealing picture, he unsnapped the locket. Both sides were blank.

"Mary Katherine took out the pictures of her papa and mama; she said," Grandmother explained, "that if she was dead to them, then they were dead to her. Mary Katherine seemed soft on the outside, but I can tell you in all surety that she was strong as steel on the inside." Grandmother sighed sadly. "The only one of her people that Mary Katherine ever heard from was her aunt. India. Her father's baby sister who lived with them. Miss India wasn't a whole lot older than Mary Katherine."

Why had he not been told all this before? Because the Fosters thought that it was irrelevant to his life? "Is this India still living?"

"So far as I know. I haven't had correspondence from her, but I did write her of your mother's passing."

"Where does she live?"

"Why, at the home place, the fine old mansion in Louisville on Third Street where your mother was raised. Now there's a ring in there. I want you to take a look at it."

Kellan found the ring his mother so seldom wore that he had forgotten about it. The ring was a sapphire set in a ring of diamonds mounted in gold.

"Your mother got that ring for her sixteenth birthday. Joanie will treasure the ring not only for its beauty but because it belonged to your mother."

When the time was right, he would give the ring to Joanie.

Having a house entirely to himself, Kellan discovered, was pure luxury.

Freedom. Freedom to act on inclination. Freedom from noise and confusion. Solitude. Time to read, to study. Solitude, to Kellan, was exhilarating.

There was only one fault with the house. It got excessively hot when the thermometer climbed above eighty degrees.

"This is a nice place," Bill commented as they sat on the back steps of the house, "but it's hotter than hell. Too bad you don't have some shade trees." Bill had come by with a couple of cases of beer and the pronouncement that it might be the only wedding present Kellan and Joanie would get from him. "You better get some kind of big fan or your nights aren't going to be what they're supposed to be."

Kellan let that remark pass.

"What you oughta get," Bill went on, "is one of those new window fans. Exhaust fans. One of those babies can pull the heat out of the entire house."

"How much are they?"

"Hell, I don't know. I'm not in the market for a fan. But I know where you can get one wholesale. Interested?"

"Not now. I don't know how much this wedding will cost. I may end up in debt up to my ass."

"I thought the bride's father was supposed to pay for all that crap. Dad always said he had all boys so he would never have to pay for a wedding."

"I've got to pay for a wedding ring and a honeymoon, and God only knows what else."

"Hell." Bill's all inclusive word. "Get that beer in the fridge. Next time I come over, I want a cold one."

As Bill walked across the back lawn toward his pickup, Kellan walked with him. "Let's go some place and drink beer."

"Can't. It's about supper time at the Dietmeier Digs. What are you and Joanie doing tonight?"

"I don't know. I haven't been informed. She's in Indianapolis today. Shopping. I almost need an appointment to get to see her. Weddings are a pain in the ass, Bill."

"Ah, come on. It isn't that bad. Hell."

"I'll remind you of that statement when you get involved in all this traditional shit."

"Don't get yourself worked up." Bill got in the pickup and pulled the door shut "I'll see you at the Dutch wedding tomorrow."

"Don't count on it." Bill's cousin's wedding was an event he wanted to pass up. It was Mrs. D.'s idea that they should attend. The fact that neither he nor Joanie had received an invitation and neither of them knew either the bride or groom seemed of zero importance to Bill's mother who had decided that Kellan—and Joanie—should take part in the family affair. Kellan walked back into the house, knowing that he wanted and loved Joanie more than anything or anybody in the world. And if Joanie wanted to spend a Saturday afternoon at a German wedding, they would go to the wedding. If he was lucky, she might not want to go.

She wanted to go. Definitely. German weddings were a blast.

No one answered the doorbell. The screen door wasn't latched so Kellan stepped inside the house and called out Joanie's name.

Clad only in the bare essentials, Joanie came to the top of the stairs and said, "Come on up. I'll need you to zip up my dress."

Only once before had Kellan been upstairs and on that occasion he had paid no attention to the surroundings. This time was different. Through the open door of the master bedroom Kellan saw a gallery-sized portrait that dominated one wall. He stepped inside for a closer look. The portrait was a stylized pose of a young woman half-sitting on the arm of a chair. Her head was lowered in an attitude of submissiveness, the hair drawn back into a low knot to show the perfectly shaped neck. The diaphanous pale mauve frock both heightened and softened the contours of her body. The neckline was scooped out to reveal the first fullness of her breasts. The bare arms were held at length, the hands clasped—again the suggestion of submission. The painting was beautiful. However, the face, to Kellan, seemed too spiritless.

"That's my mother," Joanie informed him as she came into the room. "Do I look like her?"

"A little."

"You've heard of Matisse, haven't you?"

Kellan looked at the artist's signature. It wasn't Matisse. The name was formed in elongated letters that might have begun with a Ch or a Dn. It was hard to tell.

"Zip me, please."

Kellan pulled up a zipper that started below the waist and ended at the back of the neck.

"How do I look?" she asked.

"Like a lemon drop." The dress was pale yellow.

"Is that a compliment? Well, I do like lemon drops."

His mind was on the painting. "That's not Matisse's signature on the painting."

"The artist who painted the portrait studied under Matisse. A friend of Charles.Not Matisse. The artist was Charles's friend. You are supposed to be impressed when I tell you that the artist studied under Matisse."

"Count me as one duly impressed."

"In some ways I don't know much more about my mother than you know about your father. She doesn't seem real to me, to tell the truth. She seems like a storybook character that Charles told me about. Nor can I imagine Charles living in Paris with my mother."

Joanie dashed across the hall to her room and immediately came back with an enormous pale yellow hat. She stood in front of the full-length mirror and adjusted the hat to her satisfaction.

"That's like wearing a small umbrella," Kellan remarked.

"It's a picture hat." Again she asked, "How do I look?"

"Like two lemon drops stuck together."

Kellan took her hand. "If we have to go to the wedding, it's time to leave."

After the relative coolness of the big, old house, the outdoor heat was cruel. Everything drooped from the humid heat.

Not a leaf stirred. Men were idiots, Kellan fumed, to wear suits and ties when it was ninety in the shade. He threw his suit coat and tie into the back seat. They would go on at the last possible moment. He envied Joanie in the thin, low-cut, sleeveless dress. But obviously she was no cooler than he.

"Oh, it's too hot for anything," she complained as she pressed a white-gloved finger against the beads of moisture that had popped out on her upper lip. "I don't think I can stand it." She rolled up the window on her side of the car.

"Then for the love of Christ, don't raise the window, Kellan objected.

"I have to. The wind blows my hat."

"Take the damn thing off."

"I can't. I might not be able to get it back on properly."

"What does it matter? Everyone will be looking at the bride, not you."

"Oh, no they won't. Everyone will be looking at me."

She was absolutely correct.

Bill was the usher who extended an arm to Joanie to walk her down the aisle.Clinging to him with her special mixture of aloofness and intimacy and moving her body as gracefully as if she were on the dance floor, she caused heads to turn and eyes to stare.

As Bill deposited Joanie in the pew, Bill mumbled to Kellan, "Better pay attention to what goes on. The next funeral is yours."

Miraculously, from some cavernous part of the old church, a current of cooler air permeated the sanctuary. The service, while solemn and ritualistic, was mercifully short. As soon as the bride and groom—both red-faced and robust—strode back down the aisle and out of the church, coats and ties came off. The reception was held at the bride's home, twelve miles out in the country. A receiving line was formed in the neat front yard, and the guests strung out in a long queue to take their turns at handshaking and well-wishing. Inside the house one room held heaps of wedding presents, and more were being added.

Kellan gave Joanie a woebegone look. "In my male uninterest in things social, I stayed blissfully unmindful of getting a wedding present."

Joanie spoke through a suppressed laugh, "Why didn't you just say, 'I forgot to buy a wedding present?'"

"I suppose I was trying to make excuses."

She reached in her purse and pulled out an envelope. "You can put this on the gift table; the newly weds will like what's in the card better than a wrapped present. Believe me. I know it is not etiquette to give money but…"

Kellan would not ask how much.

In the dining room of the farm house, there were loads of food on the table, and on set-up side tables: ham, turkey, slices of roast beef, piles of breads, salads.... *ad infinitum.*

Finally, the bride and groom cut the cake and were toasted with champagne. And then, the rolled-up, shirt-sleeved party began.

Beer kegs were tapped, plates were filled and refilled, cigars were passed out. Two times as many people came to the reception as had attended the ceremony, but the supply of food and drink never seemed to diminish.

Card tables were set up in the yard. Children ran amongst them, playing improvised games. A young fellow played an accordion. Later in the evening, when the air turned cool, there would be dancing. Kellan heard as much German as he did English.

"Oh sure," Bill explained. "I think the old folks think they're having more fun when they talk Dutch. It's the common language inside the home. Mom and Dad won't speak German when you or somebody like you is around. During the war, you know, the Dutch didn't want anyone thinking they were Nazi sympathizers."

Joanie posed a question. "Why do people say 'Dutch'?"

"Because they think that's an English way of saying 'Deutch'." Bill went on, "The government would have been hard- pressed to herd all the German families into concentration camps like they did the Japanese on the West Coast."

"Was it necessary, do you think," Bill asked, "for the government to put the Japanese in camps?"

Bored with Kellan and Bill's conversation, Joanie was watching a card game in progress. "Let's get up a card game." she suggested.

Kellan and Joanie learned how to play euchre. Bill and Joanie against Kellan and Bill's cousin, Louise.

They played euchre, drank beer, ate, and sweat.

"I like this game because it goes so fast," Joanie said. "It's almost as good a card game as bridge." She laid down a card. "I'll take this trick with the ace, lead the left bar, and we euchred you!"

Kellan was ready to leave.

"Give me a lift home, okay?" Bill asked.

"Where's your new buggy?" Kellan was referring to Bill's new Ford.

"I told Burt he could use it. He found a girl he wants to take home by way of a country lane."

Silence. They were remembering another ride in a new car.

"Burt can handle it," Bill said as if that were an answer to an asked question.

Ties and coats along with Joanie's big hat occupied the back seat. The three rode up front where the hot wind, sweet with the smell of corn fields, blew threw the car whipping Joanie's thick hair across her face.

"Let me fix that," Bill offered, and he took out his pocket handkerchief and tied back her hair in a pony tail. "How's that?"

"Perfect," Joanie purred.

At that point they saw a partially ditched car in a deep gully that separated the road from the corn field. Standing beside the car and waving them to stop was E.P.Portland.

"Hail, knights errant," she called out when the car came to a stop. "You've come to a damsel's rescue. I was on my way to crash the reception and partake of good German cooking, when a tire blew."

"Do you have a spare?" Kellan asked.

"Most certainly. A spare and a jack."

Bill was opening the car door. "I'll change the tire for her. You go on into town. She can take me home." He spoke of E.P. as though she were a non-person.

"Call me Elizabeth. Call me Elizabeth Perry. Call me E.P, but don't speak of me as if I were an inanimate object."

As Kellan and Joanie left, they did not hear Bill's reply to E.P.—if he had replied to her remarks.

"That was a surprising move on Bill's part," Kellan commented, "since he detests the woman."

"He isn't doing her a favor; he's doing us a favor." Joanie stretched her arms out and relaxed. "You know, if Bill ever gets a girlfriend, I may be jealous. I rather like the three of us being together."

"I rather like the two of us together. Alone. Where shall we go? To the cabin?"

"Charles is up there. Staying the night. Tomorrow he's entertaining his Sunday night bridge club at the cabin." She fished in Kellan's shirt for a cigarette. "E.P., by the way, is Charles's bridge partner."

"Then bridge is like politics. It makes for strange bedfellows."

"Oh, yes. Charles thinks E.P. is one of the most obnoxious persons in town."

"Except at cards."

"Except at bridge. She's an excellent bridge player. Almost as good as I am." Kellan liked her artless self-confidence. "Is that idle boasting or plain fact?"

"Fact. And it's a fact that I've never been a very humble person."

"Which in no way detracts from my love for you."

"I love you, Kellan."

"And where do we go when we get in town?"

"To our house." She added, realizing that Kellan thought she meant her father's house, "Yours and mine."

The coolest place in the house was the floor of the living room, and it was there that, after the love-making was over, they fell asleep on the shag carpet in the house that would be their home.

Late Monday morning Joanie phoned. "I'm on my way over," she said. Nothing more than that. Kellan had not shaved, hadn't dressed, hadn't finished reading the morning paper, had not done much of anything but sit in the kitchen in his skivvies and relish the cool breeze that came through the open window.

That's the way she found him. "Wow, don't you look sexy…" she touched his cheek, ".just enough of a stubble to make…"

He didn't let her finish, but pulled her down on his lap. "I'm going to show you just how sexy I am as soon as…"

"Not now." she ended his overture. She got up and sat down in a chair across the table from him. "Coffee?"

"I didn't feel like making coffee this morning. It's too hot."

"Oh, well, I'll just have a cigarette." She picked up the cigarette pack and lighter that were on the table. "First the gossip." She paused to light the cigarette. "Charles said that E.P. came late to duplicate bridge. She had a black eye and bruises on her face. When asked what had happened, she said she tripped on a stack of books and fell into th fireplace. Which, Charles said, was nothing but her perverse way of saying it's nobody's business. He there were bruises on her upper arms."

"She's an exhibitionist who enjoys drawing attention to herself. Being an oddity." And then he changed the subject.

"What's the other thing that's on your mind?"

"Well, last night you mentioned that you wanted to hang that gun…"

"The Kentucky rifle."

"…over the mantle in the living room. That's not the place for a gun. We want to keep it a formal living room."

"I am not going to hide the rifle in a closet."

"Please let me finish. We will buy a gun case which we will put in the room that I intend to make into your study."

"A gun case for one gun?"

"Oh, we'll just buy some guns to go with it."

"What kind of guns…a Browning automatic, or a…"

114

She either did not recognize his jibe. "Long guns with beautiful wood handles."

"Stocks."

"Stocks. You might as well know, I've already bought the gun case. From Steamboat. Wholesale. He is ordering it from a catalogue."

"You've certainly had a busy morning."

The mockery in his voice was lost on her. "When I make up my mind to do something, I get it done fast. When I saw you, I wanted you, and…well, here we are."

He loved her without reason, but reason prompted him to ask, "How much will I have to pay for the gun case?"

"I've already written Steamboat a check."

"Joanie," Kellan began, "things—the gun case, for example—are not necessary for our happiness."

"I know that. I could live with you in a tent, and I would be happy. But the fact is—we don't have to live in a tent. Or a house with a gun hanging on the wall above the mantel. The fact is that I have access to money. So swallow your pride and enjoy me and everything that comes with me."

Why not? Why couldn't he be content with this sort of life? Wasn't every component for happiness found here, with Joanie? No. He had ambitions that could be submerged in ecstasy but could not be eradicated. "I would be a liar if I said that it does not chafe my sensibilities that I can't give you everything money will buy. But you are the light of my life, and for your love I will compromise, I will sacrifice."

Joanie had tears in her eyes when she said, "I could not live without you, Kellan, if I ever lost you, I would…"

He put his hand over her mouth. "Don't say it. Don't ever say that again."

The Welles-Foster wedding was the social event of late summer. There were showers and kitchens showers and luncheons and teas. One party after another.

E.P. Portland gave a dinner-bridge. Never in his life had Kellan seen so much sterling and white linen in one home.

E.P. might be foul-mouthed and obnoxious, but just as she dressed conservatively and in good taste, so she also hosted the party with impeccable manners and appointments. There was nothing haphazard about the evening. She was gracious and well- organized and the maid moved to her biding in a no-nonsense way.

In the party where guests came as couples, Bill came as a single which, whether planned or not, made E.P. and Bill a couple. At the first opportunity,

Bill said to Kellan, "Don't get any wrong ideas. I'm only here because of you and Joanie."

Then he kidded, "Hell, come to think of it, I'm only here because of Joanie."

All evening Ken Warwick tried to catch Kellan in a position so that he could talk politics with him, and he finally had his chance when the card playing ended, and the scores were being tallied.

"Say," Ken began, "what do you think of that Whittaker Chambers? He's going to tighten the screws on those Commie sons-of-bitches, isn't he?"

Davis Courtney, who was sitting in a position to speak slyly in Kellan's ear, said of Ken through clenched teeth, "Politics is his game, erudite is his name." He cackled loudly and retreated behind a smirk.

The conversation was lost with things happening and people moving about, and thus began the exodus from that party.

Dr. Joe and Mrs. Frederick entertained with a cocktail party. Many of the guests at this affair were of Dr. Welles's age, and most of them Kellan was meeting for the first time. He seemed to be tediously repeating the same bland responses to the same bland questions over and over.

Kellan was surprised, however, when Superintendent Hiram B. Zeikoff—with his wife bobbing along beside her husband, sought him out. Oh, what a change in Mr.Zeikoff from that first cold interview. Indeed, as he introduced his wife to Kellan, he was downright fawning.

Mrs. Zeikoff, pulling uncomfortably at her cocktail dress, asked, "What subject will you be teaching?"

Zeikoff quickly answered for Kellan. "I think he can teach about any subject, Mother; he has a well-rounded education.

His transcript is about as impressive as I've ever read." Then he added in a more natural tone, "Too bad he can't coach something."

May my tongue swell and fill my mouth if I ever call Joanie, Mother, Kellan swore.

Guests converged on Kellan and Joanie, and they were separated, each the center of attention. Kellan made the right answers, asked the right questions, commented positively on everything from the weather to the war. He was full of self- assurance for he knew that he was well-liked.

Except for Charles Welles, standing with his arm about Joanie.

One year, Kellan promised himself. One year and then Joanie and I will go our own way, make our own life. Away from this town and these people.

Slowly, the crowd began to thin, but it was well past the dinner hour before the party ended. Dr. Joe was discovered dozing in an easy chair, his pudgy hands folded across his round, vested stomach, his pipe gone cold in the ash tray beside his chair.

His wife shook him gently, "Wake up, Dr. Joe. We're going to dinner now with Charles and his lovely daughter and her fiance."

Bob and Helen Fulton gave a backyard party. A cookout.

Running a bit late, Kellan and Joanie were among the last to arrive. They were greeted at the front door by Davis Courtney who happened to be near the door when they rang the bell.

"Ah, she's lovely, she's engaged, she uses Ponds," he said quoting the advertising slogan. Davis touched Joanie's arm.

"The usual crowd are assembled on the patio." He detained Kellan as Joanie moved on. "Won't be long until you have the ball and chain around your ankle, my man," Davis began; "Lynda's got a girlfriend who's hot to trot. I know of a place where the four of us can mix it up." He grinned wickedly.

"I'm not interested."

"Ah, no, not so hasty. Don't concern yourself that Lynda might talk. The little sex pot will do anything I ask in anticipation of a visit to Princeton that I've promised her. Of course," his voice took on a tone of regret, "when the time comes, the visit will have to be cancelled for some as yet unforeseen reason." He smirked, and added, "Miss Lynda would be grossly out of place at Princeton, and I would spare her the embarrassment of, uh, not quite fitting in."

"I know that feeling well," Kellan said flatly.

"Just offering a little pre-nuptial diversion. One never knows. Did I ever tell you that Joanie and I had a few rather intimate good times together?"

"Like hell you did." Kellan hurried out on the patio to find Joanie.

Shrubs and heavy foliage made the Fultons' backyard as private as the interior of their house. The group on the patio sipped drinks and watched Steamboat turn the meat on the outdoor grill. Smoke from the broiling meat hung in the warm outdoor air and blended with the cosmetic fragrances of the women. The talk was banal, easy and relaxed until Esther casually mentioned that she was pregnant.

The crowd reacted.

"Good lord, again?"

"Jeeze, Esther, you're not Catholic.

"Hey, Scott, haven't you learned what causes babies?"

"It must be in the water. Better not drink water at Scott's house."

Esther stopped the comments when she stated, "I like having babies."
Scott was stoical.

I will not let myself get trapped in a life like this, Kellan vowed. It's a
world away from the farm, but it's the wrong direction.

"Can you slow down the steaks, Bobby?" Helen asked. "E.P. and Bill will
surely be here shortly."

"How in hell can I slow down the steaks?" Steamboat asked no one in
particular.

A telephone call solved half his problem. Bill phoned with regrets. He had
to meet with the ABC commissioner about a new franchise for the
distributorship.

Kellan was amused. Only Bill would fabricate such an outlandish excuse
and expect to be believed.

At least one person was not taken in by Bill's story. Ken remarked quietly,
"We certainly have a dedicated staff on the Indiana Alcoholic Beverage
Commission. Working on a Saturday night, by golly."

"I don't mean to be bossy," Phyllis Cordet said, getting ready to be bossy,
"but I would not wait any longer for E.P. She was invited for the same time
as everyone else."

Phyllis was one half of the couple that Kellan had just met for the first
time. She was an ordinary looking woman with an extraordinary poodle
haircut which was not in the least becoming. Her husband, Clem, was a soft-
spoken Southerner from Louisiana with a mild manner and mild good looks.
The Cordets had recently returned from Louisiana, having had an extended
stay while Clem settled his deceased parents' estate.

Steamboat agreed with Phyllis. "You're damn right, Phyllis. These steaks
cost too much to let 'em get ruined. Let's eat."

"Hey!" E.P. appeared on the patio, Lonnie Lykens in tow. "Are you
people going to eat out here in the heat and humidity and share your fare with
the gnats and mosquitoes?" She addressed Bob Fulton. "My aching back,
Steamboat, I thought Helen had civilized you enough that she let you eat in
the dining room. As for the rest of you people, you look like gypsies around
a campfire." She was holding onto Lonnie's hand like she was taking a kid to
kindergarten.

For a few minutes it was too quiet.

"Go ahead and stare, good friends," E.P,. said. "And can't you see why I
often call him Adonis?" She looked up at Lonnie's face. "If you are not
Adonis, oh, but you are Adonis."

Lonnie made no response nor did his impassive expression change in the least.

E.P. went on. "Honest to God, Steamboat, can you explain why you left the manor house for the courtyard?"

Steamboat was stumbling for a smart answer, but Helen was quicker. "Feel free, E.P., to take your plate—and the young man's plate—and eat in the dining room if you will be more comfortable inside."

E.P. and Lonnie ate outside with the rest of the guests.

Lonnie had the good sense to keep his mouth shut. Or he was bored. He showed no interest in the chatter about the wedding, business, fishing, or golf. He listened intently, however, with wide-eyed interest when Scott and Davis, both of whom had been in the infantry, talk about the war. Like most vets, they kept the horrors they had witnessed submerged and dwelt on the ineptitude, bungling, and general cussedness of the infantry.

"Say, kid, when do you leave for Purdue?" Steamboat asked.

"I'm not sure. I'm not even sure I want to go to Purdue."

"Hell, kid," Steamboat advised, "You got the chance of a lifetime. How many guys from this burg ever get a chance to play basketball in the Big Ten?"

"Yeah," Lonnie agreed. He appeared not to give a hoot. "I guess you're right." He turned to E.P. "Can I have the car?"

"Of course you may. Not can, may. Just don't forget to come back and pick me up." She fished in her purse for car keys and handed them to Lonnie.

Lonnie remembered to thank Helen.

Ken Warwick, ignoring the party talk, said in all seriousness to E.P., "E.P., you are asking for trouble. The boy is a minor. You're not stupid. Think about it."

E.P. ignored Ken. "Where's Bill Dietmeier, everybody's Mister Good Guy?"

Hearing Helen's explanation of Bill's absence, E.P. snorted, "What a bunch of bullshit. "Go phone Bill, Steamboat, and tell him to get his butt over here."

"Phone him yourself."

She did.

Kellan would have bet it would be a useless phone call.

E.P. came back subdued. She took a claim on the martini pitcher and a chaise longue. She was finished with buffoonery and gave the party back to the others.

Lynda Davis pumped Joanie for all the intimate details of the wedding plans, Ken talked politics, Davis belittled Lynda in the nicest sort of way, Esther flirted, Scott tolerated, Clem cooed about his coups on the stock market. Phyllis interrupted him, stating that it was time to leave. Thus began the exodus from the cookout. Finally, there were, besides Kellan and Joanie and the Fultons, only E.P. left, her head thrown back, her mouth open, snoring steadily.

"You got the prize of the lot," Bob said to Kellan as he watched Joanie helping Helen tidy up. "She's got it all—looks, personality—she must have got it from her mother. Her old man is sure a cold bird. If I was sick, and I ain't never sick, I wouldn't go to Doc.Welles. Helen goes to him. She says he's a private person. He's private, all right. My ma used to work at the funeral home. Cleaning. Whenever there's one of those quick, private burials, it makes you wonder. Me, when I go, I want to go in a blaze of glory. I want to be laid out in the best. Lots of flowers, all my friends coming to pay their respects."

Steamboat was serious, but Kellan couldn't keep a straight face. "That's important to you?"

"Damn right. I want the works. The best." Steamboat dropped that subject when Helen and Joanie came out of the house and joined them.

"What do we do about E.P.?" Helen asked. "I don't think that boy has any intention of returning."

"If you wake her up, Helen, Joanie and I will take her home," Kellan offered.

"Let her be," Steamboat shrugged him off. "If the kid doesn't show pretty soon,I'll take her home." E.P.'s snores were deep and loud. "Jesus, she's out of it. What do you think, Helen?"

Helen looked tired. "She's completely passed out. Maybe we can get her into a bedroom and let her sleep it off." She tried rousing E.P. to no avail.

"Lead the way, Helen," Kellan said, "I'll carry her."

"She's dead weight," Steamboat said, "no need to get a hernia. You take one end— and I don't want the bottom end— and I'll take the other."

Between the two of them they removed E.P. from the chaise and got her to a guest bedroom where Helen and Joanie, who had the bed turned down, removed her shoes, and loosened her clothes. And they left her to sleep it off.

Steamboat seemed to be rejuvenated. "You know what I think I'll do, Foster? I think I'll have me a swimming pool put in where the patio is now, and then put me a big new screened in patio around the pool—say, Joanie, if I put in a swimming pool will you come over and skinny-dip with me?"

When they weren't attending a joint social function, Joanie was going to a luncheon or shower or consulting with her father over the details of the wedding.

"Shit. I just do what I'm told," Kellan complained to Bill. Bill had come by the house to take Kellan fishing, but the rods and the tackle boxes never got out of Kellan's kitchen where the two of them were drinking beer. "I'm sick of hearing about flowers and showers—hey, that rhymes. But it's not poetry, is it? Open us another beer, Bill. I got a letter from my grandmother and a whole flock of relatives are coming up for the wedding."

Bill took a beer from the refrigerator and handed it to Kellan. "I hope those Kentuckians wear shoes for you wedding,Kell."

"They're going to be in for a big shock when they see all the booze flowing freely at the reception."

"They can drink beer, can't they?"

"Wouldn't touch it with a ten-foot pole."

"You sure aren't like your family. Right now you are slightly drunk."

"I never told you this. I was illegitimate. After my mother married Garret Foster, he adopted me. For all I know, whoever he was or is, my real father might be the biggest lush in the world."

"I wouldn't worry about it." Bill's voice was casual, off hand.

"My chief concern." Kellan began, "among other chief concerns, the chieftest, the most chief, is getting the Fosters in and out of town without them preaching to all and sundry."

"I wouldn't lose any sleep over that. Doc Welles really likes to put on a show, doesn't he?"

"Oh, damn, doesn't he though," Kellan groaned. "Sometimes I think this whole thing is a mistake. I don't have to get married."

"Ah, come on. You don't mean that."

"Oh, yes I do."

"I know you better than that."

"You don't really know me at all."

"I know you as well as I want to know you."

"What does that mean?"

"Nothing."

"I'm going to be very serious with you, Bill. Very serious. I'll go along with the wedding. Okay? I'll teach here one year. Okay? Then Joanie and I will be on our way. Out of this town. Okay?"

"You don't need my approval," Bill said dryly, "but I'll bet you any amount you name that you are here in this town two years from now. Maybe in this very house."

"You'd lose that bet."

"Kell, you don't know how lucky you are. Doc is worth a lot of money.

121

Some say he made it in the stock market. That I don't know. I know he owns a lot of property around here. I never heard of a doctor who was a pauper. Plus, Joanie is going to grow up one of these days."

Kellan didn't like what he had just said about Joanie. "Joanie's got a head on her shoulders, Bill—she's got more…"

Bill didn't let him finish. "Oh, hell, don't take offense. You know what I mean."

"Let's get something straight. Joanie means as much to me as." Kellan stopped, sobered by the words he was about to speak.

"Go ahead. Say it. As much as Polly meant to me."

It was the second time since Polly's death that Kellan had heard Bill say her name. Could it be that he wanted to talk about her? "I've heard Polly was pretty and popular."

"What do **you** know about Polly?" Bill shot out.

"Only what you've told me," Kellan said. "Let's have another beer."

"The beer is kaput."

"I've got booze. I'll get that."

"Not for me."

Kellan, getting a glass and ice, said, "Joanie is different from what you think she is, Bill."

"Yeah."

"Her father is a genuine snob."

"Yeah. Say, is that old lady going to stay on at the house after Joanie moves out?"

"They don't let me in on little matters like that. You want some bourbon, Bill?" As he spoke, Kellan gestured toward the bottle, accidentally tipping it. Overly cautious, he set the bottle in the middle of the kitchen table. "If they held a contest to find the worst cook in Indiana, she would win the contest, hands down."

"That reminds me. Mom wants you and Joanie to come over for supper some night real soon. Think Joanie can work that into your plans?"

"I make my own plans." Kellan's voice sounded too large in his own ears. Like a stranger was talking.

" I'll give you a call tomorrow to remind you."

"You don't have to call me tomorrow. I'm not drunk."

"Well, you sure are doing a good job acting like a drunk. I'll phone you tomorrow."

On the morrow Kellan was sick. He tried to attribute it to over indulgence, but when the chills started, he knew what he was in for: chills, fever, sweats, three lost days.

The telephone was ringing, but he was shaking and his teeth were chattering; he couldn't answer. He wanted to get up and find more blankets, but he was so cold and out of control he couldn't move. He couldn't think. He couldn't mark time. He couldn't sleep.

He heard someone in the house.

He felt Joanie's face close to his. He felt her warm hands on his body. A mountain of covers enveloped him before he finally felt heat in his own body.

Sometime later, Dr. Welles appeared. He asked questions, forcing Kellan to concentrate when concentrating took extreme effort. Dr.Welles did the routine things that doctors do. Kellan swallowed a capsule that was poked in his mouth, and he knew that soon he would be in a drug induced sleep.

He awoke when the fever started. The room was dark except for the small light on the dresser. He didn't know he was alone.A trip to the bathroom left him feeling like he had been doing wind sprints. Exhausted, he fell back in bed.

He slept fitfully, his subconscious bringing up childhood memories. He jerked awake to the roll and pitch of the sea. He was in his own bedroom, yet he felt himself standing forward, hands on the rail of a ship, watching the bow of the ship cut through the gray water toward a bleak harbor.

Kellan did not believe in reincarnation, out-of-the-body experiences, deja vu—even though there seemed to be no reasonable explanations for the eerie detailed accounts that some people gave of former lives lived in countries they had never seen. Perhaps it was all in the genes. Maybe it was possible to inherit memories from ancestors just as physical characteristics were inherited. A wild, improbable theory.

Somewhere between irrational and rational thoughts, he dozed.

They were alone in the kitchen, closed in from winter. Gingerbread was baking in the oven and filled the room with spicy, tempting deliciousness. He sat at the kitchen table and drew pictures of airplanes in his Golden Rod tablet.

Grandmother would have scolded him for wasting his school paper, but Mother didn't. She sat down next to him and admired his drawings. "Are you going to be an artist when you grow up? Like your father?" And he corrected her saying, "Father never draws anything."

The pastel hues of dawn were coloring the bedroom, and his senses were abruptly acute to every sound in the awakening subdivision. He heard the milk truck making its stops, the morning paper being delivered, the traffic picking up. And the knowledge that his own father had been an artist was as certain as the morning.

He started to sweat. The worst was over.

Joanie came into the room. When she leaned over to kiss him, he turned his head because he knew his breath was foul and his body had the sour smell of sickness. "Not till I've showered," he said.

By the time he had finished in the bathroom, Kellan was exhausted. But he felt better. Happy that this time the duration of the sick spell was shorter. When he returned to bed, it was freshly made up, the sheets crisp and sweet-smelling. Joanie had made breakfast for him. Even though he hadn't an appetite, he ate as much as he could to please her.

"There's a shower for me this afternoon," Joanie said, "and I'd beg off, but it's being given by a friend I don't see much anymore. Actually it's being held at her mother's house because Jane, my friend, and her husband are trying to finish college—even though they have a baby. So they don't have a lot of money. But she wanted to do this for me, and I truly appreciate it." She added for Kellan's information, "I don't have many close friends my age; they all went away to war or to college, and I fell in with the older crowd. But if I'd gone away to college, I might never have met you. Oh, but some place, somewhere in time I would have met you. I guess like you were telling me: we were a match made in heaven.

After Joanie left and the house was quiet and Kellan was sleepy, Dr. Welles stopped by to see him.

He has something on his mind, Kellan thought, other than my well being. Kellan sat up and propped the pillows behind his back.

Dr. Welles lit a cigarette. There was the characteristic lift to his black eyebrows, and the faint twitching that always played about his mouth. He inhaled deeply and exhaled smoke out his nostrils. "I must talk to you about Joanie."

Kellan tensed himself to suffer through a foolish speech about the responsibilities of marriage or some such uncomfortable subject.

"The information which I am about to divulge must be held in the strictest confidence. It is for your ears only. For all of her life, I have protected Joanie from stress, made her life stable, safe, and easy. Where to begin?"

The question hung in the air until Dr. Welles took a deep breath and began.

"I met Joanie's mother in Paris. Ostensibly I was there to continue my studies,as least that's what my two parsimonious old maid aunts who financed the year abroad thought. Studying was soon secondary. I fell in with a—shall we say Bohemian— crowd, and I was not sure that I ever wanted to practice medicine. But to go on, it was toward the end of my sojourn in Paris that I met Alicia, Joanie's mother.

"One night when I'd wrapped up an evening and returned to my flat about two o'clock, the concierge knocked at my door with the message that a gentleman friend wished to see me on an important matter. The friend was Robert, an American I sometimes played tennis with. His urgent matter was a girl who had had an accident. Knowing that I was a physician, and close by, he wished me to see her.

"We walked down the boulevard and up to the flat of Robert's friend, an artist.There, along with a couple of other men, was a young woman who had taken the pains to slash her wrists. When I examined her wounds, I found them to be superficial. I treated and bandaged the wounds, satisfied that they would heal in a few days. From all indications, it appeared to be the act of one who had no intention of actually committing suicide.

"Later I learned that…that this artist was one of several young men who called themselves *The Brothers of Lord Byron*. They had planned a leisurely trip through Italy and on to Greece where they would emulate the poet and try to swim the Hellespont. If all this sounds bizarre, it was. Nevertheless it was true. The girl was distraught because she was going to be left behind. She had been living with the artist, and when he left, she would be, if not destitute, hard-pressed for funds.

"Suffice it to say that she moved in with me."

"Alicia's life, I learned, was a series of being abandoned. When she was quite young, her mother left husband and child in the United States and went to Europe where she married some lower echelon Polish nobleman. Alicia's father, harried with the strain of raising a small daughter and commuting from Connecticut to his job in New York, alternately neglected the child and lavished her with presents and affection. When he remarried, he put Alicia in boarding school much against her wishes.When she was happy and adjusted at school, he took her out of school. At home there were now two half-brothers, and Alicia's stepmother made her feel as though she were an intruder.

"When she was old enough, Alicia wrote to her mother who was then in Paris, and asked to be allowed to live with her and her step-father. The arrangement was less than satisfactory; when Alicia's mother and the count went back to Poland, Alicia stayed in Paris. Her small allowance from her father was hardly enough to live on, and she supplemented the allowance by sitting as an artist's model, which led to her moving in with the artist.

"Alicia and I loved each other, and I will not elaborate on our happiness. We were married. Alicia was eager to return to the States. She wanted to live in the Mid-west. She had this idea, this fixation, that life in small town, middle America was solid and stable. Instead, she found it dull and boring."

Dr. Welles paused to put out his cigarette. Then he continued. "Alicia and I were delighted when she found out that she was pregnant. But after our baby girl was born, Alicia showed signs of serious depression, but I attributed it to postpartum blues and to the fact that I was spending long hours establishing my practice." Dr. Welles' face looked drawn and old. "One day when the cleaning lady was here, Alicia fed the baby and put her to bed; then she told the cleaning lady to keep an eye on the baby because she needed to take a nap. When the baby was fussy, the cleaning lady knocked on Alicia's door but there was no answer. She waited a while and again knocked. Finally, she opened the door to Alicia's room. She told me later, that as soon as she saw Alicia, she knew she was dead. Alicia had overdosed on sleeping pills. The cleaning woman stayed with the baby until I was located. The good woman who cared for the baby and stayed on to care for her was Miss Eddie who will always have a home here as long as I live."

"How much of this does Joanie know?" Kellan asked.

"All of the good but none of the bad." He looked directly at Kellan. "I see no point in distressing her with the details of her mother's passing. But I think you should know."

"Mental illness isn't inherited, is it?" Kellan asked.

"The answer is no. As far as we know. Because of all these things I have told you, I have been overly protective, I admit, trying to keep her life on an even keel."

Kellan thought of the sudden, unprompted upturns and downturns in Joanie's moods. He thought of the times he had heard her say—and thought it only an extravagant declaration—*if anything ever happened to you, Kellan, I'd kill myself.*

At that moment Kellan felt a depth of love for Joanie that he had never felt before. Protective love.

He would keep her safe. He would never leave her.

To my beautiful and beloved daughter on the occasion of her wedding:
Once I tried to put into poetry my love for your mother, but what I was able to write was so mediocre that I only cheapened what was strong and beautiful. I never again tried to express myself in poetry. So today, your wedding day, I can only repeat what you've heard me say before: you are the light of my life, my joy, and my happiness. Those graceful lines from one of Shakespeare's sonnets might well have been written about you. "Shall I

compare thee to a summer's day? Thou art more lovely and more fair."
  And you, you love your Kellan more than you love me, and that is the natural order of things. Even so, I will always be your bulwark against the vicissitudes of life.
  Charles

Joanie...

The weather was unseasonably warm for the first day of December, and the sun came through the picture window in a bright shaft of light that showed up the streaks and sumdges on the wide expanse of glass.

Joanie was playing her bridge hand routinely since she had no face cards and no trumps. She was thinking about the dirty window pane. If I were hosting bridge club and my windows were dirty, I'd draw the drapes. Esther was a sloppy housekeeper. And a sloppy bridge player. She was going down on a game bid that she should have easily made. Esther didn't seem to be good at anything but having babies. And flirting.

Esther was set two tricks which ended the six hands at that table. Joanie moved to the next table where she and E.P. would play Helen Fulton and Juanita Warwick. Both good players. E.P. was getting good hands, but Joanie wasn't, and she was getting edgy.

When the playing ended and the sunshine had faded to winter gloom, in the final tally Joanie was second high.

"I don't know how you did it, Joanie," Helen commented.

"Bidding when I should have kept my mouth shut," Joanie said.

Phyllis Cordet ran her hand over her poodle haircut. "I wish to heaven, I didn't have to cook dinner tonight."

"Bobby and I are eating at the country club tonight," Helen said; "why don't you and Clem join us?"

Phyllis drew on her cigarette and sent out a great stream of smoke like a fire-breathing dragon. "It doesn't fit into this month's budget."

Oh, no, not the Cordets' budget again, Joanie inwardly groaned, as Phyllis began with the details of her monthly budget; no one gives a damn.

The party started breaking up. "Kellan and I may join you, Helen," Joanie said. "I'm not in the mood to cook either."

She took her coat from Esther who was handing out wraps from the closet in the small foyer. "Thanks for having us, Es. Everything was very nice."

As Joanie stepped outside into the deepening gloom, a blast of cold wind hit her in the face. She was rather out of sorts. She, who was never late for her periods, was late. She was not ready to have a baby. Some day. But not now when life with Kellan was so fantastic.

It was fully dark by the time Joanie got home. Kellan's car was in the driveway. His books and papers were on the dining room table. But no Kellan. Then Joanie remembered. Kellan and Bill had a basketball game to referee. They had left without her. Damn. She loved going to the games with Kellan and Bill.

At first, when she started tagging along on the refereeing trips, the high school games had bored her, but she loved being with Kellan and Bill, and they had fun on the way to the games and afterward when the guys had showered and they were on their way home, they would talk about the games. Sometimes, if it were a long ride back, they would stop somewhere for a beer. Listening to Bill and Kellan talk over the game they had just called, Joanie couldn't get in on the conversation because all she knew about basketball was how it was scored. Sometimes she asked a question like, how can you tell the difference between blocking and charging? She always felt shortchanged with their answers as if she really wouldn't understand. So Joanie had taken Kellan's IHSAA Rule Book and studied it until she thought she probably knew as much or more than they did.

At some point after that, Bill had said, "Hell, I think Joanie knows more about basketball than we do, Kell."

Unhappy at being left behind, Joanie went to the refrigerator to see if Kellan had eft her a note. He had.

Waited as long as possible for you. Bill, Janet and I are off to Shoneyville. It will be late when we get back.

You behave yourself! Love you, Kellan

"I don't believe it." She spoke to the empty room. Bill had taken Janet Smyth along. What did he see in her? She wasn't Bill's type. Joanie remembered the time Bill, when she had asked him when he was going to get a girlfriend, had said, *When I can find a girl like you.* Well, if Bill's idea of someone like me is Janet, Joanie thought, he needs help. Why in the world had Kellan introduced them? Because she was a new teacher who didn't know many people in town? Or because he thought Bill ought to have just any girl for a girlfriend?

Joanie picked up Kellan's books and papers that he had left on the dining room table and took them to his desk in the room she had turned into his study and put them neatly on the blotter. In the bedroom his clothes were scattered about. She picked up his suit coat where his presence seemed to linger and pressed it against her face. She was suddenly afraid. What if I were never to see him again? She shook that thought off as she brushed off his suit and hung it in the closet. The tie, she thought, looked shabby, and she threw it in the trash basket. I'm not staying at home. I'm going to dinner with Helen and Steamboat.

The ringing telephone cut into the silence.

It was Ken Warwick for Kellan.

Joanie explained that he was out of town, refereeing a basketball game and asked if there was a message.

"Nothing urgent. I'll contact him later."

Feeling slighted, she said to herself as she hung up the phone, it doesn't matter, Mr. Kenneth Warwick. Kellan tells me everything.

Before Joanie left for the country club, she discovered her period had started. With a sense of relief came a sort of giddy reaction. Let her men be with Janet. It would make them appreciate her all the more.

Joanie spotted Helen and Steamboat having a drink at the bar and joined them.

"Where's the better half? Steamboat joked. "Out with another woman?"

"Refereeing a game with Bill. And another woman."

"Tell me more, honey."

"Janet Smyth went along with Bill." Joanie spoke as if she had a bad taste in her mouth.

Helen was amused. "You mean Bill has a date with Janet."

Joanie shrugged off the comment.

"Janet is a nice girl," Helen said. "And I can tell you that the school board is very happy with her teaching. Personally, I hope Bill and Janet hit it off."

Seething inwardly, Joanie smiled and agreed.

"I think…" Steamboat stopped without telling them what he thought. "Oh, my God, here comes that salesman that called on me this afternoon. I told him the club had the best food in town and he ought to be my guest."

"Robert Fulton, why are you always doing things like that?"

"You tell me." Steamboat got up and brought the salesman into the bar. "This is my wife, Helen, and our friend, Joanie Foster. This is Tipton."

"John Tiplet," the salesman corrected his name. "Tip to my friends."

"Yeah." Steamboat acknowledged. "Well, Tip, we were about to go into the dining room and order dinner. Okay?"

John Tiplet was probably in his mid-thirties, Joanie guessed, neither good looking nor ugly, not particularly well dressed nor poorly dressed. He was staring at her. Did he think Steamboat had arranged for her to be there? Joanie wanted to laugh. The poor fool.

Helen was doing what she did best. Being correct. Being tactful. "And where are you from, Tip?"

"I work out of Cincinnati. Originally I'm from New York."

"I love the Big Apple," Joanie said. "It's an exciting place."

"I'm from upstate New York," Tip corrected.

The trite conversation went nowhere, making no connections that produced convivial or even easy discourse. Tip told a golfing joke that wasn't funny, at least not funny to Joanie. Jokes followed between Steamboat and Tip moving from stupid to risque, to ethnic.

"Please," Helen's face was stern, "I find very offensive derogatory ethnic jokes.Certainly we can find more pleasant and mature subjects for conversation."

"Name one," Steamboat was grinning, in a playful mood. " How to cheat…"

"Don't be crass, Robert Fulton." Helen was not in an indulgent mood.

One sharp word led to another until Helen stood up and said, "I'm sorry to be so discourteous, but I am not at all well." I must go home." She left.

She left with Steamboat hurrying after her.

Tip looked at Joanie as though he expected answers from her.

"A minor tiff," Joanie explained. "It will only lead to a glorious reconciliation. Believe me."

As for Joanie, she intended to enjoy her steak and have a dessert if Chef Vic had made his wonderful lemon chiffon pies.

Tip seemed to have lost his sense of humor. He settled his bill with the waitress; Joanie signed for her dinner and for the Fultons as well. And said goodnight to John Tiplet.

He followed her out of the club house. "Want to go somewhere for a drink?" he asked.

"No. Thanks, but no."

"I wanted to buy your dinner, so at least let…"

"No." As Joanie made for her car, he detained her.

"Bob Fulton told me that you would be good looking, someone I could…"

"He didn't tell you anything." Joanie wanted to slap him. Instead, she went briskly off to her car. And forgot John Tiplet. He wasn't a person who was important to her life.

By the time Kellan got home, she was in bed and comfortably asleep. She hardly stirred when he kissed her.

The next afternoon when Kellan came home from school, he literally threw his books and papers on the floor and sent his coat and tie in the same general direction.

"Whatever in the world is the matter with you?" Joanie asked, putting down the *Vogue* magazine and yawning lazily.

"I'm sitting in the teachers' lounge trying to get some papers graded before the next class and in comes Adele...she teaches home ec....

"Adele Pfrom. Esther Scott's cousin."

Kellan ignored Joanie's prompting, "...and she says to me, 'I saw your wife at the country club, having dinner with a gentleman and leaving with him. And I thought, I'll bet that's some of Kellan's relatives from Kentucky. And Kellan's off refereeing a basketball game.'"

Joanie was amused. "And what did you say to nosey Adele?"

"What should I have said?" he asked angrily.

"You should have said, I don't know what the hell you are talking about."

Kellan kicked one of the books. "Who was he? Did you leave with him?"

Because she had nothing to hide, and because she liked his possessiveness, Joanie was calm and patiently explained the evening to Kellan. "We can blame the whole thing on Steamboat. Or on Helen who lost her good manners and walked out and left me sitting with a perfect stranger. But don't blame me. I was hungry; I wasn't about to have my steak put in a doggy bag to bring home."

Kellan stepped over the books and sat down on the sofa. "I'm sorry I lost my temper, Joanie. Forgive me."

"You're forgiven," she said breezily, never having been alarmed at the silly little misunderstanding. She began picking up papers and arranging them.

"Blame it on my work," Kellan sighed. "I hate teaching."

And she hated those last three words.

Christmas slipped up on Joanie, and she had a multitude of things to do, not the least of which was decorating her father's house for his annual holiday open house, an affair which had become a tradition. Unlike the burden of addressing stacks of Christmas cards, decorating the house was a challenge she enjoyed. Each year she used a different theme. This season she left the huge pine tree in the living room bare except for red satin bows and red lights. On the mantle above the fireplace there was a grouping of large red candles nesting in poinsettias. Throughout the house, she had placed red candles and red poinsettias. The crowning touch, she thought, was the stairway. On each step next to the banister, she had placed a pot of poinsettias so that it became a red cascade.

Joanie stood in the foyer and admired the effect. Absolutely gorgeous. She hoped Charles would like it. And she already had an idea for next Christmas—white and silver. "What do you think?" she asked Miss Eddie who had come in to observe the progress of the decorating.

"It's all right, I guess. But it sure is going to be expensive."

Which was more or less Kellan's response when he came in from school, the last day before the Christmas break. "How do you like it?" she called down from the top balustrade.

"Aren't you over-doing it a bit?"

Joanie was concerned. If there was anything that Charles ridiculed it was pretentiousness. "Do you think it's too, too…"

"Ostentatious."

"Too ostentatious?"

"I don't know. You're the head decorator. All I know is that your father is going to have a hell of a florist's bill."

"Come upstairs. I want to ask your advice about something."

"If it's about decorating, you'd better ask Charles." But Kellan bounded upstairs rather jauntily.

Joanie wanted to avoid last year's confusion with the overflow of wraps and the availability of bathrooms. "Now, should which bedroom should I use…you aren't listening to me, Kellan."

Kellan was in Charles's bedroom looking at her mother's portrait. "Look at this signature; what name does it spell?"

Joanie did not need to look. When she was a little girl, she used to stand before the portrait and wish her mother would come alive and send Miss Eddie away. "All I can tell you is that the first four letters are CHAZ; the other letters are all run together."

"Do artists think that it increases the value of a painting to have an illegible signature?"

"Ask Charles." Joanie had given up trying to interest Kellan in the needs of the open house. "I think I hear him downstairs now. Let's go down and have a drink with him." They started downstairs. "Did you get any Christmas presents from your students?"

"I got an outlandish tie from my English class. They said it was punishment for all the hard grammar lessons. They said that evil things would happen to me if I did not wear the tie. I'll wear it to the open house."

"You will not. You will wear a black tie and be sexy as hell."

Kellan stopped her on the last step. "I've been accepted as a candidate for a doctorate in European history. After Christmas break, I'll hand in my resignation."

Joanie's pulse quickened with the foreboding vision of a dismal apartment and Kellan's back forever hunched over books and papers. Why did he want to do this? They were so happy in their little house, with things to do and places to go— why did he have to spoil it all? She tried to make her voice sound light and happy. "Whatever you want, hon." Yet she could not resist saying, "Don't you think you have an obligation to Mr. Zeikoff and the school board to honor your contract?"

Kellan grinned at her words and asked, "Just when did you become so concerned about obligations?"

Joanie felt her temper rising. "When I thought about having to live in a cramped apartment and be bored while you waste our lives studying." And turned to greet her father in the living room. "How do you like the decorations, Charles?"

"Stunning. You would make an excellent interior decorator."

Joanie seized on that. "I could do it. If I had a shop. A beautiful shop that would appeal so much to customers that they would hire me. And Kellan could be the business manager and keep the books. Why don't you finance us?"

Charles lifted his eyebrows in amusement. "Because I don't invest in losing business ventures."

Miss Eddie came into the room. "Evening, Doctor. I've got the dinner ready."

"Not yet, Miss Eddie." Charles was curt. "I'd like to enjoy at least one drink before dinner."

"Well, the rolls is already done." The tone of her voice meant don't blame me if the rolls get cold. She retreated to the kitchen.

My father, thought Joanie, is looking younger every day. Suddenly she knew what to say to discourage Kellan from going back to the university. She would say, *Charles is getting up in years, Kellan, and I'm all he has. He needs me to be near him.*

"Has everything been ordered for the open house?" Charles asked Joanie.

"I've double checked everything on the list. The only thing that hasn't been taken care of is what I'm going to wear."

"Drive into Indianapolis and get yourself whatever you want and charge it to me. You've earned it." The small twitch played about his mouth. "After all, you will be the most conspicuous and important part of the decor."

That's the way Joanie felt on the afternoon of the open house.

The dreary day had turned dark early, but inside the big house glowed with the warmth of fireplace, candlelight, and the rich, red poinsettias. Soft music made a background for the discordant voices. Joanie loved it. She loved being hostess in an elegant home, liked moving among the guests, being charming to every old biddy, like Dr. Joe's ancient mother who might well have been a reincarnation of Queen Victoria. Liked welcoming the late comers.

She opened the door to Mr. and Mrs. Davis Courtney, senior. "So very nice to have you here this evening. Is Davis arriving later?"

Louise Courtney whose thirty years in the Mid-west had done nothing to diminish her Boston accent, or her long nose, preened herself proudly and replied, "Davis is a house guest this holiday at the home of Miss Harriet Adams of Philadelphia."

Lynda Davis never had a chance, Joanie thought, and turned to Clarice, one of Miss Eddie's two nieces acting as maids for the event. "Please take Mr. and Mrs.Courtney's wraps." And then she welcomed Mr. and Mrs. Portland, E.P.'s long- suffering parents, and heartily thanked them for their generous sponsorship of the new wing of the hospital.

Janet Smyth came alone. She had been added to the guest list when Bill was dating her. I'll take Janet off the list after tonight, Joanie decided. She doesn't fit in.

Charles was greeting Janet. Good, thought Joanie, now I don't have to. And went off to mingle with other guests. And check the dining room table. And check the kitchen. And see that someone was in attendance on Mrs. Frederick, the ancient one, whose burgundy taffeta skirt spread out from the chair in which she was sitting, straight and proper, her burgundy silk hat giving her the air of royalty. At least it made her distinctive for no other woman wore a hat. Joanie had heard that she wore a hat in her own house. No problem there. Helen Fulton was paying her respects, and Dr. Joe and his wife were near at hand.

Where was Kellan?

Joanie saw that Kellan was with the Dietmeiers, newly added to the guest list. Spotting the Zeikoffs, alone and ill-at- ease, Joanie hurried to guide them into the dining room to the eggnog. They needed some loosening up.

Bill Diemeier came alone. No one had to rescue him from thorny situations. He didn't know the definition of insecurity.

"Go ahead and say it," Joanie said to Bill as he stood eyeing the staircase.

"Say what?"

"Say what a hell of a waste of money."

"What a hell of a waste of money."

Above the din they could hear Steamboat's boyish voice bragging about his new car. A Cadillac.

"Listen to that," Bill remarked, a look of tolerant exasperation on his face. "He hasn't got the brains to know most people in here could walk in and pay cash for a Cadillac. They might not happen to like Cadillacs."

"Or," Joanie added, "they're too tight with their money to cut loose for a Caddy. I heard you're buying a new Cadillac, Bill."

"Oh, yeah." He was sarcastic. "A new pickup, maybe."

"Most girls don't like to ride around in a pickup."

"I don't like most girls."

"Not even Janet?" Joanie needled.

Bill rolled his eyes. "She and I don't even speak the same language."

"Oh, I love it," Joanie grinned. "You and I speak the same language. Like, forget the eggnog, etcetera, and get yourself a beer out the kitchen fridge."

Bill nodded his head in the direction of the front door. "You've got more late guests."

He turned for the kitchen and Joanie, irritated with the crass nerve of E.P. in bringing Luke Lykens who was definitely not on the guest list. He looked like he belonged in a gym.

"We started out from Lafayette in snowstorm," E.P. explained. She had been to Purdue to bring Lonnie home for the Christmas break. "The snow stopped about ten miles north of Indy."

Joanie wasn't paying much attention. Where was Kellan?

A few friends gathered around E.P.

"How do you like Purdue?" Larry Sumner asked Lonnie.

"It's okay," Lonnie answered, looking around unabashedly at the party-goers.

"Don't be so modest, my sweet," E.P. chided. "Tell him you made the freshman basketball team. But you are flunking English comp and you'll spend your Christmas break getting tutored by none other than the scholarly E.P."

"Oh, crap, E.P.," Esther Scott was belittling; "you couldn't make it through the first year of college yourself."

E.P. squelched her. "Dummy. It wasn't academics that caused me to get kicked out of the best schools in the East, it was my nocturnal activities."

Juanita Warwick touched Joanie's shoulder. "Have you seen my husband?"

"No. Have you seen my husband?"

Scott appeared with Esther's coat, holding it out for her. "Time to go home, Es."

Reluctantly, Esther said their goodbyes.

That began the exodus.

And there was Charles escorting Janet to the door. Talking cozily to her.

And soon all the guests had left except the Warwicks.

And then there were Kellan and Ken approaching the table in the dining room.

Ken snatched a petit four from the tray that the maid was taking to the kitchen. It had been a grand open house they all agreed. They all agreed they were tired. Charles excused himself to go to his room. The Warwicks said goodnight and left. Kellan and Joanie followed, heading for their own car.

"I do not want to host another party as long as I live." Joanie sighed.

"Tell me that in the morning," Kellan came back, "and I'll believe you."

Joanie moved close to him and laid her hand on his hand that was on the steering wheel. The only thing that nagged at her serenity was the two words, graduate school.

But she lost even that concern when, after they got home, Kellan took her in his arms.

They made love passionately, extravagantly, so satiating that Joanie wanted time to stand still. "We're so beautiful together, aren't we Kellan?"

He whispered, "You make everything beautiful."

"If I ever lost you," she was almost crying, "I could not live."

"Yes, you could. You would have to."

"Do you love me?" She knew he did; she wanted to hear him say it.

"I've loved you all my life."

"You always say that, but I don't know what it means."

Somewhere their words got lost in sleep and they slept soundly until about three in the morning when they both woke up hungry and went to the kitchen to make toast.

"What do you think of politics, Joanie?" Kellan asked.

"I don't. I vote Republican because Charles is a Republican. Why?"

"Does politics bore you?"

"Let's just say it has never attracted my interest. Why?"

"I was afraid of that."

"Why?"

"Because Ken wants me to run in the primary on the Republican ticket for the Indiana State Legislature. For a seat in the House."

It took a few moments before the plausibility of his words became meaningful to Joanie. "Tell me that again," she said, and Kellan repeated what he had just said.

"I like politics," she exploded, "I love politics. I adore politics." And visions of sugar plums danced in her head. She saw herself at the State Capital in Indy, saw herself at banquets and receptions. She saw herself in the Governor's Mansion.

Going to Washington. To the White House. "Kellan, this is the most fantastic opportunity imaginable. People like you, they gravitate toward you;

they recognize your intelligence, your wisdom. You could win any election."

Kellan, amused, said, "Don't get carried away. I haven't told Ken that I would run. I don't know that I want to get into politics."

"Oh, but you do. You know you do" She contained herself. Calmed down. Wanted him to see that she was reasonable and wanted what was best for him."However, we want what is best for you in the long term. I know you will seriously consider Ken's offer and decide on the course that is right for us." But somehow, I'll make him see that running for a state office is the chance of a lifetime. "The fact is that opportunities like this are rare. And hey, you can always get out of politics if you don't like it."

Kellan didn't respond.

"What, exactly, did Ken say to you?"

"He said the Republican Party is looking for new blood. They want to get a strong hold on the legislature which might help elect a Republican governor." He went on about the political situation the state was in, but Joanie wasn't listening, although she pretended to listen.

"My gut feeling, Kellan, is that you should accept Ken's offer."

"It won't be fun and games, Joanie. I'd be away a great deal. You would be expected to campaign. You would have to be charming when you don't feel like being charming. You'd have to smile when you felt like frowning. You couldn't snap out a smart-ass answer when someone asked you a stupid question. You would have to guard every word you uttered. To everyone."

"I can do that."

"But I don't know if I can handle public life."

"What can be more public than standing up before a bunch of smart aleck teenagers every day? Dealing with their parents?"

"I think Ken should have asked you to run for office."

"I'd sure play the game to win."

"Sure you would. And you probably would win."

"Basically, in 1949 it's still a man's world, isn't it?"

"Unfortunately. But you know the old saying, *the hand that rocks the cradle rules the world.*"

"Oh, rot. Written by a man, I'll bet. Who was trying to keep some woman in her place." She didn't want to get off track. " You have something to contribute. You can help ease the burden of the poor and downtrodden. Help the state grow, lower taxes…"

"I'm not so sure I can do any of that."

"I am. I want **you** in the Indiana State House. You can go places, And I want to go with you." She got up from the table to stand behind Kellan with her arms about him and to lay her face next to his. "Go for it, Kellan, please. It's the chance of a lifetime."

"This isn't a decision we can make on impulse. We have to think about where we want to be five, ten, twenty years from now."

"What's the salary of a state representative?"

"I've been waiting for you to get practical. The salary is comparable to what I make teaching. I will get mileage and get paid for every day the legislature is in session. Also, Ken intimated that certain influential party members might have advantageous opportunities for me."

"Exactly what opportunities?"

"All of that was nebulous. Everything would be contingent upon winning the primary in May and the general election in November."

"And if you lost?"

"Back to the university to work on a doctorate."

"I won't let you lose." She didn't know anything about politics now. But she would learn fast. She already knew that Kellan was the type of person people would automatically trust. His good looks would assure him of a lot of female votes. And I would be an asset. Which of the married women in her circle of friends was an asset to her husband? Not Esther. Helen? If it weren't for the McKintley money, Steamboat wouldn't have a down payment on a bicycle. It was Helen's grace, her social skills that were a balance against Steamboat's rough manners. Steamboat learned from Helen, but he didn't know that; he thought he was God's gift to Helen. Juanita? Now there was a true asset. She watched over every aspect of Ken's life—his diet, his career, his social obligations. Which prompted the big question. Why wasn't Ken himself running for office?

"Why me?" Kellan asked aloud.

"Oh, darling, we've been over that. You are intelligent. People respect you. You are likeable. You are clean-cut, handsome—what a good image for the Grand Old Republican Party. With those words she had given herself the reason Ken wasn't running. "Ken has none of those qualities. That's why he doesn't want to run. People don't warm up to Ken. He's so standoffish. And prim like his mother." Then she thought of another possible reason. "It could be because of his diabetes."

A weak winter dawn was showing through the kitchen windows before they had exhausted themselves with speculating on what might be. They went back to bed, curled up together and slept through the morning.

Compared to the tantalizing prospects of what the new year might bring, preparations for Christmas Day seemed routine, just an item on a list of things to do. To Joanie Christmas Day had always been something of a disappointment. After the elation of opening presents, the day was somber, perhaps because she and Charles were alone without the hubbub of an extended family. Even so, it was better than going to New Jersey to spend Christmas with her Welles relatives. Her first vivid memory of Christmas in New Jersey began with the train ride. And then being passed back and forth from one relative to another and being frightened by their possessive clutches and strange, disagreeable voices. Christmas at home with no one but Charles was better than Christmas in New Jersey.

All things considered, Joanie was glad they were going to Kentucky for Christmas Day.

The roomy farmhouse was burgeoning with Foster kin—aunts, uncles, cousins—like a too-full popcorn popper unable to hold exploding grains. Every time Joanie turned around she met another new-to-her relative.

A new linoleum had added yet another layer to the strata of floor coverings in the kitchen where Grandmother and Aunt Sammie gave directions to a jumble of female relatives who elbowed about trying to help with the dinner. In Grandmother's room the men sat in a haphazard circle around the fireplace where a big beech log, newly thrown on the fire crackled in the revived flames. In the front hall a cedar tree, freshly cut from the woods and decorated with an eclectic mix of ornaments, put out a pungent fragrance that permeated the air. The parlor, as seldom used as a mausoleum, had a glowing fire in the grate, and teenagers occupied the room with the boisterous arrogance of youth. Threaded among all these folk were the little ones who were picked up, put down, their noses wiped and their behinds swatted.

Throughout the house, Aunt Sammie's taste was superimposed on the hitherto handsome plainness with crocheted doilies stiffened to stand upright in convoluted cones and ruffles on mahogany and walnut, and framed family pictures on the walls, for Uncle Kirby and Aunt Sammie had recently moved in with Grandmother Foster.

Joanie felt like one of the doilies, a flimsy kind of person amongst somber people whose chief concern was religious morality.

Before Christmas dinner was served, they all gathered in the dining room to hang their heads and squeeze their eyes shut while the Reverend Edward Foster prayed, and prayed, and prayed. Couldn't he condense his prayer?

Was it necessary to name each of them individually? Couldn't he just lump them together as family and ask one blessing for all?

Couldn't he just ask for a blessing on the United States instead of going into detail? For Charles, religion was a social appendage; he attended church because it was the proper thing to do; Christmas and Easter and a few Sundays in between.

She wondered why Kellan never went to church and why Bill never missed church.

"What did you get for Christmas, Joanie?" Aunt Sammie asked the very moment Uncle Edward pronounced a protracted amen. "I just bet Kellan got you something real special."

Somebody else's mind had wandered during the prayer.

The elderly family members sat down at the dining room table first. The children were given filled plates and sent off to sit on the stairs to eat their Christmas fare. After the elders had finished a full course meal, the table was cleared and reset and younger adults like Kellan and Joanie ate their dinner. The last to eat were the women who had done the cooking and serving. They sat down to cold and messed over food.

In the afternoon Aunt Sammie played Christmas carols on the piano in the parlor.Plink, plink, plinkety plink. The teens pressured her to play popular music. *If I Knew You Were Coming, Mona Lisa.* If there was a song she didn't know, she'd say, "Hum, it, honey," and pick and thump until she had the tune. Plink, plinkety plink, plink.

William Kirby sought out Kellan. "I know where we can get up a quick covey of partridges. I saw them yesterday down a fence row between our place and Lewises'. I think we can get them up without a dog."

Joanie wanted to go, but she had not been asked, and she didn't have suitable shoes for tramping the half-frozen fields so she was left to cope with the crush of relatives.

The gathering broke up early. They were farm people, and there were evening chores that must be done. When the last of the kinfolk, Uncle Edward and Aunt Lizzie, had left, Uncle Kirby and Aunt Sammie put on old wraps and boots and went out to do the milking. Grandmother and Joanie were left alone, sitting in front of a fire that had burned down to red hot embers.

Grandmother threw a log on the fire. "Remind me, Joanie, to give Kellan some things of his mother's before you all leave. I don't know how I overlooked them but I did. Some old Kodak pictures, and Mary Katherine's prayer book and Bible." She started to sit down but didn't. "Why, I might just as well get those things right now. That way I can't forget." She went to the cedar chest that stood under the double windows, opened it, and dug down into the interior and brought out the objects. She handed Joanie a large envelope and the two companion books.

Imprinted in gold at the bottom of each book was the name, *Mary Katherine Kellan.* Both books had on the flyleaf in lifeless brown ink, *Presented to our daughter in remembrance of her confirmation, April 11, 1906. Mother and Father*

"Did Kellan's mother," Joanie asked, "ever see her mother or father after they rejected her and sent her away?"

"No. Never. The Kellans were such an aristocratic, blue-blood family that they felt she was a disgrace to their name.

Old Mr. Alfred Kellan said, according to Mary Katherine, 'My daughter is dead to me.' And he forbade any of the family to mention her name in his presence."

"Honestly, Grandmother, I didn't know things like that happened except in old tales."

"Well, they do. Or did. People nowadays don't uphold virtue. The war has made shambles of moral values."

"Personally, I think Mary Katherine's father was mean. And stupid."

"I hold to that. On the other hand, to us it proved a blessing. We thought Garret would never marry. Lo and behold, he fell head-over-heels in love with Mary Katherine and nothing in this world would please him but to have her for his own. And oh, how I did come to love that child. She seemed a sweet, gentle soul, not a mean bone in her body. But I vow, she could be stubborn. And I often thought she called her son Kellan to spite her family."

"I hate her cruel father."

Grandmother had talked herself into being indignant. "And those Kellans called themselves Christians! Christ said we were to forgive seventy times seven. What I say is if you're going to profess the Bible then live by the Bible. All of it. Not just the part that suits you."

"To be realistic," Joanie said, "What difference does it make whether or not a man mumbles some words in a wedding ceremony? Men and women do the same thing whether they are married or unmarried."

Joanie had shocked Grandmother. "Why, child, you don't mean that. Fornication is an abomination unto the Lord. Adultery is a sin. A union that has not received the blessings of the Lord is headed for trouble." Then she went on in a softer tone, "Mankind was meant to live in families. If ever there comes a breakdown of the family then our way of life, civilization is doomed."

"Your family is the only family I've known who are so concerned **all** the time with sin and morals and what the Bible says. You Fosters live and breathe religion." Joanie did not say it critically but as a statement of fact.

Nor was Grandmother offended. Rather, her face radiated affection as she answered, "True. True as Gospel. The Fosters have been strong Methodists for generations, but I was raised an old-time Presbyterian. The Edwardses, my family, were such strict Presbyterians they made the Methodist Fosters look like libertines.I mayhaps exaggerate a mite."

"I'm a sort of libertine, Grandmother."

"Nonsense. You are a person with a sensible outlook on life. And you search for the truth. My grandson is blessed to have you for a wife."

Grandmother had a way of making her feel humble like no one else ever had. Joanie changed the subject. "Didn't Mary Katherine—Kellan's mother—ever hear just once in awhile from some of her other relatives?"

"Miss India Kellan, Mary Katherine's maiden aunt, wrote once in a blue moon.When Mary Katherine was dying, I took it upon myself to write the lady."

"She's the one you told me about?"

Grandmother started gently rocking in her chair."Maybe I did. Miss India replied to my letter only to express her sympathy. As far as I know, to this day she still lives in the home place, in old Louisville. I hear tell the neighborhood's run down. Those elegant old homes got turned into shabby apartments. Reminds me of what happened to a second cousin of mine down in Mississippi."

The monologue that she was launching was cut short when Kellan came in from hunting, and Grandmother got up to help him dress a rabbit and six quail. Joanie had no desire to participate in that activity and stayed put by the fireplace.

At bedtime she and Kellan went upstairs to his old room, unheated as were all the upstairs rooms. Joanie shivered as she got out of her warm clothes and into a flimsy gown, and her teeth were chattering as she slipped under a mountain of quilts and felt the cold sheets. "How," she asked, "did you keep from freezing to death when you werea little boy?"

Kellan seemed impervious to the cold. He took her chilly body into the circle of his warmth. "On really cold nights Mother would heat a brick in the fireplace, wrap it in flannel and put it under the covers for my feet. I'd soon have a warm nest under the covers. Getting out of bed the next morning was a different story."

Beginning to get warm and comfortable in the security of Kellan's embrace, she kissed the strong arm that held her. In the silence they could hear Aunt Sammie coughing in the adjoining bedroom.

Kellan moved his hand to her breast. "Not tonight," she whispered, stopping him.

"Why not?"

"Because Aunt Sammie might have her ear to the wall, trying to hear every move we make."

Kellan was being demanding, making her body respond.

"I didn't bring my diaphram," she whispered.

And he whispered, "So? Sooner or later we will want children."

She almost snapped out, later, but she realized he had given her the perfect excuse to push him to make up his mind about running for the state legislature. "Until you make up you mind about Ken's offer, we can't start a family. And we certainly don't want a baby if you decide to go back to school to get your Ph.D."

He didn't answer but left her alone and settled himself into a relaxed position and was soon breathing deeply and slowly in the peacefulness of sleep.

How could he sleep? Her body was pulsing with desire and her unsatisfied longing was keeping her wide awake. If I didn't love him so much, she thought, I'd hate him for being so self-controlled. Men aren't supposed to have that much self- control; he ought to be fighting to get to sleep. I have just as much self-control as he does. Maybe. All I want is for him to want me so I can show him how much self-control I have. Was she making sense? I'd touch him, and kiss him, and wake him up and....no. I'm not about to take a chance of getting pregnant. I'm going to make myself go to sleep.

Early next morning when the day was so dim it was impossible to know what kind of weather was in store, Uncle Kirby took them to the smoke house, redolent with the hickory fragrance of generations of curing meat, and had Kellan pick out a ham and some of the smoked sausage to take home. Grandmother gave them strawberry preserves and blackberry jelly. Aunt Sammie had crocheted doilies to give to Joanie, who expressed her thanks but no thanks, candidly saying that she didn't use doilies in her house.

"You hurt Aunt Sammie's feelings, Joanie," Kellan said as they drove north out of Green Forks. "Even if you never used them," he reproved, "you should have accepted her gift to you."

Joanie was defensive. "I don't know why. If I offered Aunt Sammie a.a.a whisky decanter which she would never use and she refused it, I wouldn't be offended."

"That's not the same."

"Why isn't it?"

"Because you have so much, and Aunt Sammie has so little. She likes you and admires you and wanted to show her affection. That was all she had to give. You made her feel cheap."

"I don't think so." Joanie was defending herself. And then, "Now you have made me unhappy. Made me feel guilty. I'll buy her a necklace and earring set and send it to her. I notice she always wears a lot of cheap jewelry."

"Joanie, Joanie, you just don't understand, do you?"

"Yes I do. If she sends the jewelry back to me and says she doesn't like it, we'll be even."

"Can't you accept the fact that you made a mistake?"

"I won't send her cheap jewelry. I'll send her something really nice. Expensive."

"Okay, do what you want to do."

"I really don't like your tone of voice. It sounds like you think I'm so dense that you can't make me understand what you mean."

They rode on in silence, Joanie wanting to be unhappy with anyone other than herself, feeling sorry for Aunt Sammie, and then dispirited because she was full of contrition for having hurt Aunt Sammie's feelings. But it could be that was just Kellan's idea and she really hadn't hurt Aunt Sammie's feelings at all. She would buy something pretty for Aunt Sammie and mail it to her as soon as she got home.

She wanted to talk about something else. "Grandmother gave me a prayer book and Bible that belonged to your mother. She wants you to have them."

Kellan nodded his head as if he knew about them.

The sky became bright blue the farther north they traveled, with transitory clouds that intermittently showered them with masses of large snowflakes that danced in the wind.

"Can you," Kellan suddenly asked, "easily get to the prayer book and the Bible?"

Without answering, Joanie stretched over the front seat and reached into the backseat and fished the books from a suitcase.

"Open them," Kellan said, "and see if anything might have been left inside."

The Bible opened with a clasp similar to one on a five-year diary Joanie had once been given and in which she might have written a total of five times. She riffled the pages and uncovered a sprig of pressed lily-of-the-valley faded to a dead yellow and as thin and dry as the paper pages. There was a lock of gold-brown hair tied with a teeny faded ribbon. The prayer book, however, opened to a fragile envelope. Inside was a single sheet of thin paper lined with old-fashioned handwriting.

"Read it to me."

Joanie read slowly for the script was difficult in some places to decipher. *"My dear niece, I write to you with the hope that this letter finds you and yours in good health and happiness. Your dear mother seems no better than she has been since the birth of your baby brother. I fear she was too old to withstand the ordeal of childbirth. However, Brother Alfred fails to recognize this and insists that she is growing stronger every day. He has rented a place in Florida, near Palm Beach, for the winter because he thinks the sea air will be a tonic. Your sisters will be in boarding school and with us only on holidays. Although Alfred never allows your name to be mentioned, I'm sure the family, as I, grieve for you. Allow me to say that I think you inherited a large measure of your father's strong will else you would be forever beseeching his forgiveness. Certainly you can understand the depth of shame you brought to him. By sending you away, he spared you the humiliation that you would have been subjected to amongst your family and friends. Think how mortified your sisters would have been. I grant you, it was cruel of Alfred to destroy, unopened, the letters addressed to you. But try to understand his hate for the callous man who ruined his oldest daughter. You were the apple of his eye. Oh, if only each of you would just bend a bit. How hard it must be for you to live a life deprived of all good things. I pray that the man who married you is a man of good breeding and something of a gentleman. At least he gave your baby a name. With affection, Your aunt, India J. Kellan."*

Full of ire, Joanie wanted to say, I hate those people for what they did to your mother and you, but she held her tongue. She wanted to say, like Bill would say, to hell with those hypocrites. She wanted to say, I love you and isn't that all that matters? But she kept quiet and waited for Kellan's reaction.

They rode several miles without speaking. Abruptly, Kellan lost his composure and hit the steering wheel with his fist.

"Damn it. I thought I'd finally reached the point that I didn't give a shit who my father was. Why am I so obsessed with wanting to know who he was? All I know is that my father was Chaz. Charles? Is he still alive? Is he a person whom I could be proud of or is he a bum? Or worse?"

"Does it really matter? You have it all—intelligence, good looks, good health. And me. You have me. I don't think you should ruin your happiness by worrying about who your biological father is. Or was."

"I'm not worrying."

"You just said you were obsessed."

"Obsessed and worry are not the same."

Joanie did not want to argue. She hated anything that made the smallest rift in their lives. She wanted to get on with important things Like politics.

They rode along, both quietly thinking their own thoughts. Why not, Joanie had a sudden idea, stop in Louisville and see if they could locate the old lady. At least see if she was listed in the telephone directory with the same address. She said as much to Kellan.

Kellan had regained his composure. "A letter would be better. For several reasons. And you are right. Our life together is the only thing that is truly important."

"And what we do with our lives," she quickly added. "The decisions we make." Joanie wanted to prod him into saying that he would run in the primary, but the timing wasn't right. Kellan couldn't be rushed.

She couldn't resist. "I definitely think you should enter the primary race. Kellan, you are exactly the kind of man this state needs."

Kellan reacted with a laugh. "Oh, Joanie, just when did you ever give a tinker's damn about the kind of man the state needs?"

"When the possibility of your becoming a state senator came up."

"State representative, Joanie." He was being condescending.

"I know that," she replied heatedly. "And don't talk down to me. I'm not an imbecile."

"Tell me what you are, Joanie." His voice had the gentle seductiveness that melted her heart.

"I'm a good lover."

"Without equal."

"And sometimes I give good advice. Run in the primary."

Joanie was pressing the dress that she would wear that evening to the New Year's Eve parties. Bill sat at the kitchen table and watched, drinking a beer while he waited for Kellan to change into his hunting clothes.

"Want to go along with us?" Bill invited. "I know exactly where these mallards come in. I think we can get the limit before you get cold."

She wavered. It would be fun to be out on a winter afternoon with Bill and

Kellan. But no. Earlier she had nagged at Kellan about going hunting and getting too fatigued before the parties started. "I'd like to go with you, but I'd better not since we're going to have such a big New Year's Eve celebration. You are going to celebrate New Year's Eve, aren't you, Bill?"

"Hell, Joanie, I haven't given it a thought. What's going on?"

"Actually, there are three affairs. And I know very well you've received invitations to all three." She waited for him to make some kind of response, but he only shrugged his shoulders indifferently. "The Courtneys are having a cocktail party to introduce Davis's fiance. Then there's the usual dinner-dance at the country club.After that we go to E.P.'s for her annual champagne breakfast."

"I may show up somewhere before the roosters start to crow."

"And you haven't even considered getting a date, have you?"

"Who would I ask?"

"Lynda Davis is available," she said facetiously, "now that Davis Courtney is engaged."

"Who is Davis marrying?"

"Harriet Adams. A very rich Miss Adams from Philadelphia."

"That figures. The Courtneys are the kind that look on marriage as an investment. Hell. It's their business, not mine."

"E.P. told me that Lynda Davis said that Davis Courtney..." recognizing the lack of interest in Bill's face, she stopped short. Gossip bored Bill as much as it did Kellan. Why were they like that? Charles didn't always turn a deaf ear to gossip. And Steamboat thrived on it. Homer Scott, though, would doze through a spiel of gossip.

Finished with the dress, Joanie put it on a hanger and hooked the hanger over the top of the broom closet door. She wanted Bill to be at the parties, and when she wanted something, she couldn't let it go till she got her way. "You ought to get a date for tonight, Bill. The last New Year's Eve of the Forties. End of a decade."

"Maybe I'll find a sexy broad hiding in the duck blind when we get there."

Joanie was set to tell him that she would even tolerate Janet Smyth when the ringing telephone interrupted.

It was Charles. Who got right to the point. He was taking Janet Smyth to the dinner-dance at the club and wanted to join Kellan and Joanie. With great difficulty, the words choking in her throat, she told her father that they would be delighted.

When she put the phone down, she burst out, "My father is taking Janet Smyth out tonight! Has he lost his mind? Can you imagine a more ridiculous situation? My father with Janet Smyth! Damn, damn, damn."

Kellan, geared up for duck hunting, had come into the kitchen while she was on the phone. "Don't get so worked up, Joanie. There's nothing disgraceful with your father having a date."

"Oh, god, Kellan, I don't believe you. Janet Smyth?"

"Hell, Joanie," Bill was amused, "if it doesn't work out any better for your dad than it did for me, it won't amount to a hill of beans." He was eager to get away. "Let's go, Kell. Ducks won't wait for us."

Joanie lost her exasperation as she watched her husband leaving with Bill. They were like kids skipping school, two figures clad in hunting tan and orange against a drab, cold day. She felt an irrational fear. What if there was an accident? What if Kellan got shot? What if he fell into the icy water? She felt compelled to go with him as if her presence would insure his safety. She opened the back door and called out, "Kellan…"

He turned to catch her words.

"Be careful, and be sure you are back in time to get ready for the cocktail party."

Bill yelled back, "Don't worry, Joanie, I'll have him back in plenty of time."

Make sure, she said to herself, that you have him back here for the rest of my life; I could not live without him.

Two significant things happened to Joanie on New Year's Eve besides her father being with Janet Smyth.

"Dr. Welles and Janet make quite an attractive couple, don't they?" Juanita Warwick remarked to Joanie after Charles and Janet had left the country club.

"Do you think so?" Joanie responded drily. Shouldn't he be with someone who is nearer his own age? Some with a flair for fashion?

"Dr. Welles is still a handsome man, and Janet's lovely platinum fairness compliments his dark, good looks."

Joanie would have called it milky whiteness, but she was spared from continuing the subject when Davis Courtney asked her to dance.

Davis danced very correctly but not with a natural rhythm. Dancing was something Davis did because one was supposed to dance. Davis talked while he danced whereas Joanie would rather have lost herself in the music. With Davis she had to make replies and follow his mechanical lead.

"What do you think of Harriet?" Davis asked.

"She's charming and attractive." The right thing to say.

"Ah, yes. She has all the proper qualifications. Even if she is not as beautiful as you are."

"I am beautiful, aren't I, Davis?" It was a remark made without thinking because her mind was full of strategies to get Kellan to say yes to Ken and run in the primary.

"Don't be so utterly immodest, my dear." He gave Joanie a whirl in an attempt to give variety to his dancing. "Do you think Harriet will adjust to small town life?"

"She will have a miserable life if she doesn't."

"Realistically, she has no choice but to adjust. After three generations of Courtney, Courtney, and Courtney, Attorneys at Law, this Courtney won't break the tradition." Davis switched to his proper persona. "Harriet has many interests. She is a voracious reader, she paints. Watercolors. And she does play bridge."

"That's good. And it will help if she likes basketball."

"Ah, Joanie, Joanie, regrets, regrets. Do you remember our one and only date?"

"That wasn't a date. That was an assault with intent to deflower the damsel."

"But there was the image of your father. Knife in hand. Come to castrate me." Davis gave a wicked little smirk, and his cold blue eyes gleamed as he held her away so that he could look directly into her face. "You don't know what a good lay you missed."

"And now I'll never know."

"It's not too late. We can arrange it so nobody will ever know. Ever suspect."

"Davis," Joanie said in a pedantic voice, "Will you shut up?"

"Touché, my dear," and now he was prim and proper. "You don't think for one minute that I was serious, do you?"

"You were as serious as hell."

There was his acknowledging little cackle as the music stopped, and then in the most gentlemanly fashion, he escorted Joanie back to her place at the party table.

Seeing Kellan dancing with Phyllis Cordet, Joanie felt a pang of jealously. Then, why should I be jealous of that string bean with a poodle haircut? She chided herself for her mean thoughts. Then, she doesn't have to drape herself all over him, does she? She spotted Bill, approaching the table.

"Dance with me, Bill, please."

She felt so comfortable in Bill's arms. None of Scott's heavy breathing and trembling, none of Steamboat's overt flirting, none of Ken's stiffness, none of Davis's nastiness. With Bill she never had to carry on some artificial banter or adopt some protective image. She needed no artifices or defenses with him. Just good old buddy, Bill.

Later, when she was in Kellan's embrace again, dancing with his cheek against hers, feeling the enchantment that always flowed between them, he kissed her. And then said quite casually, "I told Ken that I would run in the primary."

Surprise was followed by elation, and she wanted to shout out a cheer. Instead, she pressed herself tightly against him, feeling his corresponding intensity.

Happy 1950!

At twelve o'clock the noise makers went off, the band played *Auld Lang Syne.* Kellan kissed her. Happy, happy, New Year. Clem put dry lips on hers. Happy New Year. "Happy New Year!" Steamboat yelled and grabbed a kiss.

" Happy New Year, babe." Ken Warwick barely brushed her cheek. Scott missed her mouth and half-kissed her chin. Happy New Year, let the good times roll. Where was Bill?

Bill, holding a bottle of beer in one hand, was nonchalantly striding across the abandoned dance floor toward their party.

"Hey, you ugly Dutchman," a tipsy Esther called out; "you didn't get kissed Happy New Year."

Like stopping on a dime, Bill put the beer on the floor, and made an exaggerated checking of his watch, shook his arm, held the watch, up to his ear. Looked again. "Hell, my watch is still on South Pacific time. Why didn't someone tell me?"

Steamboat was popping the champagne. "Set your damn watch, and drink to the New Year. And get ready for breakfast at E.P's."

The Portland house, enormous as it was, was crowded and noisy. E.P. had not had so much to drink that it kept her from being the perfect hostess. She greeted and informed. "You are acquainted with the powder room downstairs, and there's also the downstairs bathroom. I've left a glowing light in the available upstairs bathrooms should necessity send you up there, please leave all rowdiness downstairs. The elders need their undisturbed rest, you understand."

Satiated with excellent food and drink, the party was idling down like an engine put in neutral, when the maid came in with the piece de resistance. Tiny crepe suzettes with flaming brandy sauce. And in walked Lonnie Lykens. wearing old jeans and a Purdue T-shirt. Out of place in dress and age.

Clem, sitting next to Joanie, drawled none too softly, "Here comes baby to get his sugar tit."

"Shame on you, Clem," Joanie teased, for Clem was never a tad vulgar.

"Bet you don't know what a sugar tit is, honey chile."

"I've got a good imagination."

Clem, slightly drunk, wasn't listening. "A sugar tit is a little old piece of cotton cloth tied up with sugar inside. Keeps baby happy till he gets the real stuff. My mammy gave me a sugar tit when I was a baby."

"Mammy?" Joanie was curious.

"Sure thing. Down in Louisiana…"

"Shut up, Clem," Phyllis ordered. "Nobody wants to hear about your backward childhood."

Clem shut up.

Joanie wanted to tell Phyllis that listening to Clem was a lot more entertaining than listening to her tell how she made a slip cover for the sofa in the family room. Oh, but life was wonderful. And she let her imagination take her through elections and inaugurals from Indianapolis to Washington before she was back to the immediate.Tomorrow she would have Kellan explain everything, every little thing about the political situation he was in, and then she would get herself organized and start finding out everything there was to know about local elections. Thinking about all this gave her a nervous bladder.Finding the downstairs powder room and bathroom occupied, she dashed upstairs and took the liberty to go into the bathroom that was off E.P's bedroom.

Relief. She washed her hands, ran a comb through her hair and was ready to rejoin the wonderful party.

So unexpected was Lonnie Lyken's grabbing her, that Joanie had no time to react before his mouth was suddenly on hers and she was twisting away, to say, "Leave me alone, are you crazy?" She tried to push him off. "You….don't do that. you're…"

"Take your dirty hands off her." It was Bill. He yanked Lonnie's arm up behind his back and held it there, tightening his hold as he talked. "If you ever so much as look at Joanie Foster again, I'll beat the hell out of you. What's wrong with you?"

"Haven't you got any sense?" He let go of Lonnie's arm.

Lonnie stood defiant as if he wanted to hit Bill.

"Don't," Bill said. "You've got yourself in enough trouble the way it is. I could kayo you with one punch." Bill gave him a shove. "Get out my sight. Go sober up."

Joanie's knees were weak. She felt guilty. What had she ever done to cause Lonnie to think he could... "Oh, Bill, I've never flirted with that kid. I've never liked him..."

"Forget it. I don't think he will ever bother you again." Bill lit a cigarette.

"Give me a drag off your cigarette, please Bill." Joanie was shaking.

"I thought you and Kellan gave up smoking."

"We did. All I need is one drag to calm me down."

Bill gave her his cigarette and left.

Joanie hated what had happened. She hated the way she had handled the situation. The evening had been so wonderful.

She consoled herself. Nothing is ever perfect.She would tell Kellan exactly what had happened.

Kellan would make everything perfect again.

New Year's Day was as somnolent as though a *Do Not Disturb* sign had been posted above the town. Afternoon came before Kellan and Joanie bestirred themselves.Jonie opened the drapes to a white landscape and softly falling snow which matched their mood of gentle contentment.

They went to Charles's for the New Year's Day dinner. To Joanie's consternation, Janet Smyth was curled up in a chair by the fireplace, cozily settled in the room like the mistress of the manor. Had she spent the night? No. Charles would not have a woman in the house all night. Would he? He wouldn't have had her in his bed would he? She couldn't bear to even think of such an awful thing. But here was Janet, serving the Bloody Marys as though she belonged. But she didn't belong. Not in this house. I wonder, Joanie mused, if she is younger than I am.

What did Charles see in her? Wispy thin girl with hair that was too blonde, eyes that were too pale. Who smiled too quickly, who was too polite, too correct. Janet managed to turn every conversation into something serious. Usually school.

My this, my students that. My principal said so-and-so. Biology is blah, blah, blah.

Joanie forced herself to be congenial when all she wanted to do was snap at Janet. Get out of my father's life. Get out of our house. Leave us alone. She complimented Janet on the outfit she was wearing.

Acknowledging the compliment, Janet said, "I made the skirt and vest."

"You sew?"

"Oh, yes. I make many of my own clothes. And I love to knit." She reached down beside her chair and pulled up a half-finished argyle sweater, large size.

How sweet. Sarcastic was Joanie's only state of mind. Charles would never wear that wonderful creation. Not as long as he had breath.

"I'm making this for my brother," Janet explained; "I meant it for a Christmas present, but I got so busy with school work that I simply did not have the time to finish it. Now it will be his birthday present."

Catching an amused expression on Kellan's face, Joanie gave him a disapproving stare. How could he be so simplistic?

Couldn't he recognize Janet as a schemer?

Resentment of Janet awakened in Joanie an early memory, one vivid recollection in the hazy shadows of memories of long train rides to New Jersey to visit fragile grandparents who sat with afghans over their laps in an overly-heated house that smelled like medicine. The one memory that was not in shades of gray was of one night when Charles went off with a lady who wore a lavender dress. Perhaps it had been New Year's Eve that long ago night. She remembered that a group of grownups—maybe relatives—and the lady in lavender had come into the stuffy house, letting in the sounds of laughter with the cold night air. They had come for Charles. *"I'll put the little girl to bed,"* the lavender lady said, and she whisked Joanie upstairs. Dangling earrings swung like pendulums from under her marcelled hair, and a long string of beads tickled Joanie's face. *"If you're lucky, missy, you'll get me for a stepmama, and I'll get your father for my sugar daddy."* Joanie loathed the smell of her perfume and was afraid of the woman. She would have called out for Charles, but the lavender woman clapped her hand over Joanie's mouth saying, *"Be quiet, you little imp if you know what's good for you."* She turned off the light and left Joanie in a pitch black room, so afraid that she covered her head and lay that way until she had to have air. Then she saw monsters in the room and cried out, but no one came. If she slept, it was an uneasy sleep for she woke up sobbing with Charles holding her. He smoothed out her twisted nightgown and kissed her and lay down beside her, stroking her with his soft hands until she was blissfully drowsy...

Kellan was talking to Janet. "Are you ready for school to resume tomorrow?"

"I don't know—I've had such a marvelous holiday. But, yes; I think I'm ready for the challenge of one more semester." She was beaming. "How about yourself? Did the graduate school plans materialize?"

"There has been a complete change of plans."

"Yes?"

"Yes, I will file soon to run in the Republican primary for State Representative."

Janet seemed caught completely unaware.

Charles didn't. "So you have decided to run," he affirmed. "I am very pleased. I told the central committee when Ken Warwick threw your name in the mix that I thought there was not a better qualified man nor a man with a better chance of beating the incumbent." He looked at Joanie. "And I also told them that Kellan's wife was the kind of woman every politician ought to have. Smart and beautiful."

Joanie basked in her father's favor, warm as the glow from the fireplace.

"Although I am not an active party worker," Charles was saying, "I realize the state needs new leadership and the Republican party needs new blood. Someone with a fresh approach and articulate enough to express his ideas so that they will be appealing. His nostrils flared ever so slightly. "As I said, I'm not a party worker, but I do contribute heavily so I'm cognizant of the affairs of the party."

Damn, Joanie said to herself, Kellan will chuck the whole thing if he thinks it was Charles's influence that gave him the nod to be a candidate. In a way, she too, did not want to think that this had come Kellan's way because of Charles. Yet, why should she stew over that? If Charles wanted to do this for her, so what?

Joanie's absorption in her private speculations had taken away the vexation that she felt toward Janet's affair—if affair was what she should call it—with Charles.

Until dinner.

The dinner had been prepared by Janet, and the meal was so expertly handled by super-efficient Miss Smyth that Joanie's resentment returned in great waves of acerbity that made the food that Kellan kept praising choke in her mouth. She could hardly stand it until the meal would end and she and Kellan could get away.

"The meal was delicious," Joanie complimented, "and we do apologize for having to eat and run, but Kellan killed two ducks yesterday, and I want to go by the Diemeiers'and ask Mrs. D how I should prepare them."

"Roasted duck isn't difficult to cook." Janet was following Joanie to the front hall closet. "You need to…"

Joanie cut her short. "I'm sure it isn't. And I have many cookbooks with explicit instructions. But I want to know how Mrs. Dietmeier cooks them because she is absolutely the greatest cook. Isn't she, Kellan?"

"Yes. But not any better than Janet. Tonight's dinner was excellent."

The navy blue night sky was clear, and a cover of bluish whiteness lay over everything. Kellan and Joanie had to plod through several inches of snow to get to the car. Joanie held her temper until the two of them were closed in the car. Then she let her ire spew out. Finally she ended her tirade with, "What can Charles see in her, Kellan? She's not even pretty."

"I think you would find that most persons would classify Janet as pretty. Sweetheart, you use your looks as the measuring scale of beauty, and if a woman doesn't measure up you dismiss her—as you've done with Janet—as plain or unattractive. With that, all you are doing is paying homage to yourself, drawing attention to your own beauty by contrast."

"I do not do that." She defended herself. But there was a grudging, inward acceptance that there was some truth in what Kellan had pointed out. "I don't have to depend on my looks to get what I want. I can do anything I want and be a success at it. And I'm going to have everything in my life just the way I want it."

"Grandmother Foster would tell you that *pride goeth before destruction, and a haughty spirit before a fall.*"

"Don't you dare preach at me!"

"God forbid." Kellan's voice was grave. "I've had enough of that to last us both a lifetime." He pulled her face close enough to kiss her lips, and the car spun in a vicious circle on the snow-slick street.

"Do that again," Joanie said. "It makes me feel sexy."

"The kiss or the spin?"

"Both."

He did.

"Don't go home," Joanie advised, noting the direction he was taking, "Let's do go to Dietmeiers.'"

"I thought going to Dietmeiers' was only an excuse."

"It was. But as I think about it, it's a pretty good idea. I haven't the foggiest notion of how to cook a duck."

Opening the front door of Dietmeiers' house (no one but a rank stranger ever knocked) Joanie's first greeting was the faint bouquet of cooking foods. So many loaves of bread, so many pots of soup, so many roasted meats had been cooked in the kitchen that the house always held a faint aroma of food.

The entire family was at home. Bill was adjusting the aerial of their newly-purchased television set and trying to convince his mother that the money spent on the set had not been wasted. Mr. D. was sitting at the dining room table playing solitaire; a radio blared in a distant part of the house. The rhythmic thumping noise that came up through the floor was, according to Bill, Karl working out in the basement.

The conversation jumped from one thing to another—the Rose Bowl, Ohio State, and what to stuff a duck with. And not the least of all, Kellan's venture into politics. From what was said, it seemed Mr. D. also had known about the central committee's decision to ask Kellan to run.

Was Mr. Dietmeier also such a heavy contributor to the party that he, too, might have had an influence in choosing Kellan to be placed on the ticket?

Mr. Dietmeier began shuffling the cards. "I knew the minute Joanie walked into the room, I'd get me a euchre game going." He brought the cards together and slapped them on the table. "What say, Joanie, you and me partners?"

"You bet," Joanie was enthusiastic. "We'll take on anybody, won't we?"

The card table was extracted from its hiding place behind the buffet and set up in the living room, but the start of the game was delayed when Karl came into the room.

"Kellan ain't the only one who's got big news. Tell us your good news, Karl," prompted Mr. Dietmeier.

Grinning self-consciously, Karl announced, "I'm getting married."

"One of them long, tall, Southern gals," Mr. Dietmeier added in a terrible imitation of a Southern accent.

"She lives in Florida," Karl explained, "but she came from Illinois. Her dad is with the Florida League."

"When is the big event?" Kellan asked.

"Sometime before spring training. It won't be a big wedding."

Mrs. Dietmeier, who had been ominously silent, added like a condemnation "She's a Baptist."

Joanie suppressed a laugh. "Well, marrying into this family, she won't stay a Baptist very long, I bet you."

Joanie and Mr. Dietmeier took on Karl and his mother and disposed of them quickly. Bill and Kellan who were watching television refused to respond to Mr. D.'s challenge so he called down Max and Burt from upstairs and made them play. They let themselves get beat as soon as possible. It was Bill and Kellan's turn.

They had beer and popcorn and lots of laughter, but the play was serious. Joanie played cards to win. And so did Mr. D. It took a lot longer than it had for the other opponents, but Joanie and Mr. D. finally defeated Bill and Kellan.

"Girl," Mr. D. said admiringly, "you and I ought to play cards for real money."

The late news came on television, but Joanie paid little attention. Nothing on the news affected her life. However, when Kellan began talking about the military build-up in Korea and about its only being a question of time until North Korea crossed the DMZ and invaded South Korea and about the effort to contain communism, Joanie spoke up.

"Let the Koreans work out their own problems," she said. "What business is it of ours what kind of government they have?"

Her question was ignored.

Bill said, " I've got a navy dossier that says I'm a reserve officer trained to handle critical spare parts. I'm single—so you suppose if I marry a widow with a bunch of kids, I'd be exempt? Hell, I'd rather be in service."

Everyone thought it was funny, but Joanie was afraid.

Kellan's involvement in politics took him away from home much more than Joanie had anticipated. Even when he was home he was studying the issues, reading—always reading. She would not harp at him. She couldn't, considering how much she had insisted that he go into politics. Often, as now, he came home preoccupied with things that had to be done.

"Will you grade a couple of sets of test papers for me?" Kellan asked.

"Only if they are objective tests."

"These are multiple choice except for one essay. If you'll do the multiple choice, I will go back and read the essays and put a grade on the papers." He went to the table where Joanie usually left the mail for him to go though. "Didn't we get any mail today?"

"It's mostly junk, I think." She found the mail on the living room couch where she had dropped it when she heard the phone ring. She gave it to Kellan.

Kellan sorted through the mail. "Did you see this letter from Miss India Kellan?" And not waiting for a response said, "Make us a drink. We may need it."

By the time Joanie returned to the living room with the drinks, Kellan had read the letter. Without a word, he handed it to Joanie.

Louisville, Kentucky

Dear Mr. Foster:
Please forgive my tardiness in replying to your letter, but at the time the letter arrived, I was quite indisposed.

Only recently have I felt well enough to take pen to paper. Your dear mother's difficulties, though so long ago, are very clear in my mind. Like many elderly folk, I often forget some simple daily task while memories of the past are vivid. Raymond Chazmarek is the name of your paternal parent. He was a young man who worked at the Yacht Club of the York Bay Resort where my brother and his family, along with me, his younger sister, spent the summer of 1921. That year my dear brother had taken us on a train excursion to visit the historic sights of Philadelphia, New York, and Boston, and we spent the remainder of the summer near York, Maine. Although my brother forbade Mary Katherine to keep company with this young man, he beguiled her into disobeying her father. Not only did he dishonor her, but he also abandoned her. It is my understanding, though I am not certain, that he went off to Paris.

Our family was nearly destroyed. We have always been an honorable family. Both Brother Alfred and his dear wife, Eugenie, departed this life years ago. Mary Katherine's little sisters have families of their own. Ann Christine is in California. Amy Louise is in St. Louis. Mary Katherine's baby brother, Douglas, whom she never saw, is attending Harvard Law School. It is my fondest hope that Douglas will return to Louisville to make this house his home. Until then, I will continue to live here at the home place. I am fortunate to have dependable, honest help.

Though I must say that help is not cheap these days.

I do hope this letter will be of some help to you.

With kind regards, I am,

(Miss) India B. Kellan

"I can't believe this letter." Joanie was irate. "Don't you think a normal person would want to see her own nephew?

She addressed you as Mr. Foster as if you were some business man."

"I am a stranger to her," Kellan offered an excuse. "She doesn't have any idea what kind of person I am. And it sounds as though she might be quite frail. At least she gave me the name I've so longed to know."

"Kellan, the signature of the artist on the painting of my mother." Joanie suggested, "...could it be possible it might be Chazmarek?"

"Possible but not probable."

"All we can do, must do, is ask Charles. And if it is Chazmarek, then the next question we will ask is was his first name Raymond."

The artist's name was Chazmarek," Charles confirmed, when Joanie and Kellan broached him, "but I have forgotten his first name; I knew him as Chaz."

"This is a letter from my mother's aunt," Kellan offered the letter to Charles; " I think you should read it."

As he read, a look of incredulity spread over Charles's face. " I don't think that I could ever have remembered Chaz's first name, but now that I'm reminded, I can tell you that indeed it was Raymond."

Excited, Joanie asked, "Does Kellan look like Raymond Chazmarek?"

"Not any more than you look like me, my darling girl. And now you are going to ask me if he ever mentioned a girl named Mary Katherine and the answer is no. At least not to me. Or if he did, I have absolutley no recollection of it. I was not in his company that much."

"But," Joanie was not satisfied with his answer, "this Chaz painted my mother's picture."

"He did her portrait before I ever met him."

"I don't understand," she said.

"Joanie, those were rakish days in Paris. Don't trouble yourself with the particulars of those days. Suffice it to say that your mother and I met in Paris. From that point on you know the rest of the story."

"I hope so," Joanie said. "I hope you are not keeping something from me the way Kellan's mother kept everything from him. Why did she not tell him about his own father?"

"My father," Kellan said it to himself as much as to Joanie and Charles, "was Garret Foster."

"My advice to both of you is that you forget the past and get on with your lives. You've an election to win." Charles was in control.

Joanie spent many hours getting herself ready to answer questions about the issues because as Kellan's wife and almost constant companion it was important that she was informed and articulate. On more than one occasion, because she was Dr. Welles's daughter, she was forced to listen to someone's complaints about a physical condition. With great effort she kept a civil tongue.

In spite of the many functions they attended together, Kellan seemed to be more and more occupied with concerns that took him or his attention away from her.

"Kellan's gone to a central committee meeting," Joanie told Bill who had come by on a bright Saturday in late March to see if Kellan wanted to go crappie fishing. "I knew this campaign would take a lot of his time, but not this much. I almost have to make an appointment to see him." She tried to make the words sound playful, but there was a raggedness that betrayed her discontent.

"Well, hell. To be honest, the water is probably still too cold for crappie." Bill pulled out a chair and sat down at the kitchen table and put his hat upside down in the middle of the table like a decorative centerpiece. "You know, Joanie, I would have bet everything I own, which is damn little, that the last thing in the world that Kellan Foster would have elected to do—excuse the pun if that's a pun—was take up politics."

"Why do you say that?" Unasked, she got a beer from the refrigerator and opened it for Bill.

"Because he's such a private person."

"He definitely is not as private a person as you are, Bill."

"Me? A private person? Naw." Bill got out his cigarettes. He held out the pack to Joanie, "You still not smoking?"

"Still not smoking. Charles has become a crusader against tobacco, so naturally he thinks no one else should smoke. Especially me. And Kellan." She leaned across the table and took the cigarette from Bill's hand. "Just one drag." She gave the cigarette back to Bill and asked, "Do you know if my father or your father had anything to do with Kellan's being asked to run?"

"All I know is that the Republican Central Committee asked Ken Warwick to run and he flat out refused. As far as I know, it was Ken that tapped Kellan."

"Wonder why Ken stays out of politics?"

"Could be he is a really, really private person." Bill yawned. "Hell, Joanie, I never waste my time trying to figure people out. The whys and the wherefores don't interest me."

Joanie had the feeling that Bill knew more than he said he did. She didn't care. All she wanted was Kellan to win the primary. "You're a gambler, Bill; what are the odds on Kellan winning?"

"The primary? Sure. But the November election is another ball game. It's hard to beat an incumbent."

"You don't think he can win in November," she interpreted.

"It's too early to tell."

"Oh, well. I'm not going to worry about the first Tuesday in November until November."

"Atta girl." Bill stuck his fishing hat on his head at a crazy angle. "Worry won't roll a wheel." He stood up. "Gotta get going and take advantage of a warm day. Next week it might snow."

With no forethought she said, "Take me with you, Bill."

"It's colder than it looks, Joanie. If a wind comes up, you'd freeze out in the open."

Joanie knew very well that thermometer readings had nothing to do with Bill's putting her off, but she went along with the pretense. "Perhaps if it's warmer tomorrow, the three of us can go fishing."

"Can't. My cousin is having her baby baptized tomorrow. There'll be a big get-together with all the relatives. Whose names I don't even know. You know how that is."

No, I don't know how it is, she thought as she watched Bill stride off across the yard toward his pickup.

Restless and tired of the house, Joanie got her sweater and went out in the yard to see if any of the bulbs she had planted last fall had come up. The sky was clear blue, the sun was warm. The first green of the bulbs had pushed up from the brown soil. Spring was in the air.

Snow came several days later—heavy, wet stuff that covered the shoots of jonquils and hyacinths and caused Joanie to get hung up in her own driveway when she was attempting to back her car out. She was in a hurry, trying to get on her way to the hospital to see Miss Eddie. In her haste, she spun the car off the driveway where it sank deeper and deeper as she tried to get free. Giving up, she went back into the house and phoned for a wrecker, which infuriated her because she figured she would have to tolerate some smug man who would be condescendingly polite to a woman driver when she knew she was a more capable driver than most men.

At least the wrecker arrived promptly.

"You had to work pretty hard to get your car hung up this bad," commented the young mechanic.

"Actually, it was quite easy," she said, staring at a point quite distant from the man who capably hooked a chain to her car and hopped back into his truck.

In only a few seconds, he had her car on the driveway and was out of the cab, writing up a bill.

"I'll mail you a check," Joanie said, "I don't want to trudge back in the house for my check book. You know us, don't you?"

"I know who you are." He was looking at her hungrily. Like she was a delectable object he could purchase in a treat shop.

She was oblivious. Just another common occurrence in her life. "Okay. Thanks.I'm in a hurry to get to the hospital."

Miss Eddie, her iron gray hair hanging in one skinny braid on the white pillow, sat rigidly upright in the semi-raised hospital bed. "It's my gall bladder," she informed Joanie. "Doctor says I have to have an operation."

"That's nothing to worry about. People live a long time without a gall bladder,"Joanie reassured her. "You'll soon be up and around."

"That's not what's bothering me. It's being here and having people work on you like you was public property." Miss Eddie twisted the sheet with her fingers. "It's mighty embarrassing."

"When nurses and doctors are doing things to you, they don't think of you personally. To them, you are like a machine that's out of order and needs to be fixed.They are probably thinking about their own personal problems."

"Mercy sakes. I sure to goodness hope that they are thinking about me and what they're doing to me. I don't want no mistakes to happen on account of they are thinking about the bills they have to pay."

"What I mean, Miss Eddie, is that hospital personnel are so accustomed to working on human bodies that it's as routine to them as doing laundry is to you. You are not embarrassed when you wash our underwear, are you?"

"It's not the same thing." She looked at Joanie accusingly, "You never did have the modesty a young lady ought to have."

Joanie could see that it was pointless to continue that line of conversation. "At any rate, it must be comforting to know that Doctor has a personal interest in your good health." Joanie, when she talked to Miss Eddie about Charles, called him Doctor as Miss Eddie always addressed him. At an early age, she had called her father Doctor also, but he had admonished her. *My name is not Doctor. Good friends are on a first name basis, and since you and I are very, very good friends, you must call me Charles just as I call you Joanie.*

"I trust Doctor," Miss Eddie was saying. "I do indeed. I wouldn't go under the kniife for any other doctor."

"Oh, it'll all be over soon, and you'll enjoy all the attention." She gestured toward a floral arrangement, "Somebody has already sent you a bouquet."

"Janet Smyth." The way Miss Eddie said it, it was an indictment.

"That was very thoughtful of her, wasn't it?" Joanie spoke in a patronizing tone. How did Janet, Joanie asked herself, know about Miss Eddie's hospitalization before I did? She asked very pointedly, "How much is Janet at our house?"

"Too much," Miss Eddie answered tartly. "She's always underfoot. Now with me in the hospital, I suppose she'll take the run of the place."

Joanie was quite frank,. "Does she ever spend the night?"

"Not to my knowledge. Both of them has reputations to uphold. She being a teacher and all. And Doctor is a respectable man. Spite of the fact that he's got some strange notions. Like having you call him by his first name. But he's respectable."

Would he sleep with Janet? Would he? He wouldn't. He couldn't. Not Charles.She could not bear to imagine Janet in Charles's bed where on Sunday mornings he used to read her the Sunday Funnies—Andy Gump, Moon Mullins, Little Orphan Annie. *Will Annie marry Daddy Warbucks? No, that would be like incest. What's incest?* Long fter she was grown up, she would go to Charles's bed on Sunday mornings and tell him all the details about her Saturday night date. Until there was Kellan.

Joanie heard footsteps and turned to the open door to see her father entering the hospital room. He had a few words with Miss Eddie and then asked Joanie if she wanted to go to the doctors' lounge for coffee.

They were the only ones in the comfortable room. Charles poured coffee for both of them and gave a cup to Joanie who thanked him and asked point blank: "Are you sleeping with Janet Smyth?"

"Did I ask you when you started sleeping with Kellan Foster?"

"I didn't think you wanted to know."

"I didn't. And neither do you want to know about Janet."

"She's young enough to be your daughter, Charles."

"You need not point out the obvious. Perhaps I have a penchant for the daughter type."He set his coffee cup on a side table. "You, my adorable pet, are suffering from jealousy. I suffered from the same affliction when you fell in love with Kellan. However, I think I handled it better than you are doing."

"I can handle the situation as well as you or anyone else can."

"Then start being friendly with Janet."

"When have I ever been rude to her?"

"Never as far as I know. But your politeness is cold enough to freeze the gates of hell."

"Miss Eddie doesn't like her."

"Miss Eddie suffers from jealously as well as from a bad gall bladder."

I'll always dislike Janet, Joanie thought, but from now on nobody on God's earth will know that except me. I'll be as sweet as an angel to her. And I'll try to find her a man more suitable to her age.

"Poetic justice," Kellan remarked when Joanie told him about Miss Eddie's impending operation.

"I don't understand," Joanie said.

"Those who live by the sword shall die by the sword."

"You are not making any sense at all."

"Anyone who cooks as poorly as Miss Eddie deserves gall bladder trouble."

"Kellan, that's mean." Her words held more amusement than reprimand.

Kellan acknowledged that he was in a mean mood. "I feel like throwing my woman on the ground, tearing off her clothes, and dragging her to my cave."

"Go ahead and see if I care."

He picked her up, and the buoyant feeling of being carried, the arousal as he nuzzled his face against her breasts brought on a tantalizing mixture of frantic desire and satisfying pleasure. She kissed the back of his neck and ran her tongue lightly across the hairline. If this should stop now, she thought, I'll die.

The doorbell was ringing.

"We won't answer it," she whispered.

"We have to. You answer the door and stall for a few minutes."

"Damnit, if you want the door answered, you answer it."

"Like this?"

She laughed at him and that kept her from dying.

"Well, Kellan," Ken Warwick began when they were situated in the living room with drinks, "something scary has come up. Your opponent, the honorable or dishonorable Denison Quigley, is supposed to have some information he can use against you."

"What kind of information?" Kellan and Joanie asked almost simultaneously.

"I heard by the grapevine that Quigley claims to have information that you once belonged to a Communist organization over in Bloomington. Mind you, nothing's out in the open yet, but we've got to know where we stand with you before…"

"You want to know if I'm a Communist?" Kellan interrupted.

"I know you are not a Communist. But you might have belonged to some pinko organization."

"The only organizations I belonged to were the fraternity and some up-and-up honorary societies. Old, established honoraries."

"According to Quigley, so the rumor goes, you belonged to a group of young intellectuals…"

Aghast, Kellan interrupted, "Oh, my god, Intellectuals for Intelligent Government. It wasn't an organization. A sham organization. It was a joke. Satire."

"Then it can be explained away." Ken studied the glass of white wine he was holding in his hand. "Do you know if there were any Communists among this pseudo organization?"

"I don't think there were any card-carrying Communists. No."

"Sympathizers?"

"Maybe. In that sort of climate it was difficult to tell a person's serious stance."

"That's too bad. You know what the mood of the country is right now."

"Do you want me to withdraw from the race?"

Joanie's heart skipped a beat.

"I will not." Kellan was defensive. "Because that would be the same as an admission of wrong doing. I did nothing wrong. It was a pick-up thing. One day after a graduate class, a group of fellows, including me, went out for beer. We started talking about the inane actions of some of our lawmakers when one of the guys jokingly suggested there ought to be an organization to promote intelligence in government. Another guy suggested we call ourselves the Intellectuals for Intelligent Government. It was a parody. A lampoon."

"A goodly number of voters don't know the meanings of those words."

"Which explains something of what we were about. Truthfully, we never held a called meeting. Various times when some of us were together we talked politics. We talked about the shortcomings of our system."

"It remains the greatest system in the world." Ken sounded like a commencement speaker.

"I agree unequivocally."

"Good," Ken said as he set his empty glass on the table. "Let's just sit on this for awhile. So far, it's only party gossip.

We'll wait for Quigley to make the first move."

That's crazy, Joanie thought. "If this gets out, it will ruin Kellan's reputation."

Ken explained, "What Quigley might try to do is convince the Republican Central Committee to pressure Kellan to withdraw. The last thing any of us wants is for the Democrats to use that kind of incendiary information against us in the November election."

Joanie had never seen Kellan's face so grave and determined as when he said, "Ken, I hope you have no doubt about political loyalties. But I will not withdraw from the primary, and if I win in the primary, I will not withdraw from the general election. I will not defer to the accusation of guilt where there is no guilt. Not even guilt by association."

The room was quiet.

Finally Ken said, "I understand. As I said before, we will sit tight and see what move Quigley makes."

Sit still and wait for a bomb to explode? Stupid. Foolish. Why did this have to happen when everything was so perfect?

After Ken left, Joanie said, "Tell me about the Intellectuals for Intelligent Government."

"You heard everything there was to tell. We were just a loose bunch of guys who occasionally met to drink beer and talk about world affairs. Including politics."

"Were some of them Communists?"

"*Maybe* is as close as I can come to the truth." And then, "Would it bother you if I said I was a Communist?"

"Communists are people too, aren't they?" It was really an answer rather than a question.

"I think Ken wants me to withdraw—what do you think?"

"I don't care what Ken wants. We're not going to let anything or anyone ruin your political career."

"At this point it is not a career. It's a pursuit."

"If, we lose, we lose," was Kellan's attitude. "There are many avenues in life."

Not for Joanie. She knew politics was the avenue that would bring them the kind of success Kellan deserved and she wanted. She would not let it slip out of their grasp.

One morning after Kellan left for school, Joanie phoned E.P. Portland.

"What do you know about Denison Quigley?" she asked E.P.

"I know he is running against your husband in the primary and that he wants that seat in the legislature any way he can get it. Why?"

"I think it's smart to know as much about your opponent as you can."

"For all I know, Quigley is as pure as milk."

"That's what we've been told. That Denison Quigley is honest and fair. That his life is above reproach." She was baiting E.P.

"Hold it. I didn't say Quigley *is* as pure as milk. I said for all I know, he's as pure as milk. There isn't a person alive who doesn't have something to hide. And anything hidden can be uncovered by a dedicated digger."

"You truly believe that?" She almost had E.P. hooked.

"Without the slightest doubt. Give me enough time, and I'll find out something about you."

"Forget me. Find out something about Quigley."

"What's in it for me?"

"An invitation to the White House—when we get there."

"Jesus, girl. When you set your sights, you set them pretty damn high."

"Why not? Kellan has it all. Brains, looks, integrity. And me."

When Joanie reflected on how she had maneuvered E.P., she didn't think she had done anything wrong, but at the same time she thought it best not to tell Kellan.She had positive ideas. She was going to suggest to Kellan that they start attending church. Maybe make an appearance at several different churches. As for herself, she thought it would be a good idea to get into some kind of volunteer work.

Joanie heard from E.P. before she had decided where she would volunteer.

"Quigley will not soon be a candidate for sainthood," E.P. informed Joanie. "He's got a mistress by the name of Daphne Dwight. A single woman with a bastard child that may or may not be Quigley's. Which is his own damn business.

However, Mr. and Mrs. Average Voter would not be inclined to cast their vote for an adulterer.Even though they themselves might be engaged in an extramarital affair. The world is peopled with hypocrites."

"Not me."

"Ah, Joanie, think. Think, girl."

"I don't have time to think about your pseudo philosophical ramblings."

"True. You haven't even had time to thank me for my valuable information."

"Thank you, Elizabeth Perry Portland. You'll be the first one on the guest list for all social functions at the White House."

E.P. laughed. "You are a little small town gal with delusions of grandeur."

The very next day Joanie drove over to the county seat, fifteen miles away, where Denison Quigley owned an appliance store.

Quigley himself came to greet her as Joanie stood near a display of refrigerators at the front of the store. He approached her with an air of self-confidence; yet as they faced each other, his face betrayed that look which was so familiar to Joanie. In its mildest form an appreciation of her looks; in its basest form, lust. Quigley quickly put on a patronizing face. "Hello, Mrs. Foster; what can I do for you?"

Joanie smiled and looked him squarely in the eye. "I thought perhaps you could give me directions to Daphne Dwight's residence."

Quigley involuntarily looked toward the open office where a woman was busy at an adding machine.

Could that be Mrs. Quigley?

"I don't know a Daphne Dwight," he said softly, opening the display refrigerator door and holding it as though for support.

"Don't play games." Joanie turned and surveyed the display room. "It's common knowledge that you visit Daphne Dwight quite often."

"I delivered an appliance to her house. Nothing more than that."

"Rather like Kellan's connection with a loose group that laughingly called themselves the Intellectuals for Intelligent Government—he may have had a couple of beers with them, but that was the extent of his involvement."

"Something like that."

"Then I suggest that you forget you ever heard of the Intellectuals for Intelligent Government, and I'll forget that Daphne Dwight is a *friend* of yours."

Quigley was livid. "I ought to…"

"Ought to what? Come on, Mr. Quigley; is it a deal? Yes or no?"

"Yes," he got out between clenched teeth.

Joanie smiled with false sweetness. "Now, worthy opponent, if you ever so much as mention Intellectuals for Intelligent Government. I'll not only tell the world about Daphne Dwight, I'll invite her to a political rally and introduce her to the voters."

"Daphne has some loyalty."

"Then it is true, isn't it, and not idle gossip?" Joanie asked, thinking, I've got him now and I'm going to nail him. "Now that we understand each other, I don't think it will be necessary to visit Daphne Dwight. But I can always phone her if I want to extend an invitation to a luncheon at the country club or some such affair. So nice to talk to you, Mr.Quigley, and find you so understanding. If I ever need a new refrigerator, I'll know where to come for a discount."

When Kellan came home from school, Joanie was in the kitchen attempting to understand and follow the directions from the cookbook that was propped up on thecounter in front of her. "If this recipe doesn't turn out, we'll have to go out for dinner,"she said by way of greeting.

"What are you cooking?"

"Something called chicken supreme. I had almost every ingredient the recipe called for so I'm giving it a try."

"It would be pretty hard to ruin chicken, wouldn't it?"

She shrugged her shoulders. "With me you never know."

"Very true."

"Kellan!"

"You said it first."

"Who knows….one of these days I may get interested in cooking and turn into a gourmet cook."

"As long as you do other things as well as you do, it doesn't matter."

"Like making love?" She turned from the kitchen counter and put her arms around his wonderful body and lifted her face up to be kissed. And it was like the first time. Exciting and erotic. "We have everything, don't we, Kellan?"

"Everything but a child."

Her heart skipped a beat. They had never talked about children. She had never thought about having a baby. She wasn't like Helen Fulton who desperately wanted a baby and couldn't get pregnant. She didn't want to be pregnant like Esther Scott who seemed to be able to shell them out like peas from a pod. I must not have an ounce of maternal instinct, she thought. She said, "After November we'll think about a baby."

"But not to please me." He kissed the palm of her hand. "You have to want one too."

"We'll both know when the time is right."

Tuesday, May 6, the day of the primary, came in cool and damp. Joanie and Kellan were up before dawn and at the polls when they opened at six o'clock. They were apart the entire day, each of them visiting different precincts. Smile. Hand out cards. Listen to comments about the weather. Smile. Smile. Be gracious to the old lady who wanted to talk about her high blood pressure because Dr. Welles was her doctor. Shake hands. Smile. Smile. She hardly paused the entire day, taking a break for coffee and a sandwich when someone insisted. She loved every minute of the exhausting day.

When the polls closed at six, she met Kellan at the Republican Headquarters where the Quigley faction was gathered on one side of the room, and the Foster faction on the other.

"I don't want to be premature in my optimism," Ken Warwick said as he handed Kellan and Joanie paper cups filled with cola, "but I can't help feeling that we've got this one wrapped up. We had a good voter turn out and that's a plus for us."

Joanie didn't need statistics. She remembered the man in bib overalls who had said that he didn't know much about politics, but Kellan Foster had an honest face. The woman whose daughter had told her to vote for her teacher.

Juanita Warwick, well-groomed and pleasant—her usual bland self, joined them at the Republican Headquarters. "You do need to come home and eat, husband dear. I've dinner ready for the table. Then you can come back and celebrate the victory. Have you had your insulin?"

Ken was impatient with mollycoddling. "Yes, wife dear." His words were like a put down. Then he brightened. "And the Fosters can join us for dinner."

"That's a splendid idea," Juanita agreed. "Please do have dinner with us."

She's probably wondering how to stretch a dinner for two to a dinner for four, Joanie thought. "You are very kind to invite us," Joanie deferred, "but I'm so excited I have no appetite. Kellan and I will eat later, when the outcome is assured."

"I understand," Juanita said. She looked directly at Joanie. "You've worked harder than anyone on this campaign. It's going to be your victory, too, Joanie."

And that's the way Joanie felt when the results were final. She was a winner.Kellan and Denison Quigley were shaking hands. The Republican faithful were congratulating them on having run a clean, honest race devoid of mud slinging.

And then the talk turned to beating the hell out of the Democrats in November.

As soon as school was out for summer vacation, Joanie and Kellan drove down to North Carolina to the Outer Banks.

They ran on the beach in golden lengths of morning light. They lay on the sand in the sun. They rode the surf and swam. In the cool night winds they clung to each other and succumbed to the hypnotic roar of the ocean. And they made love. In tenderness, in wild abandonment—never sparing, never holding back.

On June 25 North Korea invaded South Korea.

When Joanie heard the news, a cold lump of fear settled in her stomach and would not leave. Why should the United States have any business messing in the troubles that were going on in Asia? She asked that question many times in more ways than one and got the same answers in more ways than one. Communism had to be contained. Russia and China were a threat to the free world. She wanted to say, *The United States could drop atomic bombs on the USSR and China at the same time and that would contain Communism in a hurry.* She couldn't say that, of course. She'd get talked to like she was ten years old. She did say, more than once, *Why can't we let Korea work out its own problems?* And had to listen to explanations, be instructed in, explained to, informed of, made cognizant of world politics.

The role of America in the in the post war, modern world. What did all the *well-informed* really know? Nothing past what they read in the newspapers. So, she tried to keep her mouth shut, pretended to be happy, pretended to be hungry, avoided news reports. Tried to turn conversations away from war. *Correction: the police action in Korea.*

"Shit, I haven't a snowball's chance in hell," Bill Dietmeier was saying to a group gathered in the reception hall of the First Church of the Nazarene after the wedding ceremony of Larry Somner and Lynda Davis. "I'll be gone by the end of the summer."

"This is one war that's gonna pass old Homer by," Scott said. "If a wife and three kids and a new baby on the way and a back full of shrapnel won't keep me out, nothing will keep nobody out."

"Have you and Esther thought about a name for the baby?" Joanie, wanting to change the subject, asked Scott.

"Not yet. Es likes Michael or Stephen if it's a boy; Marilyn if it's a girl. She better be making up her mind."

"What's wrong with the name Homer if it's a he?" Kellan asked. "I like that name."

Joanie didn't know if Kellan was joking or serious. He acted serious.

"Everything's wrong with Homer," Scott sighed. "Only one kid in my class had a worse name than me. Horace Hindman. Hard-ass Hindman."

"Whatever happened to old Hard-ass Hindman?" Bill asked.

"Don't you know?" Scott was surprised. "He got killed early in the war. In North Africa."

War again. Couldn't they talk about anything else?

"Is it my imagination, or is Lynda looking a little full in the middle?" Joanie questioned.

Scott answered in the tired voice of authority. "I'd say about three months full."

The guests were moving toward the wedding table for cups of punch and plates of cake. All Joanie seemed to hear from the mingled voices around her was one god-damned word, war.

There seemed to be no place that she could escape the ominous talk of war.

At the country club swimming pool Joanie was catching the last tanning rays of the afternoon sun while she waited for Kellan to finish a round of golf with Steamboat, Clem, and Bill.

E.P., ignorning the posted rules prohibiting street clothes and bottles in the pool area, entered fully attired in street clothes and carrying an opened bottle of beer. She sat down on a chaise next to Joanie. "They got Lonnie," were her first words. She fished in the pocket of her cotton skirt for cigarettes and lighter. "If there was any way in the world I could get him out of the army I would. I'd lie, bribe, or blackmail. Oh, Jesus, I hope the war doesn't touch him."

"I thought everything between you and Lonnie was history."

"Our kind of relationship never really ends. It changes direction or perspective,may turn to hate, but there will always be some sort of nebulous tie."

"Where is Lonnie now?"

"Fort Leonard Wood. That hell-hole. I got a post card from him—barely legible—God, he was beautiful, wasn't he, Joanie?"

"Was?"

"Was because he will never be the same. The army will ruin him one way or another. But I was good to him."

"But were you good for him?"

"Damn right I was good for him. Without my pushing him, he would never have finished high school. He would not have tried to make it at Purdue. I spent a lot of money on that kid and I don't begrudge a penny. If I could, I'd buy him out of the army like they could do in the old days."

Joanie sat up, took off her sunglasses and looked directly at E.P. "I'm frightened to death that the Navy will recall Kellan. I don't think I can live in constant fear."

"You'll learn to live with it. Like I learned to live with guilt."

"You feel guilty about Lonnie?"

"Lonnie?" E.P. was incredulous. "I told you. I did more for that kid than he deserved. I feel guilty about the baby I gave away."

The revelation, given so casually, shocked Joanie. "E.P., I'm stunned. I had no idea. Not a clue. You had a baby?"

"The year my parents took me out of public school and sent me out East to boarding school—it wasn't a boarding school, it was a quiet little place for unwed mothers. I never saw my baby. As soon as I delivered, they took it away. I'd been told—brainwashed is a better word—that it would be better if I never saw the child. That way I would not get attached to the baby, and I could go on with my life. They said I would soon forget. Shit. I've never forgotten. Oh, I'll go for months on end and not consciously think about my baby. But sometimes, some little happening will cause me to think about that baby. How old the child is now? Was my baby a boy or a girl?"

"I'm sorry, E.P."

"Why should you be sorry?"

"You don't want my sympathy?"

"No. I want you to keep your mouth shut about my seamy life. Not because

I'm ashamed; simply because I don't like to talk about it. That's a lie. It's because of my parents. You breathe a word of this to anybody, and anybody includes your wonderful Kellan, and I'll spread a few rumors about you."

"There's nothing to spread."

"I doubt that. But I'll make up a story so eye-popping that everyone will want to believe it." She spoke without rancor.

E.P. stubbed out her cigarette and threw the butt over the swimming pool fence onto the grass. "I think I'll drive out to Fort Leonard Wood to see Lonnie."

"Stay away from him, E.P., he's no good."

"That's like saying Michelangelo's *David* is no good."

"It's a masterpiece, but I wouldn't want it in my living room. What I mean, E.P.is that Lonnie is not good for you."

"You are so pragmatic, girl, that it's frightening."

"Is war pragmatic?"

"War is pragmatic bullshit. Obscene. Vulgar. Useless. My god, Joanie, men have been fighting wars since the beginning of time, and one war just sets up another war. Why do men have to fight? Why can't they just be bitchy; like women?"

Summer moved along and the days were given to laying plans for the intense campaigning that would start in early fall.

Joanie often sat in on the skull sessions as she did now. Normally it would have been an exhilarating experience for her.

Instead, the most it did was to push fear to the back of her mind, but she was never totally free from anxiety. Once Charles had told her she was like Scarlett O'Hara whose motto was *I'll worry about that tomorrow.* Tomorrow had caught up with Joanie and was strangling the life out of her.

"In addition to Independents, we'll have to get a percentage of the Democratic votes to win the election," Ken was saying. "Which is a factor in every general election. We don't have to worry about the die-hard Republicans. We could run a scarecrow on the ticket and they'd vote for it. As for the more…"

Joanie interrupted. "Are you a die-hard, Ken?"

He grinnned. "Let's say I'm a border line die-hard."

They were waiting for Kellan and other committee members to make choices of the items to be handed out when the door to door campaigning started. Matchbooks, combs, yardsticks, note pads. Buttons for the workers.

"It's hard to believe," Joanie commented, "that this junk can get votes."

"It's a matter of making a name instantly familiar. If an uncommitted,uninformed voter walks into the polls, he will most likely vote for the name he recognizes."

"Then we are going to make Kellan Foster a household word like peanut butter."

"But there is also a segment of voters—many of them Independents—who will vote on the platform, on what he promises. Some will vote for him because of his outstanding record in the Navy."

A sudden idea dawned on Joanie. "Ken, since Kellan is running for a government office, can he be exempted from military service?"

"The Selective Service Board judges each registrant on an individual basis."

"But I belong to the Naval Reserve." Kellan had come into the room and heard the tail-end of the conversation. "If the Navy reactivates me, I'll have no recourse but to serve."

"They won't reactivate a sick man, will they?" It was a smug question which Ken and Kellan ignored.

"There is only one thing the Democrats need to win the election," Ken stated."An unpatriotic opponent."

Joanie felt like she just had a door slammed in her face.

Joanie went to her father. "Charles, can you get Kellan a medical discharge on the basis of those malaria attacks he used to have?"

"The Navy has its own examining physicians. The most I can do is write up his medical history from the time he has been my patient and recommend that he be turned down for active duty, then forward that to the examining physicians."

She felt a wave of relief.

"You are clutching at straws, Joanie."

Relief was momentary.

Bill had resigned himself to being called back. "I'll be gone by the end of July," he predicted. However, on July 19th, Bill's birthday, he still had not received any correspondence from the Navy. "They must have lost my file," Bill said as they—Kellan, Joanie, Mr. D., Burt and Max—sat around the dining room table while Mrs. D.served plates of homemade ice cream and birthday cake.

"Well, any hope Karl ever had for a Major League career is shot," Mr. D. said ruefully. "He lost his best years in the last war, and now he's in another war."

"Police action." Cynical words from Kellan.

Mrs. D. was impatient. "Why, Dad, you ought to be saying prayers of thanks every hour that Karl is stationed in the U.S. doing physical what-ch-call it. You'd have something to worry about if he was in Korea. And you ought to be thankful Max and Burt got deferments."

"I am thankful, Gert. Real thankful. But I still can't help regretting that Karl won't ever get to play baseball."

"Won't get to play baseball! Why he can play in any cow pasture he wants to when the war is over."

There was a second of silence, and then they all laughed. Except Mrs. Dietmeier.

"Hell, what's happened has happened." Bill took a swallow from his bottle of beer and set it down beside his plate of cake and ice cream. "Nobody can change anything."

Mrs. D. frowned at Bill. "You oughten to drink that old beer with those sweets."

"Why, Mom, I'm a birthday boy." Bill smiled, "Don't I get to eat and drink what I want on my birthday?"

"I don't understand how you can stomach such a mixture," Joanie said. "It makes me sick to watch you eat."

Bill grinned more broadly. "Then look the other way, Joanie."

Laughter again. Laughter came so easily at the Dietmeier house.

All the laughter went out of Joanie's life on the second of August when Kellan got his orders to report for active duty.

"I feel like Esther Scott," Joanie said.

"How's that?" Kellan asked.

"Esther said that when she got pregnant she didn't have to worry anymore about getting pregnant. I used to think it was a moronic thing to say, but now I know what she means. Exactly. Your orders are here. I don't have to worry about that anymore."

"I'm thankful I'm not leaving you pregnant."

"I wish with all my heart that I am pregnant."

"I'd worry about you, if you were pregnant."

"I don't see why life has to be so full of worries. I hate worry."

"Let's not worry. Let's hope. Hope that I will be shore based."

A couple of days later, in the still of an early morning that promised to be sweltering later on, they left for Green Forks to visit Grandmother and the family.

The family greeted them with solemn joy. Solemn because Kellan had been activated to duty yet joyful to have him at home. Why, Joanie wondered, could Kellan never accept the way they doted on him? He was special to them.

Uncle Kirby, proud of the year's crops wanted Kellan to see them. Aunt Sammie wanted to show him her new pink and yellow "shower bath" that had been added to the house. William Kirby and his enormously pregnant wife, Mae, wanted to show him how they had "fixed up" Kirby and Sammie's old house with a special bedroom for the expected baby. Grandmother had a book she had ordered especially for Kellan, a book she wanted him to promise her that he would read. *The Efficacy of Prayer.* Joanie thought Kellan looked genuinely pleased when he promised—and Kellan was a person who kept promises—that he would indeed read the book.

Through all of this, in the back of Joanie's mind she carried the wish to be pregnant. But if I'm pregnant, I'll be the neatest, trimmest pregnant woman anyone ever saw. I won't have any trouble. But if I did have trouble, serious trouble, the Navy would let him come home. Wasn't there something called a hardship discharge?

Oh, but Kellan was leaving and they kept talking about crops and canning beans and putting a roof on the house— didn't they care that it was the end of the world for her?

On a late afternoon Joanie was helping Grandmother lay out things for supper while Aunt Sammie was tending to chickens and Uncle Kirby and Kellan were helping William Kirby install a new washing machine. The gloom of the kitchen, the thought that another day had passed that took her closer to losing Kellan were too much and she burst out crying, "Oh, Grandmother, I'm so afraid."

Grandmother opened her arms to Joanie and cradled her as if she were a child. Joanie felt the warmth and love and was comforted by the old woman's strength. "How have you been able to survive so much sorrow in your life, Grandmother?"

"My help cometh from the Lord who made Heaven and Earth."

"Why did it have to be Kellan who was called back when there are others who don't have a wife?"

"All things work together for good," Grandmother quoted, *"to those who love the Lord and keep His commandments."* She patted Joanie's back soothingly. "Dear child, if I only I could give you a dose of faith."

Sounds of voices approaching the house ended the intimacy, and the women went back to the preparations for supper. Joanie felt somewhat better, and she was able to hide her anguish from Kellan.

When the visit was over, and they were saying their good-byes, Joanie overheard Kellan's words to his grandmother. "Thank you for being my family. For never withholding your care and love for me when I deserved none of it."

On the ride home, they decided that they would spend their last day and night together at the lake where their love had begun. Each told the other not to think past that.

But that was impossible. They lay in the sun by the lake and swam in the murky water, drank wine on the screened-in porch with all the night creatures sawing out their unharmonious songs. They made love like it was the first time. Like it was the last time.

"Have I left unsaid anything that I should have said to you?" Kellan asked. "Have I unknowingly hurt you in any way?"

She lay her hand on his face, tracing his features with her fingers. "No, never.Everything you are is enough to make any day a good day." There was a lapse of words while nothing but love flowed between them.

Kellan said, "As long as I have you I have the whole world."

"I still hope that you will be shore based," Joanie said, not for the first time.

"Considering what I did during the war, I may be shore based."

When the time came for their last goodbyes, there was little to be said. They had already spoken to each other everything that was important.

The first days after Kellan left, friends filled up Joanie's time with places to go and things to do, but under the surface she carried a panicky feeling that made her want to go home. As if Kellan were there, waiting for her.

Charles invited her to move back home, but he wasn't the least insistent. And she did not want to move back. She wanted to stay in the little house she shared with Kellan and touch his clothes and sob at her loss until she was out of tears and left with nothing but empty gasps. She wanted to be near the telephone in case he should call. She not only knew the definition of bereft, she was living it.

Just when she was beginning to make plans to take a train to Bremerton, Washington, to visit him, Kellan telephoned to tell her that he had been assigned to a destroyer. He would be at sea before she could get to Bremerton.

Unable to reconcile herself to half a life, Joanie was at loose ends. Searching for ways to pass away the time. Restless. She spent more time with Charles, but not as much as she might have if he were not so often with Janet Smyth.

"Doctor's gone out of town for dinner," Miss Eddie informed Joanie when she had stopped by the house to perhaps have dinner with Charles. "With Janet Smyth."

"I don't see what Doctor sees in her," Joanie said. "For one thing they are so terribly far apart in age."

"Me neither. But that don't change the situation."

For once Joanie and Miss Eddie were of the same mind. And that had not happened very often when Joanie was growing up. "Do you think if I moved back home." Joanie stopped. That wasn't a good idea. "Well, if you are not cooking dinner, I'll be on my way."

"There's plenty of leftovers. Stay and eat with me."

Joanie was struck with a sudden urge to do something for Miss Eddie. "I've got a better idea. Let's you and me go to the country club for dinner."

"Oh, land, I couldn't do that. I'd be out of place."

"How could you be out of place if you are with me?"

"Well, I..."

"Well is a hole in the ground," Joanie said as though she were in fifth grade.

Miss Eddie was so pleased to be taken out to dinner that Joanie promised herself that from now on she was going to do nice things for Miss Eddie.

That evening Joanie's period started but it was so weak that she did not give up the hope that she was pregnant. If, she wondered, I was having a baby and about to die, would the Navy let Kellan come home to see me? She fantasized. Kellan would come home to be with a dying wife, but she would miraculously recuperate and have the baby and say, *I've got a present for you.*

Joanie got an unexpected present.

It was Saturday morning, and Joanie, wearing only a short summer negligee was eating her breakfast toast in the kitchen when she saw Bill get out of the pickup and start across the back lawn. She didn't dash to change into something more decorous—after all, it was only Bill. So, trying to determine what he was carrying, she watched Bill approach the back door.

Calling out her name and opening the back door at the same time, as was his custom, Bill let himself in. He put a beagle pup down on the kitchen floor.

"You've got a new dog," Joanie said.

"No. You've got a new dog," Bill corrected. "And he'd like a saucer of milk this morning."

While Joanie was getting the milk, Bill explained, "Beagles are nice little dogs, besides being good rabbit dogs. You can get a pen built out back for him, and…"

"No pens. They look tacky…" she shut her mouth, remembering that the Deitmeiers had a dog pen in the backyard.

Bill had not caught her gaffe. Or simply didn't take offense. "The pup has had all his shots except his rabies shot. He's too young for that."

Having quickly lapped up the milk, the pup scooted the empty saucer across the floor, this way and that, in a vain effort to get more milk.

"I'm going to name you Scooter," Joanie said as she picked up the puppy. "How's that for a name, Bill?"

"He doesn't care what you name him."

"You'll have to tell me how to take care of Scooter—like when to get that rabies shot." Scooter squirmed around in her hold. "Pour yourself a cup of coffee, Bill. Or get a beer." What was it that made Bill so attractive? He was not handsome, but there wasn't a woman in town who would not put Bill at the top of the list of the town's best looking men. "Oh, no."

Joanie wailed as she felt warm wetness through her gown, "Scooter peed on me."

"I'm getting out of here," Bill said, "before you try to give that pup back to me."

September was holding on to summer, dry and hot. There was a contagious listlessness in the late afternoon so that Charles, Janet and Joanie were content to sit on the screened-in porch at their own pursuits—Charles doing the Sunday crossword puzzle, Janet doing needlepoint, and Joanie studying an assignment in Non European Studies 101. The only sounds came from the water skiers on the lake.

Deciding that working on a college degree would be an antidote to loneliness,Joanie had enrolled at Houghton. She set a goal for herself, straight A's in every course, a solid, four-point student. She would show Janet and everyone else how smart she could be when she wanted to be smart. She paused in her reading, closed her eyes and remembered Kellan—his face, his voice, his hands, his body. Against her will, a few tears escaped from her eyes.

Concern in her voice, Janet asked, "Are you all right, Joanie?"

Quick to reply, Joanie said, "I'm not *all right,* I'm half right. I won't be whole until Kellan comes home." She was peevish. She wished Janet would go away and leave her with Charles. She wanted to ask him wild, impossible questions, and hear his calm, sensible voice speak words of assurance. She wanted to beg him to shake up the very foundations of the U.S. Navy and bring Kellan home. Sadly, the most she could hope for was a letter from Kellan in Monday's mail.

There was no letter from Kellan in Monday's mail, but there was one from Grandmother Foster.

...We received a most heart-warming letter from Kellan last week, a blessing to us for he wrote at length of his love for the family and his gratitude for the home and upbringing we gave him. He went on to tell us that as far as he was concerned, the name Chazmarek was of no more importance than a name in a book. Garret was his father. And isn't it strange that we must travel so long and far on a quest only to find that the answer is at hand...

Some weekend soon, Joanie decided, I will drive down to Green Forks to spend a weekend with Grandmother. Maybe some of her patience and faith will rub off on me.

Joanie played bridge occasionally, often went out to dinner with friends, but classes and studying took up most of her time. The rollicking, good-time parties were over.

She was invited to Sunday dinner at the Dietmeiers. She woke up very early, which was unusual for her, and heard the church bell of St. Ambrose ringing for early mass. If I were a Catholic, like the Cordets, Joanie thought, I'd go to mass every morning at six and pray for Kellan. She tried to go back to sleep but couldn't. She got up, let Scooter out, put on a pot of coffee and studied for an hour. Then she got the Sunday paper, whistled Scooter back inside, and went back to bed and read the paper. She fell asleep and slept until after eleven with just enough time to dress and be at the Dietmdeiers for dinner.

The Dietmeier house was a quieter place now that Karl was back in service and Max and Burt were at IU. Yet the house was no less cheerful, and Joanie was glad to be there. She gave them news of Kellan.

"I don't think it's right that they took the men who fought in World War II," Mrs.Dietmeier complained. "Risking your life once is enough. I'd like to give the people in Washington a piece of my mind."

"Then you might not have a mind left," Mr. D. teased.

"That kind of talk is so old it's not even funny," Mrs. D said scornfully.

Bill said what he had often said before, "I don't know how in hell they missed me."

"I just might have the answer to that," Mrs. D. stated, getting up to clear the table for dessert.

No one said anything. They all knew what she meant.

"Look at all this food that's left," she said. "I can't seem to learn to cook in small amounts."

"It's Joanie's fault," Mr. D. joked. "She don't eat enough to keep a bobwhite alive."

"I'll bet you that I ate more than you did," Joanie countered.

"How much do you want to bet?" he asked.

"Well, how are we going to determine who ate the most?"

"That's a good question." Mr. Dietmeier thought a moment. "Let's bet on who eats the biggest piece of pie."

"It isn't pie," Mrs. D. said, coming back into the dining room, "it's persimmon pudding." She placed a dish in front of Joanie and one in front of Bill. "Go ahead and start," she said, "Dad and I will catch up."

"I've never eaten persimmon pudding," Joanie said.

"What? Never eaten persimmon pudding! Oh, you'll like it."

Joanie liked it, but just barely. She would have preferred Mrs. Dietmeier's fudge pie with ice cream.

When they had finished dessert, Bill announced that he was going fishing. "This might be one of the last days this fall that will be warn enough to walk the creek."

Bill was correct about the day being warm. Indian summer had given them days with temperatures in the eighties even though there had been frost earlier in the month.Already the trees were beginning to shed the yellow, red, and russet leaves that had colored their world.

"Well, Joanie, there goes our euchre game," Mr. Dietmeier grumbled; "up a creek."

"I'll go fishing with you, Bill," Joanie offered. "It's too beautiful a day to waste indoors."

"Where I'm going, Joanie, there are snakes. You would have to wear waders."

"I'll wear Kellan's."

"You and who else?"

They all laughed, but she didn't think it was funny. She said no more. Anything else would be begging. And she didn't beg anything from anyone. Ever. Oh, but that wasn't true. She would beg anyone or anything that would get Kellan back to her.

"Actually," Joanie was being blasé, "I was too impulsive. I need to study. I have a test in psychology Monday orning."

"How about a few hands of double solitaire," Mr. D. suggested; "before you go. A quarter a game?"

"Okay. But not too many hands—win or lose—I have to hit the books if I'm going to get an A in that class."

Joanie did go home to study but not because she wanted to. She wanted to be out wading the creek with Bill. Snakes? Shit. Bill, she decided, thought people might gossip if they saw or found out that the two of them spent a Sunday afternoon together. But that didn't make sense. Bill didn't give a damn about what people thought about him. Was it her reputation he was concerned about? Or did he think that Kellan would not like his best friend and his wife alone together for an afternoon? Kellan, Kellan, Kellan; she wanted him so bad she thought she would die.

She started studying in earnest.

Joanie had been studying hard for over an hour when Charles and Janet stopped by.

"Janet and I are driving in to Indianapolis tonight, for dinner, and we would like very much for you to join us."

"It's tempting. But I've got to study. I have a test tomorrow."

"I admire you for being such a dedicated student, Joanie," Janet was smiling, "but you must remember to take some time off for a bit of relaxation."

Joanie wanted to say, oh, quit being so damned goody-goody, but she held her tongue. "Don't worry about me. I might take time out to go to the Sunday movie."

"Movies are mindless," Charles pronounced; "I did my fatherly duty and took you to the movies made for kids, Joanie. And because it was such a talked about, raved about production, I went with you to see *Gone With the Wind*. And there was enough sentimental balderdash in that tour de force to last a life time."

It was Joanie's turn. "You are an intellectual snob." Joanie lit a cigarette from a new pack she bought on the way home from Dietmeiers.

"You're smoking again," Charles accused.

"When Kellan comes home, I'll quit forever."

"From the articles I have read and from what Charles has told me," Janet commented, "tobacco causes all sorts of deadly illnesses. You know, I've never smoked."

Joanie's repley was swift and tart, said before she could bite her tongue. "Then you really don't know what you've missed, do you?"

Janet did not take offense. She smiled when she said, "That's one way of looking at it."

After Charles and Janet left, Joanie made herself a drink and snacked on cheese and crackers which was about all she had in the house for dinner. She might forget to buy food for herself, but she never forgot to buy dog food for Scooter.

Joanie planned her evening. Forget the movie. Try to get started on the essay for English comp. *Changing Perspectives.* Whose perspectives? Mine? Society's? Bill Dietmeier's? She had no clue. After she wrote the essay she would go back and review her psychology notes.

She had written and crossed out three different introductory paragraphs when she heard the familiar five knocks followed by twelve knocks and one ring of the doorbell. E.P.'s signal, following Kellan's caution not to answer the door at night unless she knew who was there.

Joanie unlocked the door for E.P. to enter. "Has your perspective changed lately?"

E.P. headed for the sofa. "From what vantage point?"

"Well, let's say from looking back at the end of the war when everything was new again."

"Who cares?"

"I have to write an essay on *Changing Perspectives.*"

"Does it disappoint you that this veritable fountain of knowledge can not wax eloquent on the subject?' "

"No."

"Now I shall ask you about perspectives. How serious is a local physician—handsome, erudite, elitist and something of a stuffed shirt—about a proper and gracious young teacher?"

"I was in a decent mood until you brought that subject up."

"Sorry. All I want is for you to tell me how he can be so interested in she-who-shall-go-nameless when I'm available.

Wouldn't you like me for a stepmother?"

The question was so incongruous that it made Joanie laugh. "I can't imagine you as anybody's stepmother."

E.P., still being facetious, complained, "I'm insulted. You laughed at me. You don't laugh at she-who-shall-go- nameless."

"Seriously, E.P., I think I could easily accept a woman who was more befitting his age."

"A difference in age—there you go, changing perspectives—a difference in age can spice up the love-making, honey chile. I speak from experience. Lonnie was just seventeen the first time we did it. I, of course, taught him his superior skills. Damn, did he learn fast." E.P. stuck a cigarette in her mouth, flicked her lighter and inhaled deeply. She let out a stream of smoke as she said, "God, he was beautiful, wasn't he, Joanie? A beautiful son-of-a-bitch—but then *there isn't any beauty that hath not some strangeness in the proportion*"—so said Francis Bacon. Or Shakespeare. Or…"

"She-who-shall-go-nameless?"

"Hardly." E.P., seeming to settle in for the evening went on. "Lonnie was totally amoral. He could lie through his teeth. He had no conscience and never felt a twinge of guilt or remorse. His language was dirtier than mine. Me? I'm immoral. I know the difference between right and wrong. He didn't." E.P. was finished with that subject. "You haven't offered me a drink, Mrs. Foster."

"What would you like?"

"Do you have Scotch?"

"I have Scotch."

"Is it good Scotch?"

Provoked, Joanie went to their so-called liquor cabinet and brought out the bottle for E.P.'s inspection.

"Hmm…velly, velly, good Scotch. All I need is a glass filled with ice."

"Aren't you having a drink, sweetie?" E.P. asked when Joanie returned from the kitchen with only one glass.

"I have to study tonight."

"Go make yourself a drink. It will put you in the mood for a little fun."

"Repeat: I have to study tonight. And it is getting late." As Joanie spoke, Scooter came into the room, walked to the front door, and looked expectantly at Joanie who got up from her chair and opened the door to let the dog out.

"That damned dog has you well-trained." E.P. took a generous swallow of Scotch.

"He is not a damned dog. He's Scooter."

"Where did you get him?"

"Bill Dietmeier gave him to me."

"Ah, Bill," E.P. sighed. "What a damned, stubborn Dutchman. I did him a favor for which I received his abuse." She puffed on her cigarette. "I revealed to him the extent of Polly's screwing around while he was nobly serving his country." E.P. took another swallow of Scotch. "God, what a man—if you like men."

"And you like men." Joanie's statement begged for corroboration.

"I like beautiful people."

"I wouldn't characterize Bill Dietmeier as beautiful."

"Beauty is in the beholder's eyes, they say. Or is it that beauty is in the pocket book of the beholderee.? Perchance, I just coined a new word. Or did

I?" E.P.held up her glass of melting ice and weakened Scotch. "I don't mind if I do," she said, getting to her feet. "Don't bestir yourself, little girl, I'll get it myself."

I need to kick her out, Joanie thought, before she gets so drunk she passes out.

E.P. came gingerly back into the living room with two filled glasses sort of swaying in her grasp. "Here, my dear, drink deeply of the bacchanal delight."

No one makes me drink anything I don't want, Joanie almost said. She ignored the glass of Scotch.

"Tell me, beautiful one, what are you doing for sex, now that Kellan is gone?"

"That's none of your business." Joanie made no effort to keep the ire out of her voice.

"You're so pretty when you're angry. Isn't that what they say on the soaps?"

"I don't know what they say on soaps. I study all the time."

"Screw study."

"Oh, for heaven's sake, E.P. Shut up."

"Sexy. You absolutely exude sex in every movement of your body."

"Go home, E.P."

"You're being rude, doll."

"No, candid. I told you I have to study."

"I'll help you study."

"I'm booting you out, E.P. Go."

"Well, la-de-da...I know when I'm not wanted. If I can find my pants, I'm going home."

"Go home and sober up."

"If that pleases your royal highness. I go to a far, far, better place than I have.ever known."

After E.P. left, it took some time for Joanie to settle down.

She picked up the legal pad and her pen. Changing Perspectives. Now she knew what she wanted to write and the words came quite easily.

Scooter yipped outside the front door, and Joanie let him in. She drank a glass of milk, patted Scooter on the head, and he followed her into the bedroom and got into his basket-bed. She soon followed, tired but pleased with the paper she had written for English Comp.

Hours later, the sound of Kellan calling her name awakened Joanie. Scooter barked. And then howled as only a beagle can.

"Hush, Scooter." Joanie turned on the light. There was no Kellan. She walked through the house. So unmistakably had she heard his voice that she took Scooter and went outside. The neighborhood slept. The whole world was quiet. There was no Kellan. She dragged back to her bed and lay with wide, staring eyes. She had heard Kellan's voice as real and strong as Scooter's bark.

Joanie lay immobile, and Kellan's presence seemed to fill the room. But if she had opened her arms to him, she would have clasped nothing.

And then she knew; she had lost Kellan.

When the official word of Kellan's death came to her, it was no shock, merely a confirmation.

Bill...

Feet propped up on his desk and hands clasped behind his head, Bill Dietmeier watched the red second hand on the Burger Beer clock move inexorably around and around the dial. Which produced no philosophical thoughts only irritation that old Herman Schmundt was late to pick up his keg of beer. Herm knew damn well that they closed at eleven- thirty on Saturdays.

Bill tore off an order form, wadded it up and tossed it at a trash can that sat beside his dad's desk on the other side of the room. A perfect shot. Two points. If it had not been for the war, he said to himself, I would have made it in college basketball. Might even have made a good small guard in the pros. College maybe. Pros never. He tore off another order blank, wadded it up and hit the mark again. Nothing but net. He did the same thing three more times. Wasting order blanks, his mother would say; what do you think? Money grows on trees?

A lot of things would be different if there hadn't been a war. He would have married Polly, and they might have a bunch of kids by now. If there hadn't been a"police action" in Korea, Kellan would still be alive. Things that can't be changed need to be forgotten, he reminded himself. Life was for the living, and answers to the "Ifs" would come in the next world.

Bill's plan for his Saturday afternoon was to drive down to Louisville and go out to Churchill Downs and bet the horses. Now, damn it, because of Herm he wouldn't make the daily double; he liked to bet the daily double because if he won it, he had made the money for the rest of the day's bets.

It would serve the old geezer right, Bill thought, if I'd lock up and leave. Guess the old tight-fisted German figured no one would lock up and miss a sale. But it wouldn't work that way. If Herm came and found the place closed he'd go up home and get Dad or Mom or whoever was there to open up for him.

The red hand kept circling the dial.

At twenty-two minutes after twelve, Herm's battered pickup pulled into a parking space in front of the office. Before Herm could haul himself out of the cab, Bill went out to meet him.

"Pull her around to the loading dock, Herm."

Before Herm had brought the truck around, Bill had the beer keg on a dolly and was waiting on the loading dock to put it in Herm's pickup.

Bill rested against the fender and lit a cigarette as though the only thing in the world he wanted to do was talk to Herm, which wasn't a bad thing to do.

Bill and his dad had wanted to hunt on Herm's farm for a long time, but his place was posted. "How many girls you got left, Herm?"

"This is the last one," Herm answered. "The last god-damned wedding I got to foot the bills for."

"Hell. That's a damn shame. I was counting on you to save one of your girls for me."

Herm laughed. "Well, you're too late, boy. You done missed your chance.I had seven girls before I give up trying to get a boy. But let me tell you something. I guarantee you that any one of the seven could out work you."

"Why that wouldn't be hard. I'm always glad for anyone to out work me."

Herm's voice was humorous. "According to your daddy, you're the best worker of all his boys."

"Ah, you can't believe Dad. Don't you know that Herm?"

Herm hee-hawed. Obviously enjoying the repartee.

So Bill asked, "Herm, since you ain't got any girls left, how about birds? You got any of them little bitty quail out at your place?" It was reflex action for Bill to speak in the vernacular of the person speaking to him.

Herm spit. That meant he was getting ready to turn loose some of his money."I seen a nice sized covey yesterday." He pulled out of his overalls a large roll of bills held together by a thick, rubber band. "How much are you going to take me for?"

"Hey, just wait and settle up when you bring the keg back. The books are closed today." To be able to hold onto his money a little longer would make the old man feel good. "Herm, what would you say if I was to come out to your place and ask permission to hunt?"

Herm was pushing his roll deep inside his overalls. "Well, I'll put it this way.You and your daddy can come out, but I don't want no other town people on my property. You be sure and go up to the house and tell the missus that I said you could hunt. Otherwise, she might call the game warden. Or the sheriff."

Bill could hardly contain his elation, but he said nonchalantly, "If I can ever find the time, I just might do that. I don't know. These days a fellow has to keep his nose to the grindstone."

Herm nodded his head in agreement and climbed into the cab. "Now you folks come on out to the reception tomorrow. There'll be plenty of eats. Maybe we'll pitch some horseshoes."

"Sure thing. And if you need more beer, let us know, and we'll bring it out. He gave a wave to Herm as the truck pulled away and glanced at his watch. He was going to miss the third race, too, but considering the good fortune of getting to hunt on the Schmundt place, he didn't care. As long as he got to the Downs in time to bet My Little Pippin in the sixth race. He had been watching that horse for a long time.

As soon as he saw the twin spires of Churchill Downs against the hazy November sky, Bill felt buoyed up. Not like the nervous excitement that he felt before quail hunting, just a good, glad-to-be-alive feeling. Horses were magnificent creatures, and jockeys were incredible athletes, and a well-run race was pure pleasure. And more than all of that was the challenge of using his wits to handicap a race and win. Which was better than beer. Well, maybe not quite. The sun was very warm for late autumn so Bill left his coat in the car and hurried toward the ticket window, hearing as he got to the window the wild cheering of a completed race.

Bill always moved around quite a bit at the track, going down to the paddock area to watch the horses getting saddled up, watching one race from the grandstand, going down to the rail to watch another. Which was where he was when the bell sounded and the horses broke out of the starting gate. A race he had made no wager on.

From what seemed like the direction of his elbow came a plaintive wail, "I can't see! I can't see!"

The words were not addressed to anyone in particular, merely a loud lamentation from a small young woman who was trying to find a peephole in the crowd.

"I'll give you a boost if you like," Bill offered.

"Yes, Yes, I've got ten dollars on Whammy."

Bill picked her up and held her up so she could see. It was a short race, six furlongs. Whammy came in fifth. "Sorry you didn't win," Bill said putting her down.

"Me too. But I guess that's why they call it gambling." Her demeanor suddenly changed. "My gosh, you must think I'm crazy. I mean I don't usually go around letting strangers pick me up. I mean lift me up. Anyway, good luck." She was gone.

That's the way it goes, Bill said to himself. Come easy, go easy.

Dark clouds moved in and with them a sharp wind. The afternoon grew very chilly so Bill went into the clubhouse and found a place to sit at one of the small tables. He wanted to make sure that he had not overlooked any horse that might have a chance of beating My Little Pippin. If the odds on Pippin stayed at ten to one, he'd make out like gangbusters. He was pouring over the *Daily Racing Form* when a female voice asked, "Is anyone sitting here?" as she pulled out a chair.

She was any age from eighteen to thirty-eight. Old-young. Young-old. Too much lipstick above protruding teeth. Too much perfume. Bill hated the smell. "Sit down," he said, more interested in the *Form* than the person who occupied the chair.

"You having a good day?" she asked.

Bill didn't bother to look up. "Haven't cashed a ticket." He wouldn't tell his own mother how much he had won. Or lost. "How about yourself?"

"I cashed one show ticket."

"That's the way it goes."

She studied Bill's face as her fingers pulled at the neck of her dress so that a white strap wouldn't show. "How would you like to get acquainted with me? My place ain't far. I'm good stuff, too."

Bill shook his head sadly from side to side. "Can't honey. I got hurt in the war. I got nothing."

"Jesus God." Her face was a mixture of astonishment and disappointment. "We could do other stuff. Something. Whatever you want."

"Uh, I don't want to talk about it, okay?"

"Yeah. I'm sorry. I honest to God am sorry."

Bill reached for his billfold and got out a ten. "Here. Take this and bet it on My Little Pippin. Sixth race. It'll be the easiest money you make today."

"Well-my-God." She looked at Bill in awe. "Thanks mister." My Little Pippin won and paid $26.20. Bill had put twenty on the horse. He wondered if the toothy prostitute had bet the horse or put the ten spot in her bra.

Being a winner made it easy to bet the horses. Winners, Bill knew, came in streaks.

And, Bill thought, propositions were coming in streaks. This time it was a middle-aged, peroxide blond in an expensive suit with a mink stole. She teetered on needle thin spike heels so that as she walked her rotund body seemed dangerously near listing in any direction. Bill had noticed her before, ordering whiskey sours from the bar. Without asking, she sat down across from Bill. For a while, she played hoity-toity.

"My ex-husband raised thoroughbreds," she told Bill.

Bill didn't believe her, but he said, "Maybe you've got some hot tips."

"No. Not anymore. I didn't even bet the last race. I'm bored."

Bill's voice was expressionless. "You can always leave." Her perfume was nauseating.

She rummaged in her purse and brought out a silver cigarette case and offered Bill a cigarette—which he refused. She rummaged in the purse again and brought out a silver lighter. She lit a cigarette and blew a cloud of smoke in Bill's face. That must be some kind of foreign tobacco, he thought. The smell was as sickening as her perfume.

"I think I shall go home," she sighed, "if I can persuade a well-hung young man sitting across from me to go home with me." She blew another gust of smoke in Bill's direction. "I've got a marvelous house, a heated swimming pool...."

"And I've got the clap," Bill said, cutting her off.

"And you need not be so rude," she said.

"Just being honest." Bill was beginning to feel sick. Was it what she was smoking or something on her breath or the heavy perfume? "I wouldn't want anyone in the world to feel like I do."

She got up and listed toward Bill, putting her foul-smelling face close to his. "I think you are a lying bastard." She teetered off.

Her obnoxious scent lingered even after she disappeared into the crowd.

Bill pulled his pack of Old Gold Filters out of his pocket and laid it on the table. That's it, he said to himself; I've smoked my last cigarette. And that's the last proposition I'm getting today. I'm on my way home.

A week later when his mom was frying eggs for Bill's breakfast, she said, "Guess who telephoned before you got up."

"President Truman?"

"Someone nice."

"The President of the United States isn't nice, Mom?" If the call had been someone she didn't like she would have said that old so-and-so called.

"Joanie."

Inwardly, Bill reacted with a mixed sense of dread, pleasure, sadness— that he quickly stifled. "When did they get back?"

"Yesterday on the five-fifteen B&O." She put a plate of sausages and eggs in front of Bill. "Fix your own toast," she said. Then went on, "I think they've been gone so long, Dr. Welles will have to get introduced to his patients. If he has any left. Joanie is coming over to get that hound that won't stay put."

Scooter had been a problem. Left with Miss Eddie, he constantly ran off, back to Kellan and Joanie's house. Finally, Miss Eddie called Bill and asked him if he would put the dog in the pound or board it at the vet's. Bill brought the dog home and put him in the dog pen, but he tunneled under the fence and went back to Joanie's house. As a last resort, Bill put Scooter on a chain in the backyard. At first he howled, until Bill used some forceful discipline; he sulked, but he learned what shut up meant.

Bill asked, "Will you go out and bring Scooter in while I finish my breakfast?" He didn't want Joanie to know he kept Scooter chained.

"Dogs! We're either going to get rid of all the dogs or move to the country. I'm fed up with the mess."

Nevertheless, she did Bill's bidding.

"Anybody home?" Joanie's voice.

Bill quit his breakfast and met her in the dining room. She came to him and laid her head on his chest. "Hold me, Bill. I'm so lost. So empty."

Poor kid. But I can't help you, Bill thought, you've got to do it on your own.

Barking excitedly, Scooter ran ahead of Mrs. Dietmeier, and Joanie scooped him up, caressing his wiggling body, crying a little as she rubbed her cheek on his head. "Scooter, you're so thin."

Bill ignored the remark. He wasn't going to tell Joanie how Scooter had grieved for her.

"Take off your coat, Joanie, and come on back to the kitchen and have a cup of coffee and tell us about your trip." If there was anything that Bill hated worse than hearing about somebody's trip, it was watching the slides of somebody's trip.

"Only half a cup. And don't fret, Bill. I'm not going to launch into a travelogue. I'll just say that Europe still shows the ravages of war."

She looked so different, Bill thought. Her face was thinner—and then he realized that her hair was short. "Where did you lose your hair, Joanie?"

"In Paris. Short, short hair and long, long dangling earrings are the fashion there and Charles wanted me to have a Parisian hair cut. Do you like it?"

Bill hated it. "Takes a little getting used to." Bill remembered the time he had tied her hair in a pony tail with his handkerchief. Then her taffy-colored hair was long and silky. Whoever cut her hair ought to get a spray of buckshot in his ass. Well, hell. What's it to me?

"I ought to get my hair cut off like that," Mrs. D. said. "Be easy to shampoo and take care of."

Bill groaned inwardly, imagining his mother with such a hair cut.

Joanie said, "Your auburn hair is beautiful pulled back in what I'd call a French roll."

The older woman smiled. "I thought it was an American twist."

"It's a Big Bertha Bun," Bill said, hoping they would quit talking about hair.

"Do you have a cigarette, please, Bill?" Joanie asked. "Mine are in the car."

"I quit smoking."

"Hard to do, wasn't it?"

"Hard? No. I don't want to smoke. If I wanted to smoke, I'd still be smoking. But I'll go out to your car and get your cigarettes."

"Never mind. I won't be here long. I only came to get Scooter and bring the Dietmeier family something I got in Germany." She opened a brown package and pulled out a stein. "I can't prove the authenticity of this beer stein, but the saleswoman was very insulted when I asked if it was a copy and assured me in very good English that it was an original.

The stein had a pewter lift top adorned with the figure of a Prussian officer astride a rearing horse. Battle scenes decorated the porcelain cylinder. Across the border on the lip of the stein was the name, Peter Muller, and the date 1880-1883.

"According to the saleswoman," Joanie explained, "every soldier in a, I think she said regiment, had his own stein with his name at the top and on the side the names of the other men in his company. She heard me tell Charles that it would be great if I could find one with the name Dietmeier listed, and she methodically scanned every stein in her store and found this one.

Bill read over his mother's shoulder. Besendorfer, Brunig, Bscheider, Damm, Deimel, Dietmeier, Eibad, Endras, …

"Now, hold the bottom up to the light and look through the stein," Joanie directed.

Bill's mother looked first. "Naught, naughty," she laughed and handed the stein to Bill.

Held to the light, the translucent bottom of the stein showed the reclining figure of a naked woman. Fat was beautiful in those days, Bill thought. He didn't know what to say so he gave a soft whistle of appreciation.

Scooter reacted with an impatient yip and thumped his tail against the kitchen floor in his eagerness to be off his haunches and out for a good run.

Suddenly latching on to an excuse to end the coffee klatsch, Bill suggested, "Scooter needs some exercise. Want to take him out and see if he can run a rabbit?"

Joanie seemed withdrawn but quickly gathered herself to say, "Yes, I'd like that. Should I change clothes?"

"I don't think so. I'm not taking the gun. We'll just let Scooter have a little fun."

"Fun…" Joanie's voice was despondent, and she left her thought unfinished.

The winter cornfields were as dreary as Joanie's voice. Drab stubble. Drab everything.

"I think November is the dreariest month of the year," Joanie sighed as the pickup bumped along the township road.

"Don't you?"

To Bill, November meant hunting, and there was nothing he liked better than a cold dry season so the dogs could better work the fields. Snow was okay if it wasn't the wet kind that melted and made fields muddy. But he replied, going along with her thought, "Yeah, it's a kinda gloomy month."

Joanie reached down and rubbed Scooter's head where he lay on the floor board. "Bill, I don't think I can make it."

He knew what Joanie wanted. She wanted their personal losses to be a common denominator between them. She wanted some kind of communication that he could not give. Why dwell on something you could not change? He had to say something. "You'll make it."

She shook her head as though in disagreement. "Why did you come back here, Bill?"

"Mom's cooking, I guess."

"Oh, be serious, Bill. Why did you come back here to face all the memories."

He cut her off with a "Because," not exactly knowing what he would say, and finished with, "since I have to work somewhere, I thought I might as well work for Dad. It takes me five minutes to get to work. Unless there's a train on the Pennsy tracks. In twenty to thirty minutes I can get to places to hunt and fish. A couple of hours and I can be at the race track or a baseball stadium."

"I wish I could adjust the way you have," she said.

Bill looked out over a barren field. "Here's a good place to let Scooter run." It wasn't the place he had intended to stop, but it interrupted her train of thought. She wanted to talk about sorrow. He didn't know how to tell her that there was no way to end it. She had to learn how to live with it.

Scooter, who knew what his mission in life was, ran across the road when he was let out of the truck, slipped under the fence and streaked across the field—he had picked up a scent where Bill thought no rabbit could be.

The fence was too limp for Joanie to get a foot on and swing over, and too high for her to step over. Bill lifted her and put her down on the other side. She couldn't weigh more than a hundred pounds, he thought.

Before they went on, Joanie stopped and turned her back to the wind to light a cigarette.

"Do you ever eat?" Bill reproached. "Or do you live on cigarettes?"

"I try to eat. But I mostly live on cigarettes during the day and pills at night."

"Hell, Joanie, you can't do that…" he stopped. "Hear that?"

Scooter was baying in the distance.

"Won't be long until you can see a rabbit run across the field,." Bill pointed out the direction. "with Scooter right behind him." He noticed that Joanie was shivering. "You're cold. We'd better call the dog in and leave."

"No, don't. I'm okay."

Bill took off his coat and put it around her shoulders.

Scooter's barking was louder.

"There goes the rabbit!" Bill yelled as the rabbit whizzed across the open field with Scooter on its heels.

"What happens now?" Joanie asked.

"Scooter is wondering why a gun didn't go off." Bill whistled the dog in. No need to keep Joanie out in the cold any longer.

As they trekked back, Joanie said, This is the best day I've had since…" She didn't finish.

And Bill could say nothing.

At the fence Bill again picked Joanie up and put her down on the other side. This is about all the help I can give you, he wanted to say. You've got to help yourself.

The dog climbed into the cab like he owned the pickup and lay with his head on his front paws. Joanie bent over to rub his head, and he jumped into her lap.

Looking out at the landscape, Bill mentally marked the place. When he wanted a couple of rabbits, he'd borrow Scooter and come back. Alone. The country side was changing with more and more areas being cleared off for more corn and soy bean fields. "You know," he began as though Joanie had been aware of his thoughts, "twenty or so more years and there won't be many places left to hunt. Kinda sad, isn't it?"

"From the way I see it, life is nothing but sad." Joanie's voice was bitter.

One way you look at it, Bill thought, life is a tragedy. Everybody is heading toward a grave. But there sure are a lot of good things on the way, with a promise of better things. The heater was pouring out warm air into the cab, and Joanie loosened her coat and ran her fingers through what was left of her hair. Whoever did that to her, Bill thought, ought to be beheaded.

"Kellan liked to hunt almost as much as you do, Bill," Joanie said, and then, "Oh, but didn't the three of us have so much fun together?"

"Yeah, we sure did." He didn't want to talk about Kellan like he never wanted to talk about Polly. He had reconciled their deaths according to his belief and gotten on with his life. Joanie was clinging to the past not wanting to let it go "Don't shut Kellan out of my life," Joanie pleaded, "like Charles does. Like everyone does. Let me talk about Kellan. You talk about Kellan."

"You talk. I'll listen." That was the best he could do.

"I loved Kellan so much, Bill. The chemistry was always right between us."

He let her talk, thinking his own thoughts. Thinking he could never bare his soul to anyone the way she was doing.

Thinking about E.P.'s venomous words, *It's about time, Dietmeier, that someone told you the truth about Polly Emhuff;* he remembered that E.P. had called Polly a slut, but he remembered nothing that he said or did until he was being sick and throwing up in the john at home.

They were approaching the Dietmeiers' house when Joanie put a gloved hand on Bill's arm and said, "Thank you, Bill, for being Kellan's friend. And for being my friend. And don't fret. I promise not be a trouble to you."

"Trouble? I don't even know how to spell the word."

Trouble came with the ringing of the telephone on a blah Sunday afternoon.

Out of boredom—hunting was illegal on Sundays—Bill had devoured the sports section down to the last word and was reading the classified ads for no purpose whatsoever except to pass the time.

The phone was ringing.

When neither his father or mother seemed disposed toward answering the telephone, Bill put down the newspaper and answered.

The caller was Mel Skervan, a fellow about Bill's age, whom he knew slightly from high school and well by reputation. Mel was in and out of trouble. He had been arrested for public intoxication, for theft, for assault with a deadly weapon.

"Well, how you been, Dietmeier?" The voice was ingratiating.

"Doing the best I can," Bill replied easily. He knew what Mel was going to ask him to do. What he didn't know was how he was going to handle it.

"Say, how about doing a fellow a favor? We got us a little card game going this afternoon, and we ran out of beer. How about you slipping down to your place of business and sneaking me out a case or two?"

"I sure as hell would like to accommodate you, Mel, but you know how it is. Dad's in a tight spot where he can't afford to take the chance of getting in trouble with the State Liquor Board."

"Say, pal, what do you do when your fancy friends asks you to do 'em a little favor on a Sunday afternoon?"

"My friends don't ask me to sell them beer on Sunday." Bill was curt.

Mel got verbally abusive. He threatened. Bill hung up on him as Mel was saying, "You're going to be god-damned sorry, you son-"Trouble?" Bill's mom inquired apprehensively.

"No trouble, Mom." Bill went out of the room and out of the house before his mother could probe him with questions.

The temperature was dropping, but there was no wind so Bill wasn't cold even though he was in short sleeves. He was thinking about the situation with Mel.Hanging up on him was a mistake, but he didn't want to get his parents involved.

Anybody with fifth grade intelligence could comprehend that laws that made Sunday sales of beer illegal caused more problems than they prevented. The same thing with hunting. A man out tramping in the fields trying to find a covey of quail wasn't likely to get in trouble. Well, there wasn't a law that said he couldn't run the bird dog on a Sunday afternoon. That's what he'd do. Leave the gun at home and take the dog out and see if he could locate birds for next week.

He heard his mother call from the back door. "Telephone!"

As Bill came through the kitchen, his mother said, "It's *that old E.P.*" As though E.P. were an object instead of a human being.

"Tell her I'm not home," Bill said, yet the scowl on his mother's face made Bill, even as he spoke, head for the telephone in the dining room. His mother wouldn't lie.

E.P. was having an impromptu Sunday night poker game at her house— "honorable parents being in Florida—" and Bill was invited.

"I don't think I can make it," Bill said, mentally fumbling for an excuse He felt like telling E.P. that he knew of someone who might take his place. Old Mel would sure stink up the Portlands' elegant home. "I'd sure like to, E.P., but I've got to work on accounts tonight. Quarterly taxes you know."

E.P.'s voice was a mixture of amusement and disgust. "Oh, come on, Dietmeier, you can do better than that."

Hell, Bill said to himself, playing poker would be better than anything else I could come up with for a Sunday night—I could use some spare bucks. "Tell you what, E.P.—I'll go on down to the office and work on the books right away and come on over to your place as soon as I can." And I'll probably regret it, thirty minutes after I'm there.But hell, I'm not too smart.

The Portland house always reminded Bill of the chambers of an exclusive men's club all maroon and mahogany, but unlike a men's club, it looked unused like those furnished alcoves in a bank with tables that no one ever touched and chairs that no one ever sat in.

Even the rumpus room in the basement was gloomy. Gloomy in spite of the colorful lamp—someone had told him it was a Tiffany, whatever that was supposed to mean—that hung over the poker table, and the floor lamps by the leather sofa and chairs.

The Scotts were there. The Fultons were there. E.P.'s current attachment, Harvey Mendisonn, a rangy, horse-faced mortician recently divorced from his wife of twenty years, had taken on the role of host of the party. And Joanie Foster.

Well, it didn't take long to figure that one out. Wasn't that sweet? Bill was unhappily sardonic. Some busybody had decided it would be nice to pair up good old Bill with poor little Joanie. Why the hell couldn't people mind their own business instead of meddling in other people's lives?

As a general rule, Bill thought serious poker playing ought to be left to the men. Women tended to gossip during play or ask dumb questions. E.P. was an exception. She played poker like a man. And Joanie was an exception because she was a natural competitor. She played everything, even a game of double solitaire, to win. However, this night, Bill noticed, she played with no intensity, almost disinterestedly.

"If I owned his house," Esther Scott said in an aside to Bill while Scott was shuffling and dealing, "I'd pitch all this old dark furniture and replace it with blonde furniture. That's the latest. And I'd paint the walls yellow and orange."

Bill couldn't figure that one out. "Striped or polka dot?"

Esther looked at Bill like he was the class dummy. "I'd paint the top half yellow and the bottom part orange."

Gloom would be better, Bill thought, but said, "Gotta have sunshine all the time, don't we?"

Esther laid a heavy hand on Bill's arm. "You and I think alike, honey."

If that's true, then I'm in really big trouble, Bill figured.

Bill liked poker, and he was holding good cards and winning so he was actually having a good time. Until Harvey dealt an exotic game, what Bill called cutesy poker. Then it turned into a contest to see who could call the craziest deals. Bill would have left, but he had won so much that it would be crass to fold up and leave. So he hung in.

Conversation gradually became more important than cards, and when E.P. asked to be dealt out so she could bring in a surprise, there was Harvey at her elbow to assist her, and the game broke up.

Withdrawn and chain smoking, Joanie sat with wide, staring eyes, unwilling or unable to interact with those in the room. Bill was not the only one who recognized her dark mood. Helen and Esther barraged her with chatter as though talk were an antidote to grief.

An unfamiliar, piquant aroma drifted into the room. Good enough to make Bill decide to stick around.

"My God, what's that woman cooking?" Steamboat was also struck by the tempting aroma. "What is that, Helen? What's she cooking?"

"I don't know, Bobby." Helen was patient. "Something delicious, I'm sure."

"Yeah. Well, why would you know? All you know how to do in a kitchen is open cans." Helen stared at her husband, and Steamboat laughed to make his comment sound like a joke.

Even the dour Scott was animated. "If it's as good as it smells, I hope E.P.'s got a lot of it."

Harvey brought out a linen table cloth for the poker table, set places and brought out a fresh pitcher of beer.

E.P. came in bearing an enormous, round, flat tray. "You are all winners tonight," she announced. "It's pizza, guys and gals. I had it in New York, and I ate myself sick.And Dietmeier, you'll be happy to know that it is better with beer."

Bill admitted to himself that beer and pizza were good together.

"This is a winner," Scott declared. "We ought to consider putting pizza in the snack bar of the bowling alley." Good luck had finally come Scott's way. He was going to be the manager of the new bowling alley that was being built by Steamboat and Harvey. At last he was going to be able to get out of the factory.

"Eat up, girl," E.P. said to Joanie, "or don't you like pizza?"

Bill had been watching Joanie forcing down bites of food. He suddenly felt so sorry for her that he lost his appetite.

"This pizza kinda reminds me of that stuff we had the night us kids had that wiener roast out at Bloomby's Camp." Steamboat said, " and old man Bloomby put meat and stuff on one of those stick things…"

"Skewer," Helen prompted.

"…yeah, skewer, and roasted it like kebas, kebabs whatever you call it; you remember how good they were? Remember how you girls used to wear one of your dad's dress shirts hanging out over blue jeans? Remember? And Polly Emhuff got too close to the fire and the tail end of her shirt caught fire and blazed up before you could say jack robinson and, Bill,you remember how you pulled her down in the dirt and rolled her around to put out the fire? By damn, that was quick thinking."

"Polly wasn't hurt. But she moaned and groaned about ruining her dad's good shirt until you took your shirt off and gave it to Polly and put her burned one on. Did old Pastor Emhuff ever find out about that?"

"Boy, those were the days."

"We were a wild bunch, weren't we?" And remarks like that kept Bill from having to answer Steamboat's question. When he thought about Polly and what E.P. had said about her, his stomach cramped, and he pushed aside his plate.

"You haven't finished, have you, Dietmeier?" Harvey asked.

"I'm trying to get down to fighting size," Bill answered.

"Quit bragging," E.P. called out. "You're not much heavier than you were in high school."

"Are you still living at home with your folks?" Harvey asked Bill.

"I wanted to move in with E.P, but her parents wouldn't let me."

Steamboat heehawed. "I hear there's a lot of beds Dietmeier could put his shoes under. Now that doesn't include my wife. She's got all she can handle with yours truly."

Having not taken even a passive interest in the banter, Joanie turned to Bill.

"Will you take me home, Bill? My car is in for repairs."

Now isn't this just lucky-ducky. Her car just happens to be in for repairs. Wonder whose idea all of this was? "Sure, Joanie, I'll give you ride home."

Bill asked her, when they were in the car, "Do you want to go to your father's house?"

"No, no. I want to go to our...my house."

The neighborhood was dark, and the house was even darker. Bill walked Joanie to the front door where she fumbled in her purse, trying to find the key, and then had difficulty with the lock. Bill took the key from her hand and unlocked the door.

Besides being cold, the house emitted the stale odor that comes from being closed up for a long time. She had come here on impulse.

"Are you sure you want to stay here?" he asked.

"Yes." The answer was almost a whisper.

"Then let's set the thermostat up and get some heat in the place." As many times as Bill had been in the house, he had no idea where the thermostat was located. "Where is it?"

"What?"

"The thermostat. Where is it?"

"On the south wall in the dining room."

She acts like a zombie, Bill thought, as he set up the thermostat. He waited until the furnace clicked on. He waited until the blower kicked in. "Well, you've got heat now."

Joanie was shivering on the couch, seeming to merely be waiting for him to leave."Thanks for everything, Bill. For being Kellan's friend. For being my friend."

"Sure." Bill had no intention of getting into any conversation that smacked of intimate, personal situations. "Hang in there, kid. I'm on my way home. You sleep tight and don't let the bedbugs bite."

"Goodbye, Bill."

Bill left her, sitting on the couch with her mink coat draped around her shoulders like she was waiting to go somewhere.

He got in his car and started the engine. Something was screwy about the scene.*Goodbye, Bill.* Like it was the end of the world. He shut down the car and sprinted back to the house. Expecting the door to be locked he half fell inside when it opened with a push. Through the openness of the living room and dining room, Bill saw Joanie at the sink with a glass in her hand. Dashing to her, he caught her right hand and forced a cache of capsules to spill out. She spoke with a sobbing voice, "Oh, Bill, I've been saving those until I had enough to go to sleep and never wake up."

She wept uncontrollably, god- awful wails from the depths of her being. Bill acted instinctively with silent, tactile comforting, getting her into the living room and holding her on his lap as though she were a child. Very slowly, the crying became a whimper, and the whimper subsided into an occasional hiccup, and finally she slept.

Then Bill thought about the predicament he was in. How the hell am I going to get out of this mess? Phone Dr. Welles to come and get her? Take her to the emergency room? Take her home and tell Mom to talk some sense into her? He shifted her weight a bit. Naw, I can't do any of that. Is any of this my responsibility? Bill looked over at the mink coat spread out on the couch and remembered the time—a hundred years ago—when he had the wild notion that he would trap enough minks to have a coat made for Polly. He had told his dad that he wanted to trap to make some extra money, but his dad discouraged him, telling him how an animal would chew off its own leg to escape from a trap. Nothing would do him, but to set out a trap at Dad's old farm. He caught a muskrat. The animal was caught between the shoulders when Bill found it, alive and suffering.

He shot the muskrat, and never set another trap. Bill looked down at Joanie's puffy face. I can't shoot you, and I don't know how to help you. Joanie stirred and opened her eyes.

"What am I going to do with you?" Bill asked. "Put you on a leash?

You sure scared the hell out of me."

"I'm sorry."

"Sorry isn't the answer to our problem."

"Have you never wanted to.to end it all, Bill?"

"I don't think I have that option."

"Your religion?"

"Something like that."

"The worst part for me was coming home from Europe. Realizing that Kellan was not here, and that I would never see him again."

"Okay. So now you know. Now you know you've got to get on with your life.You've always been a fighter, Joanie."

"There's nothing to fight for."

"What am I going to do with you?" It was as serious a question as he had ever asked in his life. "If you are possessed with the idea of taking your own life, you'll find a way. And I don't want to let that happen, but how can I keep you from it?

And if you do destroy the life God gave you, I'll have to live with guilt the rest of my life. And I don't want that. I want to wake up in the mornings with nothing more on my mind than wondering if the fish will bite or if I can get to the track in time to bet the double." Bill stopped. He was saying the wrong words. Talking too much. "You always keep your promises, don't you, Joanie?"

"Important promises, yes."

"Promise me that if you ever think about taking your life, you'll tell me first. And I promise you that I will do nothing whatsoever to stop you." I'm not making sense; that's about the stupidest thing a man ever said. "What I'm trying to say is I want to help you. So if you promise to tell me, I'll know that you'll let me help you. Kellan wants you to be happy and live out your life."

Bill pushed her hair out of her face and stroked its softness. "Be strong," he said, and then like everything was normal he said in his carefree way, " and one more promise. Promise not to wake me up in the morning with any bad news; I want to sleep in."

"I promise."

"Thata girl. Now I'm going to take you home to your daddy who ought to spank your fanny. But if it's left up to me, he nor any one else in the world will ever know what happened in this house tonight, unless you tell them."

Joanie turned in his arms and clung to him for a moment. "You are my strong friend," she said. "My rock."

The Dietmeier warehouse in the early morning looked as it had on Saturday. The trucks were backed into the loading docks, ready for the day. Inside, the office was just as it had been when Bill locked up at noon last Saturday.

Bill worked quickly at his desk. It was amazing how much he could accomplish when he didn't have to put up with people. And that included his dad. Bill could run the business twice as efficiently and make more money if his dad would retire and let him run things. But it was Dad's business. And Dad wasn't about to retire. As for his brothers, Bill knew that Karl would never make it to the Big Leagues, but he seemed pretty interested in physical therapy. Max was going into optometry, and if anyone knew what Burt would do, he should be in the stock market.

Maybe I ought to do something else, Bill thought. Like what? He could laugh every time he remembered how Teacher Werke used to encourage him to go to seminary and become a pastor when he caused more trouble than any other kid in class. He never made up his mind what he wanted to do. Then the war came along and the Navy gave him a career. Then he ended up with a degree in business because he had more hours in that than any other course. I guess I'm where I belong.

Sitting in the Dietmeier Warehouse, pushing beer. Refereeing basketball games at high schools. He remembered how Joanie memorized the whole damn official's book so she could show off.

The thought of Joanie stopped Bill's rambling mind, and a feeling of uneasiness hit him like a swirl of dust on a country road, choking and stifling. I can't help her. I wish I could. Wish I could get her off my mind.

"Some son-of-a-bitch slashed a tire on every one of our trucks." Bill's dad stood in the open door, letting in a gust of cold air and a salvo of cursing.

"Ah, shit!" Bill said loud and vehemently. Mel Skerven.

"Somebody's pissed off at the Dietmeiers. Is anybody pissed off at you?"

"Not that I know of. It's random vandalism, I suppose."

"I'd sure like to take a ball bat to the ornery sneak that did this."

"Or sneaks."

"Son, are you sure that no one has a grudge against you?"

"Me? Hell, Dad, if I ran for mayor, I'd get elected unanimously."

About half past four, when the men at the feed mill got off work, Bill went down to Blackie's Tavern, a narrow dump with dingy booths along one wall and a long bar with bar stools on the other. At the back there was a juke box between two closed doors, one marked Gents and the other Ladys. The whole place smelled of cigarette smoke and stale grease. On a day when the wind was right, a person could smell Blackie's Tavern all the way to the courthouse.

Mel was in his usual spot, the first stool where he could watch passers-by through the smeared plate glass window and talk to Blackie, who, between service, leaned on the cash register. Although Mel was about Bill's age, there were deep furrows in his brow, and lines ran down either side of his mouth. A dirty railroad cap was pushed back on his oily, black hair. He also stank. Bill sat down beside him.

With a laid back demeanor, Bill asked, "How's it going, Mel?"

Mel was instantly on the defensive. "What the fuck is it to you?"

"I thought you might be able to tell me who slashed the tires on our delivery trucks."

Mel glowered. "Don't know nothing about your damned tires."

"Yes, you do, you bastard." Bill kept a quiet, civil tone. "And I ought to take you out in the alley and beat the shit out of you."

Mel turned so that his sour breath hit Bill in the face, and growled, "Yeah? You and who else you cock suc..."

Bill landed a blow on Mel's chin that banged his head on the corner of the cash register. The railroad cap dropped on the floor. Before Mel had righted himself, he pulled a switchblade from his pocket and pointed the ugly blade at Bill's stomach. With a motion so swift it was almost imperceptible, Bill sliced a blow that chopped Mel's wrist, and the knife dropped to the floor.

Bill picked up the knife. "What are you trying to do with that fucking knife? Get yourself sent to the pen for assault with a deadly weapon?"

The tavern was as quiet as church. No man so much a lifted a bottle. If a fight ensued, the patrons didn't want to miss a thing. A trickle of blood ran from Mel's mouth, and he wiped at it with his dirty sleeve.

"Now you listen to me," Bill said. "Dad's got two witnesses that are ready to swear that they saw you cutting the tires on our trucks. Now, I'm going to tell you how lucky you are. I told Dad that I hated to see you have to do time. You've got little kids at home that need a daddy." Bill waited to see if Mel had bought the story. Mel was breathing hard, mad as hell. "You know what, Skerven? You ought to thank me for doing you a favor. If it wasn't for me, you'd be in jail right now." Mel Skerven was stupid.

That there had been no interference from anyone in the place did not surprise Bill. Most of the men he could call by their first or last name, knew them one way or another. He would like to have bought a beer for the house, but that was too much like spreading largess. Mel's bluster was gone, and he looked like a whipped dog.

"Sit down, Mel, " Bill said as he himself sat down on a bar stool. "and let's you and me cool off." He handed Mel back his knife. "Bring us a couple of really cold beers, Blackie." For one of the few times in his life, beer did not taste good to Bill. But he stayed in the tavern, next to Mel, and drank his beer unhurriedly. Then he ordered another one for Mel. And left.

A couple of days later to alleviate the responsibility he felt for Joanie, Bill tried to contact her, only to learn that she had gone down to Green Forks.

"Joanie is visiting Mrs. Foster, Kellan's grandmother," Janet Smyth explained when Bill telephoned the Welles's residence. "We tried to discourage her from making the trip alone, but she insisted." Janet gave an apologetic sort of tut,tut. "And we all know how Joanie is, don't we?"

Bill wasn't certain that Janet really knew Joanie. But hell, nobody really knows another human being, he thought. We don't even know ourselves. The thought of Joanie being with Kellan's grandmother gave Bill a sense of relief. He didn't know exactly why.

Janet was continuing the conversation, speaking now rather confidently. "Dr.Welles, and I, too, for that matter—both of us are very concerned about Joanie. She's unable to come to terms with Kellan's death. It's as though she's lost all interest in herself and the world around her."

All Bill could think to say was, "Give her a little time. Joanie will make it." And he ended the conversation with, "Well, tell Joanie I called. I'll get back with her later."

Karl and his new wife, a girl he had married without benefit of a good old Dutch wedding, and who was now showing her pregnancy, came home in early December on leave. He liked the physical therapy that he was doing in the Army so much that he had definitely decided that when he was discharged, he would become a licensed physical therapist. The only person who was disappointed with Karl's decision was his father, who clung to the idea that his son would stay in baseball, make it to the big time. Karl was a realist. He knew that his best pitching years were the ones he was spending in the Army. Max got a weekend pass and came home, and Mrs. Dietmeier had a big family dinner for all the uncles and aunts and cousins. Burt telephoned while they were eating, and they all took a turn talking to him.

"This place is a hell hole," Burt told Bill, "but don't tell Mom." As though Mom might upset the entire military system by coming out to reform basic training.

The day passed so quickly it seemed that they had hardly said hello to Max, and Karl and his Dody, than they were at the train station saying good-bye.

What with one thing and another, Bill had missed too many days in hunting season, and there weren't very many days before the season closed. After everyone had gone, Bill said, "I'm going hunting tomorrow."

His dad discouraged the suggestion. "You know Mondays are busy days. I'll need you here."

"Look," Bill said jokingly, but he half meant it, "the only reason I work for you is so I can go hunting whenever I want to go."

The older man took his eyes off the television variety show and leaned over in his chair to face Bill. "I'd go with you, but I can't hunt all day anymore. And you'll want to hunt the whole day, won't you?"

"From daylight to dark." Bill didn't feel sorry for his dad because he knew if the older man really wanted to go hunting, he'd take the day off, and if he got tired, he'd have Bill bring him back to town.

"Well, there ain't much use to hunt anymore." There was regret in the old voice."No game. Used to be I could go out and bring back a bushel of quail. You'll be mighty lucky tomorrow if you can get the limit."

Bill knew his dad wasn't exaggerating about the number of quail that he used to bag when he was young. As soon as Bill was old enough to carry a gun, he had gone hunting with his dad, and even then, there was no problem finding a big covey Sometimes Bill seriously considered buying up land and letting it lie as a refuge for wild game. He had the money.

Money he had saved up for the time when he and Polly would get married.

He would force Polly out of his mind. That was best. He tried never to talk about her because he couldn't say the right things, and no one else could either.

In spite of his resolve, E.P.'s words came back to him. He wished he could take all the trash she had said about Polly and stuff it down her ugly, big mouth.

And mocking his resolve, in his mind he heard Polly say, *It's okay, Bill.* Everything was okay. That's what he had been taught, and that's what he believed. But he couldn't talk about that to other people either.

Tomorrow he was going hunting.

Bill hunted hard on Monday, and the dog worked well. By three o'clock he had the limit. All nice, big birds.

"There's not a shot in the breast of any of these birds," Bill's mom commented when she examined the dressed birds that Bill had laid out on the counter.

"That's because your son doesn't aim his gun at a bird's breast. He aims at the head."

She paid no attention to his bragging. "I'm going to invite Joanie up for a quail dinner."

"I thought I heard you say that you were sick and tired of cooking," Bill reminded her in reference to a remark she had made after the family dinner.

She ignored that remark also. "Joanie is crazy about quail, and I bet she hasn't tasted a bite of it since Kellan died. And don't say a word because I'm going to invite her whether you like it or not."

"I didn't say a word, Mom." He started to tease her. "You get so excited over everything, and you always…"

"Oh, shut up. I know what you're thinking."

Bill was thinking that he didn't want anyone arranging his life for him. Not even his mother.

As it turned out, Joanie was again out of town.

"She's gone to New York with that old E.P. to shop or see plays or something." Mrs. Dietmeier was scoffing, "What's wrong with the stores and such around here?"

Bill didn't see Joanie again until the Welles's Christmas bash.

The overly decorated Welles home had enough flowers for a funeral parlor. All that was needed was a well laid-out corpse for the nattily dressed guests to focus on. Janet Smyth was flitting around, playing the part of hostess, greeting guests, politely escorting Bill toward the dining room table. From the crystal bowl she ladled out a cup of eggnog and delicately transferred it to Bill's hand. Her hands were cold, but her cheeks were flushed with excitement, and she exuded happiness.

Bill winced as he eyed the distasteful cup that he held in his hand.

"Come with me to the kitchen and you can pour that down the drain." The voice was Joanie's. "We've got beer in the refrigerator."

She looked better. There was a smile on her face. Her hair had grown out. She was still thin, but she didn't look so emaciated as she had the last time they were together.

"You're looking great," Bill said as they went into the kitchen.

"Don't I always?"

Her spunk was back, and he said, "Hell, yes," with unfeigned enthusiasm as he poured the eggnog down the drain like a libation to the gods. "Obviously, New York must have agreed with you."

"We saw the latest musicals—*Guys and Dolls* was great, shopped. I may go back and look for a job. After Charles and Janet's wedding."

"You're kidding me."

"No I am not kidding."

"About going back to New York or about your dad marrying Janet?"

"The New York thing just popped into my head. But Charles and Janet are getting married. I can't understand...the age thing...and she's so, so passionless."

"You never know. Hey, she may be a red hot sex pot under the sheets."

"You speak from experience?" Joanie kidded.

"I was speaking academically."

"I thought you would say, none of your damn business."

"None of your damn business."

"Oh, god, it's good to be with you. Anywhere but here. If I could, I'd leave and let Janet do her thing. Whatever that is."

"Let's go."

"I'll get a coat."

"Here," said Bill taking off his suit coat and putting it on Joanie. This is almost a full length coat on you."

"Won't you get cold?"

"The car has a heater, hon," he answered with amusing irony. "Besides, I don't get cold unless the temperature is heading toward zero." Taking the bottle of beer, he nudged Joanie forward and they skipped out the back door to Bill's car.

"We'll drive out in the country. We might see a covey of quail cross the road or a rabbit." Bill's thinking was that if he had to be out, he might as well scout around for good places to hunt. Quail season would be over at the end of the month but rabbit season would be open until the end of January. "Do you have any particular place you want to go?"

"No, no particular place." She waited a few moments before she said, as though she were reading a script. "I'm all right now, Bill. I know that I could never in a million years do anything violent with a knife or a gun. That night all I wanted to do was go to sleep and never wake up."

Bill chewed on her words not understanding exactly what she meant and not knowing what to say. He said, "That's good news."

"You know," she went on, "that I went down to Kentucky and spent a few days with Grandmother Foster. She talked about Kellan. I talked about Kellan over and over and she listened. Grandmother told me how she felt

209

when she lost her husband so early in their marriage. She was comforting and inspiring. My visit with her did more for me than traveling over Europe with a broken heart."

"You'll be okay, Joanie. Want a swallow of beer?"

She took the proffered brown bottle, drank, and handed it back to Bill.

From habit, without a thought, because women so often left lipstick on the mouth of a bottle, Bill automatically wiped off the rim with his fngers.

"Bill Dietmeier!" Joanie exhorted. "Do you think I'm poison?"

"I was afraid I would get pregnant."

She giggled at his outrageously stupid absurdity. Then complained, "Damn, I forgot my cigarettes and you don't smoke anymore."

"Want to go back?"

"I never want to go back. And I am not a slave to cigarettes." But she followed that sweeping statement with, "Do you think someone might have left some cigarettes somewhere in your car?"

"There might be an ancient pack in the glove compartment. I haven't cleaned it out since I quit smoking."

She made a fruitless search about the car and then opened the glove compartment and a stash of old church bulletins fell out. No cigarettes. "What kind of prize to you get for saving the most church bulletins?"

"I'm not allowed to tell. You have to be a Lutheran to get in on secrets like that."

"I've heard about you Lutherans. Slaughtering lambs."

"We don't slaughter lambs but we have secret orgies."

"And you are the director of orgies."

"No," Bill said earnestly, "Mom is."

After they both stopped laughing, Joanie said, "I've got a favor to ask of you, Bill. You won't like it, but if…oh, look; it's snowing."

The first fat dollops of a wet snow were plopping on the hood and windshield. Bill turned on the wipers. "This is the kind of snow that ruins bird hunting."

"Why?"

"Makes the birds spooky. They don't hold. And dogs can't smell in wet snow worth a damn. Not a fresh snow like this." He turned the wipers on high. "What kind of favor, Joanie?"

"Will you be my escort for Charles's wedding?"

It could have been worse, but not very much worse. "Sure. No problem." What else could he say?

"The wedding ceremony will be private. In Charles's living room. But the reception will be at the country club. Full course dinner, orchestra, for all their friends." She huddled down in Bill's coat as if for protection. "I think my father is making the biggest mistake of his life. So does Miss Eddie, but she won't say anything. I've said too much. But it didn't do any good."

"I know you have never liked Janet, but give her a chance. I personally think it will work out all right."

"But the age difference!"

"Hell, Joanie, Janet was born old. She's the kind of girl who can spend a Sunday afternoon listening to classical records."

"How do you know?"

"Because she once asked me to come over to her apartment and spend Sunday afternoon listening to Bach or somebody."

"And of course you rushed right over."

"If memory serves me correctly, that was the afternoon I had to help my uncle count the bricks on his house."

In a very short time the world had turned white. Snow had covered the road, he roofs of barns and houses, the fields, and was filling the ditches. We'd better head back to town," Bill suggested.

There was no place to turn around so he decided to drive to the next intersection take a left then a right and be headed oward town. Before he got to the intersection a deer jumped toward the car and Bill swerved to miss the deer and the result was two wheels on the passenger side in the ditch.

"Are you all right, sweetheart? he asked.

"Of course."

"You're sure?"

"All I need is a cigarette."

Bill knew, before he got out of the car to survey the situation that it would take a tractor to pull them out. Even so, he got out anyway and stood beside the car and cussed the deer, the car, and himself for getting into such a miserable situation.

He got back into the car. "I didn't know I was such a damned poor driver. I should have let you drive the car."

Joanie brushed the snow off his hair and brushed at getting the snow off his shirt, but that only aggravated his anger, and he hit the steering wheel with his fist. He started the engine and tried a forward gear but the wheels spun uselessly. He put it in reverse and the wheels spun uselessly. He tried rocking it out by quickly putting the car first in one gear and then another. All he was doing was plowing deeper into the rut. The nearest house was a quarter of a mile away. All he could do was get out and walk up to the farm house. If no one was home, he hoped that there was a tractor in the barn with a key in the ignition. If. If he had had any sense he wouldn't have started out with a girl in flimsy dress and no coat. In half an hour it would be dark. He had no choice. Joanie insisted he put on the coat. She would keep the engine going so she could stay warm from the heater.

The snow had accumulated until it was over his shoe tops. If he had on his hunting clothes, he would be dry and warm.

But here he was, caught in a snow storm in a dress suit and dress shoes.

Before he got to the farm house the snow had changed to sleet, and a hard wind blew sharp needles of ice into his face.

His skin stung with the pelting, and his eyes watered. He thanked God for strong legs and stamina.

No one answered his knock at the front or back door of the house. He plodded across the barnyard to a shed that looked like it could house a tractor. It did. A green John Deere. With no key.

His toes and fingers ached with the cold. Should he break into the house and use their telephone? If he headed for the next farm, he might freeze before he got there.Then he knew what he would do. Go back to the car and build a big fire alongside the road. That ought to bring any farmer that could see out of his hole. There weren't any cigarettes in the car, but he knew there were all kinds of matches that he had picked up in taverns and bars. There were all those old bulletins to get a flame going.

Bill started back. His feet were freezing. His pants felt like he had peed in them. His hands were numb. He was too miserable to regret those bragging words about never being cold.

He heard the noise of an automobile approaching behind him. He stopped in his tracks to wait for it.

The car was an old Forty-one Chevy like Kellan used to have.

A cloudy window rolled down, and Mel Skerven stuck his head out. "Where you headed, Dietmeier?"

"Just out for a Sunday stroll."

"Get in. A man could freeze his balls off on a day like this."

Bill got in, too grateful to be offended by the fetid, musty smell of the interior. He pointed down the road. "That crate down there in the ditch is my car."

"Were you drunk?"

"No. Just stupid. And there's a girl in the car waiting for me."

"I thought uppity-ups like you took girls to motels. Didn't know you parked alongside a country road."

"Hell, Mel, you get whatever you can, wherever you can."

"Lordy, Lordy, don't I know it. I got me a juicy one now. I get out this way to see her about oncet a week——when I can get away from my old lady—knows how to put out, that girl does." Mel stopped the car near Bill's. "I got a chain in the trunk."

"You're a smarter bastard than I am," Bill said. "I ain't got a chain. Hell, I don't even have an overcoat."

Bill helped Mel attach the chain to the two cars and got back in his own car.

The wheels of Mel's car spun on the snow, hit gravel, and then with a violent lurch Bill's car was out of the ditch and on the road.

"Good old Forty-on Chevys," Joanie said.

Bill got out to thank Mel and offer to pay.

"Don't want your money. But say, after the favor I've did you, you'll sell me a case on Sunday if I had a need, wouldn't you?" Mel grinned like a winner and showed the gap of a missing tooth.

"Can't do that, Mel. But you sure as hell can expect to see a case or two of beer sitting on your doorstep."

"Well, take it easy," Mel said, getting back into his car. "And the next time you want to park with a pretty girl, don't get so close to the shitty ditch."

Joanie had heard Mel's last words and asked, "Did he think we were making out?"

"Yes. And I was happy to let him think it."

"Poor Bill. There goes your reputation."

She could afford to be funny. Her hands and feet weren't aching.

Joanie was smart enough to realize the he was in too much misery to want to talk, and they rode in silence.

I love this girl, Bill admitted to himself. "Joanie,....she started to speak He deferred to her. "Go ahead."

"I was thinking of how cold it gets at Grandmother Foster's. They have no heat in the upstairs bedrooms. The first time I stayed there in the wintertime and crawled in bed, it was so cold it took my breath away. I couldn't have slept if I hadn't Kellan to keep me warm. Kellan..." she didn't finish. "What were you going to say?"

"If the deer that the conservation department turned loose a few years ago keep reproducing like they are now, the state will have to open up a deer season."

"If that happens, will you hunt deer?"

"Probably. I'll hunt anything that's legal." Except you, hon. I won't mess up your life anymore than it's already fouled up.

Charles Welles and Janet Smyth were married on the last Friday in December at six-thirty in the evening in Dr. Welles's living room. In attendance were Janet's immediate family, Miss Eddie, Joanie and Bill.

Janet's father was roundness personified. He had a round, bald head so shiny it reflected the light from the bright candles, round bulging blue eyes behind rimless glasses, a roundish mouth, and a round belly. Mrs. Smyth would have been round also had she not been corseted and girdled into a shape that nature never intended. She was pale and blue-eyed with fluffy blue-white hair on which perched a round little blue hat with a veil. Little sister—Mayline, Maydine, May something—Bill never caught her exact name—was twelve years old and would undoubtedly some day look like her older sister. Older brother Jonathan was an anomaly. Tall and rangy, he had a full red beard that did not match his brownish hair. He was reticent to the point of being uncommunicative, and Bill thought he might be mentally retarded until someone said Jonathan was studying horticulture at the University of Minnesota. Perhaps he talked with plants instead of people.

Miss Eddie, strange old bird, hovered in the background, not quite family but too close to be omitted from the wedding ceremony. She did not look joyful or even comfortable as the vows were exchanged.

Who could not call Joanie beautiful?

The reception began with a champagne toast to the newly weds, followed by a shrimp cocktail appetizer and a full course dinner. Including the cutting of an elaborate wedding cake. With proper background music. An orchestra played popular tunes for dancing, and there was an open bar for drinking.

Shortly before Janet and Charles were to bid goodbye to the guests and depart on their honeymoon, Dr. Welles turned to Bill and asked him to dance with Janet. "I want to say goodbye to my daughter privately."

And he really meant privately for he disappeared with Joanie into some other part of the clubhouse.

"Charles," Janet said, pulling back from Bill to talk to him as they danced a slow number, "is taking this opportunity to tell Joanie about his new will."

"Is that right?" Bill could care less about Dr. Welles's new will.

"Yes. He's so rational, so thorough. The bulk of his estate, should something happen to him—God forbid—will be divided equally between Joanie and me, with provisions for various eventualities."

Children? Bill would have asked if he were feeling mean.

Janet giggled nervously. "Am I being macabre on my wedding night?"

"I guess," Bill said nonchalantly, "you can be anyway you want to be on your wedding night."

Janet, perhaps feeling she had been indiscreet, said, "I only mentioned the will to elucidate Charles's farsightedness and impartiality."

Bill had never figured Janet for a schemer. But the smell of dollars was a mighty powerful lure. Hell, maybe she's just got a fetish for old men.

The slow rhythms that Bill and Janet danced to, dragged to a close. When the orchestra began a piece with a new, fast- paced beat, the older couples quickly left the floor and that included Bill and Janet who went back to the bridal table.

Bill saw Charles and Joanie, arm in arm, also coming toward the table. I'd lay down a hundred dollars, Bill said to himself, that the good doctor has finagled a way to put aside a healthy sum for Joanie that Janet doesn't know about and will never know about.

At the proper moment, Charles Welles and his new bride, with proper thanks and proper good wishes to everyone; said their thanks and good wishes and everyone applauded and said goodbye to the newly weds who were leaving on their honeymoon to Hawaii.

Guests began to depart until only the hard-core party goers were left. And Joanie, the hostess, would stay until the last guest left. And Bill who could think of better things to do, would stay as long as she did.

"I'm a little drunk," Joanie said to Bill. "Do I show it?"

"What does it matter? Everyone else is drunk, too. Except me." He was serious.

At twelve-thirty the orchestra played *Goodnight, Sweetheart* and started packing up their instruments. Steamboat drunkenly tried to collect money to get the orchestra to play another hour, but the idea fizzled.

Finally, Joanie and Bill followed the last guests, E.P. and Harvey Mendisonn, out the door.

Limp and tired, Joanie rested her head against the seat of the car. "It was a wonderful reception, wasn't it, Bill?"

"One of the best."

"I love parties, don't you, Bill?" She didn't wait for a reply. "And don't you think this was a beautiful occasion?"

"Everything was beautiful."

"You're one of the beautiful people of the whole world, Bill, you know that, don't you?"

"I thought I was one of the smart people of the world," he answered.

"Smart. And beautiful. One of the world's wonderful people. Really."

"Really and truly?" Bill was being indulgent with a girl who had had one or two drinks to many.

"And I've never thanked you for everything you've done for me."

"You don't have to thank me for anything." They were in front of the Welles house, and he stopped and turned off the engine.

Joanie leaned against Bill, and put her hand on his face. "We love you, Bill. You know what I mean."

"You're kind of a special person yourself, Joanie."

"I owe you so much." She kissed his face. "Hold me."

He held her. Felt the two of them could laugh at the world and make a go of it Felt desire swell up in him. Touched her shoulder. And stopped. It wouldn't be fair.

"Everything is spinning, Bill. Two of everything. Even you. How am I ever going to get up in the morning and see the whoever they are off to wherever it is they go. Back to somewhere."

Bill helped her out of the car, walked her to the house. And without asking, took her inside and upstairs to her room. "You can stay the night," she said as she kicked her shoes off and tumbled into bed.

In the morning she would never even remember saying those words.

What might have been was over before it began.

Two days later, Bill found an earring in his car. It looked like fine jewelry to him so he stopped by the Welleses's to return it.

"Joanie's gone to Florida," Miss Eddie told Bill. "But that's her earring. I'm certain." She seemed to want to talk. "I don't think Joanie wanted to be here when Doctor and Janet return. I, myself, would be gone, but Doctor begged me to stay on. Well, Mr. and Mrs. Warwick invited Joanie to go down to Florida with them, and I encouraged her to do so. 'It'll do you a world of good to get away from here and think things out,' is what I told her."

"I agree." Bill didn't know what he had agreed to, but it ended the conversation.

Business slumped in January which was to Bill's advantage since his referreeing schedule was tightly packed. February wasn't a hell of a lot better as far as business was concerned, but he was assigned to referee a Sectional game in Indianapolis. With a little luck, he might get a Regional.

Bill knew that Joanie had returned from Florida, and he figured if she wanted to see him she knew his address and phone number. Later he heard that she had taken a job with one of the department stores in Indy. Modeling.

Bill did not get a Regional. It hurt because he knew that there wasn't an official in the State of Indiana who was better than he was.

216

His dad was philosophical. "It all boils down to who you know. That's the way the world works. You have to know the right people at the right time. It's not the end of the world."

Just the end of the season.

Just another disappointment.

Caught in the doldrums of boredom and disappointment, Bill decided he needed a change of scene. But before he could decide what he wanted to do and where he wanted to go, he met Madalyn.

He was the last in line, and she was in the teller's cage at the bank. Brown eyes, brown hair, and a million dollar smile. When it was Bill's turn, he pushed the deposit slip and money bag under the cage and said, "Where have you been all my life?"

She smiled. "Right here."

"No, you haven't. I come to the bank every Friday."

"I've been working here two and a half weeks."

"How could I have missed a smile like yours?"

Apparently pleased with the attention, she smiled and said, "I know who you are."

"You should, if you can read. It says Dietmeier Distributing Company on the deposit slip."

She was working the adding machine. "I mean I know that you are **the** Bill Dietmeier."

"And I know you are the Madalyn Louis. It says so on your nameplate. Is it Miss or Mrs.?"

"Miss," she said swiftly, flashing him a smile.

"Good. When can we get together, Miss Madalyn?"

She pushed his receipt and the empty money sack back to him. "Tonight?"

Bill had expected her to be somewhat diffident. "Tonight," he agreed. "We'll go out for dinner. Where do you live?"

"I live at 148 1/2 West Second Street. Should I dress up?"

Bill was indifferent to that question. "Whatever. I'll pick you up at seven."

She lived in a little apartment that had been made out of a couple of rooms of a large old house. Her side entrance gave the half to 148. She shared the apartment, she told Bill, with another girl who worked at the hospital until eleven.

"Where are you from, Madalyn?" Bill asked as he helped her on with her coat.

"Most recently in Indianapolis. That's where I went to business school." Then she added, "I'm kind of local. I was raised out near Pleasantfields."

"I know where that is." Pleasantfields was about seventeen miles out of town, less than that, maybe, just across the county line. It consisted of a school, a general store with gasoline pumps, a sawmill and a church. There was supposed to be good hunting around Pleasantfields.

Madalyn locked the door of her apartment and tried the knob to test its security.

Bill had not seen anything in the apartment that anyone would want to steal. Maybe she had money hidden away. A bank teller with her own money under the mattress?

Bill took her to the country club for the simple reason the club had the best food in town.

"Oh, gee," she moaned, as Bill guided her into the dining room and to a table. "if you had told me we were coming to the country club, I'd have dressed up." She was wearing a skirt and blouse with a cardigan sweater.

"There's nothing wrong with what you are wearing. You look nice. Besides, this is nothing more than a little one-horse country club. A bunch of local people trying to impress each other."

She did not seem reassured. "This is the first time I've ever been in a country club."

"Well, you'd better get used to it because I come here a lot."

The waitress was at their table. Which was the best thing about the country club. The service was prompt.

"What would you like to drink?" Bill asked Madalyn.

She hesitated. "Should I order a Tom Collins?"

"Order anything you like."

Madalyn seemed nervous. Ill at ease.

Leaning across the table and speaking in just above a whisper, Madalyn asked Bill, "Isn't that Miss Portland in the far corner, on your left?"

Bill took note. "Yeah, that's E.P. If we're lucky, maybe she won't notice us."

"And to think, her father is president of the bank where I work. Who is she with?"

"The funeral director. What's-his-name. Harvey Mendisonn."

"He's divorced, isn't he?"

"What the hell difference does it make?" Bill spoke in his usual manner, and Madalyn reacted as though he had reprimanded her.

Clara came back with their drinks, a beer and a Tom Collins. "Are you ready to order now? she asked as though they should indeed be ready. "If you are, the prime rib is better than the T-bones, and the chicken kiev is not very good." She looked impatient as if they dare not put off ordering another minute.

Madalyn hesitated.

"While she's making up her mind," Bill said of Madalyn, "I'll have the trout with whatever you want to bring with it."

Madalyn ordered prime rib. Then she explained to Bill. "I was going to order steak, but she said I shouldn't. And I don't like fish. I'm afraid of bones."

"Don't let Clara intimidate you. She's been working here for so long she thinks she owns the place. She's bossy to everyone."

"Does she boss you around?"

"Everyone bosses me around."

"Really?"

Is she going to take every word I utter for Gospel? Bill was not accustomed to explaining each and every sentence he uttered. He rationalized. Madalyn was young and inexperienced. "I was exaggerating," Bill said.

"I wanted to get a job and stay in Indianapolis," Madalyn remarked, "but the living costs were too high. I love big cities."

"I wouldn't live in a city if they paid me a thousand dollar a week."

"Really...who's that couple coming into the dining room?"

"The Fultons." And then because he thought he had been too abrupt with her, he added, "Helen Fulton's father is chairman of the board of the Citizens National, your bank's rival." The Cordets were coming in directly behind the Fultons so Bill identified them.

"I know who they are. Mrs. Cordet does their banking at our bank. You wouldn't believe how picky she is. She almost made me cry. I called her Mrs. Cor-det and she bawled me out and said her name was Cor-day."

"I believe it," Bill said absently, his mind on his own interests. "I understand that there is good grouse hunting out around Pleasantfields. Have you seen any grouse out where you live?"

"I don't know what a grouse is."

"A grouse is... " he didn't finish because the Fultons and the Cordets has stopped at their table. He made introductions, quickly angered because Phyllis Cordet gave no indication that she had ever before set eyes on Madalyn. Friendly Clem, on the other hand, made mention of having seen Madalyn in the bank.

Helen was her poised and gracious self, and as usual, Steamboat was loud and blustery. He laid a hand on Madalyn's shoulder and said, "Gotta watch this ugly Dietmeier. He might take advantage of a pretty girl like you." Helen was glaring at him. Steamboat laughed. "Just kidding, sweetie."

After the couples were out of earshot, Madalyn was full of questions. "Why do they call him Steamboat? Aren't Mrs. Fulton's light blue eyes beautiful? I wish I had black hair like hers. She and her husband are really different, aren't they?

Where are Mr. and Mrs. Cordet from? He has a real Southern accent. He's so nice and she's so mean. Why are they so different?"

"Husbands and wives are supposed to be different. That's what makes it fun." Madalyn blushed.

"And no more of this Mr. and Mrs. business. These people are my friends and therefore your friends."

Their salads came. Madalyn ate daintily. Even so, she accidentally pushed a piece of lettuce off the plate onto the white tablecloth. She retrieved the errant lettuce and put it back on the salad plate. Then she wiped at the spot with her napkin. She didn't finish her salad.

Bill had recommended the house dressing. Maybe she didn't like it. Joanie thought the country club house dressing was the best of the best. No sooner than he thought of Joanie than he saw her, moving in her effortless, seductive way as she accompanied her father and Janet into the dining room. She came directly to Bill and greeted him with a kiss. And if her walk was seductive, her kiss was merely friendly.

Bill introduced Madalyn to Joanie who, Bill knew all too well, could be distant.

Joanie begged off joining them at table. "But tell me, Bill, did you get a Regional this year?"

"Ouch."

"Sorry."

"Maybe next year. If I'm still refereeing. Are you living in Indy? I was told you were doing modeling."

"No, not living in Indy. There was very little modeling to do. And I am not a sales clerk. I'm thinking New York now."

When Joanie had given Bill a little hug and left, Madalyn asked, "Did you used to go with her?"

"No, Madalyn. She was married to a good friend of mine who was killed in Korea. She's having a rough time."

"I wish I was as cute as she is."

Bill had never thought of Joanie as cute. Didn't even like the word. Didn't think he'd used that word since the sixth grade. As for Madalyn, he thought he ought to say something to please her so he said, "You've got something she doesn't have. You've got a million dollar smile."

After dinner, Madalyn wanted to go bowling. So Bill accommodated her. The lanes were all taken.

"I'll put you down for the first open lane," Scott said. "Go on in the bar and enjoy yourselves. I'll page you when there's an open lane."

In the bar Bill ordered two beers.

He was amused at Madalyn courageously sipping at the beer. It was obvious as hell that she liked beer about as much as a bottle of poison. "Why didn't you tell me you don't like beer?"

"I'm trying to learn to like it."

"Why?"

"Because your family sells beer."

Bill caught himself before he said, that's stupid. Madalyn was young and naive. "I'll get you a Coke," he said and went to the bar to fetch.

When he set the glass in front of her he said, "You don't have to do anything to please me. I like you the way you are.

And I hope you like me the way I am because as sure as hell I'll never change."

"I really do like you the way you are. And I like meeting all your swell friends. And going to the country club. And bowling." She smiled at Bill.

They bowled until eleven-thirty. Madalyn was so full of high spirits and enthusiasm and having such a good time that he was reluctant to mention leaving. As for himself, he could think of a dozen things he had rather do than bowl. Rumor had it that there was a back room where the right people could play poker. If that was true, Bill would bet it wasn't Homer Scott's idea. Scott was too smart to take a chance on getting the place shut down. But Scott didn't own the bowling alley.

When the evening ended, they sat in Bill's car in front of Madalyn's apartment. West Second Street at midnight was desolate and dark except for the circles of light from the dim street lights.

"I'm sorry I can't ask you in," Madalyn apologized. "The Staleys don't want us unmarried girls to entertain men in the apartment. And the Staleys are so nice to us.Mrs. Staley sometimes brings us cake or pie. And the rent is cheap. I can't take a chance on getting kicked out. And ruining my reputation."

"Well, we won't upset the status quo."

"Oh, I'm afraid to try and hide it from the Staleys. I don't know where I could find another apartment. I just can't take that chance."

"What did you think I said?"

"Didn't you say, we won't let the Staleys know?"

"You misunderstood me. I don't want to get you in trouble with your landlord. There are other places we can go." When she didn't respond, Bill kissed her. Her lips were soft and pliant but without fervor. Before he could kiss her again, she pulled back and mused, "I wonder what it takes to be a model?"

"How the hell would I know?" He could not keep the irritation out of his voice.

"Bill, I'm sorry. I didn't mean to make you mad."

"I'm not mad, Madalyn. It's just the way I am." He moved from under the wheel of the car to take Madalyn in his arms. The coat she was wearing made it seem he was holding a bundle of laundry instead of a girl. He unbuttoned her coat and put his arms around her. And she let him. It was awkward. Ridiculous. Time to go home. "We are going to be with each other often, Madalyn, but not in the front seat of a car."

"That's wonderful. I love going to the country club. Going bowling. Movies.Being with you."

"Not in that order, I hope."

"Have you heard about the new 3-D movies? The ones where you have to wear those funny glasses?"

"Heard but not seen. Don't want to see."

"Do you like to go window shopping?"

"No."

Bill walked her up to the door of the apartment and kissed her goodnight. She was as limp as a rag doll, her mouth unresponsive. She was so innocent. She will learn, Bill told himself, to be the girl I want her to be.

Like distress signals, lights were shining from all the windows of the house when Bill got home. Mom and Dad who usually went to bed at 10:30 were up, and it was after one o'clock.

Had somebody died?

That unwelcome thought stirred sorrow that lay submerged under layers of daily living. He cried for Polly. And he felt the loss of Kellan. And the fright the night his brothers wrecked the car.

He looked again at those ominous lights. Burt? Karl? Max? Joanie? He stood outside in the dark and prayed until he knew he could handle whatever bad news waited for him inside the house.

Assuming a jaunty air, Bill burst into the house as though he expected nothing at all to be amiss. "What are you two old people doing up so late? Did you have a fight?"

His parents were sitting in their chairs facing the blank television set that was soundless except for the uneven hum.

"Karl called from California," his mother explained. "to tell us that Dody's baby came early. Little thing weighed just three pounds, three ounces."

"Is the baby going to make it?"

Karl said the baby is holding its own. But it's so tiny. Things can go wrong. I told Karl to get that baby baptized right there in the hospital. Just do it. And tell Dody after the deed is done."

"And how is Dody?"

"Karl says she's okay. Bill, I'm going to fly in an airplane out to California and see my first grandchild. I don't know anything about getting tickets and so forth. You are going to have to help me."

"You're going too, aren't you, Dad?"

His father took on a look of regret. "I don't think I can get away from the business right now."

"What are you talking about? You know as well as I do that I can run the business with one hand tied behind my back and one eye shut. Mom's not going to make that trip by herself. You are going with her." What made old people so reluctant to leave home base? Did they really think they were indispensable? Or was it the trepidation of separating themselves from the security of home?

They planned the trip, talked it over, and planned it again

It. That's all the baby had been called. "All this talk," Bill said, and nobody has told me if it is a boy or girl."

"A girl," his mother said, "but they haven't named her yet."

"I didn't know Dietmeiers ever produced girls," Bill commented, which was a cynical referral to a statement he often heard his father make.

March turned into April while Bill's parents were in California, and April came in wet. When the rain stopped, a cloud hung over the earth keeping everything in a state of perpetual gloom.

Bill ignored the unaccountable personal gloom he couldn't seem to shake. The progress reports from California were all glowing. Max, who had been sent to Germany, was making the best of being in the Army and was enjoying seeing the old country. Burt had escaped the front lines in Korea but detested his assignment to a MASH unit Business was good. He had Madalyn.

He didn't have Madalyn. The bank had sent her and two other employees to Chicago to learn a new machine system the bank was installing. He didn't have Madalyn, and he hadn't had Madalyn which was the way he had been taught that it should be, but which was never the way it was.

Early on, Madalyn had told him proudly that she was a nice girl. *Nice* with a definition that was not included in the dictionary. Sometime after that she had announced in the same euphemistic language that she would never go all the way with a boy until she was married. At which Bill pointed out the obvious. "I'm not a boy." Because she was young and inexperienced, he tried to be patient with her, but she was trying his patience.

Madalyn didn't need expertise to make him happy, but he sure longed for her to show a tad more eagerness, a bit of passion now and then. Well, a person couldn't have everything. Madalyn was agreeable, always smiling. He wondered if she could cook.

Bill was hungry, but he intended to finish sorting the mail that had been piling up on the dining room table. Most of it junk mail. He almost threw away the tickets for the Reds' game. Madalyn had never been to a Major League baseball game.

He put the tickets on the mantle in the living room, picked up the discarded mail and took it to the kitchen waste basket.

He instinctively went to the refrigerator, opened it and looked for something to eat as though by some miracle it had been filled with food since the last dry run. He took out a beer, uncapped it, and left. Eating out was getting monotonous.

Looking for variety, Bill went to *Mildred's Place*, a down-home type of cafe a shade better than a greasy spoon.

The last person he expected to see in *Mildred's* was E.P. She was in a booth by herself.

"Join me," she called out to Bill. "Add a measure of pleasure—notice the rhyme—to an otherwise mundane meal." As Bill sat down across from her, she said, "I come here when I want chili. It's the best chili in town. And their roast pork dinner is good. Other than that, don't bother with a menu. Or have you eaten here before?"

"A couple of times."

Bill ordered chili when the waitress took his order then wished he hadn't. No one made chili as good as his mom's.

"What do you think about the Warwicks?" E.P. asked.

"What do you mean what do I think about the Warwicks?"

"They are splitting. Divorce is in the works."

Bill who despised gossiping, nevertheless asked, "Who was cheating on whom?"

"I don't know."

"I hate to hear that. What a shame." Bill meant what he said. "They sure seemed like the perfect couple."

"There is no such thing." E.P. was serious. "What do you think caused the riff?"

"If you don't know the answer to that one," Bill replied, "I'm sure as hell no one but the Warwicks know. You are the one who always knows everybody else's business. And tells it."

"Touché. However, my friend—are we still friends if we're not still lovers? There are some occurrences about which I do keep my mouth decidedly shut. And you, Abou Ben Adhem, ought to lead all the rest in gratitude."

Bill inwardly winced, knowing what she was referring to. She held the advantage because clearly, she could remember details that he could not and did not want to remember. Yet he hoped that by chance, she might have been drunk enough that her recollections were not clear. He told himself: You can't go back and change anything that happened. so forget it.

Being his usual self, Bill asked, "Wasn't Abou Ben Adhem that good guy who loved his fellow man?"

"Ah, your erudition is impressive…and may your tribe increase.and are you…"

The waitress came with monstrous bowls of steaming chili and E.P. never finished her thought.

The chili was okay, but not as good as his mom's.

Madalyn's mother sent an invitation to Bill through Madalyn to come out to supper for Madalyn's birthday. Which was good and bad. Good because he wanted to meet her family and bad because he didn't like birthday parties. And a problem because he didn't know what to buy her for a present. He wanted to give her something of value but he didn't want to overdo it.

Bill decided that he would ask Joanie to buy the present for him. When he tried the phone, the line was busy and then he forgot, and when he remembered he decided to stop by the Welleses's on his way home from work.

Janet answered the door.

"Joanie and Dr. Welles are in New York. Didn't you know?"

Well, if I had known, I wouldn't be standing at your door. He didn't say it and stepped inside at Janet's invitation to come in. He wanted to know what was going on in Joanie's life.

"You are well aware, I know, of how Joanie is inclined to make split second decisions without giving consideration to the details and the people involved. She merely announced at dinner one night that she was going to New York. Charles would not let her go alone. And I think he was correct in making that decision…he wanted to find the right apartment for her, help her initiate her career…"

"Well, I hope things work out for the best."

"Charles phoned last night. So far, he hasn't found an agent that he considers reputable and successful enough to trust with Joanie's ambitions. Poor thing. Charles did so want me to make the trip with them, but I couldn't. You know, here at the last of the semester, I can't walk off and leave my students to a sub. I have no idea when Charles will be back."

"I'm sure you did the right thing." I'd bet a hundred bucks she was never asked to go, Bill thought, deciding that he was sitting here listening to all this because Janet was unhappy. He felt sorry for Janet.

"Was there a particular reason you need to see Joanie? I can give you a telephone number."

"Nothing important. I was going to ask her about one of Kellan's guns. Time for that when she gets back."

"I wish I knew when."

As for the gift, Bill decided to go to Weddle's Jewelry Store and let prissy Willis pick something out something.

Willis Weddle looked like a mannequin that had been animated. He spoke ingratiatingly with an affected accent. "This dainty gold bracelet will never go out of style, and the young lady will be able to wear it with any fashion statement."

Bill didn't care. Shopping made him impatient, irritable. "Whatever you say, Willis."

"Then you do want the bracelet, I assume?"

"Yeah."

"Gift wrapped?"

"Nah, never mind."

"You'll wrap it yourself, then?" As though he wanted to make certain that an article that came from his store would be properly wrapped.

"Willis, I never wrapped a gift in my life."

"There's no charge for the gift wrapping."

"Wrap it." Anything to get out.

Madalyn's parents' farm was located in a remote section of the county where the land started dropping off toward the Manock River which spread out and fingered off in a dozen directions, and the farms were small and mean to work. No sitting on a tractor that ran smoothly over fields as flat as a table top. Here were rough little hills and gullies. And lots of cover for quail.

The farm house was an old structure revamped with dark green siding and new aluminum storm windows. At the side of the house a tall metal rod jutted skyward, a television aerial at the top. Like all the houses. Like the sacred poles on the hill shrines that got the disobeying Israelites in trouble.

Inside, the house was neat though the furniture was worn. Madalyn's younger brothers—twelve year old Steve and ten year old Mike—sat stiffly on their chairs and stared at Bill, answering his friendly questions in monosyllables. Patty, the teenage younger sister, was snippy with Madalyn and surly with her mother. Madalyn's parents showed the marks of hard work yet they seemed, compared to Bill's parents, young parents.

Embarrassment was a condition which was foreign to Bill. Whatever situation he found himself in, he adapted to it. With one exception. He was totally uncomfortable with any public display of affection, especially when it involved himself. So when Madalyn chose a moment to snuggle close to him as they sat on the couch and to lock the fingers of her hand through his, look at him possessively, and rest her head on his shoulder, he felt like a cheap prize, one of those big chalk dogs they gave away at carnivals. It pissed him off. Why couldn't she show him some of that ardor when they were alone? Gently, but decisively, he removed her hand and moved slightly away from her, ostensibly to examine a framed photograph on the end table but actually to free himself from a position he found untenable.

Mrs. Louis called them to supper, and the seven crowded around a chrome dinette set that was not meant for more than six. A chest-type deep freezer took up one wall, and other than that and the dinette set, the room was bare.

They began eating without grace or ceremony.

Mr. Louis, who sat at one end of the table and had enough room to rest his arms on the table, leaned over his plate and ate in a withdrawn, methodical way that seemed to say, *you may impress the others around here, but you don't impress me a damn bit.*

"Is there pretty good hunting out here?" Bill asked. He knew there was; he was simply working up to asking Mr. Louis for permission to hunt on his property.

Mr. Louis chewed at his food, swallowed, then paused to draw air through his teeth before he made a reply. "I see game all the time. Day before yesterday

227

I seen a pheasant. First time in my life I ever seen a pheasant around here."

Could it have been a grouse? "Do you hunt?" Bill asked.

"Naw. Waste of time. Last time I killed a rabbit nobody would dress it. Squirrels is too tough to eat. Kids rather have baloney. As for quail, well, there ain't enough meat on one to pay for the shot and the grease to fry it in."

"That's about right," Bill agreed. But disagreed. No use to tell this jackass how good it was when it was fried right. Or how tender a young squirrel could be when it cooked a long time like Mom did it. No need to tell him that in the Dietmeier family quail came close to being divine.

"You hunt, do you?" Mr. Louis questioned.

"Not much," Bill replied. Not as much as I'd like to.

The Louis children, including Madalyn, appeared to be puny eaters but great Kool-aid drinkers. The food was good, and Bill was hungry. But he quit eating when Mr. Louis pushed his plate forward and leaned back in his chair with his arms folded across his chest.

Perhaps that was a signal to Mrs. Louis who got up from the table and brought out a birthday cake. A bakery cake that was decorated with pink confectionary roses and garlands of pink and green around *Happy Birthday.* Mrs. Louis set the cake in front of Madalyn and lit the candles.

"Blow out your candles, girl," Mrs. Louis directed, "but first you got to make your wish."

The older boy nudged his younger brother and whispered something to him. Sister Patty tried to look bored.

Madalyn closed her eyes, then opened them and blew out the candles.

Mrs. Louis opened the freezer and took out a carton of ice cream. With Madalyn helping, she served dinner plate dishes of cake and ice cream.

There were no presents so Bill left Willis's gift-wrapped wonder where it was, in the pocket of the coat that he haddraped over a chair when he saw that Mr. Lewis was in a work shirt.

Bill offered to help with the dishes—preferring that to sitting in the living room trying to converse with Mr. Louis. Mrs. Louis took it as a meaningless gesture until Bill went back to the kitchen, eased Patty away from the sink and took over the dish washing in the rapid-fire way he sometimes did things. Even with Patty and Madalyn both drying, they could not keep up.

"You go at them dishes like you'd had some experience," Mrs. Louis remarked.

"Lots of experience," Bill replied, not slowing down. "My brother Karl and I had to do the dishes until my two younger brothers got old enough to get that chore. That's the way it is when there aren't any girls in the family."

As soon as the dishes were done, they crowded into the living room to stare at the small television screen and watch *The Sid Caesar Show*. Conversation was limited to comments about the skits and the commercials. Mr. Louis turned the volume up, a not too subtle hint to keep the voices down.

There seemed little point in dragging out the evening. The family would be more comfortable after he left, and so would he. Bill took his leave during a commercial. And took with a grain of salt their words: "you oughten to rush off."

Madalyn, who was spending the weekend with her family, walked outside with Bill to say goodnight. A round white moon was up, and they lingered by Bill's car.

"I wish I was going back to town with you," Madalyn whined. "Mama wants me to stay over cause there's a big revival up to the church starting tomorrow. She's hoping to get Daddy there and get him saved. Daddy says he's a better person than the hypocrites that go to church and then go out and drink and cuss." She waited for Bill to say something.

Bill said nothing.

"My family likes you. They were afraid you would be uppity. I told them you were weren't the least bit stuck up. They really do like you."

If that's the way they treat somebody they like, I'd hate to be someone they didn't like went through his mind as he said, "They sure as hell had me figured wrong, didn't they?"

"They like you. You have to understand, Bill, your family has money. We don't have much. But they really like you."

Bill remembered the birthday present. He took his coat off his shoulder and tossed it to Madalyn. "Your birthday present is in the pocket."

She ran her hands through the pockets until she found the box. "Do you want me to open it?"

"I think that's the procedure for getting what's inside."

"Why do you always talk to me like that, Bill?"

"Talk to you like what?"

"Well, you always say things that make me look stupid."

Bill felt a tinge of contrition. "It's the way I talk to everybody, hon. Something you have to get used to because I'll never change." He pulled her to himself and gave her a conciliatory kiss and a gentle smack on her backside. "Now open your present. I'll switch on the headlights so you can see better."

In the bright beam of light, she tore off Willis's wonderful wrappings.

"Oh, my gosh. A bracelet. Oh, gosh, is it real?"

"I certainly hope I didn't pay for an illusion."

"You know what I mean. Is it real gold?"

"Real gold."

"Thank you, Bill. Thank you very, very much." She put the bracelet on her arm to admire it in the light. "I'm going to wear this to work Monday morning. The girls will really be envious of me now. They all think you're so cute."

There was that silly word again. "I am not cute. Most grown men aren't cute."

"Well, you know what I mean."

There wasn't much to be gained, standing out in the yard with headlights on. If I leave now, Bill guessed, I might get in on a poker game at the Sports Shack. Though it was doubtful on a Saturday night. The women usually had plans for Saturday nights. But he would drive by anyway. If there was one light on at the alley door, there was a game. Two lights, no poker. Poker games at the Sports Shack were the best kept secret in town. Not even Steamboat opened his big mouth. "Come give me your best kiss and I'll be on my way."

Madalyn obliged.

"I've got an invitation to a cocktail party," Bill told Madalyn when she phoned him on Monday. "It's an affair to honor Judge Agnew's thirty years on the bench."

"How come you got invited?"

"I bribed the president of the County Bar Association to give me an invitation—what the hell difference does it make how I got the invitation? Do you want to go or not? I have to go to represent the Dietmeier Distributing Company."

"I don't have anything nice enough to wear to a fancy cocktail party."

"Sure you do. You've got a gold bracelet."

"Quit teasing, Bill. You would be ashamed of me in my Sunday clothes. I want you to be proud of me. Of the way I look. But I can't afford to buy any clothes right now."

He felt sorry for her. "Go buy what you need and charge it to me. Dietmeier credit is good anywhere in town."

"Do you mean that?" She was excited. "You aren't teasing again, are you?"

"I mean it. Get what you need for the cocktail party."

Madalyn wasted no time in getting herself in the shops. She phoned Bill as soon as she got back to her apartment with her purchases.

"Come on over, Bill. Mrs. Staley says it will be okay for you to come in since it's not night. She says you are a steady fellow and not wild like your brothers."

"She must have me mixed up with Karl."

"Why?"

"Never mind."

The apartment was claustrophobic. Three small rooms and a bath. Bill sat down on a couch, which was a hide-a-bed where Madalyn slept, to be an audience of one for the fashion show.

First, Madalyn took a stack of bills from her purse and handed them to Bill.

He looked at the first item on the first bill. Dress with redingote. "What the hell is a redingote?"

"Look," she said, holding up a garment. This is the dress and this coat-like thing that goes with it is a redingote."

Shoes, purse, hose
Necklace and earrings
Slip, bra, panties
Skirt, blouse, sweater
Nail polish, lipstick, perfume

"You are going to look comical wearing all of this to a cocktail party. Do you wear the skirt and sweater under the red-goat or over it?" Bill was figuring a quick estimate of the total cost. "When I told you a new outfit, I was speaking in terms of a new dress. Not a new wardrobe."

"I thought you wouldn't mind if I got the skirt and sweater set. It was so cute I couldn't resist."

"I'm not particularly enamored of cute. Are you sure you got everything you need?"

Madalyn, who often could not differentiate between Bill's sometimes cutting sarcasm and his good natured teasing, had no trouble in recognizing the vexation in his words.

She defended herself. "You didn't tell me how much I could spend."

"After this I sure as hell will. Money doesn't grow on trees, you know." I sound like Mom, Bill thought, which alleviated his ill humor somewhat.

Madalyn was crying.

Bill was not moved by tears. But he wasn't going to jump on her about that. "Come here," he ordered, and she took a step and a half and stood before him. "Now give me a smile." She gave him a happy smile. "Now go lock your door. We do not want to be disturbed."

Madalyn just looked at him. Finally she said, "I can't. I fell off the roof the roof this morning."

"You what?"

"You know. I've got the curse. My monthly."

Her words had the effect of an icy shower. He asked, "Have you got a medical problem?"

"Why?"

"I don't know much about women, but I do know you have a problem that seems to be weekly instead of monthly. You need to see a doctor." At first he had attributed her shyness to innocence. Then to morality. Then to fear. And now he was thinking that she found him repugnant. If he had given her an engagement ring instead of a bracelet...that's it. She wants a guarantee of marriage Well, Madalyn, you gotta learn that nobody suckers Bill Dietmeier.

Madalyn put her arms around his neck. "I'll see a doctor. I promise."

"Do that." He had to get out in the open air. The place was stifling. Maybe he'd stop off at the VFW and get in a card game. And Bill left.

Bill thought she looked pretty enough to turn heads, as he escorted Madalyn through the receiving line. Bill, who knew nothing about style, looked about the crowded Elks Club party room and concluded that Madalyn's outfit must be in good taste for it was similar to Helen's.

"I'm going to have a martini," Madalyn said when Bill asked her what she wanted to drink. "In movies people are always drinking martinis. Dry martinis. That's what I want. They must be delicious."

"Potent would be a better word," Bill commented as he went off to the open bar to stand in wait for a martini and a beer.

"Aren't you with that little number who works at the bank?" Davis Courtney was also waiting for drinks.

"Madalyn Louis."

"Ah, yes. Smiley. I flirted like hell with her, and all I got was a smile."

"I suspect she knows you're married," Bill said.

"What's marriage got to do with it?" Davis cackled.

"If you don't know, somebody ought to tell you." With drinks in hand he left to find Madalyn.

Knowing that she had had the good sense to rebuff Davis's advances ameliorated somewhat Bill's displeasure with Madalyn. Where was she? He spotted her hovering on the edge of a shifting collection of guests, more an observer of, than a participant in, the party.

"Thank you," she said very formally, as Bill handed her the martini. "This looks refreshing."

"You might want to sip it slowly."

Too late. Shock and distaste had turned Madalyn's face into gray distress. "I can't drink this," she whispered. "What will I do?"

Bill took the offending drink and deposited on a table that at the moment was unoccupied. "I'll get a plate of hors d'oeuvres for our table."

Ken Warwick's mother came into the line behind Bill. "How are things going with you, Bill?" Her bleak tone implied that she hoped things were not going very well with him.

"Couldn't be better, Mrs. Warwick." Was divorce like a death? Should he offer condolences? "What do you hear from Ken?" Bill asked.

"He's doing splendidly. He has a great respect for the law firm he is associated with. I do worry about him nevertheless. He has special needs, you know. Juanita..." She didn't finish because someone nearby had engaged her attention.

Not quite as enthusiastically as she had requested the martini, Madalyn asked Bill, as soon as he had seated himself at the table, "Will you get me a Manhattan, Bill? I want to try one of those."

Again Bill made his way to the open bar for a Manhattan and back again with the drink.

"Has this got Coke in it?" Madalyn asked.

"I've never had a Manhattan, but I'm sure the answer is no."

This time she did sip. And made a face of dislike.

"Get the girl a stinger," E.P.'s unwelcome voice recommended. "In the meantime I'll warn the maiden of the wicked ways of the infamous Bill Dietmeier."

Bill said caustically, "We'll ignore the intrusion."

E.P. eyed Madalyn with a critical, up-and-down look. "You are a pretty, little innocent—where did Dietmeier find you?" As if she didn't already know.

"In your father's bank." Madalyn giggled. "What's the drink you said I'd like?"

" A stinger. Go get her one, Dietmeier. What's the matter with you? Were you raised in a barn?"

"The bar is out of lime juice."

"Dietmeier, you liar." Then to Madalyn in a quasi-confidentail tone, "He's the biggest liar in Indiana. Don't believe a word he says." She threw up a wave of her hand to someone. "Harvey is impatiently motioning for me. He's mad about me, don't you know."

"Believe me," Bill cautioned Madalyn, not caring whether or not the departing E.P. overheard, "have as little as possible to do with that woman. She's bad news."

"I like her. She's funny."

It seemed to Bill that the small amount of alcohol that Madalyn had consumed had loosened her up.

Shortly, E.P. reappeared and, with a little flourish, presented Madalyn with a stinger. "Now you owe me a favor, Miss Madalyn. And I always collect my debts, don't I, Dietmeier?" She stuck a cigarette in her mouth and flicked her lighter.

"Harvey's antsy to duck out of here. He's got fucking on his mind."

Madalyn's face reddened in embarrassment. She looked down at the stinger as though she were trying to detect some debris in it, and she did not see E.P. wink at Bill as she left.

"You still think E.P. is a barrel of fun?" Bill scolded.

"I never thought a nice lady like her would use that word."

"She's not a nice lady."

"Mama whipped my brother for saying that word."

"E.P. would be better off if her mama had whipped her a few times."

Bill was ready to get away from the party. For more than one reason. Chief of which was Madalyn. She had had too much to drink.

But there was Juanita Warwick approaching them.

Once more the divorce thing. Did he ignore it or offer regrets? Or congratulations?

"I wanted to say hello, Bill, and ask about your parents and the new grandbaby." Juanita's voice was soft and cordial.

"They're having a great time in California. Mom's so crazy about the baby girl that I think she doesn't want to come home next Tuesday." And then he introduced Madalyn and realizing that Juanita had come to the cocktail party alone, asked her to join them. "What can I get you from the bar?" he asked.

"You are so thoughtful, Bill. I'll have a screwdriver, please. Have to have my vitamin C."

Madalyn would also have a screwdriver.

Madalyn just loved screwdrivers.

And would have another, please.

"My dear," Juanita advised Madalyn, "it's a deceptive drink. It tastes pretty, but it carries a wallop."

When the wallop hit Madalyn, it hit hard. Bill got her out of the Elks and into the parking lot, but before he got to the car, she was vomiting in the gutter.

Bill could clean fish, skin squirrels, dress rabbits, but the thing he could absolutely not stomach was vomit. The very smell made him gag. All he could do was turn his head and hold a handkerchief to his face. When she seemed to be finished, he handed the handkerchief to Madalyn who wiped at her mouth unsteadily and held out the handkerchief.

"Throw the damn thing away," Bill mumbled, "and let's get the hell out of here."

Madalyn's head rolled around as she tried to keep it resting on the back of the car seat.

Bill wanted to get her to her place as soon as he could in case she wasn't through being sick. Did Madalyn have her key with her? Did Madalyn have her purse? She didn't. He hoped to hell her roommate was at home.

He knocked on the apartment door calling out as he did so because Madalyn had told him that after dark they wouldn't open the door unless they knew who was knocking.

"It's Bill Dietmeier. I've got your roommate out here, and she's drunker than a skunk."

It took a few minutes, but Madalyn's roommate, her hair in curlers and obviously aroused from a deep sleep, opened the door.

Skipping pleasantries, Bill said, "You are a nurse, aren't you?" as he helped the wretched girl inside. "Well, I've brought you a patient."

With wide-awake scorn, the roommaate replied through her teeth, "Thanks a lot."

He said to Madalyn, "Remember, we're going mushroom hunting tomorrow." Which probably didn't register, so he said to the roommate, "When she asks about her purse, tell her she probably left it at the Elks. I'm going back there now to see if I can locate it."

The night felt good. A soft rain as fine as mist was falling and the air carried the clean smell of spring. If the sun came out in the morning, there would be mushrooms in the afternoon. He would go to the Elks, and then stop somewhere for a couple of beers.

No need to fold up so early.

Sunday was a perfect April day. Bill went to early church so they could get an early start on the mushrooms.

"Are we going in this old pickup?" Madalyn was already stepping up and into the cab.

"One would assume so," Bill concurred.

"I'd have more fun if we were going in your car. I love sporty, new cars."

"A pickup is better for where we're going. The road is like a washboard. You are going to get your big bottom bounced around."

"I am not fat." She moved around in the cab as though she could change her environment. She picked up the church bulletin which Bill had dropped on the floor of the cab when he left church that morning. "Gosh, I didn't know you went to church."

"Why is that?"

"Well, you drink. And swear something awful…you're always saying h-e-l-l—do you go to the Lutheran Church?

Is that like the Catholics?"

"The Catholics and the Lutherans don't think so."

"What's your church like?"

"Every Sunday morning we slaughter a lamb, take out the guts, drain off the blood…."

"Shut up. You're making me sick."

"It's your hangover that's making you sick."

"I don't have a hangover."

"If you don't, you should have. You were quite drunk last night."

"I wasn't drunk. I got some bad food."

"No. You were most definitely drunk. Either learn how to drink or don't drink at all."

"Will you just shut up? I have a headache."

"What a surprise." But he didn't nettle her anymore, and let her suffer in silence.

The woods was a classified forest that lay virtually undisturbed season after season. The new foliage was a fragile green interspersed with white and pink dogwood blossoms. Pushing up through the layers of old autumn leaves were dark green may apples, jack-in-the-pulpits, and the tips of as yet unrecognizable wild plants. Bill liked the smell of the woods—an acrid, pungent mixture of decay and new life that was a better perfume than that in bottles.

They followed a path that ran between a line of bushes and a rivulet that was barely deeper than surface water.

"What am I looking for?" Madalyn asked vaguely.

Bill found it hard to fathom how a girl who had been raised in the sticks could be so dumb about the woods. He stepped off the path for a couple of paces and picked a huge sponge mushroom that was camouflaged against a rotting log. "This," he explained, holding it up, "is a mushroom. Once you spot one, very likely you will find two or three others close by." Bill dropped the prize into a sack and quickly picked two more.

"What will we do with these?" Madalyn asked.

"Eat them."

"They might be poison. Mama said the ones that are poison would kill you if you ate them."

"Look at me," Bill demanded, "I eat mushrooms. Do I look as if I'd been poisoned? Toadstools and mushrooms that look like toadstools may be poisonous. But these brown mushrooms are morels."

She did not seem to have a burning interest in morels so Bill shut up.

She lagged behind.

Suddenly her piercing scream broke the beautiful silence of the woods. "I saw a snake!"

"Did you say hello?"

She clutched at Bill, and he held her trembling body close and could feel the rapid pounding of her heart against his chest. She was full of passion now. The passion of fear. "How many people," Bill asked, "do you know who have died from a snake bite?"

"I don't know, and I don't want to be the first one."

Madalyn spent the rest of the time on the lookout for snakes. Bill, determined to find a good mess of morels, let her enjoy being afraid of snakes while he searched for the delicate fungi.

Bill remembered the time he brought Kellan and Joanie to these same woods. Joanie had never hunted mushrooms before. After she found her first mushroom, she went off on her own, determined to find more mushrooms than Kellan or Bill. She didn't find the most mushrooms, but she found the biggest. A giant of a mushroom. The largest one Bill had ever seen. They talked about taking it to the newspaper, but Bill thought it was a bad idea. The mushroom got eaten instead of photographed.

"Time to leave," Bill announced when his sack was full. "We'll take these back to the Dietmeier mansion and have fried mushrooms for Sunday supper."

It was the first time Madalyn had ever been in the Dietmeier house. With no inhibitions, she wandered around all through the downstairs, looking it over, calling out questions about his family or a decorative object or a picture. Her curiosity satisfied, she stopped in the kitchen where Bill was putting the mushrooms to soak in a pan of cold salt water. "How come your folks don't build a modern house, Bill?"

"Because it never entered their minds that they needed a new one." He shrugged his shoulders. "Maybe they like the neighborhood. I don't know—what the hell is wrong with this house?"

"Nothing. But I thought with all their money...you know what I want, Bill? I want a Bedford limestone ranch house with wall-to-wall carpeting and an enormous picture window."

"And a lamp in the picture window?" He was anything but serious. He was hungry. "I've got two steaks, plenty of beer, and the mushrooms. I'll get the skillet out. Okay?"

"No," she said petulantly. "Don't."

"What do you want to do?"

"I want to go out to eat. I like to see people."

"Well, hell, if it's people you want to see, I'll get old Mrs. Lox to line up some of the neighbors to..."

"I get so tired of you joking around all the time. I want to go to the country club."

"The only meal the club serves on Sunday is the Sunday brunch."

"Then let's go to the Village Inn. A lot of people go to the Village Inn."

"I hope so. Otherwise they won't be in business very long."

"Oh, Bill stop it." Her face drooped and she pouted.

Like an Epiphany, the light dawned on Bill. "I'm going to take you home, Madalyn. Not because you are cross from a hangover, but..."

"I won't be cross any longer. I'll be nice."

"Let me finish. We are not right for each other. Not in interests, in personalities, and Lord knows, not in sex. You back off from me like I had something contagious."

His words rattled Madalyn. "Mama told me that society boys like to get what they can out of a girl and when they get married they marry a high society girl." When Bill didn't say anything she went on. "Mama said that if you really loved me you would wait for me. And I want to be Mrs. Bill Dietmeier more than anything in the world." She was beginning to get hysterical. "And if I ever let you do it to me, you would find out I wasn't a virgin and that would ruin everything and you really wouldn't marry me. My daddy was right. Money marries money. She wept and wailed like a banshee. "You're so mean to me. I hate you."

Bill let her frenzy run its course. "I think you will agree that two people who are so far from understanding each other will be better off to be friends rather than to be married to each other. End of discussion. It's over."

She looked at him with pleading eyes. "You can do anything to me you want to do. I don't care. Look..."

"What I want to do is take you home. It's over."

Her face turned ugly. "You better not go around town calling me a whore. That's what you'll do, won't you? You'll tell all your friends I'm a whore." "Just keep your own mouth shut. Now are you coming with me or do I have to drag you to the car?"

It was not Madalyn he was angry with; it was himself.

To Bill, it seemed his parents had come home rejuvenated. Perhaps, he thought, that was because of the contrast in the way he felt. Burned out. He didn't dwell on the Madalyn thing. In some ways in spite of all of the ugliness, it was a blessing in disguise. To both of them. She needed to grow up. And he sure as hell didn't need the job.

There were two tickets to the Reds' game on the mantle. Dad and Mom could have them. Karl's baby girl, now called Deborah or Debbie, was growing like a weed, according to Bill's mother.

"You can see already," Bill's dad bragged, "that the little gal has got spunk. She may grow up to be the first girl pitcher in the Major Leagues."

"It sure would be wonderful to have the whole family together. If just for one day," Bill's mother declared. But that wouldn't happen until the war was over in Korea. "I don't understand this war," she said.

Burt was being sent to Japan for R&R.

"I hope he behaves himself," Bill's mom said as she rolled out dough for meat strudel, little pastries filled with leftover meat and deep-fried. "I sure hope he stays away from those what-do-you-call-it girls."

"Geisha," Bill helped. He heard his father outside with the bird dogs, making them respond to his demand to "hold" or "fetch" or whatever. His father had an authority with dogs like no hunter Bill knew. An instinctive sort of communication between man and dog. I'm a better shot than Dad, Bill thought, but I can't handle dogs the way he does. And I sure don't handle women very well either. And suddenly Bill knew he needed to get away. From home. From town. From everything that was familiar. He took a beer from the refrigerator and sat down at the kitchen table. He smoothed out a wrinkle in the oilcloth. "I think I'll go down to Reelfoot Lake in Tennessee," Bill said to his mother, "and fish for a week."

"So, what do Tennessee fish have that Indiana fish don't have?"

The question hung in the air unanswered for a familiar "Is anybody home?" from the front of the house and familiar footsteps through the dining room brought Joanie.

Her unexpected presence grabbed Bill with an urge of desire so intense that he had to force nonchalance into his voice.

"Look who smelled the meat strudel and came for supper. Just like a stray pup."

"Oh, boy, and does supper smell good." She came to Bill with a kiss of greeting. He pulled out a chair at the kitchen table for her to sit down. "You're the nicest thing that's walked into this kitchen since the last time you walked in," Bill said. She could take it for small talk, but he meant it sincerely. He could not think of another human being who could have walked in and made him feel as good as he felt now. "Mom, open Joanie a cold beer."

"So, Joanie, how was New York?" Mrs. D. asked.

"A lesson in reality. I was a simpleton to think I could get modeling jobs. First off, I needed to lose fifteen pounds."

"Mein Gott in Himmel; if you lost fifteen pounds you would be a stick."

"Exactly. But when I was buying clothes it was a different story. You wear your clothes so beautifully; what a superb figure you have; your face has such exquisite bone structure—all that bullshit. Excuse me, Mrs. D."

"Don't apologize. Bullshit is bullshit."

Bill had never heard his mother use the word, but she had knocked a few heads and wasted a lot of breath castigating the rest of the family for being manure mouths.

"And I couldn't get a suitable job without a college degree," Joanie went on. "I guess I'll enroll at Houghton College and get a degree in something."

Mrs. Dietmeier approved. "Now you are being sensible."

Joanie stayed for supper.

After the meal, his mother shooed Joanie and Bill out of the house, telling them that Dad could help with the dishes. "Go for a walk. You both ate too much."

Bill thought, as they walked along in the deep twilight of the warm spring night, that it would be enough to have Joanie his friend. He liked her that much. Whatever she was in the past was no more. Whatever he was in the past was no more.

This is the way they were now. Good friends.

"Tell me, Bill," Joanie began as they walked into the yellow glimmer of the street light and crossed the street to the next block, "about you. I've heard all the news about the family except you. And you've forever been one of my favorite people in the whole world."

"Nothing much changes with me. I made a hole-in-one on number 2, and considering my golfing ability that was news."

"Madalyn Louis?"

"Something I try to forget. She didn't understand me, and I sure as hell didn't understand her."

"I knew from the outset that she wasn't right for you."

"Neither was I right for her. Let's leave it at Bill Dietmeier made one hell of a mistake."

"Bill Dietmeier made one hell of a mistake. Something we won't talk about ever again."

They walked as far as the Pennsy tracks and then turned around and headed back, slowly, with only an occasional comment, not needing to keep up a conversation.

"Let's do your dad a favor and play euchre with him," Joanie suggested as they climbed the four steps to the front porch. "Your dad and I against you and your mom."

"That's unfair. You and Mom against Dad and me."

"That's unfair. You and I against your mom and dad."

"That's also unfair, but we won't tell them that."

Life, Bill thought, was good again. The next day's mail brought a reminder of Madalyn, and that wasn't good. A bill to the tune of eighty-nine dollars and fifty-cents. He looked at the date of purchase. She had bought the items the day after they broke up. Furious, Bill wanted to crash into the bank and raise hell about the bill. Embarrass her in front of whoever was in earshot.

He didn't. He wouldn't do something that might cost the girl her job. He would wait until after work and try to catch her at her apartment. But all day long at work, the thought of that bill rankled him. If she weren't so damned poor and so damned dumb, he would make her pay him back two dollars a week.

As he approached the apartment, Bill saw E.P.'s car pulling away from in front of the house. What was she doing at Madalyn's?

He parked the car and went to the door.

It took Madalyn several minutes before she answered his knocks. She opened the door for him to enter, but he stayed on the stoop. "No," he said. "You step outside."

When he took the bill out of his shirt pocket, she said before he said anything, "I'm sorry about the bill. I bought those things the day before we broke up."

"Look at the date, Madalyn; you're lying. Now you listen to me. I'm going to pay this bill. But if you ever charge anything in my name again, I'll take out an ad in the daily newspaper, half a page, saying that I am not responsible for any debts made in my name by Madalyn Louis. If you don't understand the ramifications of what I've just said, I'll go over it with you, word by word."

"Don't worry," she was snarley, "I don't need you anymore. I've got a new job in a bank in Indianapolis."

"Well that," Bill said, "is an answer to a prayer I never made."

"What do you mean by that?"

Bill was gone before she had finished the question.

If he had thought about it, he might have speculated on the connection between E.P. and Madalyn's job in Indianapolis. but it never crossed his mind.

Dietmeier Distributing Company had two seats to the Kentucky Derby, courtesy of Falls City Brewing Company. One for Joanie, one for me, Bill decided.

But Joanie was in Green Forks, visiting Kellan's grandmother, according to Janet. "She didn't say how long she would be gone," Janet said. "So I think you should ask someone else. Joanie has never learned what a calendar is for. She ended with that same apologetic sort of laugh, as though excusing herself for saying something slightly negative about Joanie.

When he played golf with the guys the next morning, he'd offer one of the tickets to the first taker.

"I've got an extra ticket to the Derby—good seats," Bill said. "Who wants it?" He took a practice swing with his driver, waiting until the rest of the foursome—Clem, Steamboat, and Scott—were ready.

Steamboat took a practice swing. "I'd take it, but the bank's got a box this year, and Helen and I are going down with her parents."

Clem couldn't take it. "Phyllis would kill me if I went to the Derby and left her at home," he drawled. "Plus we have kinfolks coming in from Louisiana."

Scott equivocated. He didn't know if he could get away from the bowling alley. He would have to check with Esther to see if she'd be home to watch the kids. Es had been under the weather lately.

"Have you got Esther pregnant again?" Steamboat muttered.

It was such a standing gibe no one noticed.

Bill teed up his ball. I'll scalp the damn ticket. He swung and the wood cracked against the ball that soared and the broken tee flew way out in front of the mound.

"My God, man; you drove Number One!" Steamboat yelled. "The little white bastard is on the edge of the green."

"I've been playing this course since we moved here in 1947, and you are the first person I've seen drive Number One"

Clem shook his head in admiration.

I could have been a hell of a good golfer, Bill thought, but I was so damned pumped up over basketball and football to consider it a sport. Aloud he said, "I guess everybody gets lucky once in awhile." And he thought of a Derby ticket going begging because he didn't have anyone to take.

Phyllis Cordet, when she found out from Clem that Bill had a Derby ticket, phoned Bill and pressured him to take Clem's cousin from Louisiana who was visiting. "Anne Emily is crazy about horses and crazy to see a Kentucky Derby. You'll like Anne Emily. You really will."

It was easier to agree to take Anne Emily than to listen to Phyllis.

Anne Emily was pretty; she was as sweet as honey with a voice as soft as butter. And she really was crazy about horses. She told Bill he was absolutely, fantastically wonderful, and she was having the most fun she had ever had in her life.

When Bill picked the Derby winner, she was ecstatic.

"Pure luck," he said. But privately thought that his winnings were attributable to his expert handicapping.

When he took Anne Emily home, or rather to the Cordets', she said, "I'm going to give you a big hug and kiss for taking me to the Derby." She did. And when a woman kissed like that, the reaction was instinctive, your arms went around her, you held her very close to yourself, you responded like nature intended you to respond, and you let her be. For Anne Emily was only fifteen. Bill left and went to the bowling alley. There ought to be somewhere where he could casually mention that he had picked the Derby winner.

Steamboat was there, loafing in the snack bar with Scott.

"How did you get along with Phyllis's sister?" Steamboat asked.

"Clem's cousin," Bill corrected.

"Well, the fact that she was Clem's cousin instead of Phyllis's sister increases the chances that you had a good time."

"Did you win any money?" Scott asked.

"I had the Derby winner, Count Turf."

"That doesn't mean you came home with any money. What's in your pocket right now is what counts"

"I haven't counted," Bill said.

"Ah, that's a lie." Steamboat was jovial.

It was a lie, but it didn't matter. To any of them.

Most of the bowling alley patrons were clearing out, it being close to closing time, when in came Harvey Mendisonn. With news. "A girl got raped tonight on the west side of town, close to the L&N tracks. At least that's where the police found her. Someone saw her and called the police."

"Do you know who she is?" Scott asked.

"The police didn't give out her name. If they knew. Probably a girl from that trailer court at the edge of town."

"What I can't understand," Steamboat said, "is why some horny bastard needs to rape a woman when there's a county full of women with the hots. Not a day goes by that some female's not advertising herself to me." Steamboat for once was not boasting. "Everyone of you guys know what I mean. Some whore sitting in a bar swinging her legs, giving you the come on. Just panting to get laid."

Harvey spoke in a professorial voice as if he had knowledge the others needed to know. "Rape is an entirely different act, Steamboat. Rape is acted out of violence, hate, retribution."

"By a sick pea brain," Steamboat scoffed. "who can't find a prostitute or a whore."

The ugliest word in the English language, Bill felt, was whore. The most degrading. The nastiest. He felt a touch of nausea. He ignored his beer and tried to ignore the talk *Polly was a whore, E.P. said. and nobody has the guts to tell you. But I'm tanked just enough to tell you. Polly Emhuff was a whore and you're...* he hit her and she fell to the ground and he kicked her. A lurch of nausea came up to his throat, and Bill headed for the Men's Room. The vomit came out of him in uncontrollable regurgitation. The taste in his mouth was as vile as bile. Another wave of sickness swelled up in him, and he vomited again. Then it was over. He flushed the toilet. And flushed it again. He turned on the water in the lavatory and washed his face and hands. Cupped water into his mouth and rinsed. He looked at himself in the mirror. How could he have been blind for so long? How could I not have remembered? *Behold, He makes all things new...*There was the reconciliation. Peace of mind. *That peace which passeth all understanding.*

"God a'mighty; it smells like somebody puked in here." Steamboat walked to a urinal and unzipped his pants.

"I did," said Bill. "Must have been the barbecue sandwich I had at the track."

"Too damn much grease in those things. You all right?"

"Sure. All I needed was to get that rot out of my system."

Bill went home with a clear conscience and the thought that he needed to get a fresh start.

Bill worked on a resume without mentioning it to his parents. Not that they would object. He had a degree in business, and his transcript was decent. The completed resume stayed in his drawer. He wasn't going to rush into anything. But he said to himself, if the right opportunity comes along, I'll seize it.

Shut up in the office working on the payroll when the world of blue sky and sunshine outside was heady with the enticements of the first of June, Bill decided he would knock it off early and let someone else mind the business.

He was concentrating so intently that when the phone rang, he was barely aware of its noise and not inclined to answer until his dad stuck his head in and told him to answer the phone.

It was Joanie. "I was about ready to hang up," she said. "I thought Dietmeier Distributing might, for some strange reason, he closed. Did I interrupt something important?"

"Hell, Joanie, do I ever do anything but loaf?"

She ignored his exaggeration. "I've sold my little house, Bill. I'm putting the things I want to keep in storage." She paused a moment. "There's a man who wants to buy Kellan's guns."

It gave Bill a queasy feeling to think of Kellan's guns being sold. "What have you got? The automatic and the twelve gauge?" Knowing she knew next to nothing about guns, he said, "Want me to come over and take a look at what you have? Are you at…"

"I'm at the little house."

When he arrived at the house, it was in the sad disarray of moving with packed boxes standing about and boxes being packed. Miss Eddie was wrapping crystal stemware with newspapers.

"Who's the good-looking gal helping you, Joanie?" Bill kidded.

Involuntarily Miss Eddie looked about expecting someone else, Then she realized Bill was talking about her. "Go on with you," she said, never stopping at her task.

"Who bought your house, Joanie?"

"E.P."

"What does she want with this house?"

"She bought it for Lonnie Lykens."

"I knew Lonnie was wounded and in the Veteran's Hospital but…"

"Lonnie will never walk again."

"Oh, Jesus; poor kid."

"E.P. is going to have this place remodeled so that it's wheelchair accessible and will accommodate a person who is confined to a wheelchair. She will probably have to spend about as much to remodel as she did for the house."

"I'll bet you lost money on the deal."

"I didn't make any money. But I don't care. If." she stopped. "You know what I mean."

"Let's look at the guns," Bill suggested.

"They are all on the kitchen table except for the Kentucky Squirrel Rifle. I took it back to Kentucky and gave it to the Fosters. It should be theirs, don't you think?"

Bill picked up the automatic. He ran his hand over the smooth stock. The barrel was clean and oiled. He was with Kellan when he bought the gun. Bill felt tears sting his eyes. He put the gun to his shoulder and sighted through it. Kellan had been so proud of this gun. "I'll buy this gun," Bill said, not wanting some stranger to have it.

"It's yours," Joanie said.

"I'll pay you."

"Do you know how much the money means to me?"

"Not a damn thing."

"Not a damn thing," she echoed.

"The twelve gauge is not worth a whole lot. And that antique dueling pistol is not an antique. Kellan bought it in an antique shop in Bloomington on the chance that it might be authentic, but we found out later that it was a replica, a gun an apprentice gunsmith makes to learn his trade."

"You keep all the guns, Bill. Kellan would want you to have them."

"Then I'll take them."

"If there is anything else of Kellan's that you want, it's yours."

You. "Let's take a break and go get some ice cream. You're ready for ice cream, aren't you, Miss Eddie?"

"Go on, you two. I want to get on with the packing. I don't want to have to come over here next week." She was talking to herself as they left. "Mrs. Doctor will give me her little list next Monday morning, and I'll have my work cut out for me."

"Ice cream sounds good, Bill. I haven't had lunch."

"Then let me buy you lunch. You've got to eat."

"You sound like your mother. No. I want ice cream."

They sat at one of the picnic tables near the ice cream stand at the park, not talking, enjoying the cool sweetness of the ice cream, licking an occasional drip that wanted to run down the side of the cone.

Joanie took the remaining ice cream off the top of her cone and talked with it in her mouth. "My next move will be to get out of Janet's hair. I make her nervous. She's jealous of me. Of my relationship to Charles. He loves me more than he loves her." She threw the remaining cone into a receptacle.

"Tomorrow," Bill said, "is the last day of the spring meet at Churchill. Want to go with me?"

"I'd love to, but I'd better not. I have so much to do."

Bill was disappointed, but he took it in stride. Disappointments seemed to be a way of life with him.

However, on Saturday morning early, Joanie phoned, "Is the invitation for the races still open?"

"You bet."

The day was a carbon copy of the previous day—warm but not hot, sunny with a blue sky breeze. The drive down to Louisville was relaxing: traffic and conversation was light.

"Janet and I do not belong in the same house together," Joanie said. "I had to get away to keep my sanity."

And Bill had mistakenly thought she wanted to be with him. Wrong again.

"If you get your own place, you and Janet will get along."

"My problem, Bill, is that I keep thinking that she's in my house and she doesn't belong in my house."

"I understand." And he did.

"If I decide to go back to Houghton, I'll get an apartment."

"You really don't know what you want to do, do you?"

"I know what I don't want to do."

"That's the important thing."

"Do you like what you're doing, Bill?"

"To be honest with you, yes, but there are times when I think I should be doing something else."

"I hope not at this moment."

"This Saturday I can't think of one thing I'd rather do than bet the horses."

"Me too."

They went through the afternoon like a couple of old handicappers, studying the *Daily Racing Form,* consulting the program, watching the odds change on the board.

At the end of the day, Joanie was a big winner.

"Hell's fire, Joanie, I know what you should do. Start booking horses."

"I'd rather be a jockey."

"Girls aren't allowed to be jockeys."

"They will be someday." She was counting her winnings. "I'm taking us to dinner at *Kunz's*. You don't have to be home at any particular time, do you?"

"I don't have to ever go home."

"Neither do I."

Renowned for its superb food and service, the restaurant's ambience of soft lights and hushed sounds was conducive to a feeling of intimacy. Even after they had finished their meal, they lingered.

"I wish this day never had to end," Joanie said.

"The day is already past." He said it as a statement of fact. not trying to be dramatic.

"Then I wish this night would never end."

"We can't make a night last a lifetime. But it could be a start." Bill saw love in her face.

"Then I want it to be a start. I love you, Bill."

Her words drained him. Drained him of all the old inhibitions—*she's Kellan's wife, she could never love me, she doesn't belong to me, she's Kellan's*—and Bill said the words. "I love you, Joanie, more than anything on God's earth."

Then being the pragmatic person that he was, he kissed her and said, "Let's get the hell out of here and go make up for lost time."

Printed in the United States
55195LVS00005B/151-153